I0700991

LEARN TO LOVE YOU

Book Cover by Emily Wittig

Title typography by Emily Wittig

Jade Hernández is an imprint of Aleera Anaya Ceres

First edition 2023

Paperback ISBN: 979-8-9869546-3-9

BLURB

D AMIáN "JUNIOR" ÁGUILA-GUTIERREZ SHOULDN'T think about his sister's mysterious best friend. She's off limits, unattainable, and more importantly, uninterested in him. Besides, he has other things to worry about. Like taking over his papá's rancho, Los Corazones. Inheriting his familia's empire is all that's expected of him, but Junior has other plans and desires, and he knows if they ever discovered the truth, it would hurt the people he cares about the most...

Mayda Jiménez has lived on the outskirts of the Águila-Gutierrez family for as long as she can remember. She's been loved by them but has never quite been one of them. She's always kept herself at arm's length, knowing if this perfect family ever found out about her mother's addictions, they'd want nothing to do with her lot. It won't stop her from pining after her best friend's brother, though. The one person in the world she knows she can never have...

When the secrets of their circumstances bring Junior and Mayda together, what started as a tentative friendship ignites into something more. Shared whispers become kisses. Kisses become passion. And passion becomes a revelation that threatens to destroy the foundation of everything they've built.

Trigger & Content Warnings

This list contains spoilers

Learn to Love You contains scenes and situations that could potentially be triggering for some readers. If any of the following disturb you, proceed with caution, if at all.

- Drug, alcohol, and substance abuse and addiction

- Child neglect in a character's past that is mentioned several times throughout the book

- Grief

- Light machismo

- Health issues (heart attack)

- The death of a parent

TROPES & KINKS

S OME TROPES AND CONSENSUAL kinks within the book are:

- Best friend's brother

- Friends to lovers

- Hair pulling

- Praise

- Soft degradation

- Car sex

- Camera sex

Author's Note

Learn to Love You is a Latinx Romance set in a fictional place in the U.S. It is not mentioned where, as I leave it open ended and up to the interpretation of the reader. There are a few places mentioned that are purely fictional and are not meant to mimic real life places. The situations, family dynamics, and culture in this book is taken from my own experience and is not meant to encompass Mexican culture as a whole. The contents within are meant fictitiously.

In this book, there is a constant use of Spanish words, endearments, and phrases. These will not always be translated into English afterwards and won't be italicized. This is a personal writing style and choice.

There is an instance in the book in which Junior (the MC) calls Mayda (the FMC) 'cusca.' While this translates online to mean 'whore' or 'slut' it is not used in that context. As an author who lives in Mexico, that term is used in my region to mean 'greedy' or 'hungry for sex' and is not meant to slut-shame in any way, shape, or form.

LEARN
TO
LOVE
YOU

CHAPTER 1

JUNIOR

MY PAPÁ NAMED OUR rancho 'Los Corazones.' He said it was because that's where a man encountered his strength. In his heart, in his family, and in his rancho. *Corazón. Familia. Rancho.* Three integral things that made up the living, breathing mechanism that was our lives.

I was the second of five, and the only son. That, of course, didn't include the ranch hands that lived on the property or Doña Gloria and her son—my best friend—Hector. The trabajadores were as much my family as my sisters and I were, given that my parents liked to *theoretically* adopt anyone they deemed worthy of carrying the Águila-Gutierrez last names.

Sunlight slanted against my bare skin, the wind whispering secrets to me as I leaned my elbows against the wooden fence. I was usually up before anyone else at the house stirred so I could be witness to this. The warm morning sun spread across the acreage of crops and farmland, gripping at Los Corazones with orange and pink fingers of light, giving our property a subtle, golden glow. It was going to be blistering later, though I didn't mind the heat any more than I minded tending to the crops and taking care of the animals. Latin blood ran through my veins, through and through.

I relished in these few moments of silence before my sisters swept through like the storms they were, filling the rancho with their exuberant laughter and mismatching personalities. I didn't live at the house with them anymore. I'd moved out to one of the smaller cabins that dotted the edge of our rancho meant for the trabajadores, but I could always hear the noise from the main house floating towards my front door. It never failed to put a smile on my face, but there was something particularly soothing about the quiet, too.

Pushing myself away from the fence, I turned and made my way up the cobblestone path where the main house greeted me. With its orange shutters, archways, and walls painted in the yellow and red tones of a sunset, it reminded me of the streets of a Mexican Pueblo Mágico every time I walked up to it. I supposed our little paradise had the workings of a magical village all on its own, a perfect mix of new and traditional, bursting at the seams with colorful rose bushes and blooms of noche buena.

I slipped inside the back door that led to the kitchen, greeted by the delicious aroma of food, the pulsing echo of music, and a woman standing over the stove, shaking her body to the beat.

"Hmm, something smells good." I closed the door behind me with a snap, causing Doña Gloria to startle, spine going rigid. She whirled almost immediately, smacking my chest with a damp dish towel.

"Me espantaste, Junior!"

Holding back my laughter, I pulled her small, plump body towards my much larger frame to press a kiss to her forehead. Affection swelled in my chest when she patted her palm against my chest in a warm greeting.

"Sorry, Doña Gloria." I tried to make myself look contrite, though my lips pressed into a thin line of amusement that I was sure she could make out immediately.

She grumbled in rapid Spanish as she peeled her body from mine. I heard whispered curses and threats of chanclasos, the dish towel twisting in her tight grip. Just the thought of getting hit with a dreaded sandal had me biting at my lips and backing up a discreet step.

I was no stranger to the wrath of mothers, even if they weren't technically mine. That was the issue with knowing her my entire life. Trust was built from the time I was in diapers and the consequences of her friendship with my mamá meant double the punishments.

I was spared a chancla to the face as she turned her stocky figure back towards the stove. "You're up early," she commented as she sprinkled salt in the pan.

"I'm always up early."

She hummed and pointed her spoon in the direction of the olla de barro simmering on the stove. "There's café in the pot, but if you want chocolate you'll have to wait."

She was a bullet in the kitchen, moving quickly and efficiently from one side to the other, multitasking like a pro. One moment she was grating cheese and the next she was chopping away at lettuce, onion, and radish.

"Do you need help?" I offered, though I knew it was in vain.

The kitchen was her domain, and she didn't let anyone except my mamá and abuela in here, and that was only because they were the jefas of the house, or else I was sure they'd have been kicked out as well.

Still, Doña Gloria beamed at me and sauntered over to pet my cheeks in her rough palms. Her affection was never lost on me, and I relished in it. "You're a good boy, mijo. Now get out of my kitchen."

Laughing, I poured myself a cup of café, taking out a second mug when I heard the door open. A quick look over my shoulder told me it was Hector, already dressed to work out in the fields, in torn-up jeans and a t-shirt. He wiped his dirty boots on the mat and pulled off his sombrero to hang on a nearby hook before he came in and pressed a kiss to his ma's cheek.

"Buenos días, ma. Thanks, bro." He took the mug I handed him, taking a sip of the café and promptly burning his tongue. "Sh—shoot," he amended when he caught his mother's glare. He flashed her a sheepish grin, showing off the dimples I'd heard my sisters whispering about more than once when they thought I couldn't hear.

What was it with their obsession with face holes?

"Since you're both here, you can set the table. Everyone else will be down shortly."

I was already moving, pulling stacks of plates from cupboards and handing them off to Hector so he could set them out in the dining room.

"What's for breakfast?" he asked as he rummaged through drawers to find utensils.

Doña Gloria cooked for our family as well as for some of the ranch hands in the afternoons at lunch hour. While our rancho had accommodations for our workers, they didn't all live on the property. They were as much a part of our lives as Doña Gloria and Hector were. Thanks to them, this place ran smoothly and because of that, my father treated them exceptionally well and offered them a home. Yet only Doña Gloria and Hector ate with us in the mornings.

"Chilaquiles. Extra spicy."

"Who's hungover?" I joked. Chilaquiles were a tradition in our household. We usually ate them after a night of heavy drinking or on Sundays after mass. Since it was Saturday, it could only mean one thing.

"That would be Gabriela and Mayda."

I almost dropped my coffee mug, my clumsy fingers grasping tightly at the handle. I cleared my throat, hoping no one saw my fumble, but a quick look at Hector's amused grin told me I wasn't as slick as I wished.

"Mayda is here?"

There was a certain tightness to the question that had me clearing my throat almost immediately. The fact that she'd mentioned her shouldn't have been surprising, but like always, a warm sensation nestled into my chest. It wrapped around her name and held on tightly, like how I'd sometimes wrap my fingers around the end of her ponytail and tug, not wanting to let go.

"They went out dancing last night. Your poor mamá was up all night waiting for them to come home." She shook her head back and forth and clucked her tongue, though a small smile touched her lips afterwards.

As far as rebelliousness went in my hermanas, Gabriela was *not*. Adventurous and opinionated, sure, but she would never purposefully make my mamá worry about her. She was the golden girl.

I opened my mouth to answer but was interrupted as loud voices reached my ears from upstairs. It was followed by pounding footsteps as my sisters bounded down. The storm was coming, and I braced myself with a smile on my lips as it finally swept through.

"Something smells delicioso!" Ximena rounded the corner first. Her tight curls were speckled in paint and tied in twin pigtails, held together with different sized paint brushes. As if she'd rolled on canvas and hastily got dressed this morning, oblivious to the rainbow staining her body. Behind her, Sofia walked in more quietly, her nose tilted as she sniffed the delicious aroma of breakfast.

Sofia and Ximena were as close in age as Gabriela and I. Ten months apart, to be exact, both twenty-three years old. Sofia was older, and though they couldn't be more different, in personalities and appearance, the two were as close as twins.

"Chilaquiles! Please tell me there's arroz con leche, too!" This came from the youngest, Valentina, who all but barreled past Ximena and Sofia in her quest to come peek in at the pots simmering on the stove. Her loose hair hung over the flames, nearly singeing the ends as she bounced on the heels of her feet.

"Cuidado, bonita." Hector grabbed her around the waist and pulled her away from the danger, only to let go just as quickly. She whirled, a bright smile painting her face and a flush brightening her cheeks. "You're gonna burn your hair all off," he scolded, though there was no real heat to his cadence.

Valentina rolled her eyes at Hector and turned away, taking care this time to twist her hair behind her neck. She tried inching towards the food again, but Doña Gloria swatted the dish towel in her direction, shooing her away.

"We have leche con chocolate," Doña Gloria snapped. "Now get out of my kitchen."

Valentina's laugh was boisterous as she leaned over to kiss Doña Gloria's cheek, murmuring, "Buenos días."

"Good morning everyone!" I looked up from my coffee mug to see my parents rounding the corner. They were usually up and ready for the day before my sisters, as much a part of the exuberant mornings as the rest of us. "Hmm, that smells delicious, Gloria," my mamá said. She looked freshly showered, her long, graying hair braided over her slender shoulder.

"Thanks, Claudia. Everyone take a seat, it's ready!"

There was chaos after that as everyone rushed past each other to take their seats at the long table. I waited, rolling my eyes at their antics, and didn't move until they were all seated. I followed after at a much slower pace to avoid the stampede of bodies, but as I did, someone else rounded the corner that separated the kitchen from the staircase, ramming into my body. I jerked my mug back, café sloshing over the rim and burning my fingers, my other hand shooting out to steady the delicate figure before she toppled backwards.

"Woah!"

Her hands pressed against my chest. Hazel eyes met my own, big and bright and framed by dark lashes and smeared with glitter and mascara. Her light brown hair was worn in waves down her shoulders, twisted and ratted like she just got out of bed without combing it. Pajamas hugged her form and I tried not to stare too hard at her curves, or at the fact that she obviously wasn't wearing a bra beneath her flimsy tank top.

Don't ogle her nipples, pendejo.

"Cuidado," I told her, my voice low.

"Junior!" The nickname I'd had since birth pushed from her lips like the softest of sighs. "Sorry!"

Gabriela came up behind her, my older sister raising her eyebrows at Mayda's and my proximity. I pulled away with a guilty smile, though every instinct that charged through my body demanded I glue myself to her. Everything about that was a bad idea. Not only because she was my sister's best friend, but because she never gave me a single inkling that she wanted me in the same way

I wanted her. I was nothing to her but someone to side eye, my flirting brushed off and ignored, laughed into a corner of solitude and want.

Despite that, my fingers *itched* to touch her again, and I gave into the almost desperate urge. With my free hand, I reached around the back of her neck. Her body tensed for a mere fraction of a second, but she didn't pull away as I lightly caressed the tips of her messy hair. The feather-light touch sent a surge of energy up my arm and a deliciously tempting voice whispered in the back of my mind. To touch. To tug. To claim.

I tightened my hand, gripping a fistful of her dark strands and I pulled, angling her neck back so our eyes met and held. Her mouth dropped open, the heart shape of her lips forming a perfect little bow.

"Don't worry about it," I whispered. And as quickly as I gripped and pulled, I released her hair, letting it glide back against her back.

I regretted letting her go the moment I did, because not a second later, her gaze flitted away, as skittish as a bird startled from a perch. "Good morning," she mumbled, already pushing past me to go into the dining room to take her seat.

I watched her go, unable to explain the longing that began to grow in my chest every time she was near. I blew out a breath, fighting some weird, primal urge inside to rush after her. To wrap my fingers around her hair once again, just so she'd keep that gaze fixated on me for just a bit longer.

The only time she ever looked at me was in those moments, and like a thief, I took as many as I could get, because I knew there was no other way she'd ever glance at me if I didn't.

Damn.

The thought was almost sobering as much as it was heartbreaking.

CHAPTER 2

MAYDA

KILL ME NOW AND *swallow me through the floor, Diosito. I don't want to live.*

Okay, I did want to live. That was a complete exaggeration, but you couldn't blame me for being embarrassed, could you? It happened every single time I was near Damián "Junior" Águila-Gutierrez. Also known as my best friend's younger brother. A measly ten months separated the two, putting all of us at the ripe age of twenty-seven.

It was inevitable I'd make a fool of myself when he was around. Just like it was inevitable that I always seemed to look like shit when he was around, too. It almost felt like a curse at this point.

I could practically feel Gabriela containing her laughter behind me as we made our way over to the dining room table where everyone else was already seated and Doña Gloria, their housekeeper, was serving heaps of steaming chilaquiles on their plates.

The smells wafted over to me and my stomach let out a soft roar. Despite having been dancing and drinking late into the night, I was wide awake and *starving*. Maybe it was just Doña Gloria's cooking. The woman was a grade A chef, a master in the kitchen, and, for as long as I'd known her, could make any and every single dish taste divine.

It was why I loved coming to the Águila-Gutierrez house. Well, one of the reasons, anyway. I'd been coming since I was an awkward, lonely kid in elementary school. Gabriela had always been loyal to a fault and the moment she saw me, she'd declared us friends, and had been dragging me to her house almost every day since.

That fierce, unwavering determination within Gabriela was just one of the reasons my best friend and I were exact opposites in almost every aspect. But even if I was nothing like the Águila-Gutierrez clan, Gabriela still tried to fit me into their little unit somehow. Like I belonged there.

Because of the deep-rooted camaraderie we'd shared for years, it was so easy to think of myself as a part of their family, especially when my own was so disgustingly absent.

Gabriela took a seat next to her youngest sister, Valentina, leaving the only two available spots for me and Junior to sit next to one another. I tried to keep the panic off my face as I took a seat next to him. While there was an adequate amount of space separating the two of us, it felt like little more than a suffocating compact of bodies that weren't meant to share the same area.

Before I could think too hard on it, Doña Gloria was there, dumping tortilla chips covered in salsa on my plate.

The smells pulled me from my momentary alarm, causing my stomach to let out an embarrassing growl and my mouth to water. *Hmm.* Chilaquiles. I really loved the dish, especially after a night of drinking. It was practically a traditional weekend meal for me at this point. Even the simplest of foods in this household always hit me like a feast, if only because it was better than anything my own mother could have ever given me.

Once I added the fixings–cheese, sour cream, onion, raddish, lettuce, and avocado–I dug into my meal, eating in silence while everyone else around me chatted animatedly in between bites.

This was another thing I liked about being here. I liked picking through the tones, comparing, analyzing every single member of their close-knit family. A lot could be taken from a single interaction with them.

Like how the four sisters looked like their mother, except in different shades, sizes, and textures. Each girl was darker than the last, their skin in varying shades of brown and tan, all with the same midnight hair, though Ximena's curls were the wildest. Tight and thin, she kept it away from her face and held up with paintbrushes while Sofia's was straight and in a single braid down her back. Valentina's was stuck somewhere in the middle. Like her genes didn't know if they wanted to be straight or curly and stopped right in between, leaving a wild mess behind. Gabriela's was wavy, cut into beautiful layers that she never left unstyled.

Whereas I came to breakfast with a bird's nest on my head. I guess I just hadn't been thinking, my brain too addled with the few tequila shots we'd tossed back the previous night.

Their voices rose and fell in crescendos around me, like different stations of a radio playing at the same time. Valentina was practically screaming in Hector's ear about the new fowl that had been born and how excited she was to care for it, while he nodded and indulged her like he always did. Mamá Claudia and Doña Gloria were speaking amongst themselves, with firm and elegant flicks of their hands and wrists. Ximena was in deep conversation with her quieter sister Sofia, and Gabriela and her father were talking about the rancho's income.

"Wild night?"

I nearly choked on a thin strip of lettuce as Junior lightly elbowed me in the side. I could feel my cheeks reddening as I turned to face his humorous grin. My tongue felt almost leaden in my mouth. That goddamn grin weakened me. I should have been immune to the charm he exuded, given all the years we'd been in one another's presence, yet being around him got harder—not easier—with time.

Junior was beautiful. I wasn't sure if you could even call men that, but he *was*. It was in the full features of his lips and the smooth texture of his brown skin, wide dark eyes and soft hair shorn short against his scalp. There was a time he was lanky, his limbs skinny, his joints knobby, head and ears almost too big for his body.

The joy of practically being raised together meant we got to witness each other's awkward phases. If you'd told me then that Junior would grow from the skinny boy who yanked on my pigtails in passing to the ripped specimen sitting next to me—who *still* yanked on my hair—well, I would have laughed.

Not so funny now, huh?

"It was pretty tame," I replied. The tightening of my fingers against my fork grounded me. If he looked at me, he'd never know how my stomach twisted into thousands of knots before exploding from the pressure of thousands of fluttering butterflies taking flight. Every single nerve-ending seemed to hum when he was near, begging for a scrap of a touch. My heart pounded until I could feel the rapid beating knotting into my throat.

I couldn't let any of that show. Not because I didn't want to, not because it was kind of embarrassing to reveal my true self around him, but out of necessity. I was born into a household that thought feelings were a nuisance, and expressing them would be more trouble than they were worth.

Junior's eyes were searching, flicking over me with a curious, assessing gaze. Like he was trying to find a lie in my words, or like he was comparing them to my disheveled, hungover appearance.

I suddenly cursed myself for not taking a brush through my hair before coming down.

"I can see that." His lips pursed as his eyes flicked back up to mine. His brown depths glittered with amusement, and I recognized the teasing almost instantly. I was all too familiar with it.

I turned back to my plate, a part of me wishing the floor could just swallow me whole already while I shoveled another forkful into my mouth, my every movement methodical and practiced.

Junior just liked to ruffle my feathers, to see what kind of a reaction he could get out of me. It had been like an ongoing game between us since childhood. I was always the shy one, eclipsed by his sister's blinding light, quietly trailing after her, always the voice of reason. Calm. Collected. Mature for my age. He'd taken to jesting, making me want to blush at every turn even if my body would never give him the satisfaction of that.

I liked that routine between us, because Junior had never been hurtful. Not like the other boys at school. Not just because his mother would have taken a belt to his behind if she'd found out he was being mean to anyone, but also because Junior had always been a genuinely good guy.

Conversation flowed after that relatively easily around me. Gabriela chimed in about our "wild" night out at a club in the city, a place we frequented a few times a month.

"What were you out celebrating this time?" Hector asked laughingly.

Gabriela brought her mug of café up to her lips. "It was a celebration and mourning put together in honor of Mayda. She goes back to work in a few weeks and needed a night out before all the craziness starts."

"Aw, cariño that's wonderful," Mamá Claudia, the Águila-Gutierrez matriarch, crooned in my direction. "Are you excited about your new post?"

Genuine pride shone in her eyes that made me swallow back emotions for a second. It was a look she'd been giving me my entire life and it got to me every single time. It was more than my own mother ever gave me, that was for sure.

"It's a dream come true," I answered honestly.

I'd always wanted to be a school counselor, and after years of applying, I *finally* got the job.

"She has to go in today and set her office up," Gabriela continued.

An uneasy feeling slid down my spine as I caught the glint in her eye and heard the mischievous tone of her voice. She was up to something. I recognized that look. It was the same shine she always got before she dragged me into one of her crazy schemes.

"It's in a few hours, but I have to help papá with the accounting today and I can't take her. And since her car isn't here..." She trailed off, letting her family fill in the blank.

I barely contained myself from mouthing *What the fuck are you doing?*

"You can't be late on your first day." Mamá Claudia set her mug down on the table, giving me the practiced, overly dramatic look of a surprised telenovela star. She thrived on punctuality and being late was a nightmare for her. For a moment, she got a pensive look on her face before she snapped her fingers as an idea burst. "Junior can take you!"

My fork clattered against my plate, eyes widening. I took in Gabriela's smug expression. It was all I needed to see to know that this was planned.

Bitch.

I made sure my eyes conveyed that particular message loud and clear, and she stifled her laughter behind her hand.

"I couldn't impose…"

"Nonsense! How else would you get there? An Uber? No, no, no. Junior will help you."

"I wouldn't want to cut into his work time," I argued weakly.

"Está bien," Papá Damian cut in. "He can spare a few hours."

My fingers twisted into my napkin and I all but ripped the cloth at the seams. "But—"

"It's okay, Mayda." Junior's hand came down to rest over mine, his touch easing and eliciting anxiety all at once. My heart pounded up to my throat, and I turned to meet his warm gaze and easy smile. "I'll take you."

"I don't want to monopolize your time…"

"Nonsense!" his mom called out from across the table. "You're family, too, mija."

In the end it was that single word that did me in.

Family.

I'd known them since I was a child and was related to them all but by blood. That's what it felt like sometimes, but it was often easy to place myself on the outside of their little unit. Like an orphan staring from a windowpane at something I'd always wished I had. Like it was my greatest desire within my grasp, grazing at the tips of my fingers hovering not quite within my reach.

And I treated it like it was mine just the same.

I gave them an indulgent smile and slid my hand out from under Junior's, missing his warmth almost immediately. I chastised myself for feeling that way. It wasn't like that's where his touch belonged. Just like I didn't quite belong at their table and yet there I was. Belonging, but not. Tolerated, but loved. *Ni de aquí, ni de allá.* The words had never resonated more so than they did in moments like this. When I felt like I didn't belong here, there, or anywhere else. At this point, it felt like it was a habit for them to have me at their table.

And some habits were just harder to break.

CHAPTER 3

JUNIOR

I WAS WAITING FOR Mayda while she got ready, leaning my shoulder against the side of my black Chevy, when my papá approached.

He was dressed in his jeans and work boots, a sombrero on his head to shield him from the sun. Not like it ever made much of a difference with this heat. It beat down against us with unrelenting pressure and left us sweating and red-faced, darkening our skin. Hats just seemed like a part of the uniform at this point, with no real purpose.

"No te tardes," Papá said, his voice stern. It was a complete contradiction to his open and loving expression at breakfast earlier. He was all hard lines and seriousness now as he ordered me to hurry back. The face he wore in my presence was always so different from the mask he donned in front of others.

"I won't be long," I promised.

He nodded once. "Good. You have things to do here on the rancho. When you get back, I need you to talk with Gabriela so she can show you how payment works and you can discuss inventory."

I tried not to tense, but the slightest tightening of my body was inevitable. I knew he noticed it, because his eyes narrowed on me, breathing me in like he would the smoke from those old Cuban cigars he liked to keep in his office.

My sisters often joked that as the first-born son, I was the favorite. That being born a man somehow earned me special treatment. Perhaps to others it would appear that way, but the reality was that if you were born first in a Mexican household, you were beholden and indebted to your parents. They raised you differently from your youngest siblings, funneled more responsibilities onto your shoulders, demanded more of you because you were the example the other children would follow.

I wasn't oblivious to the distinction between Gabriela and I, though. My prerogatives weren't limited to kitchen duty or diaper-changing like hers had been, but that didn't make my struggles as their 'protector' any less valid. Especially when that role was thrust upon me by my papá, and to refuse the path laid out for me meant his censure and my consternation.

Relaxing my features, I ran a hand through my closely cropped hair. My stomach twisted with frustration and a sense of foreboding.

I loved my papá, I truly did. Familia was important, they were everything. Like any Latine, we sometimes defined ourselves by the roots we put down. By how close we were and how much we valued and were loyal to those in our lives. We were as close as could be, and while I loved the rancho, and while I was proud of what we had all built, a struggle lived inside me.

The struggle of wanting more, of wanting something different, while at the same time balancing on that edge that would keep me tightly knit to them, to my papá and his legacy. As his only son, it rested on my shoulders to keep the rancho going after him.

It shouldn't have been hard. My papá had been grooming me for this since I could walk. I knew what to do, I knew how to work the fields just like any other trabajador here. Contrary to the wealth of the house, I didn't grow up sucking on a silver spoon. We didn't struggle by any means. Not like others struggled, like Doña Gloria after her husband died. But he taught me humility by sending me out to work with the others. Like *he* did and still does.

Because what kind of a jefe would I be if I wasn't willing to get my hands dirty?

The philosophy made sense, in retrospect. So I busted ass at the crack of dawn with the rest of them and I learned never to complain. Never to contradict.

Now, though, my father was training me in other ways. I knew the rancho and I knew the workers. It was time to learn about the business side of things.

That was usually Gabriela's domain. She was an accountant and took care of all matters pertaining to the rancho. She helped to bring in the money. Numbers were her thing. She paid the wages, the taxes, did inventory, and everything else. My papá had a hand in it, and now he wanted to drag me into it as well.

It was one thing to work the fields and tend to the animals. It felt like another commitment entirely to start taking over that aspect of the business. It was a huge step. One that had me jerking back and staggering, only to feel my papá's massive hand against my shoulder, teetering me forward into something I wasn't ready for.

Something I didn't think I'd ever be ready for.

"Great," I answered, hoping he wouldn't hear the skepticism in my voice.

He wasn't Mamá. She could smell bullshit from a mile away. Or maybe he did and just didn't care about my tentative misgivings. He had a way of ignoring my discomfort like it was an Olympic sport. Out of sight, out of mind.

"Perfecto." He clapped me on the back. "Then we are going to meet with our suppliers, and I'll teach you how to buy and breed the best stallions on this side of the border."

"Sounds great, papá."

His lips curled from beneath his thick, graying mustache in a smile, his dark brows raising over brown eyes. He looked like he wanted to speak again, to say something else, but I was spared as Mayda walked towards the truck.

A bag was slung over a slender shoulder, her hair freshly combed and showered. Clad in tight jeans and a soft pink and gray cardigan, she walked in an almost tentative way towards me, her eyes guarded. For a moment, my papá fell away and I was lost in the hazel color of her eyes.

My entire family had eyes that ranged from the color of molten honey to brown to black. Hers were different, yet it wasn't the color that fascinated me. It was the secrets she garnered in their depths.

When we were younger, I used to yank on the back of her ponytail to get her attention. She would never flinch, never scream at me for it. She'd been calm and collected even then, tossing a strait-laced expression over her shoulder like she couldn't be bothered with my antics.

She wore a mask, even in her eyes, and I was desperate to pull it off and catch a glimpse of what lay underneath. I'd always been curious. Granted, I knew—we all knew—from Gabriela that Mayda's home life left much to be desired, but we didn't know details. Mayda was closed off. And we didn't pry.

She was like a perfect porcelain statue that I was almost too afraid to touch sometimes, out of fear that she would break. A thought that came and went fleetingly. She wasn't weak or easily breakable.

The truth was, I didn't know *what* she was beyond the icy, crisp demeanor.

Her footsteps slowed as she approached us, her worn flats scuffling against the rocky ground. She paused, and a slow smile curled at the edges of her mouth.

I lived for those smiles, for the softness of her face when she started to let her guard down. She pointed that smile in my direction first before turning to my papá.

"Thanks so much, Señor Águila. I promise I won't keep him long." Her tone should have been teasing, but she said it so softly, seriously, leaving no doubt in my mind that she meant to not monopolize my time.

I didn't know why that stung.

It always felt like she was trying so quickly to get rid of me.

"I told you many times to call me Papá Damián."

Mayda's eyes flashed. It was shockingly brief before the mask pulled tightly at the edges again. She didn't say anything to reply to that, though she did give the slightest nod with her head.

That was answer enough for papá. He turned to me, the jovial expression he wore when facing Mayda morphing into something stern as it tore through me like a knife. It made me tense and give him a terse nod before turning away from him to face Mayda.

"Ready to go?" I snapped without meaning to. Her guarded expression turned surprised, then hard as she nodded. I didn't give myself a moment to feel guilty for snapping because I was already turning, briskly opening the passenger side door.

Mayda slid inside carefully like she did everything else. Once she was settled inside, I slammed the door and rounded the other side, hopping in. Only after we were both buckled in did I peel out of the rancho, leaving my father and his expectations behind in a cloud of dust.

Chapter 4

MAYDA

"**D**on't talk to me. I hate you right now."

I slid the brush through my hair, pulling at the ratted tangles and wincing every time. The yanks at my scalp took me back to my childhood. Back when my mom would slam a brush against my head in retaliation every time I moved and messed up her braids. It would happen a few times before she finally gave up, tore the careful construct of arranged hair, and let me go to school with it down in waves against my shoulders.

Pulling at the tangles now felt like my own way of punishing myself for being stupid enough to walk into breakfast with a bird's nest in the first place.

"You love me," Gabriela replied before she leaned forward in the mirror of her vanity and swiped lip gloss over her full, heart shaped lips. She finished and smacked her mouth, blowing a kiss to her reflection before smoothing the ends of her hair over her shoulders.

I'd always admired her sense of style. One would think that because we were opposites, me quiet and calm, her loud and boisterous, that she would dress as wild as her personality. But that wasn't the case. Yes, Gabriela was wild at heart. She was opinionated and headstrong, but she gave off bad ass jefa vibes and every day she dressed like she was ready to destroy the patriarchy.

She wore dark slacks with a pink blouse and a single string of pearls around her neck. She didn't wear earrings or anything she deemed frivolous around her wrists. Her makeup was simple, her gaze sharp.

She looked ready to conquer the world while I stood next to her in jeans, a pastel-colored cardigan, and old flats.

We were like yin and yang, she and I.

"I can't believe you pulled that stunt," I complained, setting the brush down on the little table.

Gabriela emitted a rude noise. "Please, you should be thanking me. I know you have the hots for my brother."

It didn't matter how many times she said the words, they never failed to make me blush like I was in middle school all over again.

"Now you'll have the chance to be alone with him for a bit," she went on, oblivious to my discomfort.

Me and my best friend's brother? No. Absolutely not.

"I don't have the... *hots*... for Junior," I said adamantly, stumbling a little over the word. "Besides, that goes against girl code. I'm sure of it."

Gabriela scoffed. "Screw girl code. You know how I feel about that. It was created by some jealous pendejas who would rather see everyone around them suffer than allow others to live their happiness. What kind of an asshole would I be if I told you not to date my brother when you've obviously been mooning over him our whole lives?"

Her words managed to both amuse and offend me at the same time.

Typical Gabriela. She didn't believe in unspoken codes. She was so frank and honest and believed in going after what you wanted. In her world that was probably the case. We lived on different planets and I was looking through a telescope at her brightness.

Besides, I hadn't been *mooning* after Junior. The audacity!

"Yeah, well, I don't know what you're trying to accomplish here. I don't like him and even if I did, he would never look at me twice. So there."

I hated how the words burned on my throat and how true they felt, at least the latter. Junior was... untouchable. He always had been. Him and Gabriela had been insanely popular in school because of the confident way they carried themselves. Junior had been on the school's basketball and soccer teams and had girls fawning over him all the time. Gabriela had exuded beauty and power, and the fact that she'd enrolled in so many clubs—debate, chess, and soccer? She would have been reigning queen of the school were it not for the baggage she dragged around like a shadow.

Me.

I was that baggage.

So even if I wanted him, I would never fit or deserve him simply because of who I was and where I came from. I didn't have a big, beautiful family. I was never the smartest in my class like Gabriela. I was plain. Tarnished copper, compared to their glittering gold.

"Alright." Gabriela stood to her full height, towering over my smaller stature by a whole foot, placing her hands on her hips. She had the stare mastered to mimic her mother's, and it was equally frightening as when Mamá Claudia did it. It made me want to whither. "Get this one thing straight, Mayda Jiménez. You are beautiful, and kind, and amazing. My brother couldn't find anyone better than you even if Diosito himself dropped a woman from the sky right in front of him. You will be with Junior one day and we will be sisters *officially*. Got that?" She'd started to point the end of her lip gloss at me like she meant to stab me with it.

I held my hands up in mock surrender. "Cálmate," I said. "Calm down, it's no big deal."

Gabriela's eyes narrowed "I know when you're shit talking yourself in that pretty little head of yours. I won't stand for it. So just get with the program, grab your bag, and go charm the pants off my brother so you can get married already. Geez." She tossed the lip gloss with irritation, which only made me chuckle as I bent to grab my overnight bag and slung it over my shoulder.

This had been an on-going battle that had only seemed to escalate over the years. My best friend had never been the type to say "Ew, you have a crush on my brother!" and shame me for it, no matter how badly I denied it. The first time Junior had yanked on my ponytail in passing, Gabriela's eyes had lit up with promise. The next day, with a bright, scheming smile, she'd declared, "One day you will marry Junior and we can be sisters de verdad."

De verdad.

For real.

A longing had burst inside my five-year-old heart at those words. But then her own sisters had been born. Ximena and then Sofia, one after the other and ten months apart, as appeared to be the norm with the Águila-Gutierrez siblings. It seemed Gabriela had gotten her wish. She had sisters *for real.* But she never pushed me away, and she said she still wanted *me* because I was closer to her age than the others. Because I was her favorite.

I was never sure if she truly meant those words, but hell if Gabriela didn't have a way of making me feel special.

It was one of the things I loved the most about her.

"I can't believe you're ditching me."

"I have work to do, y tú también. So stop complaining." With a final flick of her hair, she turned towards her bedroom door. "Now get out and go flirt with Junior."

I scoffed as I left her room, stopping to say goodbye to Mamá Claudia and Gabriela's abuelita. I hated interrupting them while they were bustling around the house, even more so while they were watching their favorite morning novela, but I still stopped and said goodbye, since leaving without doing that would have been taboo. She probably would have kicked me out and never let me back in if I dared.

After saying my goodbyes, I headed out the door, walking down the graveled path to where Junior's truck was parked to find him speaking with his father. I slowed my gait, looking between the two. I observed them for a moment, noting their similarities and differences.

All of the women of the Águila-Gutierrez family looked like very different versions of the same painting, or at the very least, different variations of a single color. But Junior looked like his father, and I could catch a glimpse of what Junior would be when he was older. Señor Águila had a strong build and a slightly rounded stomach. He wasn't the tallest; in fact, Junior loomed over him by quite a bit. But they had the same strong, straight nose and fierce jawlines. While Junior kept his face clean shaven, Señor Águila's upper lip was peppered with a graying mustache. Their eyes were similar, drawn in the same shape, same thick, dark lashes, and a color that rivaled molten pools of honey every time the sunlight hit them. My steps faltered and I tried to keep my expression neutral, satisfied that it wouldn't change in time to the crazy pounding of my stupid heart whenever he was near.

But then he turned and looked at me and his whole body seemed to soften. I hated noticing that. Hated how Gabriela's words about Junior and I getting married played in my head when I knew just how impossible it was. But I couldn't deny the softness of his expression. How his body seemed to tilt towards me. Or the feelings he provoked in my belly as he stared into my eyes like he was trying to find a chip in my armor.

He always looked at me like that.

Like he could strip away all my secrets with a passing glance. What I didn't know was why he wanted them, or what he planned to do with them if he ever had them.

The fear of that alone had me tearing my gaze away from him to look at his father, a soft smile pulling at my lips.

"Thanks for having me over, Señor Águila."

"I told you many times to call me Papá Damián."

I tensed a fraction, hoping they didn't notice. He had told me to call him that, but I couldn't bring myself to. Not because I felt like it was a betrayal to my own father, screw that guy, but because Damián was also Junior's name, and I didn't want to sound like a freaking pervert.

He just smiled at me before turning back to Junior. The two shared a look and I noticed how Junior tensed up before turning to me and snapping.

"Ready to go?"

Well, shit.

The sharpness coming off him could slice me into pieces. So much for Gabriela's master plan. Not like I had been intent on it in the first place. Hell no. I wasn't going to be making a fool of myself in front of Junior by attempting—pathetically—to flirt with him.

He opened the passenger side door for me, and I slipped inside methodically, putting my seatbelt on before he slammed the door. He got in on his side and peeled out so quickly I jerked against my seatbelt.

What the hell?

I looked at him from my peripheral and noted the white-knuckled grip he had on the steering wheel and the slight flare of his nostrils. Something was upsetting him. I wasn't sure what he and his father were talking about, but that would explain this sudden anger.

I didn't want to think about it though, because regardless of what his sister wanted, Junior and I were barely friends. We barely spoke to one another unless Gabriela was there because things had a funny way of getting very awkward very quickly.

Like right now, for example.

So I pressed my lips tightly together and I shut up and focused on the ride ahead. But as the ride progressed and he veered off into the highway, Junior's shoulders began to relax, his fingers loosening against the wheel. I knew he was calm the moment he let out his next deep breath.

"Sorry," he said. "I shouldn't have snapped at you."

I didn't reply except to lift a shoulder in a shrug. There wasn't anything I could say. Everyone had a right to their feelings, good or bad, and at least he was conscious enough to apologize when he felt he was in the wrong.

In my experience, not everyone was like that.

"Hey."

I jerked my attention from the rosary hanging from the mirror, swinging like a pendulum, to find him side-glancing me.

"I'm sorry, Mayda," he repeated. "I was an asshole."

"It's okay, Junior."

He let out another breath that escaped into a chuckle. "Shit, that was easy. My sisters would have slammed my face into the steering wheel."

"Well, it's a good thing I'm not your sister then," I replied with an almost teasing tone.

"Yeah." He chuckled. "Good thing." The words were spoken low, so low they held an entrancing edge to them that made me want to shiver. My breath caught in my throat at the heated flash in his eyes a single moment before he turned his attention back to the road.

What the hell was that?

A reprieve from that heated stare had me looking out the window, trying to discreetly catch my breath. For a moment it felt like...

"So, tell me about your new job," Junior began.

My job was a great subject for the much-needed distraction. It helped to tear me from the fantasies my mind conjured up.

"I'm starting on as a school counselor," I explained. "I've been working office jobs for so long hoping to get here one day. It feels pretty surreal that I actually made it after applying to so many schools."

I worked hard to become a counselor. I knew people didn't think it was an important job, especially not at an elementary school, but it was. Young minds were always the most impressionable, and if there was a possibility that I could help at least one student on the pathway to a better life? It was worth it.

I wasn't aware I'd said those words aloud until Junior's hand came to rest against my thigh. "You're doing a great thing," he whispered.

But I couldn't focus on his words when his hand. Was. On. My. Thigh.

Shit.

The touch was warm and grounding, much like his presence. Meanwhile, I felt like I couldn't breathe. For a second, I entertained a fantasy where his hand slid up higher to press between my legs, easing the ache he caused with his mere presence.

"Thanks," I choked out.

Seeming to realize what he was doing, his hand slipped away from me quickly to press back against the wheel. I noted the way the fingers on that hand tightened and I wondered if he felt like contact with me burned. It certainly burned me. Even through my jeans, I could feel the presence of his touch like a heavy brand.

But it didn't bother me at all.

In fact, a selfish part of me wanted his hand there again.

"Some people would probably tell you to work with CPS instead."

His sudden words broke me out of whatever spell he'd placed under me. An immediate scoff pushed from my lips that I tried to snuff just as quickly as it was released.

Junior's eyes darted to me, then back to the road. "Don't have a high opinion of them?"

"Oh, no, I do. It's just…" I tried to convene my thoughts and internal monologue, carefully picking apart and organizing my sentences before I spoke them. "I think the system is disgustingly broken."

He waved a hand between us, a silentious order to elaborate.

"Think about it. If a parent can't afford to take care of their child, the government takes them away and places them under the care of a foster family, giving that family monthly checks and food stamps. Monetary aid that could have been given to the child's parent in the first place. In what world does that system make any sense at all? Not to mention the blatant abuse that occurs within these homes and the fact that so many of those teens end up homeless or back with parents unable and unwilling to change or care for them the way they deserve! Not to mention, the parents that actually love their children being forced away from them!"

A prolonged silence filled the space in which I fought to catch my breath.

"I guess I never thought about it." His fingers thrummed against the wheel and he nibbled on his bottom lip. "I mean, how could I? I grew up privileged, I guess. I don't know the struggles of others." For a second, he sounded disgusted with himself, and a part of me wanted to reach across and placate him with a hand to his knee like he had me. But I didn't. He was right. He *was* privileged. That didn't make him a bad person, though. It just meant that he had a lot to learn about the world.

"The number of POC and BIPOC children screwed over by the system is astounding. Besides giving them over to white families and having their cultures erased, it just *ensures* systematic poverty. With the system overflowing with kids, they're too tired to care about a single one of them." My voice cracked on the last word, a sliver of my emotions bleeding through. I forced myself to look away, watching the scenery pass by while I tried to get my shit together.

I'd researched foster care extensively as a kid and would have done *anything* to avoid it.

"So, you think you're better suited to help at the school?" he asked, pulling my attention back to him.

"I know it probably sounds fantastical, and logically I know that I won't be able to help *every* child, but I want to make a difference. Even if it's just for one kid. School is a sanctuary for some, and they need that safe haven, just like they need teachers and counselors to talk to."

I'd needed that. I was speaking from my own experiences, and from many others. School was *my* haven besides the

Águila-Gutierrez household. It was where I could flourish in my studies, where I didn't have to worry about the crippling fear of staggering footsteps and angry words and punishments.

"Eres increíble, Mayda," Junior whispered finally. "Truly incredible."

The praise had a flush crawling up my neck and staining my cheeks. I probably looked a really unattractive shade, and I was desperate to change the subject. While I was proud of my work and what I aspired to be, talking about it with Junior felt intimate in a way that frightened me. Only Gabriela knew my hopes and dreams, and even then, she knew whatever little pieces I gifted her. His attention made me feel awkward, and without my best friend present as a buffer, I feared he'd easily be able to gauge every emotion on my face.

I shrugged. "So, what about you?"

Drum, drum, drum. His fingers tapped away at the wheel. "What about me?"

"What are *your* future plans?"

The drumming stuttered off-beat before he white-knuckled the wheel and cleared his throat. He flashed me a side smirk before returning his focus to the road, though I noticed his demeanor had changed. I was in tune with his mannerisms, yet the change was so subtle, I almost hadn't caught it.

"You know." His shoulder lifted in a shrug. "Taking care of el rancho."

"Lots of work goes into that."

"Yup."

His one-worded answer was off-putting as well as telling. I was toeing a line of a subject he didn't want to discuss. While curiosity burned holes through my insides, I backed off, respecting his bit of privacy. It didn't matter how much I wanted to know; we weren't *that* close. I had no right or reason to pry. Besides, I had my own secrets.

We all did.

Some more dreadful than others.

Eventually we fell back into comfortable conversation that died down all too soon as we got closer to my place. Even as Junior tried to keep it going, relishing in our brief moment of camaraderie, I couldn't bring myself to play along anymore. Self-consciousness coiled in my gut as I realized this was the first time he'd ever been in my neighborhood. This was the first time, in all the time we'd known one another, he would see my house.

Gabriela and her sisters had been here on occasion—during quick pit stops to pick up my things—and while Gabriela didn't mind the humble, broken-down place I'd lived in since I was a kid, I preferred to keep this part of my life separate from theirs. Mine was embarrassing. Not because the house wasn't as lavish as theirs, but because it was hollow inside. Dead.

And because of *who* I lived with.

The broken shingles and cracked windows looked disgustingly dreary and pathetic. The place made me feel small in ways I didn't think I was capable of feeling anymore. It was hard not to compare the opulence of the ranch to this. Hell, even Junior's small home outside of the main house was better kept than mine.

I could feel my cheeks burning as he pulled up to my driveway. He put the truck in park and stared out the window at my place, his brows furrowed together. I wanted to know what he was thinking, but at the same time, I was sure I would've died of mortification if I deep-dived into his thoughts. Having him here was embarrassing enough as is; I didn't need to hear his internal musings about my shitty place.

I cleared my throat, pressing the button on my seat belt so it would slide back into place. Gripping the strap of my overnight bag tightly, I refused to meet Junior's eyes.

"Thanks for the ride," I said. "I guess I'll... I'll see you some other time." I couldn't open the door fast enough. My fingers fumbled as they shook against the handle. My breaths were shallow and demanding and my face was flaming.

"Mayda..."

His voice cut through the sound of me pushing open the truck door. I froze, one leg already out of the vehicle. I didn't want to face him and see pity on his face, but not to look at him would make me seem like the coward I was.

So I took a deep breath and turned to meet his gaze, only to find him smirking at me.

"¿No te vas a despedir de mi?"

I nearly swallowed my tongue at the deep timbre and perfect Spanish pushing past his lips.

I was Puerto Rican on my mom's side, but she never taught me to speak a lick of Spanish, even if she could speak it herself. She was just never around enough to bother educating me on the language, let alone my heritage. But one didn't spend time at the Águila-Gutierrez household and not pick up bits and pieces of it.

Their house was a clash of cultures, Mexican and American. Their parents were so involved with their children's lives that it was unfathomable they didn't know their own roots. I envied that sometimes, wished my mom would have cared enough to teach me something, anything.

Regardless, I knew what Junior was saying.

Aren't you going to say goodbye to me?

I nearly sputtered. I knew he was teasing just like he always did because he wanted to see me flustered. I couldn't show him just what his words made me feel as I slid my leg back into the truck and scooted towards him.

In Mexican—or rather, in most Latine cultures—we greeted and said our goodbyes with a kiss to the cheek. I'd done it hundreds, if not thousands, of times before, but this felt different.

It felt intimate.

With my lips a whisper away from his skin, I pressed a quick kiss to his cheek. His face turned as I moved, though, lips skimming against the corner of my mouth. I froze and his touch lingered. We stayed like that for a single breath before I pulled away.

Fireworks danced beneath my skin, causing the hairs on my arms to rise. I resisted the urge to slide my palms against my body to ease that burning ache that rapidly built.

Junior's own pupils were flaring, his eyes trained on my mouth. This had never happened before. I didn't mean the desire. That was quintessentially my own. It breathed within me, a life I couldn't extinguish no matter how hard I tried. I'd spent so many nights burning with it, wishing his hands were there to ease the ache, having to make do with my own.

It was the charged air between us like crackles of electricity. It made everything more perceptible. My feelings. My emotions. My nipples ached within my bra, and my core throbbed to the beating of my heart and harsh breaths. Everything about this was almost suffocating and entirely too overwhelming.

"Thanks again." I broke the spell, and his eyes went up to mine again. "See you..."

His mouth opened and closed then opened again. Finally, he nodded but didn't say anything else, so I jumped out of the truck and slammed the door, making sure to walk calmly up to my house. I dug into my pocket for the key, my hands trembling as I opened it and stepped inside.

I took a moment without him in my presence to breathe deeply and get my emotions under control. It was so hard to do around him. Each day I felt my mask slipping more and more, and I was terrified that one day, he'd be able to read it as easily as Gabriela could.

I couldn't let that happen.

I dropped my bag on the floor and began gathering my things I needed for my office. It took me all of ten minutes to get everything in two different boxes, as I'd already prepped most of it beforehand. Hefting one in my arms, I juggled it and my car keys as I stepped back outside.

Only to find Junior still parked out front.

He jumped out of the truck and sauntered towards me, his hips all but moving seductively as he approached. "Let me help." Before I could protest, he was pulling the box from my arms to his.

"Um... don't you have to go to work?" I asked.

"Trying to get rid of me?" He winked back. "Let me help you, Mayda. I can drive you to work and help you get your office settled."

I could practically hear Gabriela laughing maniacally in my ear, urging me to say yes and put the moves on him, but my own logical thoughts won out. My brows furrowed. "I couldn't ask that of you. You've already done enough..."

Junior's eyes rolled. "Giving you a ride isn't what I'd call 'enough'. Come on, Mayda. Quiero ayudar. I'll take you to school, help you set up, and then bring you back."

My own eyes narrowed at the offer, trying to gauge why he wanted to help me so badly. Junior was always very selfless and very kind. In school, if we walked in the same direction, he would always offer to carry my bag and books, even while he held mountains of his own plus his basketball or soccer equipment. He was chivalrous. But I didn't like feeling like a burden any more than I had to.

"Why?"

He was already moving towards the truck. "Why what?" He opened the door and set the boxes in the back seat before turning with raised eyebrows.

"Why do you want to help?" I hated how snippy the words sounded and how ungrateful they tasted on my tongue. I winced; I couldn't help it.

It was hard accepting help. Anytime anyone tried, they always wanted something in return. There was always some ulterior motive that came with their offers. It was the one thing my mom had taught me that was hard to get rid of.

It was hard enough being friends with Gabriela, staying at her house, eating her food. I learned to roll with it because she was my best friend, and I tried to give kindness back to her as much as she gave it to me. Junior was different.

I wasn't sure if his kindness came with a price, and I hated myself for thinking it did. He had never implied that it did, so why was my mind going in that direction now?

He studied me a moment before answering and when he did, he leaned forward and smirked. "The truth is, I'm helping you for selfish reasons."

I knew it.

I swallowed, and it felt like there was a lump caught in my throat.

"I want to see you in action. I want to see you at school, I want to see all the great things you plan on doing..."

My chest heaved with those words, though trepidation still crawled down my spine. It seemed almost too good to be true, and I didn't want to hope that he was actually being honest. "I'm just going to set up my office... I—I'm not actually starting work..."

He smiled, flashing straight, white teeth. "I know." Then he sobered for a second. "You made me realize that I know nothing about the real world. I've been living in the rancho's bubble." His gaze swept over my house then back to me. "I'm embarrassed. To know so little about the system, about *you*. How is it, Mayda, that we've known each other for years and it still feels like I don't know a thing about you? Can't you just give me this?"

If he was anything like his sister, I knew he wasn't going to give up so easily. It would be better to give in, to let him take me to the school and back again without a fight.

I didn't show it in my expression as I agreed, but my stomach rumbled with nervous butterflies. Unwilling to admit it, a part of me was excited and reluctant to be spending more time with him, just the two of us. That he wanted to *know* me, even if there wasn't much worth knowing.

CHAPTER 5

JUNIOR

I INSERTED MYSELF INTO her day purely out of selfish reasons. I hadn't meant to. We'd said our adioses, she'd gone inside, and I had my foot poised over the gas pedal, ready to peel out of her neighborhood. But something stopped me. A number of confounding reasons prevented me from pressing down and going back to the rancho and all the responsibilities that awaited me there.

In all the time I'd known Mayda, I hadn't looked too closely at her place. I knew she came from a humble household, but I hadn't remembered it looking *this* shabby before. The walls and windows had never looked so splintered, the paint so chipped, the neighborhood so dreary. And the closer we got to her place, the more I noticed Mayda retreating into herself, avoiding conversation, sinking into her seat.

I couldn't recall ever seeing her look so *sad*.

It pushed me back to our earlier conversation about my life and the privilege I'd known. Oblivious to the turmoil of others while I've been locked inside my own version of a palace. Just the thought that I had no real pinche idea what it was like for others kept me rooted where I was.

I didn't even have any real idea what it was like for Mayda.

Perhaps that was why I wanted to stay. For Mayda. To know her. I wanted to spend time with her while simultaneously staying away from my papá for a few hours as well.

Like I said, purely selfish.

And then there was that kiss.

I'd kissed Mayda on the cheek thousands of times before whenever we said hola or adiós. But never like that. It was always quick, just a fast press of our faces together. Her lips had certainly never touched my cheek like that, and mine had certainly never lingered in places they shouldn't, so close that I could smell and nearly taste the mint of her toothpaste on the corner of her mouth.

It had just felt *right*.

And that scared the shit out of me. Because for a brief fucking second, she had felt like a dream come true grasped within the palms of my hands. And like smoke, that dream vanished. I was left reminding myself she wasn't mine, this aloof, mysterious woman that I truly didn't know.

We were both quiet as I drove towards the elementary school. We lived in a small town with a small population where everyone knew everyone. We went to that school when we were kids, and it felt strange parking in the lot. Even stranger to see it nearly empty.

"Only a few of us are coming in today," Mayda supplied as she unbuckled and went to open the back door for the boxes. I followed closely behind, reaching to grab the heaviest one. I'd take both of them, but I knew she wouldn't allow that. Stubborn woman. "A few of the teachers are still on vacation."

"Does Mrs. Roberts still work here?" I asked.

A small smile touched her lips as her hip connected with the truck door, slamming it closed. "She does."

"Damn. That woman was evil."

Her laugh trickled from her throat, mesmerizing me on the spot. "You were so loud in her class. I remember."

"It was so *boring*. She called my parents in so many times. My mamá took the belt to my backside more than once because of the shit I pulled." It stung back then and had me howling like an animal, but I knew I deserved it. Especially because I set the class pet loose in her drawer. Hearing her scream and fall back in her chair when she opened it to find a gerbil gnawing at her pencils was hilarious.

"You never pulled a stunt like the gerbil again, though," Mayda said like she was reading my mind.

"My papá threatened to ship me off to military school. I believed him, so I stopped with my shenanigans."

I remembered being so pissed at my papá. Sometimes, if I thought about all those situations—and everything he'd ever threatened me with—I felt nauseous. Being his only son meant he was stricter with me than he was with any of my other siblings. The legacy of our family fell solely on my shoulders, and I was meant to carry it out with dignity and hard work.

He'd told me to get my shit together, so I did, even at a young age.

Swallowing the lump in my throat, I got quiet as Mayda led me towards the entrance of the school. The scent of the place brought back so many memories of when we came here. Muscle memory guided me straight past the principal's office and into the counselor's office. She procured a key from her pocket and opened the door.

The office was smaller than I remembered. It was funny how looking at things through the lens of a child could make the world seem so vast but looking at the same things as an adult gave you a different perspective entirely. The room itself was stripped naked to nothing but the bare bones of a desk, a computer, and a chair.

"What happened to the previous counselor?" I placed the box on the desk next to the other one she'd set down.

"She retired, *finally*," Mayda replied, digging into a box to start pulling out her personal items. As she set them out along the desk, I realized she'd brought everything from motivational posters about honesty, emotions, friendship, and perseverance.

Seeing them filled me with a strange pang of longing, especially when she pulled out a poster of an adult hugging a child, the words 'It's okay to ask for help' spread out in big lettering.

Right then, I wished I'd had a teacher like Mayda growing up. Someone who cared enough to say those words to me. If I'd been encouraged from a young age, maybe it would have given me the courage to confess to my papá the truth about what I wanted with my life. Maybe then I wouldn't need to hide the fact that I was secretly taking online college courses.

With the rancho forced to be my main focus, college just wasn't in the cards for me. Eventually, I'd started getting antsy, and the drowning feeling of worthlessness had been powerful enough to push me into action. Like I was meant for more. I enrolled in online courses in secret for years. I obtained my major in child development. Like Mayda, I could apply for a job as a counselor or child psychologist if I wanted to, but the real desire was pushing myself further. So I decided to take more classes, hoping that it'd spark more than just desire in me. I was hoping for the courage to finally get out there and do something with my degree that could actually be helpful.

Yet I was stagnant. My throat wanted to tighten at the thought, but I managed to stave off those emotions, opting instead to watch Mayda.

She moved with purpose, like she'd had everything mapped out beforehand and knew where she wanted her stuff to go. "She was getting on in years. Unfortunately for her, but luckily for me." She made a soft noise of disapproval. "No offense, but the woman was not counselor material."

"Oh, I believe you." I nodded, a smile twisting the edges of my mouth.

Her eyes shot up in my direction. "Are you laughing at me, Junior?"

"Jamás," I replied. "I would never think to laugh at you, cariño."

The moniker slipped from my lips without meaning to. As soon as it did, I was gifted with the sight of her cheeks reddening, the flush crawling up her neck. It was hard to break through her tough armor. Like she'd wrapped herself entirely in layered walls of steel with barbed wire and broken glass at the top.

To see how a mere slip of the tongue had her biting on her lips and turning away from me made my smile grow broader. If I'd known that calling her honey would have brought this reaction out of her, I would have called her it a lot sooner.

"Well, I won't get anything done if I just stand here." She laughed awkwardly and whirled from me. I watched with a smile as she started getting to work. Her movements were brisk, fast, and efficient, and when I caught a glimpse of her face again, she was in perfect concentration mode.

As if I hadn't spoken to her at all or flustered her in the slightest.

Well, fuck.

I wanted to be insulted that she could so easily write me off, but I was used to the sharp sting of her rejection. I was just a blip in the road to her.

Standing to the side had me feeling more than a little useless as she quickly and efficiently began stapling the posters to the walls.

"What do you want me to do?"

She stopped mid-staple and turned, finally acknowledging that I was there to help. "Maybe you could organize the files in the drawers alphabetically? We have the names of every student on file. When school starts, I want to have a session with each one to get to know them and write down observations."

I opened the drawer and whistled. "That's a lot of students."

She threw me a sheepish smile. "I know, but I don't believe anyone should ever be left out." Her voice took on a sad, almost wistful tone that made me stop and stare at her.

When she spoke about her job and the kids, she did it with such caring cadence that it was hard *not* to be lulled into feeling the same. I wondered why she felt so strongly about it. Was it because of her own home life? Had it been bad that she now felt the need to save other children?

Seeing this side of her was like pulling away part of a layer, and I was fascinated with every second of it. I wanted to know more about her on a level that not everyone knew. She was like an obsession; she always had been. Because she was so calm, so *cool* I just wanted more every time I was with her.

"I think the kids will be lucky to have you," I said sincerely.

She seemed almost startled that I'd say that but then smiled in a grateful way that made me want to swipe my thumb against her bottom lip. Every day this curiosity and desire burned hotter inside of me. I was like a thief, trying to steal little bits and pieces of her. Any pieces I could get. Any pieces she could give me.

Like her time. Like a kiss near the edge of her mouth.

I wanted so much more.

Whatever else she was willing to give.

We finished within a few hours until everything was meticulously placed. I'd texted my father thirty minutes into our work to let him know I would be longer because Mayda needed my help. It wasn't exactly a lie, and maybe I was a coward for using her name to shield me from his anger, but it worked. At least momentarily. I would probably get shit for ditching work when I got home, but it was worth it.

By the time we finished in her office, locking it up again and getting back inside my truck, it was nearing lunch time. We drove in silence back to her place, the radio on low. My fingers flexed and my stomach fluttered with nerves as I worked up the courage to ask her out to eat.

I wanted more time with her. Time I probably didn't deserve and shouldn't steal, but I wanted regardless.

"Thanks for helping out today," she whispered shyly.

"Anytime, Mayda. You ever need someone to help you, count on me."

"Mhm..."

She didn't sound like she believed me.

"En serio," I urged. She didn't say anything, and just when I was about to open my mouth and ask her to join me for lunch, we arrived at her house. As soon as the truck was parked, she was quick to unbuckle and slip out. I followed, intent on carrying the empty boxes inside and asking her to have lunch with me. She seemed more relaxed now than she had been hours ago when I came to drop her off at her house that first time. She was even humming as she opened the door and let me inside.

Following after her, I was surprised when she suddenly stopped, and I almost rammed into her back. My feet skidded against her floor, nearly dropping the boxes and startling when she let out a curse.

"Shit!"

I peeked over her shoulder to see what she was looking at.

There, in her living room, lying on the couch, was her mother.

I'd seen Luciana Jiménez many times in my childhood, so I knew this was her. There was a vague familiarity between her and Mayda, but there was something off about the woman I used to know as her mother. She looked... she looked sickly. Her skin clung to a skeletal frame, and her hair looked dry and stringy. Her eyes looked too big for her thin face, and shadows rimmed them, her cheeks were hollow and her lips were cracked and bleeding. She lay half-on, half-off of the couch, and there was white, bubbly saliva on the corners of her mouth.

"Shit, shit, shit." Mayda ran towards the couch and loomed over her mom, grabbing her arms in a tight grip. I stood frozen, watching, and it was like she'd forgotten I existed as her gaze swept over her mother's skin.

Even from where I stood, I could make out the welts all across her arms.

It made my whole body freeze and tense up.

"Mom!" Mayda lightly slapped her hand across her mother's face in rapid succession. "Mom! Can you hear me?"

Her mother stirred, batting her away. "Mayda... s'at you?" Her eyes peeked open. "Thought you were at Briela'sss..."

Mayda's whole demeanor changed in an instant. Her voice came out in quiet, hissing fury. "Mom, what the hell did you take this time?"

Her mother giggled and shoved her away weakly. "I'm the mother, not you. Fuck off."

The hairs on the back of my neck stood on end at the way she was speaking to her daughter. What the *hell*?

I put the boxes down by the door and stepped deeper into the room. It seemed to catch her mother's attention, because she turned to me and giggled. "Finally tapping that? 'Bout time, May...da..."

Her words had Mayda's attention snapping straight to me like she was just now remembering I was there. Her face flushed and emotions flashed across her expression, one after the other. For once, her whole façade had ripped away, the steel walls finally melting and the real her was glaringly obvious beneath the quiet.

I got the full onslaught of a big secret. Pain, embarrassment, shock. It all rippled through the space that separated us and hit me like an oncoming tractor.

I'd wanted emotions. I'd wanted to steal them.

Just not like this.

I had the urge to go forward and help, but Mayda was already storming in my direction, shoving me back by the shoulders. I stumbled by the vehemence in the gesture and the wildness in her eyes.

"You need to leave," she demanded.

"Mayda, I can help."

"No, Junior," she said fiercely. "You can't."

She shoved me over the threshold and, without another word, slammed the door in my face. I stood there, baffled for a brief moment, staring at the chipping, cracked paint on the door of her house.

Suddenly, everything about her made so much more sense. About why she never spoke of her mom, her house, her closed-off personality...

Her mom was a damn junkie.

My fists tightened at my sides. I wanted to slam them through the threshold, force my way inside and offer my help whether she wanted it or not. But I knew that if I did that, she would never forgive me. This was a personal matter, one she wanted me far away from.

So, with one last lingering look at her door, I walked back to my truck and drove away. My hands tightened on the wheel, my heart thundered in my chest, stomach rolling painfully as I finally understood why Mayda seemed to have so many secrets.

CHAPTER 6

MAYDA

MY FACE BURNED WITH humiliation as I stared at the chipped wood of the closed door. My mom's groans coming from behind me only served as a sharp reminder of how different Junior and I were.

I went through the day with him wearing clouded glasses, content to let the fog press around us and drown out the outside world. For a moment it felt like we were actually friends, maybe even something more. I'd let my guard down. But reality was such a harsh thing. It was like finding myself on a peaceful flight only to crash-land in disaster without a parachute to steady my fall.

Tears pricked behind my eyelids, threatening to slip. I couldn't let them. I couldn't let myself get swept up in the day we'd shared when my life was groaning behind me.

Steeling my resolve and shoving away the tears, I slowly turned.

Seeing my mother like this hit me in the chest every single time. You'd think I would have trained myself to be numb to her drugged-out tirades, to the needle marks trailing along her skin, the alcohol and stench of weed on her breath and clothes.

She hadn't always been this way. It was hard to remember those times, because I'd never felt like she'd ever been the loving mother I wanted. Back then, she hadn't stumbled around on drunken feet and she still cared enough about me to fix me meager meals of boiled hot dogs. When she was feeling really fancy, she whipped up some mofongo or bollitas.

Those were the better days.

Around the time I turned eleven or so, she changed. She didn't pick me up from school anymore because she claimed she had to work, and I was old enough to walk or take the bus. I always thought it was because she knew Gabriela took me to her house afterwards and her parents always dropped me back off at home hours later. She figured if others were taking care of me then she didn't have to.

Her disappearances became more frequent with time. Gabriela's parents rarely asked me questions about my mom, though I knew they wanted to. I figured they knew something was up, but they were so kind to me regardless. Sometimes I felt like they thought as long as I was away from whatever shitty home situation I was so obviously in, they didn't need to pry.

I was grateful for that at least.

Not even Gabriela knew the extent of my mother's problems. I'd alluded to it a few times, but I'd never felt comfortable talking to her about my mom's frequent late nights or when she suddenly arrived in skimpy clothes and smelling funny.

Even then I knew it was bad. Gabriela's family was so normal and so united that it made me open my eyes to the reality of my own skewed way of living. I wanted so desperately to confide in someone about my life, but I knew that if I did, they would take my mom away from me.

She may have been a neglectful drunk, but she was still my mom. I didn't want to be separated from her or tossed into a system because I knew that was exactly where I'd go. I didn't have any other relatives in the States. My grandparents lived in Puerto Rico and, as far as I knew, wanted nothing to do with my mom and her devious ways. I didn't even really know who my father was, so I doubted the government would either.

I'd taken to picking up the pieces of our broken life in secret. After Gabriela's parents dropped me off in the afternoons, I'd do my homework, clean the house. The fridge was always stacked with hot dogs and boxed macaroni. Sometimes, the Águila-Gutierrez's would send me home with butter containers of arroz and frijoles. Those became my meals and my mom's when she stumbled in, sometimes at three in the morning.

I slept on the couch more often than not, waiting for her to come home. She always did, and she did it in her stumbling, almost begrudging way. When she looked at me, I could always feel a bit of hatred burning in her eyes. Like I was the reason she came back and she blamed me for it.

That didn't stop me from taking care of her, though. From sitting her on the couch and slipping her heels from her feet or helping her out of her skimpy dress and putting pajama bottoms and holey t-shirts over her. I ignored the markings over her body. Bruises and red marks that didn't belong over what had once been perfect skin.

It became our normal, a routine, until pretty soon I was the one taking care of her. I'd make her meals, remind her to pay rent on time, keep the house clean, while she went off and did whatever.

It happened so often that she forgot she was the one who was supposed to take care of *me*.

So, yeah, maybe that made me bitter as I watched her roll on our old couch and start gagging over the side of it. Maybe it made me hate her a little more every time she came home like this. But mostly, I was just embarrassed that she was still doing it.

Even worse that Junior had to witness it.

I wanted to groan all over again but instead got to work, opening the closet and grabbing the emergency bucket I kept inside for these moments. I placed it under my mom just in time for her to start spewing vomit inside.

I didn't bother rubbing her back or offering her comfort. She didn't deserve that after she ruined my day.

"Mayda..." she groaned into the bucket. "Mi dulce niña. What would I do without you?" She pushed herself up, wiping her lips against the back of her boney hand before laying down on the couch. Her hooded eyes watched me and a small smile tugged at her mouth.

I was familiar enough with those words and they tugged at my heart, making me ache all over.

My sweet girl.

I closed my eyes, pinching the bridge of my nose. When I opened them again, it was to find her bottom lip trembling. I sat at her feet and rubbed a palm along her leg.

"I'm here for you, mom. Always have been, always will be."

I couldn't really be mad at her for ruining my day. I'd been delusional, caught up in my own version of a fairytale without realizing that it was a really skewed, messed up version anyway. My prince had gone back to his castle, and I was nothing more than Cinderella waiting for a ball that would never come.

"Come on, mom, let's get you in the shower." I tried to pull her up with me, but she didn't want to budge. "Mom... Come on."

In her high irritability, her hand struck out and cracked me across the face. "Fuck off, Mayda. Always in my business."

My face burned from pain and humiliation. I hated this part of her addiction most of all. She could get nasty when I tried to make her do things she didn't want to do. But she *had* to get in the bath. I had to bring her body temperature down and clean the vomit out of her hair.

It was a struggle to get her in shower, and I came out of the ordeal scratched to shit and with a few bruises over my body. At least it was done and she was sleeping.

And tomorrow would be another day.

CHAPTER 7

JUNIOR

GRIME COVERED MY BODY, dust invaded my hair despite the sombrero, and I was dripping sweat from nearly every crevice. My father had been upset I arrived late to work. I could see it in his eyes, but he didn't say a word. There had been a lot to do, after all. Animals to feed, stalls to clean out, fields to comb through, tractors to fix...

El rancho was like a machine. It wouldn't work if things weren't running smoothly and measures had to be taken every single day to ensure that Los Corazones remained one of the most prosperous ranches on this side of the border.

Our work days were long and grueling, so by the time it finished, I was glad to slink towards my house and jump in the shower.

Usually I enjoyed the task of caring for the horses. They'd always been my favorite animals since I was a kid, and even now there was something almost therapeutic about them. I found tranquility in brushing them down and talking to them in a way I didn't find with anyone else.

Anyone else except Mayda.

She'd been on my mind all day. I couldn't stop thinking about her face when she kicked me out, or the harsh edge of her voice as she tried to wake her mom up. Her mom, who was a junkie. I couldn't help but wonder, as the water sluiced down my back like knives, if she'd always been like that.

Even when we were kids.

Her being closed off suddenly made so much more sense to me. How we'd never seen her mom at any school event. Had the woman ever even been around at all?

I hurried through the motions of my shower, scrubbing until I was squeaky clean. After drying off and slipping on a pair of pajama bottoms, I slid on my bed, grabbing my phone from the nightstand. I powered it up and opened my text messages, fingers hovering over Mayda's name.

I'd never texted her before. At least not for her. Sometimes Gabriela would use Mayda's phone and shoot me messages when her own ran out of battery. We'd known each other for years so having her number wasn't odd. What was odd was the fact that I never texted *her* before if it wasn't in relation to my sister.

That was about to change.

I typed up a message quickly and hit send.

It was a pretty basic message and still I wondered if it would seem too personal to her. She'd kicked me out of her house quickly enough. I remembered the look on her face, the horrified expression as she realized I was there.

If this was some long-kept secret, then I could understand her wariness. But I wanted to know that she'd be alright.

I waited for a few minutes, staring at my screen. My breath caught in my throat when those chat bubbles popped up to indicate she was typing.

I expelled the breath I'd been holding, brows furrowing at the message. It was cold, curt, and I could feel even through the phone that she didn't want to talk about it. She was shutting me out and I didn't like that. I respected her right for privacy but there was a burning need in me to help.

I hoped this message would be met with more enthusiasm. I should have known better.

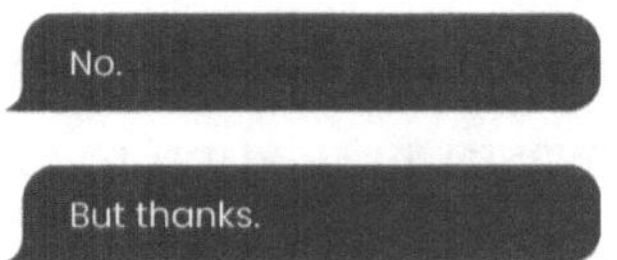

I was going to have to ask her outright.

The chat bubble popped up then disappeared then popped up again. It happened many times, like she was deleting every single word she typed up. It lasted a few minutes until I finally received a reply.

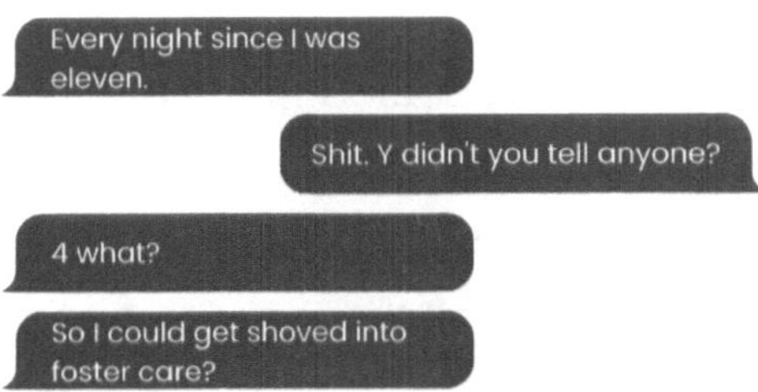

My fingers tightened on my phone as I tried to imagine that happening.

Realization dawned on me. Her dislike for the system, her knowledge and passion for it. Had she spent our youth investigating what would happen to her if she was ever put into a foster home? Had she lied awake in fear and horror at the thought that it could happen at any moment of the day?

And if she had, then what?

Being separated from Mayda was out of the question. She was as much my family as my sisters, though what I felt for her was so not sisterly. She still belonged with us. She was an Águila-Gutierrez in all but name. Losing her to the system would have been unfathomable.

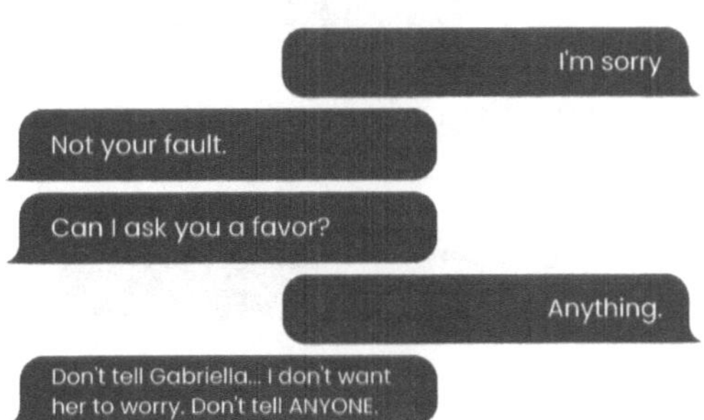

I waited a beat, my breath caught in my throat. Keeping her secret seemed imperative. I understood that. I had secrets of my own too. But this was *huge*. It was something that needed to be shared. With someone. Anyone. So we could help her *and* her mother.

I couldn't imagine the toll something like that could take on a person. The weight of that secret.

She didn't have to deal with it alone.

I was about to suggest we talk to someone when messages from Mayda came through.

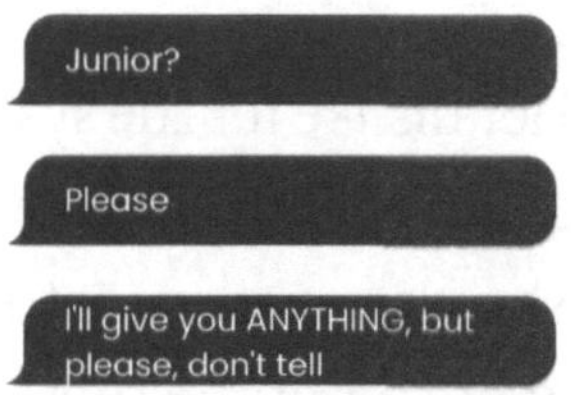

I blinked at the word. Anything? Gritting my teeth, I took a breath. I hated that she felt the need to beg me for my silence. That she thought I was so untrustworthy that she had to give me anything in exchange.

The chat dots appeared and disappeared.

It was the least I could offer.

The bubbles appeared and a text came through.

Pero, what a necia. Stubborn woman.

I don't doubt that. But I'm here if you need anything.

And then, before I could chicken out...

You know I worry about you too.

It took a while for her to get back to me, and the whole time I felt like I was holding my breath.

Why?

It was one little question, and still it knocked me on my ass. I stared at it, long and hard. She didn't know. She had no idea why I tugged at her ponytail, why she intrigued me, why my eyes followed her around a room. Maybe I didn't know it until that moment, until the question glared at me from the screen of my phone.

My fingers shook as I typed out an answer, only to delete it. I sat up in bed, feeling shaken. I wanted to be honest with her, but I also didn't want to scare her away. Besides, what I had to say shouldn't be said over text. I wasn't even sure if it would be met with disgust. Mayda had never looked twice at me. Like I was beneath her notice because I was nothing more than her best friend's brother.

Was I pathetic to have been pining after the one girl I always felt I couldn't have? Sure, I'd had girlfriends throughout my life, some of them serious, some of them lasting years. Maybe they'd never worked out because they weren't her.

They weren't Mayda.

Mayda didn't want me. She'd barely agreed to let me take her to her house today and she'd only done it grudgingly.

Instead of replying, I tossed my phone back on my night stand and got up to my desk. My body suddenly felt wired, too hot and cold, and my mind was racing. I knew if I laid down, I wouldn't be able to fall asleep anyway, so I might as well get some work done.

Powering up my laptop, I signed into my online courses and got to work on some homework.

I never went to college even though I wanted to. It wasn't because my parents were discouraging, not exactly. My papá just boasted about how happy he was that I was finally graduating high school and would be taking over Los Corazones, that it would stay in our family.

I couldn't bring myself to tell him I didn't want it.

So I went along with his plans for me without complaining, even if they weren't exactly what I wanted for myself.

The sound of my door opening and closing startled me. My hand grabbed my laptop, slamming it down. I rolled in my chair, turning with my heart pounding up to my throat.

"Jesús Cristo. Pinche pendejo, me espantaste!" I clutched my hand against my chest, heaving in breaths as Hector's laughing figure strolled into my room. Not even my calling him a fucking bastard and telling him he'd scared me deterred him from walking deeper into the room.

"I knocked, but you didn't answer." He flopped on the end of my bed. "Did you think I was your papá?" There was a bit of mischief in his voice that I chose to ignore.

Hector was my best friend so he knew what I'd been trying to hide on that laptop. He knew everything my papá didn't know. He was the only person I felt I could confide in; he kept my secrets and I kept his.

There was not a childhood memory I had that Hector wasn't a part of. He was so ingrained in my life that I didn't think there'd ever been a time without him. He was my brother. Mi hermano.

I knew his mamá didn't like that we called ourselves that. She had a weird view about her station and Hector's versus ours. As if we were fucking royalty or something. While she treated me as well as a son, sometimes I could still feel the differences in the way she treated me and how she treated Hector.

Like I was the boss' son. Which, okay, I was, but I didn't like to be reminded of it. I didn't like the special treatment, the careful placement of herself and Hector on the outside of our lives sometimes. Like they belonged, but not fully.

It was the same with Mayda, now that I thought about it.

"You doing homework?"

I spun in my chair and opened my laptop again. "Yeah."

I could feel Hector's eyes drilling on my back and I knew him so well, I figured what he was going to say before he even said it.

"I don't get why you just don't tell him the truth."

I sighed and closed my laptop again before spinning to look at Hector. He was clad in dark sweats and a shirt. Freshly showered, his dark hair pressed against his cheeks.

It was hard talking to Hector about my papá. He didn't understand where I was coming from because he didn't have a father himself. His papá died when he was eight. He didn't have anyone to impress. He didn't need to follow in anyone's footsteps or worry about disappointing a legacy because his papá was already gone.

That probably made me an asshole, and I was likely being bitter. I didn't know a damn thing about what his situation felt like, so making those assumptions was stupid of me, but I couldn't stop myself.

"It's complicated," I said.

"How? Your parents are the most understanding people I've ever known. I don't see why you have to live a lie."

"You're right. You *don't.*" I hated snapping at him. Hated how he tensed up at my words. I wanted to apologize, but I couldn't bring myself to. Not even when he slowly unfurled from my bed and stared at me with wide, sad eyes. When it was evident I wasn't going to say another word, he walked out of my house, the door clicking closed softly behind him.

My face heated with shame at the way I'd spoken to him. I only snapped because he was right and I hated that he was.

I don't see why you have to live a lie.

I didn't want to, but I wasn't sure if anyone could understand what I really wanted to do with my life.

No one except Mayda, maybe.

Finding my courage, I grabbed my phone and typed out two things and sent them before shutting my phone off.

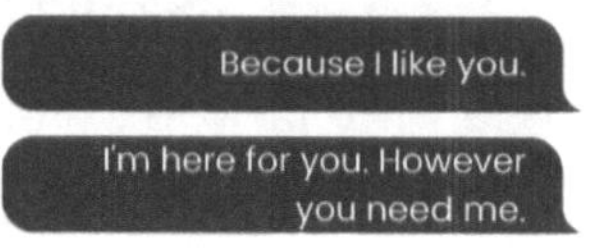

CHAPTER 8

MAYDA

I STAYED UP ALL night to check on my mom and make sure she didn't choke on her own vomit. When I finally settled for bed to find a text from Junior, it had pushed away all exhaustion from my body. A few back and forth messages had my heart pounding with anxiety until I was sure he wouldn't rat me out to Gabriela.

I still couldn't believe he had been a witness to my humiliating life. At their house, I could easily forget who I was and where I came from. I could pretend to be what they all thought me to be. Dragging him into my truth was something I never wanted to do. I'd almost expected him to run as far away as possible, but he'd been sweet, supportive.

I shouldn't have questioned why.

Then he wouldn't have sent the final texts that left me tossing and turning all night.

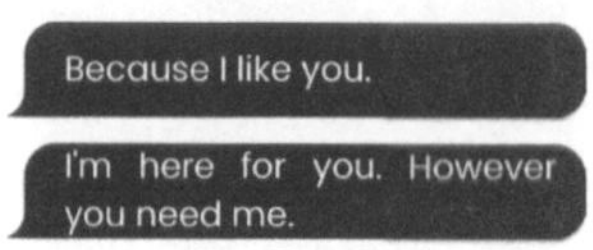

What had he meant by that? He liked me? He meant as a friend, right? Or was it something more? I was trying not to let myself drown in the fantasy that he represented, the fairy tale of him that I'd always wished would come true.

It was like living my whole life covered in rags and waking up to a simple message that turned an impoverished maid into a princess.

I tried not to get my hopes up about his pronouncement, but I couldn't help it. How many times had I stayed awake wishing for those words exactly, knowing they'd never come true because I was all but invisible? But they'd happened, and now I found myself analyzing every aspect of them, turning them over and over again in my mind because I couldn't quite believe they were true.

But the evidence was right there in my text messages.

Because I like you.

My heart beat faster every time I reread those words, and I'd reread them hundreds of times since he sent them. Still, I couldn't bring myself to reply. I was tongue-tied, unsure of what to say. What if I told him I liked him too, bared my heart when he didn't mean what I was hoping he meant?

Besides, I had other things to worry about that tore my attention away from the messages that morning—and at that point it was just too late to reply anyway.

After sleeping for a total of about three hours, I got up to go check on my mom only to find her gone. This was as normal as her random, drugged out appearances, and still they never failed to make me upset. She could have at least said goodbye to me before she went off on her next *adventure*. She could have at least thanked me for staying up all night, holding her hair back as she emptied the contents of her stomach into the toilets and buckets throughout the house.

She was ungrateful, or maybe she was embarrassed, I didn't know, but she always slipped out the next day so it shouldn't have been surprising. In my rage, I had the urge to change the locks. Next time she wanted to come and crash here, she could sleep on the porch or go somewhere else once she found it barred against her.

As soon as the thought appeared, my own guilt chased it away. Regardless of her selfishness, I couldn't bring myself to push her away. I worried enough about her, and at least she came home sometimes. I would have worried more if I changed the locks. Then she'd have absolutely nowhere to go.

No matter how pissed she made me, I couldn't do that to my mom.

She *was* my mom, after all.

After my first bout of anger passed, I decided to keep myself busy. To take my mind off both my mom and Junior, I cleaned the house from top to bottom with bleach. It was therapeutic, like cleaning away the stench of her vomit I was cleansing the space of those bad energies. Hours into it, I felt myself relaxing.

Using my broom as a partner, I swept and danced my way across the floor to Marc Antony's voice as my soundtrack. It was a little something of the Águila-Gutierrez family that stayed with me for weekend cleaning days.

I swiveled my hips as I pushed the trash into the dust pan, belting out the lyrics in my own cracking voice.

Just as I was finishing, my phone started screeching from the table. I wiped my hands on the sides of my jeans before going to answer. My heart beat the whole time until I saw Gabriela's name. I couldn't deny a brief flash of disappointment.

What had I been expecting?

Okay, I'd be lying if I said I wasn't hoping it would be Junior, but there was no way he'd call me. Not after I ignored his messages. Even if I wanted to reply, it was just too late to respond to them now.

"What's up?" I answered.

"Stop cleaning, get showered, and come over," Gabriela said by way of greeting.

Chuckling, I walked over to turn the volume down on my speakers. Without the background noise, I could hear the commotion coming from Gabriela's end of the conversation.

"Why?" I pressed my hip against the side of the table, smiling as I imagined her on the other end.

"Valentina, quitáte," she snapped. "Stop it!" There was a shuffling on the other end before she focused her attention back on me again. "So are you coming over or what?"

I sighed. "Why am I coming over?" She knew I wouldn't deny that chance. Whenever she invited me, I always said yes, even when I felt reluctant to do so. I didn't want her family to think I was taking advantage of them.

"*Beeecaaaaause,*" she dragged out, and I could just picture her on the other end rolling her eyes at me. "You want to eat some carnes asadas. It'll be a small get-together."

"Uh huh."

The definition of a small get-together for the Águila-Gutierrezes was a full-fledged party by other people's comparison. They invited their family, their workers, and had a ton of food and beer. If I said no, I knew it would offend Mamá Claudia and she wouldn't let me hear the end of it.

"What's the occasion?"

"We start picking the crops next week!"

"Ah."

Every time the crops were successful and it came time to pick them and send them off in trucks to the farmer's market, restaurants, or bigger department stores, they celebrated. It was a way of thanking their ranch hands for all their hard work and to keep them interested in working there.

"A happy worker means successful crops," Señor Águila always said.

I looked down at my outfit. I was covered in grime and grease, my t-shirt clinging against the sweat on my skin. I winced at the ugly picture I made.

"Give me a bit. I'm going to shower then I'll be over to help."

Gabriela made an impatient noise on the other end. "Hurry up! We miss you!"

"*Sí! Apurateeeee, Maydaaaa!*" I heard Valentina's screeching voice from the other end. She'd likely pulled the phone away from Gabriela to scream into the receiver.

I found myself chuckling. A wave of love washed over me. I adored the sisters. Even though I was an outsider, they'd all accepted me like I was their own. Even her sisters were always so kind and welcoming and treated me like I was one of them.

Inadequate and undeserving as I was.

"Bye! See you in a bit!' I hung up before Valentina could go off on a tangent like she was prone to doing. The seventeen-year old was adorable and full of so much energy and would have gone for hours if I hadn't hung up.

I quickly showered and dressed in a pretty floral, knee length dress with thin straps. I spread cream through my thick locks then passed a brush through the knots. I usually didn't take a lot of time with my appearance, content with throwing on jeans and a cardigan or a t-shirt.

I knew the real reason I decided to rummage through my make-up and add a bit of concealer to the shadows beneath my eyes and take a wand to my lashes. That reason was Junior. I felt equal parts nervous and pathetic as I got ready, thinking of him and the words burned into my retinas from the night before.

Would I see him there? Would he mention the message? Ay, Diosito... I poked myself in the eye with the mascara wand and let out a low curse. Would I make a fool of myself?

Crap. Maybe getting dressed up was a bad idea...

I was debating changing my whole outfit when my phone shrieked with a message from Gabriela again. Too late. If she was sending me a follow up message, it was because I'd already taken too long and she thought I was bailing. If I took longer, she'd jump in a car and come drag me back to her house.

I reached for my purse, shoving my phone into it, and grabbing my car keys. I all but rushed out of the house, locking the door behind me before jumping into my car and pulling out of my drive.

My fingers shook against the steering wheel and took steadying breaths the whole way, calming myself and keeping my cool mask in place. By the time I arrived at the rancho, I felt steadier. I was no longer shaking and felt ready to confront whatever came. Not confident exactly, but definitely calm and collected.

I just had to avoid thinking about the texts from last night and everything would be okay. I could immerse myself in helping everyone with the preparations to distract myself. It would be easy, considering there were dozens of cars parked all along the rancho's drive.

The front door was wide open and inviting, so I didn't bother to knock as I walked through and made my way towards the kitchen where most of the clan were piled together, bustling and talking loudly over one another.

Gabriela caught sight of me. "Finally! Come help me take the salsas out!"

It took me about ten minutes before I could help her because I had to stop and say hello to everyone, gifting them with kisses on the cheeks. Of course, that ended up reminding me of the day before, of Junior's lips hovering near the edge of my mouth as I said goodbye.

By the time I finished, Gabriela was vibrating with impatience. She handed me a tub of red salsa and I obediently followed her out to the back. Tables and chairs had been set up, along with speakers and three different grills where they were frying carnes asadas, longaniza, elote, papas, and jalapeños for rajas. There was another table with cups and plates, arroz, salsa, fried onions, and tortillas.

Gabriela led me to that table, where we arranged the salsas.

Everyone was lending a helping hand and laughing, and I took a second to bask in the familiarity of this. It felt like one giant family, even if not everyone was related. They set up coolers with beers and sodas, messed around with the stereo, stood around the grill laughing with cold coronas in hand.

For the next twenty minutes, I helped them get everything set up and caught no sight of Junior. A sensation like disappointment wormed its way in my chest that I ignored as I helped make the guacamole and took out the fried chips.

Then the party started in earnest and I found myself sucked into the fray of their fun. No matter how boisterous the gathering was, no matter how many people piled into the yard or how loud they got with every passing hour, I never felt the crushing weight of the noise.

It didn't matter the different radio stations of personality. The Águila-Gutierrez family were a balm. There was a certain tranquility about them that was hypnotizing and made me feel, like always, that this was my favorite place in the whole world.

CHAPTER 9

MAYDA

Hours passed and I still didn't catch sight of Junior, even while I was actively looking through the sea of faces. I was distracted, and Gabriela had noticed. I tried to play it off, dancing with her, Hector, and her sisters any time they drug me out onto the dance floor. I moved through salsas and cumbias. Mamá Claudia had taught me along with her daughters the footwork of it, but no one was a better dancer than Sofia.

Gabriela's sister flowed with the music and moved like it lived in her soul and you couldn't keep her from dancing even after the melody stopped. Not that it ever did. They played song after song and I moved until my feet felt pinched in my flats.

I had to pull away and sit at a table with a groan as Gabriela took a seat next to me. Even though she'd been dancing more than me, there was hardly a sheen of sweat on her. Her hair and makeup were perfect and her smile was wide even while her eyes narrowed on me.

"So…"

My brows rose. "So?"

She gave me an exasperated look. "So, what happened with my tonto brother yesterday? Did you flirt? Did you make a move? Did *he*?"

The press of his mouth near mine was imprinted on my skin. The flash of what I mistook for desire in his dark eyes. The way I shoved him out of my door and then the messages right after.

Not for the first time, I wondered if the message had been in pity because of what he'd witnessed.

My eyes searched Gabriela's face, looking for any sign of the truth I'd hidden from her. Junior had promised he wouldn't say anything, and it seemed like he'd kept that promise. She would have assaulted me with questions if she knew. At least I didn't have to worry about her knowing what my mom was really like.

"Nothing happened," I said with a shrug, hoping the heat I felt inside wasn't crawling up my neck as we spoke.

"Really? Because he got home pretty late…"

My body tensed up. "I hope he didn't get in trouble with your dad."

Gabriela shoved my shoulder. "Geez, relax. You're always so uptight. Everything was fine, but I want el chisme."

El chisme was the tea. She wanted something piping hot I could spill into her nosey cup, but there was nothing. Nothing except a cryptic message that I hadn't bothered replying to and was now turning over in my head.

"Nothing happened. Junior doesn't like me."

Even though I had a message in my phone that said otherwise.

I still couldn't believe it, if only because I hadn't seen him since I arrived.

"Did he say that to you?" Her voice dropped low and she scooted forward in her seat so our knees touched. "Because if he did, I'll drop kick him in sus pinches huevos."

"Gabriela!" I slapped her leg, causing her to smirk. "Leave his balls *alone*."

"I think my mamá would be on my side in this instance. You know she loves you."

My heart squeezed at the confession. It nearly brought tears burning to the backs of my eyelids. I hated how it always made me emotional. Her family treated me like I belonged when my own mother didn't even treat me that way.

"I promise you, Gabi, nothing happened." I squeezed the words out past the emotion in my throat.

What was one more lie?

"Really?" She gave me a skeptical look. "Then why are you wearing a skirt?"

Shit.

Nothing got past her.

"Uh—"

I was spared having to reply when Hector sauntered over and grabbed Gabi's hand, pulling her out with a laugh. She followed, shooting me a look that said our conversation wasn't over.

While she danced with Hector, my gaze combed through the party. I was being needy and borderlined on desperate. I knew that. Still, looking for him was like a drug. I should have asked Gabriela where he was, if he was even here, but my firm need to keep anyone else from knowing what I felt held strong.

It was a strange sense of both pride and humiliation. It seemed it didn't matter how many times Gabriela told me she wanted me as a sister. I knew where I came from. I knew what blood coursed through my veins compared to theirs. I didn't think I'd ever feel worthy of being in their circle, much less a member of their family.

Abandoning my search for Junior, I turned my attention behind me when I felt a hand brush against my shoulder. My smile was immediate and genuine.

"Mayda, can you do me a favor and make a plate for Mamá Mari? I have to run to the store. I don't think we have enough soda."

I resisted the urge to look at the coolers still filled to the brim with soda. She was always worrying they'd run out and there'd be nothing left to give to the guests. It was better not to argue with her.

I got to my feet. "Of course! No problem at all."

"Gracias, mi dulce niña."

The endearment sent a slice of cold down my spine. It prickled and stabbed, and I tried to keep the apprehension from showing in my expression. I was a master at containing my emotions by now. It had been born of growing up too early, of having to pretend like everything at home was alright and that I was happy living with a mother who neglected me.

But that endearment? It was what my mother called me, and it made my blood run cold every time I heard it come from Mamá Claudia's lips.

I all but fled from her, making my way to the grills where I piled a plate high with a bit of everything before I wove my way around the swaying bodies to Mamá Mari, rather, Abuelita Mari.

Abuelita Mari was by no means a frail, old woman. She was old, yes, and wrinkles creased through her skin like balled up paper. Her hair was long and gray, and it braided down her back with red ribbon. Although she walked with a cane and her back hunched and she heaved with every step, her eyes were bright and full of life.

The honeyed depths danced along with the rhythm of the party, and her smile was wide with laughter.

"Your plate, abuelita."

"Gracias, mija." She took it and began chewing in slow bites.

I didn't stay around to chat with her. Gabriela was still dancing, being twirled by Hector. He switched partners, dancing between her and Valentina, and their laughter followed me as I snuck away from the party, back to where the houses for the ranch hands were situated.

Maybe I was hoping to find Junior back here. I could explain why I never texted back and if I was brave enough, ask him what exactly he meant by the words in the messages.

I stopped near the little house I knew was his. It was closest to the main house and all the lights inside were off. I debated knocking for a moment, lifting my hand almost tentatively. From here, the pulsing beat of the music was little more than a dull throb, so when I heard the sudden harsh hissing of voices, I startled.

I recognized the low timbres of both voices as they argued back and forth. The sounds came from around the house.

I shouldn't have snuck closer, but curiosity burned and pushed my feet forward. My head peeked around the corner where I could see Señor Águila and Junior near the wooden fence that surrounded a good chunk of the property.

I'd seen Señor Águila upset probably only once in all the time I'd known him. Mamá Claudia was more likely to scream at someone in the house than he was, so seeing him and Junior go head to head was like seeing a blue moon rise over the sky.

I inched closer, capturing bits and snippets of their conversations. I almost flinched at the rapid fire of Spanish being released from señor Águila's mouth.

"...dejáte de pendejadas..."

The words had me biting the inside of my cheek. I understood enough Spanish to know that he was cussing, that he was pissed. *Cut the bullshit.* And I wondered, with my heart beating up to my throat, if Junior had the same type of relationship that my own mom and I had.

I didn't want to believe it. Señor Águila was always so nice to me. But the evidence was here, in the harsh spitting of his words away from prying ears. It was in the downcast way Junior's shoulders were set and in the energy vibrating around the two of them.

My heart clenched at the pain I could just make out on Junior's face, even in the shadows.

I needed to turn back, to go back to the party and talk and dance with Gabriela, but I couldn't bring myself to move.

Who was I kidding? I didn't want to move.

So I stayed right where I was and tried to listen in on their conversation.

CHAPTER 10

JUNIOR

MAYDA NEVER TEXTED ME back. The next morning, I'd turned on my phone, anxious to see the screen shining with something akin to hope.

With something that read like, "I like you too."

But there'd been nothing. Nada. Panic had seized me as I typed out a message I'd been preparing to send. A 'haha, just kidding.' But I wasn't kidding and I didn't want to lie to her, so I deleted the words before my stupid fingers could decide to press send.

The empty messages haunted me throughout the day. We hadn't worked the rancho, but around the house to get ready for the asada to celebrate the fact that the crops were going out to the market and the stores.

I should have been knee-deep in prep with the rest of them, but I sequestered myself in my house to study for an upcoming test. It took me hours, much to my papá's chagrin.

Instead of yelling at me for not being up at the crack of dawn to help him, he quietly sent me on my way to keep me busy with preparations, sending me to and from the store over and over again.

In between red lights and as I pulled into the parking lot of grocery stores, I whipped out my phone every time to see that I had no new messages.

I banged my forehead against the steering wheel.

"What have I done?" I looked up to the sky, hoping Diosito would send a bolt of lightning down and maim me for my stupidity. Unfortunately, it didn't happen.

No matter how much I kept busy, Mayda wasn't far from my mind. The brief glimpse I had of her vulnerability crippled and distracted me from anything else. I wasn't quite sure she was being honest when she said she was okay, and a big part of me wanted to be the shoulder she could lean on.

I'd probably botched that up with my confession.

Top that on with the fact that I had a paper due and a test to take?

I was really, really distracted.

When I could finally escape my mother's clutches and party planning, I rushed back to my house and powered up my laptop. My fingers sped across the keys, my mind working in overdrive as I finished up the last of my report.

I could hear music coming from outside and knew the party had started. I wanted to go out and look for Mayda, but I needed to finish this first. By the time I did, my eyes felt bleary and I was anxious to see her.

As soon as I walked out of my house, though, I was met with my father. His quiet, demanding presence nearly made me jump out of my skin.

"Papá," I breathed. "¿Qué pasa?"

Clad in a nicer version of his work clothes, my papá's eyes roamed over me. It made me tense and I wondered if whatever he saw he found lacking, though I didn't ask. His dark gaze flicked back up to me and he jerked his head to the side.

"We have to talk," he said.

I followed him to the side of my house. He was leading me towards the fence that surrounded the property. I knew what he was doing. He was pulling me away towards the privacy of the fast-approaching shadows because he didn't want anyone—probably my mamá—to see us talking.

Which could only mean one thing.

He was primed and ready to argue.

I tried to steel myself against it, but it felt impossible.

When he turned and pierced me with that glare, my steps almost faltered.

"What are you doing, Junior?" he demanded.

My fingers slide against the sides of my jeans. "Going to the asada..."

His scowl only deepened. "Don't play stupid. You disappeared for *hours*. Your mamá needed your help up at the house. I needed your help."

My face felt like it was suddenly too hot. Pricks of discomfort stabbed against the backs of my eyelids. I hated disappointing him. It didn't matter if it was doing something I didn't want to do, I felt a sense of responsibility. Maybe it had been placed there by him and the rest of my family. Maybe Hector was right and I was stupid for living a lie, but it sat there nonetheless. It demanded I listen, that I be nothing less than perfect in all ways. So every time I fell short and my papá looked at me with that disappointed expression, it burned.

"I'm sorry. I had something to take care of."

"In your house?" His thick brows pulled together with disbelief. "Like what?"

My mouth opened, but no reply came. What could I even say to that? Tell him I enrolled in school behind his back? He would be pissed; mamá would be pissed that I'd lied to them for years. Hell, even my sisters would probably want to take a belt to my ass for lying.

No one ever told me the truth would be this hard.

At my lack of response, my papá growled. "I can't believe this. It's like you're a little kid all over again."

His anger was a palpable thing, something that within moments could become all-consuming and tear through me like a machine on a warpath. I couldn't brace myself against it as he flung so much at me within the next few moments.

"The trabajadores need to see you here, helping, showing an interest in our traditions. Instead of helping, you holed yourself up in your house. Do you know how that looks to everyone? Do you know what they'll say about you? About us? You're set to inherit all of this, so what you do reflects on me, too. Do you think they'll want a jefe who is a lazy cabrón?"

The words pierced past every flimsy barrier I'd erected and crumbled them down. He wasn't yelling, and he wasn't *really* insulting me, yet it tasted like an insult anyway because they were faults against my character, against my decisions, and they made me feel as if I'd failed him and everyone else.

"I helped, pa. I just had to do something."

"Stop making excuses, Junior!" This time he did raise his voice, and I was glad we were far enough away from the party and that the music was blaring loudly so they didn't hear him shout. "You've been avoiding talking about the future since I told you

you're taking over. What's wrong with you? Don't you want Los Corazones? Don't you want this legacy I built for you, for this family?"

Guilt crawled up my body until I suffocated on it. He knew exactly what to say to make me feel like this. Like I was all but worthless, like I was driving the legacy to the ground. It was in his look, in the subtlety of the way he worded things.

Don't you want it? Sorrowful eyes would stare at me.

I built this from the ground up for you. His voice would crack, and the splinters of the sound would pierce my skin.

I felt myself sinking further and deeper into a hole that I couldn't come out of. I wanted to tell him the truth. I should have right then and there. I didn't want Los Corazones. Not the way he wanted me to take care of it. I couldn't imagine dealing with the numbers, with the workers. I already worked the fields, and I was used to it, but it didn't bring me *joy*.

Because of that alone, I felt like I didn't deserve the place. My papá loved Los Corazones, and he could build it up because he loved what he did. I feared I'd bring it to the ground with my lack of enthusiasm. How could I do that to them? But also, how could I turn away from this?

From legacy.

"Of course I want Los Corazones." The words tasted vile in the back of my throat because of how untrue they were.

"¡Entonces dejáte de pendejadas y ponte a trabajar!"

Cut the bullshit and start working.

The words were cutting, spat with vehemence.

"You have an image to keep up, Damián. You have to be on top of things. That means no more ditching us in the middle of work or in the middle of stuff like this. You have to show them you want this, entiendes?"

I swallowed past the ever-rising lump in my throat. "Yes," I answered. "I understand."

He clapped me on the back, a gesture I thought was meant for comfort. Too bad none came. "It's not like you have anything else important. What's more important than Los Corazones?" He tried for levity in his tone, but it didn't quite reach his eyes.

I forced my smile. "You're right."

Another clap on my shoulder and he walked away, leaving me alone in the darkness.

His absence made me want to scream. Instead, I felt choked. My mood souring, I stormed away. I had to get myself under control before going out to the party and seeing everyone. He was right, after all. We had an image to maintain. He wanted us to look like the perfect father and son duo.

I rounded the corner of my house and stopped short as I rammed into someone.

Déjà vu overpowered me for an instant as my hand reached out to steady the delicate body in front of me. Hands slid up my chest and she gasped, "Junior!"

Unlike the last time I'd run into Mayda like this, I didn't let her go immediately. In fact, the sight of her was so startling, I felt like I'd lost my ability to speak for a moment.

I drank her in, eyes roving over her from head to toe.

She was usually the least frivolous person I knew, always wearing jeans and t-shirts. I'd heard my sister complaining about her attire more than once, even though I thought she looked absolutely amazing in anything she wore.

Tonight, she was breathtaking.

Her dress was simple in material and pattern. It wasn't meant to entice or seduce, as it touched a little past her knees. She wasn't in heels or showing miles of skin, but I still felt myself getting hard regardless. I still felt myself allured by her.

"Mayda…"

I pulled my hands away, the movement slow as I didn't want to let her go. But I had to, because those lack of text messages were glaringly prominent now.

As if we were both thinking the same thing, her head dipped and she tucked a strand of hair behind her ear. "Junior, hi."

She appeared cool and collected just like she always did. When I looked closer, though, I could almost make out the slightest trembling of her fingers. Maybe she wasn't as unaffected as I thought.

A part of me wanted to test that theory.

A second part of me realized, with a jolt, that I'd forgotten my anger completely at the mere sight of her.

"Mayda…" I cleared my throat, scratching at the back of my neck at an imaginary itch there. I'd never felt as awkward around her as I did right then, because of the messages and because I wasn't sure if she'd heard my papá and I arguing. "How are you?"

She looked up at me through dark lashes, each one the curving point of a star. I was captivated by the hazel color and surprised to find her depths… open. She didn't look vulnerable exactly, not like she had the day before. This was a different, wide-eyed wonder, and maybe something else too.

That something else worried me, as did the awkward shrug of her shoulders.

Pendejo, I cursed myself. I probably screwed up our tentative little relationship with those messages.

"I'm okay."

There was a pause where neither of us seemed to know what to say.

"Look, Juni—"

"Look, Mayd—"

We both froze.

"You firs—"

"You firs—"

This had smiles cracking on our tense lips. Instead of speaking, I waved a hand in her direction indicating that she should speak first.

She tucked another errant strand of hair behind her ear.

"I'm sorry I didn't reply to your texts."

"Why didn't you?" The question came out before I could tame it. I wanted to know what she had to say. To know if I was deluding myself into thinking we had some sort of chemistry between us. If she told me she didn't like me, I would back off. It would hurt, but I wouldn't bother her with anything again.

"I—" Her eyes were wide, like it was a question she hadn't been expecting and wasn't quite sure how to answer. But then her eyes softened and there was acceptance there, of the truth, whatever that may be. "I was nervous, and I wasn't sure what you meant by the words."

Shit.

Maybe I should have been more specific?

I had the opportunity now to tell her how I felt, but it didn't feel like the right moment to confess.

My hand shot out, grabbing her wrist. She startled at the movement, and I smiled to ease her nerves. The pulse against her skin pounded on my own, probably the only sign of nerves she'd show. My thumb slid across her skin and a moment later, I dared to thread our fingers together.

It was the closest we'd ever been. This touch seemed more intimate than our cheeks touching with every hola and adiós. Hell, it felt more intimate than my mouth lingering against her skin the day before. It was a connection, and it surged through me and settled in the space of my heart.

My alma, my soul.

"Come with me?" It was a question and a plea rolled into one. If she told me to let her go, I would. I'd let her go and not look back, but if she said yes, then there was hope.

I held my breath as she took her bottom lip between her teeth. I tried not to react to the erotic picture she made or the desire that coursed through me at the sight. But then she squeezed my hand back and nodded, and I dragged her into my house.

The lights were off, but I could make my way through the shadows easily. I kept close to her so she wouldn't trip on any discarded items on the floor or bump into my wayward furniture. Once we were in my room, I flicked the light on.

My heart pounded in my chest and my throat closed up. This was my sacred space, and hardly anyone ever came in here. I had never brought a woman back here and not even my family had set foot in here since I moved in, if only because I spent more time at the main house anyway.

This room held all my secrets. I knew what big of a leap this was when there was nothing established between us. We weren't in a relationship, our friendship was invisible, tentative at best, but there was *something* here. And I wanted to share this with her.

Mayda looked around my room with wide eyes, her posture nervous. I knew she was thinking the same thing I was. That she was in my sacred space, and she didn't know what to make of it.

"Junior..." Her voice trembled. I saw her eyes stray to the bed, a question in her depths.

"Jesus, Mayda, *no*. I didn't bring you in here for that." Still, my body stirred just at the thought.

"Oh..."

I swore I could hear disappointment lacing through the word, but surely I was imagining it. Not wanting to fuel my imagination, I led her towards my desk and sat her down on the rolling chair.

"Junior, what's going on?" Her bright eyes searched me, and I felt her gaze sear down to my soul. "Does this have to do with your dad? I—I didn't mean to eavesdrop..." Her face flushed and I gave pause. I'd never seen her flustered or embarrassed.

Fuck, I was like a kid on Halloween, starving for treats. I wanted to shove my hand into the whole bowl and come away with a mountain of sweets. I wanted everything she gave me.

Everything.

Only, her words registered and I cleared through the haze of desire my mind pulled me under to smile ruefully at her.

"I don't care that you eavesdropped, Mayda," I said. "But I did want to explain..."

Mayda crossed her hands on her lap and sat up straighter, her attention perking.

A chuckle rumbled through my chest. "You look like such a school counselor sitting like that."

She uncrossed her hands, expression falling.

"Didn't say it was a bad thing, cariño."

"Oh."

"Yes, well, I guess I should explain what you heard out there. My papá wants me to take over Los Corazones." I paused, rubbing a hand across my chest like there was a phantom ache and I was trying to ease it.

Mayda, of course, picked up on my discomfort. Her head tilted a fraction to the side, she blinked and said, "But you don't want it."

My body sagged. "No."

Saying it out loud felt phenomenal and terrifying. Finally admitting to what had been living in my heart for years hurt as much as it brought relief. I almost expected a bolt of lightning to shoot down on me. For the floor to open up and swallow me whole. Or, at the very least, for a demon to drag me to hell for this sin.

Mayda's gaze softened as she drank me in. "You're making your dad think that you do want it," she observed. "Why?"

I'd never talked to anyone about this before. I physically couldn't. Anytime I tried, my throat tightened up, my heart pounded, and my hands shook. Like my body was rejecting the words I wanted to say by making me physically ill.

With Mayda it was different, easy. I didn't feel nervous. The words, when spoken, came out quickly. Everything I'd wanted to say for so long that had been bottled up poured out of me.

"That's all he ever wanted for me, and the rancho is all I've ever known. He's always been so proud of me when I tend to the rancho, prouder than whenever I played basketball or soccer, or made good grades. His eyes actually light up when I'm with him in those fields, when I take care of the trabajadores, when I take charge. He wants me to want this as badly as he does, and if I tell him I don't want it, I'll feel like... like..."

"Like you're betraying him?" Her voice was gentle, soothing.

"Yeah, exactly like that."

The echo of the chair sliding across the floor was penetrating in the silence. Mayda started forward until our knees were touching. She leaned forward and grabbed my hands in hers. Her grip was firm and demanding just like her eyes. She enraptured me in them.

"Junior, why do you think your dad would be upset with you? As far as I've seen, your parents want all of you to be happy."

My fingers tightened on hers. "I know that," I said. "But I think he wants me to be like him. Hell, he even gave me his *name*. What will happen when I tell him I don't want this legacy he built for me, for us? I don't want to hurt him, and I don't want him to look at me like I'm a disappointment. Like I won't measure up to what he is. That I won't *be* like him."

"Ah, so your fear is being a disappointment. Why would he be disappointed? What would you rather do than work at the ranch?"

"I don't know, Mayda! I don't know what I would do with my life!" I tore my hands from hers, causing her to roll backwards. I pushed myself to my feet, going and opening one of my desk drawers to pull out a framed diploma and handed it to her.

She took it reverently, smoothing her fingers over the edges of the frame. Her eyes blew wide with surprise as she took in the name on my paper.

"I have a degree I don't know what to do with."

"Junior... when?"

I closed my eyes and tried to push away the tightness at my throat, to no avail. I opened them again. "A few months after I graduated, maybe. I knew I wanted to do something else, so I did it in secret. I used my earnings, student loans, took online courses... I got my degree in child development, but I wanted more, so I'm taking more courses—"

"You're taking *more* online courses?" she asked, her jaw dropping.

"Yes. I should be finished with those in about six months..."

"Junior, that's amazing! You could be a child psychologist—"

"Yes, but I don't *want* that."

She blinked. "You don't?"

"It's hard to explain. I love kids, I want to help them, but not in the same way you do. Shit, I can't even help myself. What if I fuck up their lives, Mayda? And what about the rancho? My family?"

Her eyebrows rose. "What about them? Junior, they're adults and so are you. You can do whatever you want."

I wanted to walk out, to run away from the conversation that I dragged her into, but I couldn't.

"Los Corazones won't fall apart if you aren't at the head of it, Junior," Mayda whispered. "Your dad will find a way. I think you're being too hard on yourself."

I sighed. Maybe she was right. Maybe they'd be cool about it.

Or maybe my papá would disown me.

Mayda's eyes narrowed as if she could read my every thought. Slowly, she stood and placed my diploma back into the drawer I tore it out of, closed it, and turned to me.

"You don't have to make a decision today, Junior. You don't have to tell them anything right now. Hell, you don't even have to think about it right now if you don't want to. Eventually, yes, but not right now." Her hand slid up my arm and squeezed.

Her touch brought comfort. Her very presence was my own personal balm.

I let out a breath. "Papá thinks college is a waste of time, that it's better to learn a trade and work to support my family. He thinks it's because we're Mexican and don't have the same opportunities out there that others do." At least, that was his thought process when it came to *me*. My sisters were different. He wanted them to study and thrive. As a man, I had to work because when my parents couldn't do that any longer, it fell on me to help take care of them financially. To become the man of the house.

Pain flashed in her eyes, or maybe it echoed from my body towards her own, I couldn't be sure. All I knew was that it was there. And it hurt.

"I don't know about that," she whispered. "But if it means anything, I think you'd be a great educator, an amazing helper. You're incredible, Junior. I admire you. I... I—" She broke off, biting her bottom lip.

I so badly wanted to know what she had to say, but she looked like she was retreating, pushing herself away from the feelings I was starting to suspect were there. I didn't want her to, but that wasn't my decision. Maybe with time, she would tell me.

In the meantime...

My hand rose to cradle her face. Her breath hitched and she released her lip. I swore I could hear her heart pounding, or maybe that was my own beating savagely against my chest. "Can we keep this between us? Don't tell Gabriela...?"

She seemed to lean into my touch. "Don't worry, your secret is safe with me."

CHAPTER 11

JUNIOR

T HE MOMENT MY PAPá switched out beer for tequila, I knew we were doomed.

"Esto va para largo." Hector grinned from my side, swallowing down the rest of his drink just as my papá made his way to the table. He offered us both a cuba, shooting me a smile as if our earlier conversation had never happened. I tried not to let that thought settle heavily in my chest as I clinked glasses with Hector and took a small sip.

The music was booming through the yard, a fast-paced cumbia, and the dancing feet made the entire ground feel like it was shaking. Everyone dancing moved at different rhythms and in different styles, and the joy was infectious as I watched.

Valentina approached our table, holding her hands out to Hector. "Dance with me!" she ordered and didn't wait for him to reply before she grabbed his arm and yanked him out of his seat. He stumbled after her, and they lost themselves in the sea of dancing bodies and music.

I took another swig of my cuba, letting the tequila and soda settle in my throat while my eyes scanned the crowd. The current song stopped playing after a few more minutes and some couples dispersed while others remained where they were.

La Buenona by *Nativo Show* started playing immediately after, causing a chill to sweep over my body. The hairs on my arms rose and the back of my neck prickled as excitement swept through me. I loved this song.

Like an instinct I couldn't fight, my eyes scanned the crowd, landing on Mayda; like I knew exactly where she was, my body honed in to her every move. I wanted to believe that she felt the same when her gaze connected to mine at the same moment.

Her smile was tentative, but it was her eyes that really shone. Slowly, I set my drink down on the table and, never breaking eye contact, jerked my chin in the direction of the dance floor. I stood and walked in that direction, watching as she slowly went to meet me in the middle.

"How are your cumbias?" I asked her, smirk twisting my mouth.

She chortled, her cheeks flushing in a way I knew had nothing to do with the alcohol. "As good as ever."

My mamá, Doña Claudia, and Abuelita Mari taught us all how to dance. We'd only been eight when it started. Every gathering meant tequila, music, and the teasing that came with it. I remembered them trying to force us to learn.

"Ximena, go dance with your brother!"

"Guácala!" My younger sister would fake gagging noises and then wear a scowl when they inevitably forced us together, teaching the both of us how to move our feet side by side. It was always awkward and stiff and uncomfortable.

We eventually grew out of it, but Mayda was no doubt remembering the lessons just as I was.

I pulled her to me, my palm pressing against her hip, hand taking hers. I held her close, so close that our lower bodies touched. It elicited a gasp from her delicate mouth, and I was sure she could feel the raging hard-on I sported beneath my jeans. I swallowed, waiting to see if she'd pull away, put distance between us like she tended to do. But she didn't. Her eyes met mine, and for a second I wondered if the expression I saw was something akin to desire. Maybe I wanted to believe it, because there was something between us now. Shared secrets that had brought us closer than we'd ever been before. Our feet began moving in tandem as I led her to the rhythm of the music. My lips mouthed the words of the song while she tilted her head back and laughed, causing the words to catch in my throat.

Her laughter was the most beautiful melody, and I'd be content to listen to it for the rest of my days.

I twirled and dipped her, cutting off the thoughts that suddenly scared me. And it was a fear that gripped me as we finished our dance. Even as the music died down and my hands couldn't stray away from her body, that fear only seemed to increment and my heart pounded as realization began to set in.

But I tried not to let my emotions play across my face, though I feared she'd already seen them.

Instead, I let my fingers wrap around the end of her smooth hair and tugged slightly, tilting her gaze to mine.

"Another?" I asked.

She smiled breathlessly at me. "Another."

"Abuelita, do you want me to help you inside?"

It was getting late, and while the party was still going, her eyes were fighting to stay open. At my words, though, she glanced over at me slowly, her thin mouth pulling up into a wrinkled smile.

"I'm fine, mijo. I want to watch."

I didn't want to bother her with my concern, so I just leaned forward and wrapped her blanket tighter around her shoulders.

"Let me know if you need anything?"

I knew she wouldn't. Abuelita was quiet. She reminded me a bit of Sofia and Ximena in that way. Like she tried to limit herself to the sidelines and watch everyone else have a good time, despite her own discomfort.

Hell, maybe that's where I got it from.

"I will," she assured me. "Go have fun, mijo. Mayda looks hungry. You should feed her. She's too skinny."

I tried not to roll my eyes. "Sure thing, abuelita."

I didn't take Mayda a plate, though. She was sitting with Gabriela, whispering and cackling together like they tended to do. I veered my way instead towards Hector. I'd already monopolized enough of Mayda's time and would probably do so again when more songs I liked began playing.

As it was, the party had already started to die down. Guests had said their adioses and taken plates wrapped with food. I'd stood by my papá's side as they thanked us for the party, though standing there made me uncomfortable.

They looked at me like I was important. Not just as the jefe's son, but like I was their boss as well. And my papá just clapped me on the back, like I had every right to stand at his side. As if he were proud of me even when the heavy weight of his disappointment from earlier still pressed down to my bones.

I just smiled, though the action hurt my face, and counted down the seconds until I could leave his presence without speaking another word.

It was always easier to smile through it, to pretend like everything was alright even when it wasn't. To let his expectations drop onto me, filling me to the brim. Because what was the point of having a son if I didn't follow in his footsteps, right?

With a heavy sigh, I plopped down next to Hector. My friend already looked like the alcohol was getting to him. His eyes looked unfocused, his smile too tight. It'd been a while since I'd seen him let loose.

"You okay?" I asked.

"Fuck, maaaan." He ran a hand over his face, heaving out a sigh. "I should probably cut back, huh?"

Far be it my duty to tell him what he should or shouldn't do. "What's bugging you?"

"What makes you think anything's bugging me?" His eyes didn't meet mine. I noticed they swept over the party, going over my sisters, stopping on my parents.

Ah, fuck.

I knew what was bothering him. He got very melancholy when he drank and tended to brood in silence. When we were in high school, we used to sneak out and go to parties when we could. Every time Hector would drink, he brooded. And it was always because of his dad.

"I think maybe you should call it a night," I suggested quietly.

It seemed to break him out of whatever stupor he was in. He turned to me slowly, the expression leaving his face, a smile replacing it. "Yeah," he agreed, releasing a small chuckle. "I probably should."

"Need help getting to your place?"

He stood up, his legs wobbling slightly before he righted himself. I fought the urge to reach out for him, tightening my hands against my sides.

Hector wasn't a violent drunk, but he was one who got irritated easily. "I got it." He waved me off. "I need to see if my mamá needs anything." He walked away, not bothering to look back as he waded his way through the bones of a dying get-together to reach his mamá.

Doña Gloria watched him approach, her eyes narrowing with each step he took. When he was finally in front of her, she immediately started letting out a slew of rapid-fire Spanish, though the words were too quiet for me to hear. She berated him and he just frowned at her before pushing past her, down over to the direction of their shared house. A moment after, Doña Gloria sighed and walked after him.

I wondered what that was about.

All my life I'd watched her be strict with him. It wasn't new to see her berating him, particularly when he was drinking. It had happened so long throughout our lifetime that I didn't think anything of it.

"Hey."

I startled, looking up bare, tan legs, the edge of a floral dress, and up into Mayda's big eyes. She stared down at me shyly, her hands hidden behind her back.

"Hey." I leaned back.

"Is Hector okay?" Her gaze strayed to where he'd been standing by his mamá. "That looked serious."

"I'm not sure."

And it made me realize I'd been a real shitty friend to him. I'd been so busy with my own shit that I hadn't inquired about his own emotions and well-being. Fuck, I hadn't even apologized for snapping at him in my house before.

She turned back to me, this time her smile was strained. "Seems like everyone's got parental problems around here, huh?" I knew she meant it as a joke, but there was a tightness to her voice that I didn't like. I knew she was thinking about her own mom and what I'd witnessed the other day.

It felt weird, feeling sorry for myself when Mayda had things so much worse. I was bitching about my papá at every turn, but at least he was present in my life. At least I knew who he was. At least he *had* dreams to give me—even if they weren't my own.

Mayda was left in the nightmare of picking up the pieces of her own mamá's messes.

"Guess we aren't so special after all," I joked.

That did make her laugh. She held out her hands then, expectant, her eyebrows raised in a rare sight of mischievousness. I reached for her immediately, placing my palms over hers.

"One last dance before the party ends and we have to go back to reality?"

I stood, pulling her close by the waist so our bodies touched.

"Sounds like a plan."

Chapter 12

MAYDA

I STUMBLED INTO THE kitchen the next morning, or rather, afternoon. The party had led off well into the early morning, and I'd stayed awake for all of it. Even though I didn't drink more than two beers, as I liked to measure my alcohol intake, I still felt *way* too tired.

Perfect contrast to what I felt last night.

Because last night? I felt *alive* for the first time in a long time. My skin was on fire. It wasn't because of the two beers or even the spicy foods that incinerated my tongue. It was Junior. Plain and simple.

After we left his house and wandered back to the party, each of us going our separate ways, it felt like there was a camaraderie between us. Like the secrets that joined us had somehow made us stronger, pushed us closer. And close we stayed. Like two magnets being drawn together, we gravitated towards one another throughout the night. Sometimes we talked and ate, but mostly we danced.

His hand wrapped around my waist, pushing our bodies close together as we moved to the corridos, fast paced music that required a lot of quick footwork and endless twirls.

He held me like I belonged in his arms, and he looked at me the same way. His touch and stares branded me down to my soul.

I relished in that closeness most of all.

Especially in the way his dick felt through our clothes. I tried to pretend I couldn't feel it, but holy shit, it was hard to ignore it when he grinded it against me while we danced. And I, cusca that I was, didn't pull away. In fact, I'd pushed *closer.* A part of me had wished that there were no barriers between us at all. The kiss of our lower bodies caused a friction against my skirt that almost had me moaning and begging for more.

I didn't ask him to explain his text messages to me. It seemed just too obvious after we spoke and then danced like our bodies tried becoming one. He *liked* me. In the same sense that I liked him. I didn't want to deny my feelings for him anymore, but I didn't want to accept them just yet either.

I felt like I was on the edge of a tightrope. Waiting. For what, I didn't know. For him to make a move? For more confirmation? For me to become worthy of being with him?

His touches and glances had been subtle, and more than what we'd ever given each other before. But they still made me feel high.

So, despite being exhausted, by the time I slid into my seat the next afternoon at the dining table, I still felt a sense of giddiness. Like I was in the clouds. Not even the scents of heated leftovers on the stove or Doña Gloria's afternoon music could rouse me.

The Águila-Gutierrez clan slowly bounded down the stairs, stumbling and rubbing at their eyes, one by one. Gabriela showed up, but Junior still hadn't. I tried not to look at the back door longingly and caught myself when Gabriela took a seat next to me, shoving her elbow into my side.

"Ow!" My attention snapped to her. "Rude!"

"Don't give me that, Mayda." She pointed her fork in my direction. The utensil was speared with a piece of meat. She looked prepared to slap me with it, too. "What's going on with you and Junior?"

Her proclamation was met with silence. Literal. Silence. Everyone stopped what they were doing to turn their curious gazes in our direction. Forks clattered against their plates and eyes burned holes through my forehead.

Particularly from the sisters.

"I don't know what you mean." I picked up my own fork and knife and cut through my own leftover asada.

"Don't be a liar, Mayda Jiménez, it doesn't suit you."

"I'm not lying!"

I *was* lying. Mainly because I was still on unsure footing and didn't know what we were. We were closer, that was for sure, but we weren't on the level Gabriela wanted us to be on. I was unsure if we'd ever be *that* close. If we'd ever be what she wanted us to be. For now, we shared secrets and a kindling desire for one another that I wasn't sure we would act on.

"I saw the two of you come out of his place," Gabriela poked, hissing low, though I knew everyone heard her.

At that my face flushed, and I sent her a glare. There was that familiar glint in her eye that screamed of mischief. As if I didn't know what she was doing. She was outing me in front of everyone on purpose because she thought it would make me more inclined to tell the truth.

Traitor.

"What were you doing in his house, Mayda?" She twined her fingers together, resting her elbows atop the table and her chin atop her hand. "He never lets anyone in there."

Fuck.

I couldn't very well tell them what we were really doing there. If I didn't say anything, they would think we were up to something we weren't supposed to. I could feel Mamá Claudia's eyes on me, and I tried not to cringe. It didn't matter how nice they were to me, I didn't think they would be understanding if they thought we were having sex in his house... on her property.

Shit, fuck, damn.

"It wasn't—"

"I think Mayda and Junior would make such pretty babies." Everyone seemed to startle at Abuelita Mari's words. She smiled brightly, her wrinkled fingers firm as she stabbed her fork into a piece of meat on her plate.

"They *would* make the cutest babies," Valentina agreed, equally bright. "Can you imagine? I'd be the best tia."

My face flushed. I felt mortified. I wanted the floor to suck me through and not spit me out until they were all gone.

But then it just got worse.

Because Junior and Hector walked through the door, and he caught the vestiges of our conversation and he looked at me. Our eyes held, gazes locking, and his smile just made my face flush brighter. Even as the embarrassment crawled through my system, it was overpowered by a burning rush of *need*.

I was surprised I felt it amidst everyone, but it was there, demanding attention. Beneath my borrowed t-shirt, my nipples puckered against the fabric and the ache between my legs that never really abated built in intensity, throbbing, needing. I swore his eyes flashed dark with his own desire, pinning me in place, drying the words in my throat before I could even speak them.

A second later, the expression was gone, and he laughed lightly at something Hector muttered from behind him and walked into the house. He didn't hesitate to take a seat next to me. Like that's exactly where he belonged.

Our shoulders brushed together, and my breath whooshed from my lungs.

Gabriela noticed. Her eyes narrowed, but she didn't push with her questions again. Maybe because Junior was here, and he tempered her nosiness. Or maybe because the evil bitch was plotting. I swore, she wanted to kill me every time she spoke. She'd never been this damn persistent in the past.

Brunch went by in relative quiet after that and by the time we were finished, just sitting around and talking about the party last night, my nerves were better.

Until Gabriela spoke again.

"Let's go out!" she declared, shoving her shoulder into mine. I shot her a glare at all the jostling so soon after I'd just eaten, which went ignored. She was bouncing on the edge of her seat, a wide grin splayed over her pretty lips. "Soon we won't have time to see each other. Let's go dancing."

"We just went dancing." Truth be told, I didn't want to go again. Going to the clubs meant Gabriela could let her hair loose, which meant she would be shoving shots into my hand and demanding I pour them back.

She never got me drunk in those outings, and she never got beyond a little tipsy herself. In our whole friendship, she'd only ever seen me slightly tipsy one time but never shit-faced. She never pushed, but she always got this glint in her eye like she wanted to test my limits and see how far I was willing to go, maybe push me a little further.

She didn't know my mom was a drunk and that she was the reason I was averse to hitting anything heavier than beer or tequila. She always asked if there was a reason and I always made up the same excuse that someone had to stay sober to watch out for her ass.

"We should go *again*," Gabriela said, flipping her hair over her shoulder. "We could meet hot guys!"

I fought back my cringe at the boisterous words. They traveled down the length of the table, and I knew the moment they reached Junior's ears because Gabriela's smirk kicked up even though she didn't take her eyes off me. And those eyes screamed what her mouth wouldn't say.

You know, since there's nothing going on between you two?

Bitch, bitch, bitch! My eyes narrowed and shot lasers at her.

"Hot guys?" Señor Águila muttered the words like a curse, and I tore my gaze away from my she-demon soon-to-be ex-best friend long enough to look at the family head. Junior sat next to him and they wore matching expressions of distaste.

My lips thinned to avoid smirking at the way Junior's eyes were thunderous on his sister. Like I wasn't the only one not up for the idea.

"Dancing sounds amazing!" Sofia, who was otherwise the shyest of the sisters, shouted from across the table. Her dark brown eyes lit up with promise and excitement.

"You danced last night!" Junior cut in, looking at his sisters while avoiding my gaze.

"Yeah, but it was with family and the trabajadores, not hot guys." Ximena pulled out a paintbrush from her tight curls and chewed on the end of it. "Dancing at a club has a different vibe."

"You don't even *like* dancing!" Junior grumbled, leaning close to try and snatch her paintbrush away.

She snapped it out of his grip before his fingers could close over it. Her eyes narrowed and she pointed the thing at him in accusation. "I don't, but like I said, the *vibes* are different. I need a change of pace to help boost my inspiration for this new piece I'm working on." She turned, efficiently dismissing her brother to smile at Gabriela. "Count me in."

"Hot guys..." Señor Águila grumbled again, running a hand over his face. His panic-stricken expression was enough to make me want to laugh because it was like he was just now realizing his daughters were grown and could go out to clubs and *meet* said hot guys.

"I want to go, too!"

Well, all except for...

"You're too young for that," Hector teased from Valentina's side. He'd been silent the entire time, content to watch until the youngest sister spoke up.

Laughter caught in my throat at the pout she threw his way. He ignored her and turned back to his meal, the cold shoulder making Valentina's own slump down and her dark eyes flash with anger.

She'd always had a crush on Hector, something that had never been given to fruition due to their age difference—she was only seventeen, and Hector was my age. Sometimes I wondered if that wouldn't change when she turned eighteen. Hector was protective of the youngest sister, for sure. I could always catch the glimpses of disappointment in Valentina's eyes when he kept her at arm's length, treating her like a child instead of a woman like she so hard tried to portray.

I feel you, girl.

At least, I felt that before yesterday and the day before.

Somewhere down the line, mine and Junior's relationship had morphed like a butterfly bursting slowly from a cocoon. I was eager to see if it would take off in flight.

My eyes met his again. His jaw worked tightly, and his hands were wrapped into fists on top of the table. I couldn't read what he was trying to convey because he tore his eyes away a moment later to glare at Gabriela again.

"It's settled!" she said, oblivious to her brother's rage. Or, if she was aware of it, she didn't make it known. "We're going. And you—" She pointed at me. "You are going to get dolled up and meet someone. It's high time you found yourself a boyfriend."

I don't want just any boyfriend.

The words I meant to say got stuck in my throat at the same time Junior stood abruptly, his chair scraping back against the floor. All eyes jumped to him, but he didn't meet them as he stormed away from the table and out of the house, slamming the back door closed behind him.

I want Junior.

CHAPTER 13

JUNIOR

IT DIDN'T MATTER THAT there had been a party yesterday or that we were up until the early hours of the morning drinking. All it took was a single cold beer to cure our hangovers and then we were all back out there in the fields, prepping the soil for the crops to be picked.

The sun beat down against my bare skin, causing me a discomfort that I almost welcomed. If only to take my mind off the swirling thoughts that plagued me. The words Gabriela spoke at the table replayed in my mind, making my hands pierce the soil all too aggressively, a grumble pressing my lips.

Hot guys.

A fucking *boyfriend.*

As if I hadn't molded her against my body the night before and felt her heat through her fucking skirt. As if we hadn't felt one another's arousal like a tangible thing that lived between us. And

Mayda did nothing to contradict Gabriela's words. To tell her that she didn't want a boyfriend, that she had no interest in going out and finding one.

She sat there, avoiding my gaze.

Aloof.

Mysterious.

All the doubts I'd ever had about her and her interest in me came rearing their ugly heads, like a hydra monster. Just when I thought I'd cut off one insecurity and we'd stepped into a new chapter of understanding, more heads arose, leaving me floundering all over again.

I wanted her, and I feared she was too blind to see it. Just like I feared telling her would make her somehow pity me, like by speaking more than just a simple 'I like you' through a text message would push the truth forward. Then I'd truly find out that she had no interest in me at all because I was her best friend's brother. That I somehow just wasn't *enough*.

I never was enough.

"¿Que te pasa?" Hector asked, eyeing the way I tossed my tools into the dirt and pushed myself to an annoyed stand. Even as he asked the question, his dark gaze was knowing.

"Nada."

Nothing was wrong. The lie could slip easily from my mouth, as I was so used to fucking hiding my feelings anyway. Hombres didn't show emotions. We pushed our turmoils to the back of our minds in the hopes that they disappeared. It was such a fucking toxic way of thinking, but somehow I couldn't let it go.

Hector shook his head in my direction, like he knew exactly what was on my mind. Why wouldn't he? My best friend knew me better than anyone else. He scoffed. "Estás bien pendejo." The words were unkind, and I wanted to snap back at the tough love he gave in his own way, but there was nothing I could say when I knew he was right.

I *was* a fucking dumbass.

"Junior!" My papá appeared, shielded from the sun with his large sombrero, a sheen of sweat dripping over his forehead. His right-hand man was at his side. Don Filiberto—Don Beto—was an older man with thick, graying sideburns and hazel eyes. Don Beto smiled at me from beneath that bushy mustache as he handed me a cold corona. "This heat está cabrón." He handed another beer off to Hector.

I was inclined to agree on his assessment of the weather.

"Makes a man want to retire," my papá laughed. It was followed by a clap on the back that jerked me forward. "Once Junior here takes over, though, I'll be able to kick back in the shade with a cold beer."

The heavy implications of his words made my gut churn even worse, turning the beer sour in my stomach. I could feel Hector's gaze on the side of my face, almost like he was urging me to take the moment to come clean to him and tell him what I really felt.

I just swallowed a sip and gave my Don Beto and my papá a tight nod. It was met with beaming smiles of pride and words of encouragement that slipped into one ear and out another. I was already too lost in my own thoughts to focus on what they were saying around me.

I hated this. Hated the pretending. I hated feeling like my very lies were choking the life out of me only to fill everyone else's cups. With every lie that pushed past my lips, I lost bits and pieces of myself and I knew that if I kept this up, eventually, there would be nothing left of me at all.

I sat my grimy ass down on my mamá's couch with a blessed sigh. She shot me a glare from the kitchen and I pretended to ignore it. It was a grueling day on the rancho, and I was both physically and mentally exhausted. I should have made my way to my place to hop in the shower, done some homework, and then crashed.

I couldn't even move.

And I'd be lying if I said I didn't want to see—

A storm of voices impacted the entire house, and like a wave cresting against the earth, my sisters came rushing down the stairs, their heels clicking against the wooden floors of the staircase. They were nearly a blur of fabrics and swishing of dresses, all except Valentina, who sulked behind them in jeans and a t-shirt, her arms crossed petulantly against her chest.

Valentina plopped herself unceremoniously on the couch next to me, grumbling something about injustice. I rolled my eyes and wrapped an arm around her shoulders. "Tranquila, hermanita."

She groaned and shoved me away. "Junior, you stink, go away."

Of course, that just made me rub myself against her even more. The day's sweat and dirt slid against her skin. She shrieked in protest and tried shoving me away.

"Stop it! You're a whole man-child!"

"That's not very nice." I all but tackled her in retaliation onto the couch cushions, doggy piling onto her body and shoving my pit in her face.

She cried out for our mamá and our hermanas, but everyone cackled alongside me and nobody came to her aid.

It was then that Gabriela whooshed down the stairs with Mayda at her heels.

The sight of Mayda gave me pause. My movements froze. My breath caught. My heart stuttered in my chest. Valentina took advantage of my distraction to wiggle her small body out from beneath me. Her palm cracked down against my forehead in retribution and she darted away from me.

I didn't reach for her, though. I sat up straight, rubbing my palm across the mark she'd likely left behind. My eyes followed Mayda as she bounded down the stairs, heels in hand. I watched as she took a seat on the couch across from me, sliding her delicate feet into her strappy, black footwear.

She was a fucking vision.

Clad in a seductive red piece that hugged her frame, the swells of her breasts rose as she breathed. Her long, wavy hair tickled her lush skin, the ends begging to be wrapped around my fist. I swallowed, eyes trailing down the length of her as she stood up, taking in every little detail from the dip of her hips to her toned, tanned legs.

My dick stirred to life in my jeans.

And she still hadn't even acknowledged my presence at all. Her gaze darted everywhere except for me, and there was a pang in my chest at the thought.

"We're leaving now, ma!" Gabriela called out.

"Tengan cuidado, and call me if you need a ride."

"Sofia is our designated driver tonight," Gabriela reassured her that they'd be careful.

They spoke a few words, but I couldn't hear. The only thing that existed in my ears was white noise, and the only thing that lived branded into my brain was the sight of Mayda as she started to walk away, giving me a glimpse of her rounded backside. Of her locks of hair swaying down her back.

But not her eyes.

Not her attention.

And not a glimpse of what I really wanted to see.

Chapter 14

MAYDA

THE CLUB REVERBERATED AS music blasted against the walls and feet bounded up and down in unabashed dancing. It was the hottest club in the city and rivaled all others because of one reason only. It did theme nights. The thing was, no one ever knew what theme the night would bring until you stepped inside and felt the pulsing beat of the music. Dress-codes didn't matter. Only the music.

Tonight was disco.

Boogie Wonderland pooled out from the speakers and had club goers sliding, twirling, and hip thrusting in an array of colorful skirts. While I enjoyed the ambiance and was having a good time, my mind kept rushing back to the moments before we'd left the rancho.

When I'd walked down the stairs, clad in a skintight red dress, courtesy of Gabriela, it was to find Junior in the living room, his eyes drinking in every step my exposed legs took down. They trailed up, leaving a path of fire wherever his dark eyes touched until they stopped on my face.

I was caked in makeup, the winged liner sharp enough to cut through my inhibitions and make me feel pretty. Ximena, with her skilled eye for colors and detail, had been the one to contour everyone's faces. She'd worked wonders, making me look fierce and giving me a smoky eye I'd only ever seen and slobbered over on Pinterest.

When Junior's eyes landed on me fully, I knew the hours of getting ready had been worth it.

His eyes and nostrils flared and the carefree expression he usually always wore changed into something more dangerous. Like a predator who'd caught sight of his prey. Why did that thought send a thrill through my body?

I'd pretended not to notice his glances, but it was hard not to. It was all I could feel, all I could practically taste. It made my face heat, and I waited for him to acknowledge me, to say *something*.

But he never did.

So I'd left with the girls and was in the club, sitting at the bar with Gabriela and watching Sofia and Ximena dance together. They were a captivating pair. Due to how close they were in age and appearance, people often thought they were twins. Ximena's hair was unrulier, her body thick, and while she wasn't skilled at dancing, her quiet enthusiasm made up for it. There was no doubt though that Sofia was absolutely breathtaking once the music came on. Every eye was on her, following the roll of her hips, the rise and dip of her hands, even the deliberate placement of her fingers...

"You haven't looked for a single hot guy since we've been here!" Gabriela shouted the accusation in my ear.

I shot her a look of exasperation. "That's because I'm not interested."

Her palm came down to slap against my thigh. "I knew it!" she shrieked, loud even over the music. "Something happened with Junior!"

This again? I rolled my eyes and whirled away from her. "Nothing happened!"

"Let's say I believe you." The margarita on her breath fanned against my cheek, startling me. "Then why aren't you out there looking for someone to dance with?"

"Gee, maybe because I don't need a man to be complete?"

Gabriela cackled. "What you need is a good dicking."

"Gabi!" I stared at her, aghast.

"What? Don't tell me it's not true. You're so uptight. So is Junior, for that matter. While I don't want to think about my brother's sex life, I think you'd both do each other some good if you know what I mean." Her eyebrows waggled and she looked so ridiculous, I laughed.

"You're relentless, you know that? Fine." I pushed myself off of the seat and stood. "If it makes you happy, I'll go dance."

"You do that. Go dry hump on the dance floor."

I threw my hand up over my shoulder, flipping her the finger, as I sauntered over towards her sisters. They welcomed me into their dance circle with cheers, and I threw my head back and laughed as we started moving.

I bounced right alongside them, my legs sliding, mimicking old school disco moves. As the tempo of the music changed, I felt hands glide up the sides of my hips and pull me close. My back met a hard chest and my body tensed, my feet faltering. Once the shock wore off, which was like two point five seconds later, I whirled in the person's hold and glared at the man behind me.

He flashed me a smile that did nothing for me. Sure, he was handsome, but it wasn't enough to make my heart beat faster or my thighs to press together to try and stave off desire.

Maybe Gabriela was right and I needed to get laid, but not with Mr. Touchy Feely here.

"No thanks," I told him, registering his falling smile, then turned away, back to Ximena and Sofia. But when Mr. Touchy Feely left, more men came up to take his place until it felt like I was fighting off annoying, flirty dudes all night.

A lot of them were attractive, a lot of them weren't. But it didn't matter what they looked like, because they weren't what I wanted. They weren't a long, straight nose or short dark hair. They weren't caring smiles or full lips. They weren't long fingers that reached out to tug on the ends of my hair.

The thing was, I'd had boyfriends before, but none that had ever lasted long enough for feelings to grow. I'd kept everyone at arm's length my whole life. I told myself it was because of my life, because of my baggage.

It was there, with music shaking through my nervous system and another man walking away, that I realized it *wasn't* because of that.

It was because none of the men in my life had been the one I truly desired.

All my life, Junior had been something untouchable, something I didn't want to tarnish with my fucked up life. All my life I'd wanted him. Now, things were changing. I thought of his lips on mine. Of his truth and my truth mingling in the quiet spaces of his house. The heat of his eyes as he took in my appearance.

I wasn't naïve enough to wonder what it had been. I knew he wanted me too. He'd confided in me secrets no one else knew.

He told me he *liked* me.

Now I just had to be brave enough to confess to him that I liked him too.

CHAPTER 15

JUNIOR

PICTURING MAYDA AT THE club, meeting 'hot guys' as my sister had put it, made my stomach go in knots. It made my head spin. It made me want to fucking *punch* something.

Then seeing her walk down in a skintight red dress? Fuck. I just knew men were going to be all over her that night, salivating like wild animals. I wanted to pick her up and throw her over my shoulder, take her to my house and keep her locked up there and away from the eyes of other men. Another part of me wanted to go with them and make sure no one dared to come close.

What kind of fucked up thoughts were those? They were machista, at best, and not my finest head space.

I couldn't act on *any* of that, as much as I wanted to. She didn't belong to me. She wasn't my girlfriend. She'd barely even hinted that it was what she wanted. I had no way to know if I was alone in my feelings or not.

Instead of giving in to my impulses, I'd walked away. Every fucking time, I walked away.

Now, I was stuck inside my house, with the image of how sexy she looked in that outfit, that makeup, while I tried to get homework done. I almost succeeded, too, but my phone beeped with a text.

I picked it up with a sigh, seeing a message from Gabi. I opened it and my blood went cold. My feet planted firmly on the floor from shock, my spine going rigid straight.

Gabi sent me a single picture. A picture of Mayda at the club. Dark around the edges, but with the angle of the strobe lights, I could make out her dancing form perfectly enough to glimpse at her open sensuality. The way her head was tossed back, her lips tilted in one of her rare, care-free smiles. She was beautiful. Scratch that, she was fucking sexy and wild with abandon. Of course, that was no surprise. What was surprising was the fact that there was a man pressed close behind her. I couldn't make out his features, but I could see his hands against her hips.

Something feral awakened in me at the sight. It made me want to bang against my chest like a caveman and take my fist to his nose.

My phone pinged again, and I grudgingly looked down on it and found Gabi's words laughing at me.

Fuck.

I wanted to toss my phone, but I couldn't seem to relinquish the tight grip I had around it as much as I couldn't stop staring. At those hands. On. Her. Hips. Those should have been *my* hands. That should have been my body pressed against hers, making her smile like that.

Gabriela's words taunted me.

You snooze, you lose, pendejo.

Wasn't that the fucking truth? And for the sudden life of me, as I stared at this picture, I couldn't remember why I'd never dared to make a move. Any and every excuse I'd ever conjured up regarding it suddenly felt so lame, so stupid that I wanted to slap myself upside the head.

Because she's my sister's best friend. When had Gabi ever given any indication that she didn't want us together? If anything, she always seemed to push us together instead of apart.

Because she doesn't like me back. How do I even fucking know that? I never even *asked.*

All my life, I'd played things safe. I'd gone along with what others wanted for me instead of taking the fucking leap into the unknown and look where it had gotten me. I was a coward, but Mayda? She made me feel brave. She made me want to take that plunge just to see what I'd find at the bottom.

My breath came out in short spurts as the realization hit me.

I wanted to tell her how I felt. I wanted to give in to the chance. And who knew, maybe she would feel the same way about me. Maybe she had wanted me as much as I wanted her this entire time. The point was, I'd never know unless I put myself on the line and spoke my truth.

And for Mayda?

For Mayda I would take that plunge.

I only hoped she'd be waiting for me when I reached the other side.

CHAPTER 16

MAYDA

THE RANCHO WAS QUIET, the dark room filled with nothing but the echoing of Gabriela's soft, steady breathing. I couldn't sleep. No matter how many sheep I counted or how long I closed my eyes, it evaded me.

Rubbing the heels of my hands against my eyes, I sighed and threw my legs off over the side of the bed, creeping out slowly. I reached for a spare robe Gabriela kept in her room for me and slid the smooth silk over my arms. The sleeves reached my wrists, while the hem touched just above my knees. It hid the sleep shorts and tank top I was wearing, at least, though the material seemed to make the sharp tips of my nipples more prominent.

We'd gotten in a few hours ago. After removing the heavy layers of makeup and taking a brush to my hair, Gabriela and I laid in her bed. She was asleep within moments, while I tried not to toss and turn.

My body felt like it was on fire and my tongue felt heavy as it stuck to the roof of my mouth. I blamed it on the tequila shots. There hadn't been that many, but it always left me feeling strange after I drank them. Like something was wrong with my body.

As quietly as I could, I slipped out of the room, closing the door behind me. The hallway was dark, and the floorboards creaked softly as I put my weight against them. Not wanting to wake anyone up, I hurriedly took the stairs and bounded down to the dimly lit kitchen.

I always felt awkward walking into the kitchen at night when no one else was here. It felt like I was somehow intruding. Like I was a burglar creeping through a place I didn't belong. Grabbing a glass from a cupboard, I went to the sink to fill it with water.

I took a hefty gulp, downed it, then leaned over the sink for a refill. It was at that moment when the door to the kitchen opened and I startled, a soft cry of surprise bursting past my lips. My hand trembled and the cup wavered, sloshing water over the sides of the rim. I dropped it in the sink and whirled.

"Shit!" I pressed my hand to my chest, trying to steady the rapid beating of my heart. "Junior, you scared me!"

He was swathed in the buttery glow of the porch light. It slanted over his body, and I found myself captivated by the picture he made. He wore a t-shirt that was tight against his frame, hugging his chest and upper arms so I could make out the exact shape of his pecs. Every ridge and bump that tapered down was all a result of hard work instead of gym time. Sweatpants swung low on his hips and...

Fuck me.

Gray sweatpants.

I wanted to groan and barely resisted the urge as he closed the door and stepped into the kitchen.

"Sorry," he whispered. "I didn't mean to startle you."

"What are you doing here?" I asked, then winced at myself for the question. This *was* his family's house. He had more right to be in this kitchen than I did. "Sorry, stupid question."

He stepped forward. That nervous sensation that had died down suddenly built back up, and I felt my heart beat up to my throat. His proximity did that to me. It made my belly tremble, made my fingers shake.

Junior all but prowled towards me, his eyes flaring in the dark. It was only thanks to the night light they kept plugged into the kitchen that I could see his expression at all, and it had me stepping away until my back hit the edge of the sink.

He stopped in front of me, placing his arms on either side of me so I was caged in. "It's not a stupid question, Mayda." A whisper of minty breath blew the words across my skin. There was an edge to them, to *him*, one I wasn't familiar with and didn't know how to navigate or face.

I was used to the playfulness, the smile, the fingers tugging at my hair to get my attention and demand more of me.

Not this... heat.

I found I didn't mind this unknown side of him at all.

"I actually came to talk to you."

My mind was too slow to catch up to those words. When they did, I blinked slowly up at him, brows pulling together in confusion. "You... were?"

He nodded. "Yup..." The pop of the P had my eyes darting to his full lips before catching myself and going back up to his gaze. Too late. He'd noticed. Dark eyes danced with mirth in the shadows of the kitchen, with the heady undercoat of desire.

"How did you know I'd be in the kitchen?" It felt imperative we keep whispering, even when everyone else was a whole floor above us, even when we were the only two here. This felt like a secret, like something was about to irrevocably change between us, and I didn't want to risk an interruption that would break this moment.

"I didn't know. I couldn't sleep and came over hoping..." He broke off, tilting his head to the side as if he was deciding what exactly to confess to me.

I found myself wanting to grab at his shirt front. I wanted it all. All of him and everything he had to say. His truth and my truth together.

"I was hoping you'd be awake too."

I swallowed the lump of nerves in my throat. The moment pulsed between us like a steady beat. It was different, not because of the proximity but because of everything we'd shared the past few days. Our secrets whispered between us, encircled us, bringing us together. But it was more than that.

It was like everything I ever held back from myself when it came to Junior was screaming at me now.

And it was as if he felt the same.

Still, I found myself asking, "Why?" I truly wanted to know the answer. I wanted to know if he felt what I felt. If my feelings weren't in vain. A part of me knew, but I wanted confirmation.

His arms lowered at his sides, and he straightened. Fear gripped me, making me worry that he was going to pull away from me, walk out of the door. He didn't do either of those things. Instead, his hands spanned against my hips, his palms searing through the silky material of the flimsy robe.

"Did you have fun tonight?" he asked, an edge to his voice.

I didn't know how he even expected my mind to register the question when his hands were on my freaking body, his thumbs trailing circles against my hip bones. It was a torment, one I had to yank my attention away from to actually answer.

"Uh... um... yeah..."

His hands stilled a moment before they kept up their slow, explorative movements. They suddenly weren't just in one place but gliding up and down my sides, leaving a trail of fire in its wake.

"Really?" he hummed. "You enjoyed that man's hands on your hips?"

My body went taut. My eyes widened. "What?"

"Gabi sent me a picture of you. You were dancing with someone." There was a pause as he cocked his head to the side. "Did you hook up with him?"

Circles twirled through my thoughts and tumbled them all together until I couldn't think straight. I didn't miss the note of jealousy in his voice, and I wasn't sure if I should feel humiliated by his line of questioning, wonder what he was getting at, or feel elated that he thought about me at all. There was also a steady, rising anger at Gabi, knowing she'd likely snapped a picture of me and Mr. Touchy Feely when I wasn't looking.

"I—is that even your business?"

A low growl rumbled from his chest that felt animalistic. It vibrated through my own chest, down to my core. His fingers tightened their grip. We were pressed close, but it didn't feel close enough. I couldn't feel the hard panes of his body, just his heat.

I wanted to angle my hips towards him but stopped myself.

"No," he breathed, and disappointment was a shock down my system like a cold jolt of water. "But I want it to be my business, Mayda. You have to know, you can't be *blind*..."

"Know *what*?"

But I already did. I just wanted to hear him say the words. I wanted that implosion, as it was everything I ever needed. For once, there were no inhibitions, no holding back. It was us, in the dark, with our secrets spilling over the edges of the containers we kept them in.

"You have to know that I l—that I like you. That I've liked you for years and you're the one I want, the *only* one I want."

The hands tracing figures against my body stilled their methodic movements. A whimper threatened to keen from my throat, and it was only by some miracle that I managed to bite it back as he pulled away from me. I didn't have to wait long before one of his hands was reaching behind me, grappling for the ends of my hair and *pulling*.

It was like every inch of me had nerve endings, and I could feel the shock of his firm hold through my system. This touch wasn't like the others. This wasn't a playful tug. This wasn't teasing between friends.

This evoked so much more.

A thrill shot down my spine as he pushed me forward with his hips. The sink bit into my lower back, the cold edge a contrast to the warmth that emanated from him. Arousal coated my skin like a second layer. It burrowed deep, pulsing hotly at my core. Throbbing. Aching.

A breath of need trembled from my lips.

With my neck craned back, I could see deep in his eyes. See his demand for an answer. To *acknowledge* him.

His words were the match, and my hissing whisper of a response were the gasoline.

"I want you, too."

I couldn't be sure who moved first, but move we did. We met in the middle, our mouths meshing in an inelegant clash of need. The breath vanished from my lungs the moment his pillowy lips landed against mine. Soft yet firm, Junior pillaged, his tongue prying apart the seam of my lips to delve inside my mouth.

His fingers dove into the strands at the back of my neck, tangling into the messy web to hold me firmly against him. Our bodies didn't know the meaning of the word space. The closer he pressed, the more my body arched into his, the more he folded me over the sink.

My hands grappled for purchase against his shoulders and his arm encircled my waist. A whisper of possession lived within the grip he had on me. We melded together one moment, and the next, he was yanking me away from the sink, his body disappearing for a spinning flash of a second as he whirled me and pressed me against the front of the kitchen counter.

My body slapped against the granite surface, a cry I didn't dare unleash on my lips. My heaving chest rose and fell against the cold. I warmed as Junior crowded behind me. First, his hips pressed against my ass, grinding my lower body against the edge of the counter and creating a friction I craved. Then he grasped my hair, yanking me up with a firm gentleness that finally had sounds of pleasure peeling from my throat.

With my back pressed to his front, the threat of falling into a puddle at his feet was real. "Junior," I pleaded, the sound harsh in the darkness of the kitchen.

"Dame tu boca," he commanded, his hand leaving my hair to wrap around my throat. He palmed my neck, putting pressure against my windpipe until all sound left me. Until I was nothing but a mess of desperation and desire. "Give me your mouth, cariño."

I turned my head sideways at his command and he lowered, his lips just a whisper away. I waited for his mouth to descend on mine, my eyes fluttering, my core tightening.

His lips skimmed across mine and he whispered words against my flesh. "You're mine, amor."

The endearment had my entire center heating. I felt the wetness dampen my panties, my legs quivering beneath me.

"Fucking *mine*."

He finally took my mouth in a searing kiss I felt down to my toes. It was a devouring. The wet mess of our tongues flicking together hungrily was the only sound to be heard. My heart beat a frantic rhythm, the pressure of my pulse pushing against the skin of his hand. He groaned, grinding his hips against my ass.

A gentle tug at my front and I could feel the silk robe slipping away, and then his hand dove between my body and the edge of the counter. His fingers teased the edge of my sleep shorts, and I tried to break away from his mouth to catch my fucking breath, but he growled, holding me to him by the throat.

Like he refused to ever let me go.

We'd taken too long to get to this moment for either of us to pull away now.

So I let myself struggle for breath and relished in this rapture. The rough calluses of his fingertips slid against my skin, right in the space where the hem of my shirt met my shorts. I was aware of every move, memorizing every single spot he touched. It heated me; fingerprints branded onto my skin. When he swooped beneath the elastic of my shorts and panties to touch my flesh, my palms slapped against his body, nails digging in like claws to hold tight.

Finally, Junior pulled away and I gulped down breath after breath. His stubbled cheek scraped my skin raw as he pressed against me, groaning low in his throat. His fingers slid between the seam of my pussy, teasing the wetness that spread against my curls.

"Fuck." His hoarse voice echoed in my ear. "Fuck, estás *empapada*. Your cunt is *soaked* for me." He bit down on the lobe of my ear then down to my neck, leaving a wet trail wherever his lips touched. He spread my folds with his fingers, hovering over the edge of my entrance. My own hips canted to meet him, but he denied me.

"Junior…" It sounded like a whine, a plea.

"Tell me, Mayda, have you always gotten this wet for me?" He inserted one finger as the question rattled through my brain, and I lost all coherent thought as my body welcomed him. "Do you always soak your panties under your demure little outfits while you never look my way?"

Yes.

I choked on the word, a part of me not wanting him to know that I'd always been a pining, pathetic little creature. His hand slipped away from my throat and entangled within my roots. I wanted to cry out at the roughness, but not in pain. No. I knew Junior would never hurt me. It was hard containing this desire to scream and writhe and wake up everyone on the whole fucking rancho.

"Mírame, Mayda."

We locked eyes and the depth of emotion I saw in his made me want to shy away like I always did. Always afraid to look. Always afraid of what I'd find. But this time, I braved his stare and saw what I was probably too dumb to admit to myself this entire time.

"Dime la verdad."

He wanted me to tell him the truth, but the truth of my feelings would scare him. Hell, they scared *me*. Too intense. They ran too hot, for too long and with too much.

But I gave him the one truth he wanted at that moment.

"Yes," I whispered. "You don't even need to talk and my panties get soaked."

His growl was drowned out as our lips collided once more. The sounds deafened and his fingers finally slipped inside me, smoothing against my insides. I moaned into his mouth and he curled inside me, thrusting in and out in a rhythm that made my head spin. My hips met every thrust, my entire body pulled taut as I chased both friction and release.

His thumb tapped against my clit, pressing and tracing circles all while he speared me, scissoring, eliciting gratification with every move. I stood on the tips of my toes, rubbing myself against him.

I was drowning. He was shoving me beneath the depths, depriving me of oxygen and yet somehow trying to give me life at the same time. He pulled me to that delicious edge of bliss, fingers sliding through my wetness and piercing deep in a way that made a keen trap in my throat.

He pulled away just enough to slap his palm over my mouth to muffle my cries. His harsh breaths pushed against my warm face. He played me like an instrument, and I teetered precariously on the ledge...

"Quiero tus gritos," he whispered against my ear. "Un dia, me darás todo lo que me puedas dar. Por ahora, quiero sentirte, Mayda."

In the end, it was those words that did me in. My addled brain tried to translate while his fingers moved within me, and when they finally did, I fell and gave him just what it was he demanded.

I want your screams. One day, you'll give me everything you can give. For now, I want to feel you, Mayda.

Feel me he did.

Tremors wracked my body as my orgasm overpowered every single nerve inside my body. I fell apart in his arms, my bones becoming nothing but a languid mess. My entire being trembled, and when he pulled out of me, I almost cried out at the feeling of missing him inside. But he left, bringing his hand up to our eye-level. Even in the dark I could tell his fingers were glistening.

Slowly, he slid his other hand from my mouth to cup my jaw.

"I want to taste you."

And he did just that. Bringing his fingers to his lips, he sucked them into his mouth, groaning as he licked the evidence of my arousal and my orgasm from his skin. It was filthy, and I'd never seen anything hotter. As he pulled his fingers away, a trail of his saliva went with it and before I knew it, his fingers were pressing into my own mouth.

The sharp taste assaulted my tongue, and my lips closed over his fingers with a groan, sucking down to the end and back again. He pulled them away with a pop and turned me in his arms. The quickness of the movement almost made my knees buckle beneath me, but Junior was there once again, cupping the underside of my ass.

A groan rumbled through his throat, and a moment later he was lifting me, perching me on the edge of the counter. My thighs managed to wrap around him, pulling him close while his arms braced on either side of me.

The ridge of his cock pressed hard against my center, and I let out a startled cry of desire at the sensation. I was still sensitive, and that simple touch sent aftershocks through my system. We rubbed lazily against one another, his hands a roaming force against my body.

I reached between us, my hands cupping the rigid bulge through his sweatpants. I palmed him through the material, hand closing and tightening as I slid down his impressive length.

He huffed a breath, gaze catching on mine. My movements stuttered, as I didn't know what to make of his expression.

Full of awe and wonder.

Emotion clogged in my throat.

I never thought when I finally gave in it would feel like this. It was better. It was everything I needed. To feel wanted, to feel beautiful.

Slowly, he lowered his forehead to mine. "Come back to my place," he whispered.

My thighs tightened in response to the pleading tone of his voice. I knew if I went with him, we would cross that line. There would be no going back from that. Even after my own release had left me languid and agreeable, I still felt *wired* beneath my skin. I wanted his touch. I wanted to be without the barriers of clothing between us. Skin on skin.

Unfortunately, logical thinking reared its way between us.

I sighed, sliding my thighs away from him. "I can't."

Seeing that I was touching down for a standing position, he released me almost reluctantly and stepped back so I could get my bearings. His brows pulled together and in the dimness of the kitchen, I could make out the uncertainty. I didn't like that I'd put that expression there so I stepped forward, taking his hand. Needing that touch to show him that I was still here with him.

The pulses at our wrists moved in wild tandem, and it was more intimate than his fingers inside me.

"If I go back with you, your sister will ask questions since I went to bed in her room for the night."

He made a huff.

"You know she can be chismosa. She *will* demand answers and I'd like to figure us out before..."

He silenced me with a kiss. They tore apart my words, left my head spinning all over again. When he pulled away, his lips lingered over mine. "I understand," he whispered against my skin. He gave us a small space of distance, his smile wide. "Us, huh?"

My eyes rolled and I pushed at his shoulder, though a tension I didn't realize was there eased in my chest a fraction. I didn't want what had just happened between us to be awkward. I didn't want the sunrise to come with regrets. We'd danced around each other for so long it was like awkwardness was all we knew, but it was like a single kiss washed all that away.

Somehow.

Maybe that was all we'd needed this whole time.

"If you want that..."

"Jesus, Mayda, of course I want that. Us. It has a nice ring to it."

I breathed a sigh. "Okay, good." I pressed close to him, my palms skimming up his chest. I stood on the tips of my toes, giving him a small peck on the lips. I didn't want to pull away, but I forced my feet to comply. I knew if I delved any deeper into his mouth, we'd be lost again. "We're an 'us.'" I smiled, because the word did taste good on my tongue. "Goodnight, Junior."

I walked away and his voice carried after me. Soft, and full of hope.

"Buenas noches... Mayda..."

Chapter 17

JUNIOR

SHE'D TASTED LIKE HEAVEN and felt even better in my arms. I'd wanted to pull her closer with each kiss because it didn't feel like we could possibly be close enough. Like this was all some sort of delirious dream and within an instant she could be ripped from me and I'd wake up aching and alone.

But it hadn't been a dream. It'd been real. The taste of her lingered against my tongue long after she walked away. Elation buzzed through my blood, making it impossible to sleep as all exhaustion had been chased away with a single touch from her.

I'd done it.

I'd taken the plunge and she'd been waiting for me just like I'd hoped. To think, I'd held back my feelings for so long out of fear when all along she'd seen me, too.

Instead of going back to my house, I decided to take a walk around the property, letting my thoughts settle over me. It was eye-opening, that kiss, the way our bodies melded together with an ease and familiarity. It made something expand inside my chest.

Hope.

I'd believed her oblivious for so fucking long and by taking the plunge, I'd realized something fundamental. Something that could have changed my life had I only been brave enough to do it sooner. That realization made me think that maybe I could tell my papá the truth and it wouldn't be as bad as I thought. For once, anxiety didn't cripple me at the thought. Not with the tingling on my swollen lips still prominent. Not with the feel of her ass, her hips, still burning against my palms. Not with the scent of her pussy still fresh on my fingers.

I'd wanted so much more than the imprint of her touch on my body, though, and the words had blurted past my lips before I could stop them.

"Come back to my place."

I hadn't planned on doing any of that when I'd walked up to the house. But then she was there, and I imagined someone else's hands on her, and I couldn't take it. I had to know if I was alone in my burning. The absolute elation I felt when she whispered those words I'd been dying to hear for what felt like a whole lifetime.

Just remembering them made me crave her all over again. I wanted to hear her mewls echo across a room, see the bliss come across her face as she fell apart in my arms.

But she was right. It had been a dangerous game to touch her at my parents' house. Anyone could have walked in on us. We had to take things slow. After so long of dancing around one another, we needed to find our balance, our normal.

An us.

I smiled at the word.

Us.

It belonged. It was right. Shit, I should have listened to Gabriela ages ago and made a move.

I wandered for half an hour before I finally went back home and slipped in bed. I slept with a smile on my lips. When I woke, I felt like I'd gotten the best rest I'd ever had, but I knew it was merely because of Mayda, and the buzz of being with her still bursting through my veins.

I went through the motions of my morning routine as quickly as I possibly could, but by the time I made it to the kitchen, it was already filled with my familia.

"Buenos días!" I announced, grabbing a plate for myself just as Gabriela and Mayda bounded down the steps.

Mayda froze at the bottom, her eyes zeroing in on me.

Mine did the same.

I wasn't sure how long we stayed like that.

It could have been minutes. It could have been only seconds. The flush that crawled up her cheeks brightened her face, and she didn't move until Gabi's hands shoved lightly against her back. Mayda stumbled forward into the kitchen and righted herself, smoothing her palms down the front of her t-shirt.

"Good morning," she mumbled, darting her gaze away from mine.

I wondered if she was thinking about what it felt like to have my fingers inside her smooth, wet cunt.

I smirked and reached into the cupboard for two more plates, handing one off to Gabi. Mayda went to reach for hers, but I held it out of reach. "Let me serve you."

Her eyes widened and she let out a strangled squeak that I was sure were words. I found it endearing. She was always so aloof and to know that I was the one who made her feel like this? Fucking heaven. The urge to lean over and take her lips in mine was strong, but I managed not to devour her in front of an already suspicious Gabriela.

I turned to the stove and began piling food onto both plates. I barely saw what it was and didn't care. I was happy for the first time in a long time.

I held both plates in my hands. She tried to take it from me, but I held that just out of her reach as well. Instead of frowning with annoyance, her face flushed a deeper shade. I wanted to lick the heat from her skin. I wanted to touch her again. To treat her right and give her everything she deserved. To fuck her until she screamed my name.

Mayda deserved to be treated like a queen.

I'd always tried to be kind. Back when we were in school, if we were going to the same class, I would carry her things, hold open doors, hold out her chair. My mamá had always instilled manners into us from a young age. And growing up with all sisters, she tried to wring old machista cycles from our household as best as she could. Besides wanting to help, I genuinely wanted to spend time in Mayda's company. She would argue, but it wasn't until she realized I wouldn't relent that she begrudgingly let me help.

She hadn't ever blushed then. Now that there was an *us*, I liked that it made her face warm. I liked that she didn't argue, and she let me do this small thing for her.

I let her walk ahead of me and into the dining room where everyone else was already sitting. She circled the table towards three empty seats reserved for us. Placing her plate quickly on the table, I hauled the chair back with my foot for her.

She breezed by me, the soft floral scent permeating my nostrils. Smiling at the familiarity of it, I took my own seat, oblivious to everyone else around us. Only Mayda existed right then. Even when chatter came to life around me, even when my parents and sisters spoke to me, I only gave them noncommittal answers, as my entire focus was on one person alone.

I never knew it was possible to feel an ache of happiness, yet there it was, pushing up against my chest and crawling through my whole body. It made me realize I'd been living life in an almost numb state. No wonder fairytales always ended in a kiss, because all it took was Mayda's lips touching my own to wake me up.

My hand reached out, brushing aside errant strands of hair that slid over her cheek and tucking them behind her ears. My fingers lingered against her, like a magnet, my body drawn to her every movement. My own was perfectly attuned to every move, every breath. She gave a sharp inhale at my proximity and froze.

Her eyes darted towards me, the heat in them making me lean towards her so my lips brushed the lobe of her ear.

"I'm going to head out to work, but we have unfinished business later, sí?" When I reluctantly pulled away, the flush had taken up residence on her cheeks again and she was biting her bottom lip, giving a subtle nod. Smiling, I stood from my seat, rapping my knuckles against the surface of the table. "Pa, I'm going to get a head start on work."

I barely glanced at him to catch his beaming smile of pride.

"Te acompaño," he said.

"Yo también."

Soon, both my papá and Hector were standing, their breakfasts finished. I wanted to lean down and press a kiss to Mayda's mouth but resisted the urge. Instead, I gave her one last smile before I turned and headed to the door with a skip in my step.

I just knew today was going to be a good day.

CHAPTER 18

MAYDA

EVERY EYE AROUND THE table trailed after Junior until the door closed behind him, his dad, and Hector. Then, they snapped straight to me, and I could feel my already flushing face burn hotter.

This was precisely what I hadn't wanted. The attention of his family as they tried to gauge what had just happened. Why the lingering touches, why he'd bent to whisper in my ear.

While I'd given up my own inhibitions and decided to take a chance where he was concerned, I'd wanted to keep it a secret. Just enough to garner the courage to tell Gabi, and then maybe his family. So I could steel myself against any scrutiny I might have faced.

There was still the slightest bit of insecurities in me. I still didn't feel worthy of him, of this family. I'd wanted to come to terms with that before the ball dropped. Which was why I'd told

Junior I wanted to figure us out first. I wanted to see if it would be something lasting or if it was just a moment. Unfortunately, his own enthusiasm had probably just outed us. Though I had to admit, seeing his happiness was endearing, and it gave me hope that even if this was so new, maybe we could work out.

The way he'd stared at me, made me think of a future I wasn't sure if I deserved. Of years down the line. Of sleepovers, of Christmases together, of *children.* God, how far my mind wandered. But it was hard to ignore that look in his eyes. I didn't even think he was aware of it, of the way it scorched through my skin and made my armor crack, bit by broken bit.

Like he couldn't get enough of me. Mayda Jiménez, with her poor history, junkie mom, and mile-long secrets. Even in all my flaws, he looked at me like I was worth something. Even seeing what he saw the other day, he'd still kissed me and branded the taste of himself into my very soul.

I picked up my fork and tossed my huevos rancheros around on my plate, smearing them in the frijoles refritos, the yolk of the egg pooled brightly against the darker beans, which I suddenly found to be a very fascinating work of art that I was sure Ximena would appreciate.

"Ooookay, are you gonna address what just happened?"

I sighed. Leave it up to Gabi to bring up what I was trying to avoid.

I shoveled beans onto my fork, shrugging. "I don't know what you're talking about."

Gabi's palm slapped down against my hand, making the fork clatter from my grasp and fall into my plate, splattering yolk against my t-shirt. Okay, technically it was *her* t-shirt. Semantics.

"Cut the crap, Jiménez. Junior was practically salivating over you. He does that anyway, but today it was more..." She paused, as if searching for the right word.

"Obvious?" Valentina snickered.

"Yeah. Obvious. So, did something happen between you and Junior?"

Crap.

A quick sweep around the table and I found everyone's eyes on me. All the sisters, Mamá Claudia, Doña Gloria, Abuelita Mari... They burned with a threatening force that made me want to crumble. All of my structures became weak inside.

I wanted to lie, but I couldn't. I'd been lying to them my whole life, omitting truths about my life at home, about my mother, about everything. I wasn't sure I could lie to them about this too.

So I braced myself, wondering if the confession that followed would be met with disdain or disappointment from the others.

"Well... we..." I cleared my throat, but nothing was strong enough to get past the knot stuck there. "We... we *kissed.*" Though I whispered the word, it cut through the room, seeming to choke everyone to silence.

Shit.

I closed my eyes, feeling tears burn behind my eyelids. When I opened them again, I was prepared to be kicked out, to stand up, go pack my bag, and leave.

Except...

Gabriela was the first to shriek.

Her chair scraped back as she stood up, her squeal nearly shattering my ear drums. The next thing I knew I was swallowed in a hug. "Yes! I knew it! I knew you two were meant to be together!"

Her scream was a catalyst that pushed everyone else into movement. Pretty soon, I was pulled from my chair and wrapped into warm hugs from the sisters, one after another.

"Finally!"

"I was wondering when he'd grow the balls to make a move!"

"Valentina! Language!"

"What? It's true!"

"Oh my gosh, I am so happy!"

"Felicidades, mija." Abuelita Mari's firm grip enveloped me. She patted my cheek with her rough, wrinkled palm.

Then I was facing Mamá Claudia, who smiled through the tears in her eyes. "Mi dulce niña," she whispered. The words tore at my already fragile heart. "We had hoped for so long..." She broke off, taking a breath. "You know we consider you family already. I tell it to you often enough, but I want to say it again. Welcome to the family, mija."

If this was how they reacted to a kiss, I'd hoped they didn't discover that he made me come against the kitchen counter. They were sure to start planning a baby shower if I did.

Even as I thought that, tears pushed past my eyes and slid down my cheeks as she held me close. She was soft, her grip firm, and I couldn't help but compare her to my own mother, who only a few days before had been clawing at my face. Who'd been telling me to fuck off.

This. This was what a mother's touch was supposed to be. It was warm and caring and welcoming. It was everything I'd ever wanted, needed. I just didn't know how desperately until right then.

She was reluctant to pull away from me, but when she did, Gabi took her place, smiling warmly. "We're going to be sisters," she whispered, like she had so long ago. "De verdad."

"It's not like that. We're still new," I argued feebly. "I don't even know where it's going yet..."

Gabi's brows rose and everyone quieted. I knew I'd said the wrong thing and tried not to feel chastised by their gazes. We'd only just kissed last night, and while I was hopeful, I didn't want to get my hopes too high. Junior could realize we were a mistake, that I wasn't the person he'd pictured in his mind. We'd barely even had a conversation about it, and they were already planning the wedding in their heads.

"So, what's it like?" Gabi demanded, placing a hand on her hip.

I knew that pose. It was her getting worked up to being angry pose. Any other day, her antics would have been amusing, but today being on the end of them given the situation made me nervous. Especially with every woman of her family watching.

"I... I don't *know*."

"Well, I do. My brother has had a crush on you since we were six, Mayda. He knows it, my parents know it, and I think somewhere deep down, you know it too."

"I—"

"I've been watching, Mayda," Gabi interrupted. "For years he's been tugging at the end of your hair just so you'd look his way. You're both so damn stubborn. He was always vying for your attention and you were always avoiding his because you thought there would never be anything there. Well, there is. He likes you, and you like him. There's nothing complicated about it, and I want you to stop denying it, I want you to enjoy it and accept what's coming. Oh, and please... don't hurt my brother by thinking you deserve anything less than what you do."

I didn't know what to say to that tirade. My mouth hung open, the tears trailing a sticky pathway down my cheeks. Why had I thought the Águila-Gutierrez family would be anything other than accepting of me? They'd brought me into their lives since I was a kid and hadn't wanted anything in return except for my happiness. I guess it was truly hard to get rid of the stigma your childhood brought on. It was hard to get past what my mom had ingrained within me for the longest time. That I was undeserving of anything good.

I'd believed it all my life. But weren't the people standing before me proof enough that I did have something good? I'd been the one holding my breath this whole time, waiting for them to ditch me like my mom always ditched me. They hadn't. Of course, they didn't know the whole story, but Junior did, and he'd still accepted me. He accepted me because he'd been raised by kind and caring people.

He'd been molded by them to be as kind and gentle hearted as they were.

Why had I been so stupid?

Why had I ever thought I didn't belong?

"We want you in our family, Mayda," Sofia whispered, twisting the ends of her hair, looking at me nervously. In fact, they all were, and it hit me.

Had my avoidance of a relationship with Junior, my aloof and cold demeanor, made them feel like I was the one who was unaccepting? Had the same fears that flowed through me lived within them this whole time as well?

God.

I really was a pendeja.

"Thank you," I whispered. Those single words made their expressions soften and I smiled, hoping that this time, the good things in my life would last.

I'd make sure of it.

CHAPTER 19

JUNIOR

WHISTLING, I BARELY FELT the ache in my hands as we worked. Acres of land surrounded us, the fields ripe with corn stocks. Expert hands worked quickly, pulling corn, placing them in the endless woven baskets on the ground, and moving down to the next one.

Once we finished picking miles of corn, half of us would clean it and separate it into inventory for stores, while the other half would work on pulling the stocks out of the earth to prep the ground for the new season and new foods that would need planting.

Not even the blistering heat could upset my mood.

I worked alongside Hector, the two of us quickly going through our routine in moderate silence.

"So, you and Mayda, por fin."

I smirked at his words. *Finally.*

"Sí," I said. "Por fin."

"I'm happy for you. Took you long enough to make a move. We all thought it wasn't ever gonna happen."

My head whipped back. "Who is we? What the hell?"

Hector tossed corn into the basket. "Don't get offended. You have the *worst* game I've ever seen. We even started taking bets on it."

There were a few snickers from the eavesdropping workers near us. Carlos, a worker of mine and Hector's age, coughed into his arm, while José muttered about his losses under his breath.

"Because that's *not* supposed to offend me." My eyes rolled. "Do you viejas have nothing better to do than talk chismes all day?"

"Well, I'll have you know that I bet you wouldn't have the cojones to make a move, and you made me a lot of money."

He dodged a corn I tossed at him. "Vieja chismosa," I spat.

He laughed rather than bristled at being called an old, gossiping lady. "Come on, you've been into her for years and never did anything about it even though she was into you."

"She wasn't..." I froze. She'd told me in little words herself last night that she wanted me too, but we hadn't actually had a chance to talk yet.

"Come on, are you blind? She was always running away, playing it cool when you were near, but her eyes don't lie. They were always following you around when you weren't looking."

Had they? I thought back, trying to think of an instance. Had that been her cool demeanor? She pretended I didn't affect her while trying to hide her feelings for me.

Moreover, had everyone but me known about it?

"¿Porque carajos no me dijiste?" I demanded. *Why the fuck didn't you tell me?* I shot accusatory glares at the rest of the trabajadores, but their attention quickly diverted to the task at hand.

Hector snorted. "You wouldn't have believed us. Anyway, that's shit you need to figure out on your own. Love is a battle and it's every man for himself."

I pulled a face. "Sounds like you're speaking from experience."

He went quiet after that, his expression pulling tightly. I observed my friend while he steadily avoided my gaze. And I wondered if he had anyone, he felt that way about. Someone he burned for like I burned for Mayda? I wanted to ask him, but he bent and hefted the heavy basket into his arms.

"I'm gonna go dump this," he stated as he lugged it away. I watched him go, chewing on the inside of my mouth, wondering who he had a crush on, if he even had one. And if he did, why hadn't he told me about it?

I shook it off. Surely, that's something my best friend would have shared with me. He had nothing to hide from me, just like I had nothing to hide from him.

Anyway, he was right. Back then, I would have never believed anyone who told me Mayda liked me. Now, I was more attentive. I knew what her gasps of desire sounded like. How she trembled when she came. I thought back to every time I'd tug at her hair or appear by her side. The only shimmer of emotion, that tiny gasp.

I knew now what I never would have known then.

She liked me.

She'd wanted me all this time.

And now that I had her, I planned on keeping her.

Forever.

By the time lunch rolled around, the trabajadores slowly trickled away in clusters to take their breaks. I hurried towards the house alone, hoping to find Mayda still there. I stopped long enough to talk to my papá quickly before I washed my hands and face. Unfortunately, there was nothing I could do about the sweaty shirt and dust clinging to my skin.

I went into the kitchen, and not even the smells of delicious food could distract me from finding Mayda. I waved hello to Doña Gloria and my mamá, going into the dining room. My sisters were there, but Mayda wasn't.

"Where's Mayda?" I asked Valentina.

She must have noticed the determined urgency in my voice because she didn't take a moment to tease me. She pointed to the living room. I rushed into the living room, tossing one of the couch cushions at Gabi.

"Hey!"

"Go away, tonta. I need a moment alone with Mayda."

The arguments didn't come like I expected they would. Gabi scrambled to her feet and left to the dining room with the rest of my sisters.

It wasn't until she was gone that Mayda slowly stood, looking at me from head to toe.

The same desire that had flared between us the previous night came to life once again. I could feel my cock straining inside my jeans, all but weeping to have her hands on me again. Even for a moment.

"Junior… I…" She cleared her throat. "I know I said we'd wait to figure us out first, but after breakfast they all asked and… I told them."

I watched her carefully. Her structures were crumbling. "Does it upset you that they know?"

"Of course not. I guess I wasn't sure what they'd think about me and…"

"I could have told you they would have accepted you. You didn't have to stress about that."

She chuckled softly. "Yeah, I guess you're right."

We stared at each other a moment longer. It wasn't awkward, more like there was a certain awareness pulsing between the two of us and she was waiting to see what I'd do or debating if she should do it first.

I beat her to it.

"Come on a date with me. I'm taking Saturday off. I'll pick you up at your house," I said.

Mayda blinked those hazel eyes in surprise. "Saturday? But—"

"We can do dinner at my place. I already talked to papá, and he's giving me the rest of the day off. I'll take you home after if you want or walk you up to Gabi's room. I just want to spend time with you alone."

Her smile was slow to curl, and the sight of it nearly knocked me on my ass. It made *me* breathless.

"Okay. I'll go over and cook—"

"No."

"No?"

I took a step closer to her. "I'm inviting *you*, Mayda. Let *me* cook for *you*."

Her face brightened and she stammered. "Y-you don't have to do that."

"I know I don't have to. I want to. Mayda..." I was close enough to touch her now. My hands came down on her shoulders, pulling her closer so our bodies were kissing. "You deserve someone to dote on you. Let me do that." Pressing my finger to her chin, I tilted her head up. "Okay?"

She swallowed, let out a breath, and said, "Okay."

Relief washed over my body. She wasn't pushing me away. She wasn't telling me we'd been a mistake. In fact, she was looking at me like she wanted more. Like maybe, just maybe, she couldn't quite get enough.

I couldn't either.

"Good."

I bent down and took her mouth in mine.

I didn't care that my family was in the dining room, likely eavesdropping on this intimate moment. All I knew was Mayda and the taste of her mouth and how she felt against me as her hands lifted and wrapped around my neck, her fingers playing with the hair there.

Tingles coursed through my body like the rapid rush of a waterfall. I pulled her closer, one arm wrapping around her waist to hold our pelvises together, the other tugging lightly at the ends of her hair.

I wouldn't have broken the kiss, if not for the sudden whistles and catcalls coming from the dining room. My sisters fell through the door laughing and cheering at us.

Mayda buried her face in the front of my shirt, taking in a shuddering breath. "Oh my God," she whispered with mortification.

I tugged at the end of her dark hair, angling her head so she was looking up at me. Finally, I was breaking through her resolve. The tone of her voice and the flush crawling up her neck let me know that.

I knew right then that I wanted to peel every single layer away. That I would do whatever it took to get to the vulnerable spots beneath. I wanted to tear past those defenses.

I wanted Mayda Jiménez to fall madly in love with me.

Because I was already madly in love with her.

Chapter 20

MAYDA

T HE WEEK WENT BY in a blur. I spent most of it hurrying through the motions of prepping for the start of the school year alongside the other staff. Monday was our first day and I never thought anything could be as nerve-wracking as starting the job of my dreams.

Until the day of my date with Junior came around.

I'd gone around running errands, stocking up on groceries and basic necessities. By the time I arrived at home, my nerves were shot through the roof. Going on a date was the next step in our newfound relationship—making me come against the kitchen counter notwithstanding. Regardless of all we'd been through together, this was new and different. This was official, and my fingers shook as I grasped the paper bags in my arms and juggled them towards my front door.

My soul almost jolted out of my skin when I entered and caught sight of my mom in the kitchen. Gravity nearly took over, pulling the bags from my unsuspecting hands before I jolted and grasped them tightly.

"Mom."

She turned to me, gifting me with a rare, almost lucid smile. "Mi dulce niña," she greeted.

My heart squeezed at the familiar endearment, but I shook it off and the memories it evoked. "Mom, what are you doing?"

She blew out a breath. "I'm cleaning, what does it look like?" She bent over the stove, taking a scrub brush against the stains.

I slowly walked over and set the bags down on the counter. My gaze didn't leave her as I searched for signs of sickness or fever. It had been a long time since I'd actually seen her in any state other than erratic and strung out on whatever she was able to get her hands on. The alcohol made her mean, the drugs made her sleepy, and when she was bent on a craving, she became vicious and violent.

Throughout the years, I'd learned not to keep much of value in our own home. My mom didn't have a job, which meant she didn't have money, but I knew she always found creative means to get what it was she wanted. More than once things had gone missing, and I knew without having to ask where the jewelry, the speakers, even her old China had gone.

There were moments laced with sparsity, some even that felt too good to be true. Moments like this, when she'd flash a smile in my direction and I'd catch the briefest glimpse of the woman she used to be before she turned to drugs for solace in an otherwise lonely life.

Those junctures in time used to bring me a measure of happiness. Now, it only reminded me that I was just the tiniest blip on her radar. It didn't matter how much her smile lit up when she saw me. It only mattered that once the sides of her mouth flipped back into a frown, she would crawl back to her one true love.

And all it did was break my heart to know that I was never good enough to be her consolation, and I never would be.

I eyed her warily and said nothing as I began unpacking the groceries. The thunk of every sauce and bean jar against the counter served as a soundtrack in the room. The *scrape, scrape, scrape* of the scrub brush grated down my spine, making me realize I was on edge around her.

The truth was, I didn't trust these moments, because I always knew what came after. I was balanced on a precipice, looking at a dangerous drop below that led to nowhere but darkness and inevitable ruination.

"So…" She finally broke the uncomfortable silence between us, her eyes straying in my direction. She stilled, blowing a long strand of graying hair from her face. It was hard to believe that this once-beautiful woman had been reduced to the creature that stood before me right now. Blisters dotted against her forearms like shameless constellations, a once-full figure now skeletal and malnourished. Even the light in her eyes had dulled, like tarnished copper gone black all over. "Any plans tonight?" She smirked at me, though her lips trembled.

I wondered how long it would be before she asked me for money. I noticed the slight sheen of sweat against her forehead. I should have turned her away right then. Told her to get out. Told her that I spent what little I had saved from my old job on groceries, and I didn't start my counseling job until Monday and payday was still a long way away.

So why did I find myself responding? "I have a date tonight."

Her weary eyes widened almost comically. "Really…?"

I'd never actually confided in her about my dating life before. I never confided in anyone save for Gabriela, and even then it was infrequent, as she despised everyone I'd ever been with. If only because they weren't her brother and interfered with her long-term plans.

"Do I know the lucky guy?"

I cleared my throat and turned away, though I could feel the heat rising up my neck. "It's with Junior, actually."

Her shocked little gasp had me turning to her again. She probably had no memory of slapping me in front of him the other day. That was no surprise. She only remembered things at her own convenience.

"With Junior? *Really*?" She stepped closer to me, holding her arms opened at her sides like it was an offering I should accept. "Congratulations! I know how much you like him!" She went in for a hug, and I stood limp as her bony arms wrapped around me weakly. The smell of body odor and alcohol shot up my nostrils, and the mere whiff of it had bile rising in the back of my throat.

Then came the anger. Like a tide rising along the ocean, I couldn't control it. It crashed, splattering through my insides until the backs of my teeth snapped together painfully. My temples throbbed as she stepped away, and the vitriol that pooled from my lips was of my own making.

"What do you really want?"

She blinked in surprise at the snapped question. "What do you mean?"

I pulled out my wallet, yanking out whatever crumbled bills I had left. I wasn't in command of my own body. The anger became its own sentient being, burrowing deep into muscle and bone and soul, filling me with resentment and hatred.

"I mean, why the fuck are you here? How much do you want from me this time?" I waved all of ten dollars in front of her. "I guess I shouldn't be mad that you're here playing nice before you ask me to front you cash for your fucking addiction." The bills slipped from my fingertips as I tossed them. They fluttered between us to the floor.

I was surprised she didn't dive after them.

"Mayda!" Her fingers rose to her throat, a flash of pain crossing her eyes, as she stared at me in shock.

Fake. All of her was just so fucking fake.

"That's the only fucking reason you ever come around. At least you aren't stealing my stereo or headphones, huh? Guess I should be grateful."

I didn't recognize the person I was right then, but I couldn't stop it. I couldn't stop the words as they spilled out of me. The hurt. The rage. It was a wound that had never fully closed, still gaping and bleeding, rotting me from the inside.

The hurt in her eyes was replaced just as quickly with her own bout of wrath. "Mayda Jiménez, I am your *mother*. How dare you speak to me that way?"

I threw my head back and laughed, the sound entirely without mirth and filled with cruelty, but nothing could ever be as cruel as her abandonment. "My *mother*? That's rich. You're only my mother when it's convenient. When you need the cash for your next fix. Where were you when I actually needed you? Where were you when I was practically starving and there was nothing here but moldy bread and cold hot dogs? Where were you when the lights got shut off because you forgot to pay our bills? *Where the fuck were you when I needed you?!*"

It was too much. All of it was entirely too much. I wasn't aware I was crying until salt hit my lips. I swallowed my own tears, took a deep breath, but the rage was still nailed inside of me, stuck and bent at an odd angle, and I didn't have the strength to pull it out myself.

My chest heaved and I waited for her to say something. What, I didn't know. I didn't know what I wanted to hear. An apology? An apology wouldn't fix her negligent behavior all those years ago. It wouldn't give me nights with a sober mother who held me when I cried and fed me when I was hungry. An apology would do nothing for me, so the point was fucking moot.

I waited in the pressing beats of the silence and I knew it was coming, but her lack of a response disappointed me anyway.

She took a breath and stepped away. "Fine. I'll just... get out of your hair then if I'm such a terrible person."

I said nothing to her gaslighting comment. All it did was make the fight deflate out of me. I could do nothing but shake my head and walk away. I moved in a numb state, aware that it was time to get ready for my date with Junior. So I went through the motions, even if my heart wasn't in it. I thought about canceling but stopped myself. I wouldn't let my mother take another thing away from me. So I hopped in the shower and let the tears roll down my face. It wasn't until I'd dressed and done my hair and makeup that I went back downstairs.

Only to find my mom, and the money on the floor, gone.

CHAPTER 21

MAYDA

MY SKIRT SWISHED AROUND my ankles with every turn of my rapid pacing. Anxiety hummed beneath my skin, pulsing, creating an echo of my heart within the hollow cavity of my chest, as loud as a drum beat banging through empty space. I tried to breathe, counting backwards in my mind. When that didn't work, I analyzed every fake scenario I could in my mind until my hands started to shake.

What the fuck was I doing, going on a date with Junior?

My empty wallet almost laughed at me in mocking cruelty from my purse. The lack of money was glaringly obvious, and he'd show up here in his beautiful truck, wearing his winning smile, taking me on a date that I wasn't sure I deserved.

Fuck.

Stop.

I shoved my fingers through the roots of my own hair and tugged, like I could yank my own errant thoughts out with a single pull. I needed to get my shit together. The only reason those thoughts were racing through my mind was because I was nervous, and I was doing exactly what I said I wouldn't. Letting my mother fuck shit up for me once again.

Get a fucking grip, Mayda.

I deserved happiness. I deserved to go on a fucking date, have a good time. Just like I'd deserved a childhood. She robbed my youth, my time, my things. I wouldn't let this be robbed from me too. So I vowed I'd enjoy myself.

Just as the thought flittered through my mind, I heard the sound of a truck appear then park out in the driveway. My heart bottomed out to my stomach, and a tightness grew in my throat that made it hard to swallow past.

The palms of my hands slid across the material of my skirt. I held my breath, hearing the door slam. Moments later, there was the quick rap, rap, rap of knuckles against wood.

Jitters trailing through my body, I grabbed my purse, sweater, and keys and went to open it. Junior stood on the other side, dressed in a form-fitting t-shirt and jeans that hugged his strong thighs and calves. Snakeskin botas de vaquero covered his feet. Cream with traditional floral designs in a darker brown, the tips pointed slightly upwards. He made quite the vision in front of me and, quite frankly, he took my breath away.

"Junior."

His eyes roved over me, heated in their perusal. They started from the bottom of my flat-clad feet all the way to the roots of my hair. When he finally met my eyes, he smirked. "You look beautiful."

Those words were enough to ease every single fiber of anxiety that had coursed through me before his arrival. My body leaned towards him of its own volition. His own responded, hands gripping my upper arms and pulling me flush against his chest. When our lips met, a deep sigh relaxed through me. It felt right. Perfect. It was like seeing a ray of sunshine between dreary clouds after a storm.

The kiss itself was short and sweet. He was the first to pull away. "Ready to go?" He tugged gently on my hand, pulling me past the entrance of my door.

I followed, only briefly turning away from him so I could lock up behind me. Then we were in his truck and heading towards the rancho.

I fidgeted where I sat for a brief moment before his hand came down on my bare knee. Just like that, the warmth seeping through my skin, I felt at ease.

"How was your week?" he asked.

We'd texted back and forth a couple of times, though we hadn't spoken about anything substantial. The both of us had been busy. He'd been helping around the rancho and picking crops as well as several homework assignments and tests. I'd been busy getting ready for the start of the school year, helping those that were late for enrollment get settled.

"Hectic," I replied with a sigh, sinking into the cushion of the truck. "Yours?"

"Hmm..." His thumb trailed circles against my skin. It felt like a single-minded promise that had goosebumps spreading over my body, my thighs quivering. "Better now that I'm with you."

I wanted to snort at what seemed to be a line, but he sounded so sincere that I believed they were truth. "Wow, whipping the compliments out a little early, don't you think?"

He tossed his head back and laughed, and I enjoyed watching the workings of his beautiful throat. Junior turned and sent me a wink that nearly melted my panties. "It is *never* too early para decirte lo guapa que estás."

His rapid switch from English to Spanish had my brain reeling, and when my mind caught up to what he said, I felt a flush crawl up the apples of my cheeks and take residence there.

"Stop!" I pleaded, bringing my hand up to cover my mouth. As if that could stave off the pleasant embarrassment of his words.

His hand squeezed my knee before pulling away to grip the steering wheel. "I can't. It's just... nice to see you actually react to me now. You were always so calm and collected." His eyes darted to me before going back to the road. "Quiero más momentos así."

I want more moments like this.

I quietly stewed in those sweet words for the rest of the drive. By the time we made it to the rancho, the sun was already starting to set, basking the land in tones of gold and orange. After he parked and helped me out on the passenger side, I stood for a moment, taking the scenery in.

Los Corazones always seemed like it was part of a fantasy, a fairy tale. I was lucky enough to be a part of it. This little bit of magic never ceased to amaze me. For a moment, neither of us said a thing, content to watch the sun lower. Finally, Junior turned to me. "Ready?"

I took my hand in his. He hadn't parked near his parents' house and instead had taken the small gravel pathway towards his own. I was grateful to avoid the rambunctious noise that bled through the walls of the main house, at least for tonight.

"Come inside," Junior urged, holding the door open wide. I swept past him and immediately paused at the threshold as a blast of warm deliciousness hit me. The pervading smells coming from within made my stomach growl like an angry monster.

"Something smells so *good*..."

He led me towards his small dining room, and I froze for a moment as I took everything in. The candles, lit and flickering, cast dancing firelight against the dark wood of the table and the array of trays and foods there.

For a second, I was speechless as I took it all in, my purse falling to the floor in my shock.

Mofongo con camarones, arroz con grandules, papas rellenas, and pasteles were all laid out like a feast. I took a tentative step forward, inhaling the scents. They hit something inside me. Some emotional cord I didn't even know I had. Like he'd reached inside my chest and squeezed my heart with his fist.

Tears sprung to my eyes, and I didn't even get a chance to lift my hands to swipe them away before Junior was there, rubbing the back of his neck in a sheepish gesture.

"Junior... did... did you make all this?" My voice was tight with emotion.

"Doña Gloria helped a bit. And by helped, I mean she yelled at me and supervised like she's some Puerto Rican culinary expert." His eyes rolled, but I didn't miss the soft affection for her in his voice. "Do you... do you like it?"

Like didn't even begin to describe it. He'd gone above and beyond what I'd expected. I wasn't sure exactly why I'd been expecting a simple steak-and-potatoes dinner, as seemed to be the norm with men. While it was romantic, if a little cliché, this was...

It was better.

It showed that he truly did care, that he'd paid attention to me all these years. Because he'd made a buffet of all my favorite Puerto Rican dishes.

"I *love* it, Junior. Thank you."

His smile was almost bashful as he pulled out a chair for me to take. I did so, smoothing out the material of my dress in my lap. He took his seat beside me, but not before placing food onto a fancy dinner plate, serving me a little bit of everything.

"Wine?"

At my slow nod, he poured some into my glass then his, then sat back on his chair. We stared at one another, and it was like being in the kitchen last week all over again. There wasn't anything awkward, but we were gauging one another, waiting for something that was close but not quite within our grasp.

I broke our stare-down first, looking at my plate. I cut into the mofongo, as it was my absolute favorite, picking up the fried plantain topped with shrimp and sauce and took a bite. An explosion of flavors burst against my tongue, and the moan I let out was probably indecent.

I didn't care.

"Ay, Dios, Junior..." Sauce dripped onto my fingers, and I licked it away without shame. "It's so good..." I looked up to find his gaze riveted on my mouth, his pupils blown wide and nostrils flaring.

As soon as he caught me staring, he shifted in his seat.

"Um..." He cleared his throat. "I'm glad you like it..."

"It reminds me of when I was a kid." The memories came to me at once, back before things had gotten so bad.

Junior must have read the tone of my voice. He leaned forward. "Did your mom make this for you?"

I was glad he didn't ask about her addiction. In some ways, it was easier to answer about what she'd been like before. In other ways, it was harder, because it forced me to remember she wasn't the same person she had been. She wasn't the same mother who'd brushed my hair, who made me dinner.

There'd always been an ache in my chest where that mom had been. A part of me wanted her back in my life, but I'd buried that woman a long time ago, accepting that she'd never be who she once was. Because someone else had taken her place.

"Whenever she got extra tips from waitressing and could afford to buy anything other than hot dogs." I waved a hand in front of the meal. "For me, this was a feast. It still is and it reminds me of happier times with my mom."

His eyes softened along the edges, and he reached out to take my hand in his.

I couldn't help my next words, the heavy confession that had always weighed on me, searching for escape. "She used to sing while she cooked. I loved hearing her in those moments. Sometimes, she would look over her shoulder at me and smile. That was before she lost her job and everything changed." My gaze avoided his for a second, and instead I focused on the steaming bowl of arroz con grandules. "Eating this makes me remember those happy moments."

The tears were unbidden as they slid down my cheeks. Embarrassed, I reached a hand up to swipe them away. It was ridiculous that a few kisses, a forbidden touch in the dark kitchen, and our first date had crumpled my walls entirely. I was ashamed of myself that I'd bared my soul like that to him.

"Sorry," I whispered. "That's not first date material, is it?"

His chuckle was merely an expulsion of breath. "More like third date material."

I laughed at the ease he made me feel.

"Hey, Mayda, it's okay. Maybe this first date can be what you remember when you see these foods from now on. Remember it as the night I charmed you completely."

I tossed my head back and laughed. "Ha! You're pretty confident in yourself for someone who spent years of his life pulling my hair, huh?"

He sat back and I missed his touch. "I wouldn't say *pull* more like, a slight *tug* to get your attention."

I snorted, digging into my meal. In between bites, I said, "If that's your idea of charming, you need to up your game."

I didn't mean it. Not really. I relished in the whispered touches of his fingers against my hair. It was like the tips had nerve endings, and I felt it each and every time. Prayed for it, even.

"Why does everyone keep saying that?" he demanded. "Is my game really that bad?"

I pinched my forefinger and thumb together. "Un poquito."

His eyes flared again, and I felt caught inside the depths of his gaze, making the laughter die in my throat. "Laugh away, Mayda," he whispered. "You're just giving me incentive to prove you wrong."

I gulped, feeling something heavy press around us. Desire mingled with something else I wanted to question, but I couldn't because Junior dug back into his meal. As if the words he'd just uttered had never left his lips.

As if they hadn't affected me, making my thighs press together to ease the ache building at my core.

As if they'd never really been whispered between us at all.

CHAPTER 22

JUNIOR

SHE DEVOURED THE DINNER I made for her. Between every bite, her groans filled in little echoes across my dining room, a melody of never-ending pleasure. Every time she hummed, I could feel my cock growing tighter in my jeans. I could hardly stand it, and yet I picked apart those sounds, savoring them like I wanted to savor her.

They reminded me of our night together in the kitchen. The sounds I couldn't hear muffled behind the palm of my hand as she fell apart. I'd be lying if I said I didn't want another taste of that.

The wine flowed slowly. Mayda had never been big on drinking, and now that I knew why, I didn't offer her more than two glasses, and I didn't drink more than that myself either. We didn't need it to ease the nerves that flowed between us. That came gradually with conversation, a game where we picked apart the little things neither of us knew about the other, pushing them alongside chats about memories of the past.

And it worked well between us.

Until the conversation slowly began to die down. Until the silence pressed in the spaces between us, making my chest grow tighter with each passing breath. My tongue flicked along my bottom lip in a slow movement, my attempt at staving away the parched feel of them.

Mayda's eyes flared, and I wanted to pretend I didn't notice the way her hazel eyes tracked the movement or the way her shoulders lifted just as her breath hitched. She cleared her throat and, with trembling hands, set aside the glass of water that she held.

All night I'd been dipped in awareness. It had banged against the cage I'd locked it inside, begging to get out, to be set free. Waiting for the right time. I'd only shut it up because Mayda wanted to take things slowly, to get to know one another as an us. As a unit.

"Well..." She smoothed her palms along the tops of her thighs, straightening the wrinkles of her skirt. My eyes glued in on the skin at her knees, and I had the sudden urge to kiss along her skin and find every sensitive spot I could within the span of a few minutes.

A heady sense of want burned inside me, needing that outlet.

Throughout the night, our chairs had pushed closer and closer together somehow. The both of us inching but not taking. Like we were waiting for the other to make a move. Like we had been our entire lives.

I was done waiting.

"Mayda." Our eyes caught.

Desire flared.

My cock hardened.

Her breath stilled.

The next few moments happened slowly. My hands dove towards her legs, my rough calluses against the smoothness of her calves. I explored with my palms in an upward movement until I reached the backs of her knees, enclosing my fingers around her skin.

"Junior..."

I hooked my feet to the insides of the legs of the chair and yanked it forward. Her body jolted and I pulled her legs, so she all but straddled onto my lap and left her seat completely. Her palms collided against my chest to steady herself, but instead of pushing herself away, she curved her body into mine, her chest brushing against my own.

I kept the firm pressure against the backs of her knees, never once breaking away from her wide gaze.

"We took it slow," I whispered. "We took it slow for years." My hands slid up higher, pushing the hem of her dress as they went, bunching it up between us. I stilled on the backs of her thighs. "Don't you think that's enough time wasted?"

Her wide eyes went wider. Her fingers teased my t-shirt, pulling off invisible specks of lint. "I'm afraid." The confession glided between us in a fear-intoned, broken way that had my grip tightening.

"Of me?"

She shook her head, and the hair I loved so much flowed down against her collarbones with the action. "Of us. Of this. That you might not want me afterwards."

There was a moment where the pressure in my chest expanded painfully until it burst.

"Oh, Mayda." I leaned up so my breath whispered across her mouth. Her essence was but a fraction away, and all I longed for was to savor it on my tongue. "I will *always* want you."

My kiss wasn't gentle. It was a snapping of teeth and lips. Inelegant in every possible way. It was impatient. It was every frustration packed from years before finally bursting at the seams. It was every kiss I'd ever wanted to steal and my disappointment every time she looked away.

Our mouths opened together, tongues tangling, our groans mingling through the room. And suddenly, one kiss wasn't enough. I didn't think anything would ever be enough when it came to her. I wanted to steal every fucking thing she had to offer. I wanted more than just her lips.

I wanted it all.

I curled my body up, grasping her tightly to me as I pushed to a stand.

A yelp sounded against my mouth and Mayda held tightly to me as I whirled towards the table. "Legs around me," I ordered. She did it immediately, wrapping both legs around my waist. The position pressed us closer, grinding us together.

A groan sounded from my throat.

"Hold tight."

My arm shot out, sweeping away all the dishes in our way to clear a spot for her. Her breathing grew erratic amongst the clattering of glass as I laid her down against the tabletop and pried her legs off my body.

"W-what are you doing?"

I smirked at her and bent to my knees. My face was level with her waist, and I couldn't resist running my lips across the inside of her knee.

"We had dinner already," I told her, tongue tracing circles against her flesh. "Now it's time for dessert."

"Oh, God." She sprawled her arms out at her sides, gripping the edge of the table.

My shoulders pushed her legs wider apart. They dangled at the end, her flats slipping from her feet to thud to the floor. With her skirt bunched up near her waist, I got a perfect eye-level view of her red lace panties. A damp spot darkened the center and I pushed forward on my knees until the tip of my nose touched that intimate spot.

"Junior?" Her thighs quivered as she fought to hold them apart, hardly letting her skin touch me.

She was still afraid. Still afraid to let go.

That was okay.

Because I was going to make her scream until she was fucking hoarse.

I buried my nose to her center, inhaling deeply, my nose pushing deep into her cunt through the lace. Fuck. This color against her creamy, golden skin?

I bit into the lace and her skin, biting hard enough to leave a mark. Maybe it was primal of me, but I didn't give a fuck. I wanted to go through my day knowing what she hid beneath her skirts. I was going to leave bits of myself over every inch of her fucking skin.

Body convulsing against mine at the contact, I pressed down against her lower belly, keeping her pinned to the table. "No te muevas," I ordered. "I want to taste your cunt. If you'll let me."

"Ay, Dios mio." Her head thrashed side to side. "Yes. Yes, please."

I took my hand away from her belly and grabbed the outside of her thighs, pushing them closer around me, so I was all but enveloped in her skin.

One lick and I was drunk on the sensation of needing her. Her panties grasped in my fingers, I tugged. The lace dug into her skin, marking her flesh red until the material gave and ripped. The scraps pulled away and I tossed them to the side.

Bare before me I leaned forward. The urge to hurry and taste gripped me. I'd waited so long, driven by a stupid fear. But now that I had her in front of me, I wanted to savor her.

With a languid lick, I stroked upwards between her folds, pressing the tip of my tongue against the hood of her cleft. Using my thumb, I pulled her hood back and licked the nub of her clit. She writhed against me, hips jerking, hand slapping against the wet surface of the table.

But I wanted her fingers to dive into my hair and tug. I wanted her screams and her claws. I wanted her wild and wanton and *free*.

I sucked her clit into my mouth, spreading her wide with my fingertips and playing with the wet desire that dripped from her center. I teased the inside of her flesh before I slid a single finger inside. Her tight walls hugged me, and her groan was still too low for my liking.

I inserted a second finger, rubbing against her walls. She moved against me, angling her hips against my fingers in a silent command, letting me know without words what and where she liked it. I was a quick study, listening to her breathy, quiet cries, curling my fingers deeper inside her.

Her hips canted off the table, slapping against my lips. I let go of her clit with a pop, starting to pull away. Sensing my intention, her hands finally slammed down against the back of my head, pushing me back down against her center while simultaneously pushing her hips against me.

And finally, finally, she breathed out, "Junior…"

Her hips gyrated in a desperate plea for me to go on, to move, her blunt nails marking my scalp.

"No." I started to pull away again. "Not until you say my name."

"Junior—"

"My real name, Mayda." I curled my fingers within her, a threat and a promise, and maybe something more. Her hips lifted with my movements, her fingers holding me tightly. "Come on, cariño." I leaned forward, circling her clit with my tongue. "Scream my name like a good little slut."

Her thighs quivered around me, her entire body pulled taut. Wanting to snap. Needing to snap. But I controlled if she could or not.

"Damián..." It was nothing more than a breathless whisper.

My fingers curled again. "Muy bien, cariño. Very good. Again." I rewarded her by playing with her clit.

"Damián..."

"Louder, cariño."

I wanted the sky to fucking hear her.

I wanted everyone to know that Mayda was mine.

"Damián!"

Yes.

Yes.

I dove back down, moving my fingers, a firm rhythm that I mimicked with my tongue. Her taste against me was an explosion, making my dick tight and weepy with need. And she matched my enthusiasm, grinding and crying out, my name a prayer on her lips.

When I finally felt her begin to fall, I pulled her clit into my mouth until she exploded, screaming my name. With a smile of triumph, I sucked harder, wringing out every last drop of ecstasy until she tried to pull away in the aftermath.

"Damián," she pleaded. "Please."

My fingers squelched as I removed them from her heat, itching to dive back in as soon as they were gone.

Slowly, her hands slid away from my head to fall back to the table. Her pleas and whimpers died down to harsh breathing. Her body shook but laid languidly against the table.

I stood, my knees aching, legs trembling, my dick hard and making my movements stiff as I loomed over her.

I bent over her body. Her lids fluttered open a fraction and a smile teased the edges of her mouth.

"Good?" My lips skimmed hers.

She sighed, making a sated, whimpering sound. "Good," she agreed with a sigh. "The *best*."

Emotion swelled in my chest and I bent down to kiss her again. What was meant to be a mere touch of our lips became so much more as she opened her mouth against mine, her tongue dancing in slow movements. She pulled me close, draping her arms around my neck and curving her body into mine.

My dick jumped at attention from behind my jeans. My hips jerked, though the edge of the table kept us apart. Every place Mayda began to touch, she did so with reverence. Every press a slow kindling, building higher. Palms sliding against the skin at my neck, down my chest, hovering between us, right near the spot I desperately wanted her to be.

A growl of need rose in my chest as she pulled away from me.

"Damián."

"Yeah?"

"Take me to the bedroom."

CHAPTER 23

MAYDA

THE BACK OF MY dress was damp. My bones had all but turned into mush inside me, aftershocks of the orgasm still jolting across the expanse of my skin like pricks of lightning.

Junior had starred in one too many of my late night fantasies, but nothing had ever felt as good as when he stuck his tongue inside me and worked me until I exploded. It had felt far too good, that even with my entire self suffering from over-sensitivity, I wanted more of that feeling. More of him.

He kissed me, and I was sure it was meant to be chaste and full of affection, a quick press of lips on lips. But, selfish as I was, I took more. My tongue slid against his and he matched my eagerness, stroke for stroke.

He didn't demand I reciprocate, though I felt his hips move, impeded by the barrier that was the edge of the table. He couldn't grind into my center, couldn't give my clit the attention it wept for. When my hands slid from the nape of his neck, down his chest, hovering near his pants, I finally managed to pull myself away.

"Damián." It wasn't a question.

"Yeah?"

"Take me to the bedroom."

His eyes heated the moment the words were past my lips. His fingers wove their way through my hair, tugging my head back so I was staring deep into his eyes. "You don't want to get fucked on this table, cariño?"

My breath caught at the filthy words coming out of his mouth. This was a different Junior, one I wasn't familiar with. Outside of these moments, he was nice, gentle, sometimes a little awkward. This Junior was dominating and dirty.

And I liked it.

I confessed, I'd never been called a good little slut before. I never thought it'd be something I actually liked, but as soon as he confidently said those words, my mind reeled and I was a goner.

"I'm not opposed to it…" My own response was shaky at best. I shifted, my thighs burning from being shoved open, and my back was starting to get cold. Though I could deal with it, if it meant finally getting a glimpse of his dick, of finally having him *inside* me.

"Are you uncomfortable, cariño?" His hands spanned down to my hips. "Don't worry. Yo te cuidaré."

The words warmed me, the promise that he'd take care of me. It wasn't a second later that he was lifting me from the table and we were moving out of his dining room. If I thought this little break from running my hands over his body would douse the desire we both felt, it didn't.

The fact that he was taking care of my own comfort, moving us slowly to the bedroom with his eyes never once leaving mine, only heightened everything I was already feeling into bigger sensations.

He didn't speak, but all the words we'd gone so long without saying pulsed between us anyway.

When we reached his bedroom, he hoisted me higher as he lifted his booted foot, kicking the wood open. The frame snapped back against the wall and he stormed inside. The aggression of his footsteps made me think he'd toss me onto the bed and start ravishing me immediately.

He didn't.

He was gentle with me, setting me down against the mattress and among his mound of pillows. My body lay half-propped up against the cushioning. He sat over me on his haunches, the intensity of his attention making my face warm.

I tried to sit up, to reach for him, but his hand clamped down around my throat, squeezing. It wasn't threatening. It wasn't even painful, but I could feel myself start getting soaked from between my thighs with need.

"Relax." With that firm grip, Junior pushed me back down. "I promised I was going to take care of you, didn't I?" A whimper threatened to burst from me, but I swallowed it back, my throat working against the palm of his hand. "That means I'm going to undress you." He leaned down, so his lips caressed the shell of my ear. "Then, I'm going to fuck you so hard you'll still feel me inside you for days."

He pulled away from me then, leaving me trembling and yearning for more. My legs splayed across the length of the mattress, skin tickled against the fur of his thick blanket. That small bit of touch made me sigh before that released breath caught back in my throat as Junior began to strip.

My thighs locked together in an attempt to stave off the wet pulsing that occurred there, but it just heated and thrummed harder and faster the longer I stared at him.

I'd always thought Junior was beautiful, with his angular sort of features, cutting cheek bones, aquiline nose, and dark penetrative eyes... But as he slowly began to undress, I was reminded just how beautiful he *really* was.

With every article of clothing he discarded, it was a slow revelation, a slow burn of flames that twisted and writhed within me as I took him in. From the curvature of his well-toned arms and the shadowy hint of muscles down his abdomen. Lithe fingers pulled at his belt, sliding the leather from the loops. He folded it between his palms, snapping it together and making me jolt.

Mirth shone in his eyes before he slid the belt from his palms and it clunked to the floor. "¿Te gusta?" He undid his top button and slid the zipper down.

He was asking me if I liked it? If I liked the dark promise in his eyes of exploration, adventure, and so much more to come? I could only nod while biting at my lips.

"That's good to know." He pushed his jeans and boxers down in one swoop, bending to pull them off his legs. When he stood back up, it was so I could take him in, in all his glory.

"Ay, holy shit." I wasn't aware the words blurted out of my mouth until his lips curved up into a smile.

And really, why shouldn't he look so fucking smug?

I'd usually been careful about averting my gaze from his dick since I'd known him. And that was usually because Gabi always watched me with hawk-like precision, trying to find any angle she could possibly work in her plot to push us together. Besides, we'd never been truly alone for me to actually admire the outline of it pressed against his jeans. Not really. Had I caught glimpses of it? Yes. Had I been desperate to see it ever since he grinded that part of his anatomy against me in the kitchen?

Also yes.

Now it was in front of me, and my fucking mouth went dry.

His cock was absolute perfection. It jutted upwards, curved, long, and skinny. His foreskin pulled back from the red, weeping tip, and I had the sudden urge to run my tongue over that tip, to lap up the liquid desire that settled against him, evidence that we'd wanted each other all this time.

He climbed on the bed then, crawling up my body and gripping the straps of my dress. He eased them off my shoulders and I lifted up on the pillows so he could reach the zipper at my back. The *zrrrpp* as he slid it down to my lower back had every nerve on my skin tingling with alertness. The material loosened against my body, and I didn't bother holding it up against my chest because Junior's hand clasped around my neck once more. He shoved me backwards with a gentle firmness that had my core throbbing.

"I'm going to make you feel so good, Mayda," he promised once I was back against the pillows. He grabbed the hem of my dress and yanked. I lifted my hips to aid him in the endeavor, and he tossed it off to the side.

I laid beneath him, bare save for the red lace bra cupping my breasts. But even that was soon discarded with his expert finger-tips.

Once I was completely naked, it was like a dam burst between us. Like we'd been holding back, waiting for this moment in time exactly. I curved into him, lifting my hips so I could feel the length of his cock slide over my wet folds. He leaned down, grasping at my hair with a desperation I felt all the way down to my marrow. Our mouths met, hungry and devouring, a clash of teeth and tongue. It was raw and brutal, his fingers digging through my hair and pulling me closer, like he meant to entwine body and soul until there was nothing left but the bare bones of our desire.

We hardly came up for air. Content to explore our hunger with our mouths. Yet we grinded, my nails scraping across his skin, gripping at his lower back to urge him to move. He undulated against me, our flesh slapping together in a steady rhythm that echoed throughout the room.

The warmth of his dick teased against my clit and I reached a greedy hand between us to grasp at his length. He scorched my palm where I touched him, branding every nerve within me. I gasped against his lips and he let out a feral groan as he pulled away.

"Mayda..." His voice was heady with need.

I tightened my grip and slid my hand down against the smooth length. When I reached the head, my thumb flicked across the rounded tip, smearing the precum against smooth flesh. His hips jerked into the movement and he grunted.

"Fuck, Mayda, your hands are fucking magia."

I smiled at that, gifting him with another languid stroke. He grunted at my teasing, eyes flaring, before his palm came down, choking away the smile from my lips as his fingers dug into my neck. I gasped, my breath cut off as he tightened his hold.

I shouldn't have found this so arousing, and yet I did. Being pushed just to a very delicate edge of helplessness. For once, I didn't panic, but I relished in this. Because of him. Because I trusted him. And the tighter he squeezed, the more my pussy pulsed, all but begging for him to enter me.

My hips thrust up and I positioned his dick near my entrance, teasing my folds with his own wetness.

"Look at you writhing beneath me, desperate for me to feed you my cock."

My whole body quivered.

"Is that what you want, cariño? You want my cock?"

"Yesss." I hissed past the beginnings of pain.

"Yes, what?"

"Yes Damián."

"Fuck!" He yanked his hand away as if I'd burned him, and for once he seemed graceless as he reached into the drawer of his nightstand, fumbling through the insides until he pulled out a condom. The foil crinkled between his fingers and I watched as he tore it open with his teeth. I pulled my hand away, watching as he rolled the latex over his cock and then dove back down to take my mouth in his once more.

Framing my face in his hands, he angled my head back so he could dive deeper, tongue flicking against mine, the strokes maddeningly delicious.

I was already wound too tight, and Junior still didn't enter me. He drew it out even more, savoring this between us. His fingers touched the ends of my hair, bringing the long strands over my chest. He traced a path along my collarbones, leaving a sensitive, tickling sensation in its wake. I arched up into the touch, *needing* more. The ends of my hair passed over the swells of my breasts, down, down to the peaks of my brown-pink nipples. A single caress of my hair against the tips sent a full body shiver, starting at the back of my neck, rolling down my spine.

He alternated between nipples, playing and tickling both with the ends of my own hair until I was a writhing mess beneath him.

"Damián," I begged. "Please, please, please."

"Ssh." He released my hair to cradle my cheek. Our eyes held, searching, though for what, I couldn't be sure. "Te tengo." Two words, spoken like a promise that cleaved my heart into pieces only to build it back up again.

I have you.

"Te tengo."

His cock pressed to my entrance.

"Te tengo."

I have you.

I'd never felt more vulnerable than I did in that instant.

He entered me in a hard thrust, and I cried out at the sensation of being filled to the brim. I'd been empty before, and now that he was there, I could see stars flying across the galaxy.

And it felt like home.

"Yes." I held onto his shoulders, digging my nails in, urging my hips up to meet his as he began to move. "Yes, Damián, move, please."

He did as I bade, the snapping movement of his hips sliding his length in and out. I clenched around him, squeezing him deeper into me.

"Fuck, Mayda." A curse and a reverence, mushed together in a guttural sound that made gooseflesh rise along my arms.

My insides became a swirl of chaos. Of ecstacy pinballing back and forth through my very center. He undulated and curled, hitting my clit and driving electricity and static through my core. It pulled taut within me.

Before it could snap, before I could fall into that bliss I so desperately desired, he pulled away. I whimpered, reaching for him, feeling empty and needy without him inside.

He gripped my hips, blunt nails digging into me. His movements were rough as he maneuvered me, flipping me so I was face down against his mattress.

My groan was muffled beneath the pillows, arms slashing out for purchase against something, anything.

Junior molded my body to his own benefit, lifting my hips so my ass was in the air. My knees buried within the covers, and he spread my thighs wider with his. His cock slapped against the skin of my ass, the promise in the movement clear.

"Your skin is beautiful." Junior's palm slid up the length of my back, gripping the roots of my hair at the back of my neck. "I can't wait to paint it with my cum."

My face flamed and I bit down onto the pillows as he entered me in a hard thrust from behind. His body doubled over mine a fraction. He kept his grip on my hair, yanking my head up, one hand on my hip, as he began his deliciously brutal assault.

My neck ached, a bite of pain prickling my scalp the harder he pulled. It was pain in the best of ways. It spread through me as he speared his cock within my heat.

The slapping of our bodies grew louder, his grip tightened, and he gave a hard yank, pulling my body upwards so my back pressed to his chest and I was all but sitting in his lap.

He released my hair to grab my breasts, teasing, twisting, and pinching my erect nipples. His fingers spanned across my jaw, twisting my head to the side.

"Beso," he demanded, a growl.

My mouth opened, hot breath spanning the space between us as he bent and claimed my mouth for his own.

It was sloppy and hungry, my moans silenced by his demanding thrusts. While he kissed, he played, using me like an instrument. I nearly jumped as his fingers pinched my clit and his hips followed up, forcing into me.

"Scream my name." His teeth claimed my neck, biting down until I knew he'd leave marks against my skin.

I felt myself being led, no, not led, *shoved* towards that place I so desperately wanted to be.

His fingers dug into my clit, thrumming it faster and faster. His own motions became jerky and inelegant, snapping in quick succession as he climbed towards his own release.

"Scream it, Mayda. I want everyone to hear you. I want everyone to fucking know you're mine."

I cried out.

"Yes. Yes. I've waited for you for so long, Mayda. Pathetic. Just standing by and watching you live your life without looking my way. Never knowing—fuck!" He pinched my clit and that final time was all it took for my release to crash upon me.

Wave after wave of pleasure rolled through my entire fucking being.

"Damián!" His name escaped my lips with the explosion of my release.

"Yes, Mayda." He pumped into me, faster and faster. "I never knew, but now I do. Now that I know—" He cut off with a growl. Still trembling, I could only do as his hands demanded.

He shoved me down against the pillows once again, only now he pulled out of me. I couldn't see what he was doing, but the moment I felt jets of warm liquid hit my back, I knew he'd ripped off the condom and painted my skin just like he promised he would.

A curse slipped between us. He pulled away and crashed next to me on the bed. I managed to lift my head and turn my cheek so I was staring.

Junior leaned forward and kissed me. Hungrily.

"I'm never letting you go, Mayda. Not now that I know what we can be. You want to take it slow? We already have. You want to learn what kind of love we can have between us? Fine. But I know I want you. Por siempre."

The backs of my eyelids pricked with emotions.

The part of me that wondered if this was too soon was chased away by his words and the vehemence in them. He was right. So much time wasted, so much time full of my insecurities, of his own.

We could have been learning each other all this time.

But he was right.

Now we had the promise of por siempre.

Of forever.

"Por siempre," I agreed.

He smiled and kissed me again.

Chapter 24

MAYDA

With my bare feet tucked under me, I leaned against the arm of the couch, wearing nothing more than Junior's t-shirt. It barely covered past my waist, but I'd tossed the idea of modesty out hours ago.

After he'd cleaned me up, wiping a damp cloth along my back, every gentle swipe cleaning his release from my skin. When he finished, he'd turned me to my back, leaning over me on his elbows, a smile touching his full lips. I found myself mimicking the gesture with full force. It felt like it had been such a long time since I'd been truly happy. This moment had me floating towards the sky.

"Hola," he whispered, sounding as in awe of the situation as I felt.

I giggled. "Hey."

"Do you want something to drink?"

I'd agreed, slipping on a shirt from his closet while he covered himself with a pair of boxer shorts.

It was how we found ourselves currently in his living room, sipping bubbly cider face to face on the couch.

I took a sip and placed the cup down on the coffee table.

"What really made you want to be a counselor?" he asked, leaning his cheek against his palm.

The answer came easily. "My mom."

The silence pressed between us and Junior's hand lowered. "If you don't want to talk about it..."

"No, it's okay. It's the truth. Everyone always asked me that question, but I never really answered honestly before. I didn't want anyone to think less of me because of her."

"They wouldn't."

I gave him a rueful sort of smile. "Some people did back then. But my mom wasn't always like... what she is now. It's been so long though that I can't picture her as anything else anymore. When it came time to fill out applications, I'd already known that I didn't want other kids to live like I did." I lowered my hand, thinking about all the kids who followed in their parents' footsteps, who grew up to be what they swore they never would. "I always wondered if I had someone to talk to, what would have happened. Would they have helped my mom get sober? Would they have shipped me off so they didn't have to deal with me?"

"My mamá would have adopted you," Junior said, with such surety it warmed my heart. "She would have torn down the entire government with her bare hands to get you to us. You have to believe that we've always cared about you."

"I know that now." I played with the hem of his t-shirt. "Back then I just felt like a burden."

Junior put aside his drink to come closer. He took the other side of me on the couch and pulled me close. I fell against him, my legs opening so I straddled his lap. His hands didn't stray above or below my waist, though. He kept them firmly gripped, trailing comforting circles against my body.

"Nunca," he whispered, his voice rough with emotion. "You were never that."

My fingers teased the buttons of his collar shirt, but I didn't dare undo them. Fear gripped me and propelled me to utter my next words. "I used to hope that she would overdose and never come home. I would hope your family would adopt me instead."

There it was. My darkest secret. The reason I never felt good enough for him or his family. I'd always been surrounded by such genuinely kind people, and to have my own dark, violent thoughts flowing through me? How could I stain their lives with my taint? I was dirty, and because of those thoughts, I didn't deserve to be a part of the Águila-Gutierrez fold.

He tensed beneath me. I wondered if he'd be disgusted. If he'd shove me away.

"Mayda, cariño, it all makes so much sense now." His voice was soft, understanding.

It nearly broke me.

"What does?"

"Why you are still taking care of her after all this time. You feel guilty about those thoughts and you want to make it better by caring for her."

My whole body seemed to seize with the words because... hell, he was *right*. I was trying to atone for my sinful thoughts by always taking care of her, even when deep down, a big part of me always wished that when she went to sleep at night, drugs pumping through her veins, that the next morning she just wouldn't wake up.

What kind of a daughter did that make me?

I pushed my palms against his chest. "I'm a terrible, evil person." I tried to pull away, but Junior held me firmly, not letting me up.

"You are not, Mayda. You're not evil. You're just sad and confused. You want your mom. Fuck, you *deserve* a mom who is going to love and care about you the way my mamá does for my sisters and you. So what if you had a bad thought? Who doesn't? That doesn't make you evil. I know that despite it all, you still love her."

And that was the gist of it, wasn't it? I still loved her. Despite everything she put me through, I loved her so much. Besides the drugs that slithered through her veins and to her heart, there was a piece of *me* as well, just like a piece of her lived within me. It was something I wouldn't ever be able to get rid of.

And I wasn't sure I even wanted to.

Instead of tears, I let out a slow breath, my smile curling slowly. "See?" I poked his chest. "I told you you'd be a good counselor."

He barked out a laugh, the sound rumbling against my own body. "You're the only one who would think that."

I scoffed, pressing my palms against his shoulders to hold him down against the cushions. "If you gave others the chance to know, they'd think so too."

His brows pulled together, expression hardening. "Mayda..."

Sensing I was charting into rocky territory, I backpedaled. "You don't have to tell them. But... maybe you could apply for a position somewhere. Do what you love."

He shifted beneath me, shaking his head in an adamant response. "I don't know what I love, Mayda. I love the rancho, but not in the way my papá wants me to. I want to do something worthwhile, follow a different path, but..." He sighed, gripping me close like I was the only thing grounding him to the truth of his feelings. "I don't know if I can, Mayda." The way he was unsure of his own greatness broke my heart. For a second, I wished he could see himself through my eyes.

Then he'd know just how amazing he truly was.

"I think you underestimate yourself. You could do amazing things, if you only tried."

He let out a breath, a pained look crossing over his features. He swallowed, his throat bobbing up and down. "Is it stupid to say I'm afraid? That no one will believe in me? I have this fear inside that I'll disappoint the careful plans my parents have for my future. That by going against it, that makes me ungrateful."

His eyes opened when my palms caressed his cheeks. I leaned down so we were only a breath apart. "I believe in you. The world could turn their backs on you, but know that I won't. Nunca."

"Mayda..."

His head lifted to capture my lips in a kiss. There was nothing tentative about his touch. While gentle, it was firm and demanding as he sipped slow kisses, eliciting soft moans from the back of my throat. Desire flowed through me like a cup with too much water.

I was drowning and needed that first breath of air, that first touch of him that would bring me back to life. His blunt nails dug into my sides, the hem of his shirt riding up and bunching beneath my breasts, my bare pussy grinding down against his boxers.

His body rolled up into a sitting position. He caught me around my waist, our chests pressing closer. His tongue flicked slowly against my own until he picked up the tempo, demanding more of me that I was all too willing to give.

Pain mingled with pleasure as he dug his fingers harder into me, his groans deep and guttural. My body arched against his, and his lips pulled away from mine to trail wet kisses down the curve of my neck. When he reached the neckline of the shirt, he paused.

My fingers slipped into his hair, tugging, groaning, pushing his mouth against my skin. I was desperate for a touch. I'd deprived myself of him for so long, that now I felt like I couldn't get enough. We were just an explosion waiting to happen. And I wanted to erupt.

"Junior..." I complained. He didn't know how much I needed him. How much my whole body ached, how it always had for the simplest of touches, of his fingers brushing against my hair.

"When we're together, call me Damián," he reminded me, tongue sliding up to the pulse at my throat.

"Damián." My voice was breathy and needy. I knew then without a doubt that I'd never, ever call his father Papá Damián so long as I lived precisely because of this.

Me saying his name must have been the dam bursting on his self-restraint. He gripped me to him, pushing my waist down against his so I could feel his hardness through his boxers. Groaning, I rubbed myself against him, craving that friction. He didn't let me have what I needed.

He hoisted me up by the waist, urging me upwards while he slid down slightly against the arm of the couch. He gripped one of my thighs tightly, lifting so he could prop my leg against the arm, positioning me so my pussy was level with his face.

One hand on his shoulder, the other on the couch, I hovered above him.

"Ride my face, Mayda. Wet my mouth until you come."

CHAPTER 25

JUNIOR

SO WHAT IF I steered the subject away from myself and distracted Mayda with the promise of orgasms? So what if the mere idea of straying from the carefully constricted path my parents laid out for me made my insides swell with anxiety? So what if I was living an entire fucking lie that only Mayda knew about? So what if I was way too cowardly to own up to what it was I really wanted?

None of that fucking mattered.

Because Mayda was riding my face like her life depended on it.

Her pussy was currently in my mouth, and I lapped it up with my tongue, holding her thighs up to keep her perfectly balanced, while she took her own pleasure against me. She writhed against my mouth, angling her clit over my tongue and moving so I'd put pressure against her there.

Her every wish was my command.

I stroked her clit with my tongue, taking it between my lips to suction and provide the pressure she seemed to want. Her cries banged through my ears like a drum, her hips jerked, and I sucked hard, long, and fast until the crest of her orgasm shattered around us. Still, I didn't relent. I wanted more of this vulnerability, something I never dared associate with Mayda before.

I tongued her clit harder, circling it until she was begging, too sensitive, and trying to writhe away from me. But I held on, pushing her by the backs of the thighs until she was all but sitting on my face, my tongue moving in fast, deep strokes through her folds, tasting her release, staining my chin with her desire.

"Damián," she pleaded. "I can't…"

"One more." I took one of her folds into my mouth, sucking, releasing, doing the same to the other. "Just one more."

But even that felt like it would never be enough. I would always demand more. Always push her to her limits.

Maybe that was hypocritical of me when I wasn't willing to do the same. I was willing to tell her my deepest secret but not talk about it. But not take her advice. I was destined to be a cowardly bastard.

But in these moments, at least, I felt I could be more.

"One more."

I needed her release like I needed to fucking breathe. I wanted to prove to myself, to her, that I could do something, if anything, right. I'd wring the pleasure out of her body until she was mindless in my arms.

"Uno más, cariño." A stroke over her clit, a squeeze of her trembling thighs. She shuddered, sagging against me. Her placid body was still, so I did the work. Stroking, sucking, making her cry out as her fingers tore into the couch and the skin on my shoulder.

And I felt it. the trembling of her thighs that told me she was all too close to that edge. I took her clit into my mouth once again. I sucked, pressed the flat of my tongue against the nub and—

"Damián!"

It was a cry of ecstasy that had her whole body bowing over me. I adjusted myself, sitting up to let her body slide down against mine. Boneless, shaking, a heap of wrung out desire with no energy left to spend.

I wrapped her limbs around me, holding her close. My fingers toyed with the ends of her hair, letting the strands rise and fall across her back. She sighed, and soon her erratic breathing evened out, and I knew she'd fallen asleep.

My lips met the hot skin at her temple. "Nunca te dejaré ir."

The promise wove itself around us like invisible threads of fate, tightening an unbreakable knot that could never be severed.

By me, or by anyone else.

"I'm never letting you go."

CHAPTER 26

JUNIOR

THE SUN'S RAYS SLANTED through the blinds and washed across the comfort of my blankets. It bathed the room in a buttery, orange glow, chasing away the shadows with the promise of a new day.

I groaned, rubbing my palm across my face as the early light pushed out traces of exhaustion that threatened to close my lids. With a languid stretch, I turned, hitting the warmth of a delicate body that curled into mine.

I smiled down at Mayda's sleeping figure and pressed a kiss to her forehead. Her messy hair tickled my nostrils and she blew out a heavy breath in sleep.

I'd lost count of the number of orgasms I'd pulled from her body last night. After she'd fallen asleep, I'd let her rest. But the moment her eyes opened, I was on her again. Against the wall, on the floor, and again in the bed until we'd both fallen into a heap of exhaustion.

My whole body felt well spent, my mood light and airy. I knew I had to get up. I had to go work the rancho, tend to the horses, and I still had homework and reports to wade through that I was behind on because of work. But I couldn't bring myself to give a single fuck about any of that.

How could I, when everything I wanted was right here at my side?

Wrapping my arms around Mayda, I pulled her close, inhaling our mingled scents. I liked it. I liked my scent pervading her skin. Like it belonged there. And it did.

We belonged like this. Together. Enveloped tightly in one another.

So yeah.

Work could fucking wait.

I awoke to kisses being peppered across my chest. My eyes flew open to catch sight of Mayda's dark hair curtaining my chest. Her gaze lifted, eyelashes fanning across her cheeks. Her hazel gaze greeted me, her lips curling into a smile as they slid across my skin in languid strokes.

"Good morning," she whispered, her body sliding lower now that she had my attention.

I smirked. "Where are you going?"

She huffed out a breath, her hair flying only to slip back down in place over her face. "I want to give you a proper good morning." She kissed my abdomen. Lower still.

I could feel myself already hard, a perpetual state of being while I was in her presence. That desire would never abate, it seemed.

Mayda paused right beneath my belly button, staring up with a questioning look in her eyes. "Is this okay?"

My fingers tangled into her waves, pushing them aside so I could see the flush on her cheeks. The uncertainty in her eyes, though, I didn't like.

"Fuck, Mayda." I fisted the ends of her hair to give me a better view. "Wake me up like this every day for the rest of our lives."

She smiled and then continued kissing a path down.

I didn't give myself time to think about the words I'd just spoken, the promise of forever. By all means, those words should have sent her running for the fucking hills. They should have frightened her, made her skittish. We were new, as she liked to claim, but that didn't mean I didn't know what I wanted.

Maybe in my life, in my career, I was indecisive. But never about her.

And just then, I could picture it so clearly.

Our future. A wedding. Kids.

I wanted all of it.

Her lips closed around the tip of my dick, and just like that all thoughts flew straight out of my brain. She hummed against the tip, tongue sliding over the slit and lapping up my precum. The wet slide of her mouth closing over my shaft sent my hips flying up, a grunt of satisfaction leaving my throat. The action pushed my cock deeper inside her mouth. Her tongue slipped against the underside of my shaft, teasing the sensitive vein, flicking as she began to bob up and down against me.

She sucked me deep into her throat, creating a tingling sensation at my lower belly that spread across my waist. My dick jerked inside her mouth as she sucked me. My fist tightened in her hair.

I wanted her to move faster, to close her mouth around me and scrape me with her teeth.

"Fuck." Like she could read my mind, she gave the slightest graze with her teeth, scraping across the sensitive skin. I closed my fist closer to her scalp, gripping her head and taking control. Pushing into her, I held her head still as I began jerking myself into her mouth, taking my pleasure and watching her mouth split wide as I forced my way into her.

She made a humming noise around me, the vibration moving through my entire system. I cried out, feeling my balls tighten. My thrusts became jerky and quick with every slam of my hips upwards, her chin slapped against my balls. Soon the room was filled with nothing but the wet slurping of her mouth and my own ragged breaths.

I felt my body pulled to the edge, the pleasure rising to unbearable heights that wanted to be set free, to freefall and spiral into that drop of ecstasy that only she could take me there. Her lips and tongue pushed me towards that point of no return.

"Mayda," I warned, hips stuttering. "Mayda I'm going to—"

She swallowed me whole. The tip of her nose touched my stomach, taking me deep, bottoming out. The tip of me touched the back of her throat. She hummed again and I came, shooting my release down her throat.

She swallowed, the workings of her throat closing around my tip.

It undid me. Sent my head in a mindless spin. I felt a hoarse cry push out of my throat, my muscles spasming as my body spent. I forced myself to let go of her head before I hurt her with the force of my release. I grabbed my blankets instead, digging into the furs.

"Mayda, Mayda, Mayda." Her name became a prayer on my lips. A repetition and a reverence and a plea to Dios for an uncertain and rocky future that loomed over the horizon that I reached out and grasped tightly, unwilling to let go.

When I finished, I became a boneless heap, my body melting onto the bed. Slowly, Mayda pulled her lips from my length, popping off the tip. She lifted her hand, wiping the wet corner of her mouth with the side of her thumb.

Fuck, what this woman did to me.

"Come here." My voice was nothing more than a guttural rasp. I reached a hand out, caressing the ends of her hair in a beckoning. I was fascinated with the strands as they slipped through my fingers. Swinging closer as she crawled above me, her arms on either side of my body to hold herself above me.

"Good morning," she murmured with a smile.

The best of mornings, actually. I didn't say that, though. I gripped her by the hips and moved, flipping her so that her body was pressed down on the mattress and I was above her this time. She let out a soft gasp as my lips closed around her nipples, teasing with quick strokes of my tongue, one and then the other.

I made my way down her body, peppering her with kisses like she'd done to me. I dipped my tongue into her belly button, teasing her skin until her entire body quivered with want. Only then did I go lower, slipping between her folds.

"Damián?"

"Ssh." I held her down by the hips. "Let me give you a proper good morning."

We lay with our legs entwined, lazily stroking our fingers across each other's skin. It was late into the morning; we both had things to do. We needed to get up and go about our days, but neither of us seemed to be able to do that.

At least, I didn't.

Mayda had already tried to escape my clutches twice, and it only resulted in more orgasms than either of us could count.

"We really should get up," she whispered, not for the first time.

"Mhm, probably." I had a rancho to look after, homework to do. Deadlines were looming, and all of them just made my stomach twist into knots. Being here with Mayda settled my thoughts, and I'd be content to stay here forever.

"Junior, I'm serious."

She sounded anything but serious. She sounded well-fucked, actually, her words lazy and content.

"So am I." My hand slid up the curves of her side, stopping just under the swell of her breast.

Her breath hitched as my thumb traced lazy strokes along her skin, teasing the edge of her nipple. I couldn't get enough of her skin. I wanted to drown in it. In her. And I never wanted to leave.

"We have things to do today." Even as she said the words, she leaned into my touch, body curving into mine.

"What kind of things?" I thumbed her nipple, fascinated with the way it pebbled into a sharp peak.

"Hmm... We have work to do... mmm..." Her voice trailed off as I took her nipple between my fingers, giving it a soft twist.

"Yeah, such important matters we have on our schedules," I teased, palming and squeezing her breast. The sharp point scraped my palm, evidence of her desire.

"I'm being serious," she protested feebly. But she didn't push me away. She pressed closer.

"Yeah, I know. So let's get up."

She still didn't move.

Her eyelids fluttered with every stroke of my fingers. I dove down, tracing the shape with my tongue, pulling a groan from her. Her fingers scraped against my scalp, her breasts thrust forward as she demanded more from me. We turned together on the bed and I draped her across my body. Her folds slid against my erect cock as she sat down on my thighs.

"Ride me, Mayda," I told her. "Ride me before we go our separate ways."

Her eyes rolled at the use of my overly-dramatic tone. She slapped her palms down against my bare chest, digging crescent marks into my flesh. Her hips rolled, her slit sliding against my length.

"Fine," she conceded. "But just one ride. One—"

I had the condom out of the foil and rolled onto my cock before she could finish admonishing. As soon as the protection was in place, I grabbed her hips and pulled her down while I jerked up, piercing her to the hilt.

She gasped at the intrusion, her nails curling into me.

"Ride me, Mayda. Now."

Her hips began to roll. Our waists rubbed against one another with each undulation. She was slow in her movements, lazy in a way that told me she was in no hurry to leave the blissful comfort we'd both created here. Languorous, we moved together, our eyes locking and almost afraid to look away. She tightened her thighs around me, her body shuddering with each roll as she moved, her clit stroking against my body.

"Damián." Her sigh pressed through my body. I canted my hips deeper into her. "Damián, I—"

My fingers dug into her hips. "Say it," I ordered. "Say it."

Her eyes slammed closed, and I could make out the tears sliding from the corners. She closed her sight away from the emotion, from the words she wanted to say. Because it was too soon? Because she was afraid to say it?

I wanted the words.

But maybe I was just as cowardly, as I couldn't bring myself to say them just then either.

And as our orgasms came over the both of us and she collapsed against my chest, it didn't matter that neither of us said what we wanted to say. Because we knew. We knew.

And the silences said more than words ever could.

CHAPTER 27

JUNIOR

W E EVENTUALLY PULLED AWAY from one another, leaving the bed long enough to shower together and then get dressed. Mayda didn't have any extra clothes, so she'd slipped on the same dress from the night before.

"Do you want to go get breakfast?" I asked. "I'm sure Doña Gloria kept some warm for us."

I was rewarded with a flush. "I don't know, Junior." Her shoulders were practically up to her ears. "I don't know if I want everyone knowing I stayed the night." She avoided my gaze as she combed her fingers through her locks.

I didn't like that. I could feel her retreating from me since we got out of the shower and got dressed. As if with the reality of our lives approaching, she was remembering the reasons she'd avoided me all these years and was falling back into old habits.

"Hey." When she didn't turn to look at me, I crowded into her space, gripping her wrists, drawing her gaze to me. Her eyes were wide, and I wondered if that was fear I saw there. "You know my family loves you, right?"

She blew out a slow breath. "I know."

"Do you?"

Her eyes met mine, unwavering. "I do."

Smiling, I pressed a kiss to her forehead. "Just making sure." I pulled away again. "But, if you want to avoid any awkward teasing from my sisters, we can skip breakfast at the main house and I'll drive you home?"

I figured the teasing was what she was most worried about. Hell, it was too early—ha—to deal with the storm that were the women of my family, so I totally understood wanting to avoid that.

"I'd appreciate that."

"Great. Just tell me when you're ready and we can get going."

While I was able to avoid my sister's teasing, I wasn't able to avoid my papá's wrath. I'd dropped Mayda off, and after minutes of making out in my truck before she finally peeled herself away from me and said goodbye, I rushed back home and quickly got to work on a few assignments I had due.

What was only meant to be thirty minutes of my time had taken longer than I thought. Hours later, I was finally pulling on my work clothes and meeting the trabajadores on the field, only to be met by the stern glares of the jefe.

He didn't say anything to me in front of the others, but I could feel his glares boring into me throughout the day. I went through the motions, combing down horses, mucking stalls, milking cows, and combing through the crops. His disappointment was an arrow lodged between my shoulder blades, noticeable, painful, and the more I wandered without tending to it, the more at risk I was.

I walked around like a living dead man all day. Hector and the other trabajadores noticed my grim mood. Everyone except my best friend kept a wide berth.

"I thought you'd look happier, considering you finally got laid," he jested.

"Cállate, cabrón." I flipped him the finger, not in the mood for his ribbing. "At least I can *get* laid. You only have your hand to keep you company."

He cackled. "And when I'm rubbing one out, I'm thinking of your girl."

It was such a fucking old joke. One we apparently hadn't grown out of. It was right up there with your mama jokes, and went side by side with piropos, vulgarities.

"If dreaming about my girl is the only way you can get your shit up, I feel sorry for you. Anyway, you sound like a fucking fifth grader. Shut up."

He snorted. "Seriously, though. You finally got the girl, what crawled up your ass?"

I sighed. The bastard never knew when to walk away. Always pushing and pushing. Especially when I wasn't in the mood.

"Not now, Hector."

"En serio, you've waited for her forever. Is she not up to par or some shit?"

I tossed a bail of hale with too much force and whirled on him, pointing an accusatory finger. "Cállate before I punch you in the face."

He smirked in that teasing way of his that made me jerk forward and grab him by the shirt. He held his hands up, laughing. "Jesus, I'm just fucking with you." I released him with a scoff and went back to picking up another bail. When I tossed it again, his tone softened. "You okay, bro?"

I wasn't.

But before I could even tell him a fragment of what I was feeling, my papá's voice rang out from behind me. I nearly tripped in my rush to whirl around, and I almost flinched at the sight of disapproval pulling at his features.

"Junior, tenemos que hablar."

No one in their right mind liked listening to those words. *We need to talk.* They sent a chill down my spine, made anxiety twist my guts up into knots.

I dusted my gloved hands off on my jeans, ignoring Hector's pointed look as I followed my papá out of the barn. I knew what my friend's gaze would say, what he would urge me to do if he had the chance to discreetly whisper it in passing.

But I couldn't do what Hector and Mayda told me to do.

Neither of them understood.

We walked, my papá a few steps ahead of me, and made it to the smallest cabin on the property. It was close to the main house, and he used it as his and Gabi's office space.

I caught sight of my sister on the phone through the open door of her office. She waved absently to me as I passed by, focused on whoever was on the other end and tapping her pen against the desk. She disappeared quickly from view as we went into the second, larger office space.

He went to sit behind his desk, a king sitting upon his throne. Meanwhile, I closed the door quietly behind me, hearing the click of it like a damn sword coming down on my own head.

"Sit down."

Usually I could gauge his mood by the tone of his voice. It was gravelly, like rocks scraping unpleasantly together. His gaze was hooded, lips pressed into a firm line. I knew he was pissed. Disappointed. And ready to rip through me.

I was used to this. It felt almost like an everyday occurrence. And it never mattered how hard I tried. He'd never praise me for the things I did right, but he'd always berate me for all the things I did wrong. Because being perfect was something that was expected of me. Nobody ever remembered when you were perfect, good.

They could only ever point out the bad.

I felt like I was under a fucking microscope as he took me in while I sat in front of him like a teen at detention.

There was a long stretch of silence between us in which he stared at me, and when he finally broke it, it was with a heavy sigh.

"When I came to America, I had nothing."

I swallowed past the lump in my throat. I was very familiar with this speech. It was the same every single time.

"I had nothing but a dream and your mamá's love and support. I busted my ass working hard to provide for my family. I almost killed myself to build Los Corazones from the ground up. But in the beginning, I had nothing." He rubbed his fingers across his mustache in thought and took me in. Gaze assessing. Judging. "I worked hard for you so that you could have everything I didn't have. You understand that, right?"

It was hard to speak past the emotion clogging my throat. I barely managed to choke out, "I understand."

"Do you?" His brows pulled together. "I don't think you do. I don't think you understand the blood, sweat, and tears that went into creating Los Corazones. I think you're ungrateful."

The words felt like a spear through my fucking chest. I hated hearing them. I hated feeling diminished, but most of all I hated feeling like maybe he was right. A part of me wanted to fight the words. To argue. To tell him that I was doing everything he asked of me. I'd given up so much of my time and my hopes and dreams to be here on the rancho with my familia. But he couldn't see that. All he could see was how I didn't live up to par to his idea of perfection.

It didn't matter how much I sacrificed; it would never be good enough. Because I was born with everything he didn't have, and everything he'd fought to give me, it meant I had to be even greater than he ever was and only then would I match up to his idea of success.

Unfortunately, I was nothing. I would never be as hard-working as him, because I hadn't been born in poverty. I hadn't had to live my life scraping the bottom of the fucking barrel in order to get ahead. And because of that, it meant I was lazy. Ungrateful.

But he never took into account that if he'd wanted me to bust my ass, he shouldn't have given me his empire in the first place. He should have let me fight to live like he had to do. Maybe then I would have been good enough for him.

"I'm not," I gritted out, my nails digging into the material inside of my gloves.

"Entonces, ¿por qué carajos me sales con estúpideces?"

That was the big question, wasn't it? Why I was always doing stupid shit. To him, homework would be. It would be a betrayal, which was why, even with the confession poised on the tip of my tongue, I forced myself to swallow that shit back. Shove it deep down. Lock it away. Ignore it and maybe the festering pain would finally go away.

"Papá, I was with Mayda." I leaned forward, and the excuse sounded weak, even to me. I was a fucking coward for hiding behind her. For using her as a shield against him.

Only this time, it didn't work.

His palms splayed across his desk. "I'm happy for you, mijo. I really am. Mayda is a nice girl. You know your mamá and I adore her and she'd make a good daughter-in-law."

That, at least, was something.

"But you can't get so wrapped up in this thing you have and ignore your responsibilities here on the rancho. You have to show your dedication. What would the trabajadores think?"

I gritted my teeth against that, just like I always did. It only ever mattered what our workers thought of us. Who cared if I couldn't sleep at night? If I sometimes had to skip tests because I had to pull crops from the field and shoot the shit with Hector, José, and Don Beto? It only mattered what they thought of me.

When you were an immigrant from Mexico, with several eyes constantly on top of you just waiting for you to fuck up, it was no wonder he worried about how everyone in the family acted.

"I'm sorry," I told him. Because saying that was easier than saying everything that lived in the recesses of my heart. "It won't happen again."

He stared at me, long and hard once again. I wasn't sure he was going to let me off the hook, not with the way his penetrative stare lodged through me. Eventually, he sighed and it sounded strangely like resignation.

"Vete." He waved me off with his fingers. Then he turned away, like he was too tired to even look at me.

Pushing myself to my feet, I whirled and left his office, careful not to slam the door behind me like I really wanted to. As I walked past Gabi's office, her voice stopped me and simultaneously halting the burning feeling behind my eyelids. I stepped backwards and turned, looking into her open office door.

"Come in," she ordered.

"What do you want? I have work to do."

Her eyes rolled with annoyance before she pierced me with a glare. Great. That was the look she got that meant she wouldn't stop until she got exactly what it was she wanted. It was easier to give into those instead of fighting it. So I did just that.

When I walked in, she crossed her elbows up on the table, gripping at her elbows and leaning forward. Her eyebrows rose high on her forehead as she took me in, though that could have been on account of the too-tight bun she'd combed her hair into.

"So..." she drawled.

"So?"

"I noticed you didn't come to breakfast this morning. You *always* come to breakfast."

"What, is that a crime?" I snapped back defensively, not in the mood for her shit either. My tolerance at the moment was entirely too low.

"Nope." She popped the P in a dramatic fashion. "But I noticed that Mayda ignored my texts all night and this morning. She *never* ignores my texts."

Fuck, I did not want to have this conversation with my goddamn sister. "Fuck, Gabi, I'm leaving."

Before I could stand up, she slammed her palm down against her desk. The action alone kept me firmly planted in my seat.

I wasn't afraid of my sister, but she could be fucking brutal. A bruja when she wanted to be.

"Look, cut the shit, Junior. I know you guys slept together."

I cringed at the hint of accusation. "Jesus, Gabi. I don't want to talk about this with you."

"Yeah, well, I don't want to talk about your dick either. But just because you're my brother doesn't mean you're exempt from me threatening to fucking murderize you if you break my best friend's heart. You realize that, right?"

"I'm not going to hurt her."

Her eyes narrowed. "I will kill you, Junior. I will chase you around the house with a knife until you run into it."

"I'm not going to fucking hurt her."

Her gaze narrowed a moment longer, reminding me so much of my papá that it was eerie. She straightened up papers on her desk, aligning them just so. Everything on her desk was immaculate. Anal, I teased her.

"Good," she said finally. "Now get out of my office. I have work to do."

I rolled my eyes as I stood. "Fea," I insulted under my breath.

"I heard that."

I stuck my tongue out at her. "You were supposed to."

She cussed me out in Spanish and I flipped her the finger as I left.

Our interaction didn't leave me feeling lighter, however.

If anything, it left me feeling like there was a rock lodged perpetually in my chest and no amount of shoving down or ignoring would ever make that shit go away.

CHAPTER 28

MAYDA

THE SCHOOL YEAR STARTED in a whirlwind of nerves and excitement. While I was giddy and all but flying on the tips of my toes throughout the week, a lot of the students wandered with bored, tired stares. Others walked the halls with big smiles on their faces, content to be back in an environment filled with friends and found family.

It reminded me of me and warmed my heart in ways I didn't know was possible.

As planned, I set up appointments with the students to begin my interview-meet process. A lot of them stared at me like I'd lost my damned mind and my chipper greetings made them cringe. And it made me wonder if I'd turned into those peppy teachers that all the other kids always bitched about in school.

Shit.

I wasn't sure if that was a way I wanted to build trust, but I was trying. It took me the better part of a few weeks to get through the entire student body. It was a small school, and it didn't boast that many students, but it was still an arduous process.

I'd made notes on each student, starring and setting aside the folders for the ones I meant to take extra time with or give follow-up interviews to.

I really thought I had something going here, a method I thought could work where I could focus on every single kid and their needs.

At least, that's what I thought until Principal Jenkins poked his head into my office.

"Ms. Jiménez." His clear eyes peered around my space, sniffing with derision as he took in my motivational posters.

My entire body tensed at the obvious judgment he was displaying, but I didn't let it show on my face.

"Principal Jenkins, please come in." Even as I said the words, he was already in and seated across from me.

My back teeth grinded together, but I kept the smile plastered to my face.

"Is there something I can do for you, Principal Jenkins?"

He wiped a finger across my desk, rubbing it against his thumb like he was flicking invisible dust. I wasn't sure what dust he thought he found. I'd cleaned the desk this morning.

"Ms. Jiménez, it's come to my attention that the past few weeks you've been calling in every student for meetings."

I beamed. "I have, yes."

"Hmm. That's most unusual."

"Sorry, sir? I don't see what's so unusual about getting to know every student and their situation. It will help us make their transition in school so much smoother."

"Listen, you're new around here, and I'm sure you think you'll have a positive impact on some of these kids, but the reality is that we can't help them all. Focus on the ones you *can*."

I stared at him with genuine confusion. "But how do you know I can't help them if we haven't even tried yet?"

His bright green eyes shone with what could only be described as mirth. He let out a huff and reached across the desk to press his sweaty palm against mine, giving me a firm pat. I resisted the urge to jerk my hand away and wipe it down on the material of my cardigan.

"I've been doing this for a long, long time, Ms. Jiménez. Longer than you've even been alive, I reckon. I know what I'm talking about." He stood up. "Don't waste your time."

And that was that.

He turned and stalked out of my office, leaving a suffocating, angry silence in his wake. I stared at the spot he'd vacated, feeling my anger rise higher and higher the longer the minutes of the clock mounted on the wall ticked by.

I wanted to be the type of person who could shrug off his negativity, ignore it and just keep doing what I'd planned on doing all along, regardless of what he had to say on the matter. Unfortunately, I wasn't that type of person. I let the anger fester, I let it stew, and I let it warp me.

I knew that being a teacher, or even a part of the staff, was so vastly different, a world all on its own orbit. It made me wonder if they'd always been like this. If these were the types of thoughts the teachers had about me back in the day?

Had they looked at me and thought, 'Poor little Mayda, with her negligent mother and sad home life. She's too far gone to help, so let's focus on the ones we can?'

Who were they—who was Principal Jenkins—to decide who was worth saving? Who was he to dictate who could and couldn't be helped? That was the whole point of my job. To help any and everyone.

In any fucking way I could. No matter their background. Every single student at this school deserved that and more. They deserved to be cared about. They deserved a shoulder to cry on when the ones at home failed them.

I'd deserved that once upon a time, too.

But the difference between my younger self and the kids at the school now was that they hadn't had *me*.

And I was going to flip Principal Jenkins the proverbial middle finger and do whatever the fuck I wanted. Because there was a sea of kids out there, and every single one of them was worthy of love, guidance, and a voice.

And I planned to give it all to them.

My purse landed onto the passenger seat with an angry thud. My fingers drummed against the steering wheel a second before my forehead thunked against it. A shot of pain spliced through my head and pounded at my temples.

It had been a *day*.

Despite wanting Principal Jenkins' words to fill me with motivation like I'd originally thought they would, they'd just filled me with self-doubt. Every move I made, I overanalyzed. It felt like I'd gone the rest of the day under a microscope, being watched from the shadows.

It made me jumpy, and it had made an ache throb increasingly at my temples and from behind my eyes.

Now, all I wanted was to get home and throw myself in bed. I didn't care that it was the middle of the afternoon. I was getting on in years. Sure, twenty-seven wasn't *old*, but my body was starting to feel it. Creaking bones, lower back pain, the works.

The joys of being in your late twenties.

With a sigh, I finally willed myself to pull out of the school parking lot. It was all but dead, only a few teachers straggling through the lot and ready to go home. I was cautious as I started the drive home, lost in my thoughts until a shrill ring sounded from deep in my purse.

I let it ring, unwilling to cause an accident for trying to reach for the damn thing. It continued its annoying cry, stopping, only to start back up again. And again. It silenced, and it was about fifteen minutes later, when I was pulling up my drive and parking, that I finally reached for the mobile.

Three missed calls from Junior.

My heart sped up at the sight of them. We hadn't seen one another since he'd dropped me off after our night together. I hadn't been around the rancho at all because we'd both been buried neck deep in work. We had texted on and off in the mornings and at nights, but otherwise, I hadn't actually talked to him.

I quickly redialed and pressed the phone between my ear and shoulder, grabbing my bag and hopping out of the car.

He answered on the second ring.

"Are you ignoring me now that you got what you wanted from me?" he teased.

Just the sound of his voice and those words had my mood lightening. I laughed, inserting my key into the front door. "You caught me, how did you know?"

He fake gasped. "I'm offended. You just used me for my dick and left me."

I closed the door behind me. "If it makes you feel better, it was a very good dick."

"That does make up for your abandonment, at least."

We laughed together as I went about putting my things away. There was no sign of my mom anywhere. I hadn't seen her in a few weeks, but that was normal. She disappeared, or only came by when I wasn't home, the evidence of her life in the crumbs on the counter, missing food, or the messed up front closet with tossed shoes.

I kicked off my shoes and walked to the kitchen. "How was your day? Shouldn't you be working right now?" Señor Águila ran long hours, and usually the workers ended their day by six or later. They were compensated very well for their time, though, and received good health benefits.

There was a shuffle on the other end of the line, and I imagined Junior getting comfortable.

"I had a test today, so I told my papá I was busy."

I wanted to pry and ask if he'd told his dad about school yet but refrained. I knew it wouldn't be met well, and I also already knew what the answer would be. We hadn't dived deep into that topic of conversation yet, but I knew Junior's feelings on the matter. He was as stubborn as a donkey, but I didn't have the right to tell him what to do.

"How did your test go?" I asked instead, genuinely curious.

He sighed, and for a second he sounded very forlorn. "Papá has me working long hours. I didn't get as much studying in as I liked so I feel like I barely scraped by."

"I'm sorry."

"Not your fault."

"It still sucks."

"I guess. How was your day?"

I groaned, not sure I wanted to talk about it and bring back that anger.

"That bad, huh?"

I busied myself with pulling leftovers out from the fridge. While I contemplated my answers, I popped the top off and put it in the microwave. While it spun and heated, I leaned against the counter.

"Principal Jenkins told me not to bother helping the 'lost causes' and to focus more on the ones that actually have a chance."

Junior let out an immediate curse. "Viejo pendejo."

"Right?" I sighed, rubbing my temple. "It was just so disheartening, to be honest. How can anyone think that about those kids? If anything, they need our help the most." My voice cracked on the last word and I had to pause and clear my throat.

I was a little embarrassed to be met with silence on the other end, but if I knew Junior, he was carefully contemplating his reply.

"Are you okay, Mayda?"

The question had a bundle of nerves lodge into my throat.

I hated to be seen as weak. I'd always been careful to keep my composure around him and his family throughout my life. I knew things were different now. We were different now, but that didn't take away years of instinct.

"Fine."

"Talk to me, cariño. You know I'm here for you. That's what boyfriends are for, you know."

Something in my chest warmed at the liberal use of the word boyfriend. It'd be a lie if I said I hadn't wondered what we were now. One date didn't a relationship make. Not even sex was sometimes enough to tie yourself to another person, no matter how intimate the act.

That single sentence threw away any insecurities and doubts I may have had regarding where we stood.

"Boyfriend, huh?"

"Yup. Boyfriend. No backsies. I'm yours now and you can't get rid of me."

"I wasn't planning on it."

We were quiet a moment before the microwave beeped. Junior heard my loud ass machine and chuckled. "Are you having dinner? Do you want to call me back when you're done?"

I didn't want to leave him too soon. "How about we video chat?" I suggested instead.

A second later, there was a click and the incoming beep of a call. I accepted immediately and Junior's face filled the screen.

My smile was an immediate mirror to his own. Seeing his bright smile a balm to my otherwise shitty day.

"Hey, you," he greeted, as if we hadn't just been speaking on the phone moments before. "I miss your face. I miss *you*."

"I miss you too."

"Now, eat your dinner, cariño. Can't have you going hungry on my watch."

Once I was settled at the table, I ate my meal in silence, Junior propped up, watching me and filling the silence with his own animated chatter.

This was one of the things I had always loved about him. He was extroverted in the best way, and it drew me to him. He could fill the spaces of the silence between us with the most random topics, and I was content to merely listen.

Finished with my meal, I went down the hall to my room, closing the door behind me. I had to change my clothes, get out the last bit of ick of the day.

"Hold on." I propped my phone up against my dresser, camera facing my bed, before I moved out of frame to grab an old t-shirt and some sweats.

"Mayda?"

Clothes in hand, I peeked back in the frame of the camera. "Yeah?"

His smirk met me, his voice lowering to little more than a mischievous whisper. "Are you changing?"

"I was about to, you know, before you interrupted me."

His eyebrows kicked up and he took his bottom lip between his teeth, biting down on the corner. That damn movement weakened me at the knees in inexplicable ways. "Can I watch?"

The question knocked the breath from my chest. Desire was an immediate sensation, a throb pulsing in my core. My fingers shook, causing the clothes to fall from my grasp. I suddenly felt nervous and anxious, both sensations warring in my chest.

My fists curled into the folds of my skirt. There was heat in his gaze, the same kind that had been there the other night we'd spent together. In the little icon on the top of my phone, my own face reflected back at me. The rising flush on my cheeks, my lips parted as I breathed hard. I barely cast a glance at myself before my gaze was drawn back to Junior once again.

He waited patiently, not pressuring me into anything.

That was another thing I loved about him.

"You don't have to," he whispered finally, giving me an out.

Was I brave enough to do this? He'd seen every inch of me already, but there was something different about doing it on camera. There was an extra layer of vulnerability to this. One I wasn't familiar with.

"I've never..." My breath caught as the confession got stuck in my throat.

His expression switched to shock before smoothing over. "Never?"

I shrugged.

I wasn't a blushing virgin, obviously. Junior hadn't been my first. I'd explored my sexuality long before him and had had many partners in the past. But there had never been anyone I completely trusted, especially not with something as delicate as camera sex—I'd never even sent a nude or let others take pictures of me.

That kind of thing could always get ugly super fast. You could never be too sure who to trust, if they'd secretly record you while you were baring yourself before them.

"We don't have to," he repeated.

I must have hesitated for too long for him to say that, but in a split second I made my decision.

"I trust you." I faced the camera completely, stepping backwards a little until the backs of my calves hit the edge of my bed. The jolt of it brought me back to reality, causing shyness to set in. I hugged my elbows, taking a breath. "Don't laugh at me, okay?"

"Cariño, I wouldn't do that."

I knew he wouldn't, but shivers still trailed down my body. It took me a moment to gather my courage.

"Maybe you should sit down?" Junior suggested softly.

I did what he asked, sitting myself on the edge of the bed. It felt good to receive direction, when I was too shy to make the moves I wanted to do myself.

On the camera, Junior adjusted his phone. There was a shakiness as he propped his phone up somewhere and leaned back, giving me a view of him on his bed. The bed he'd made me come in several times.

"Unbutton your cardigan?" He framed the words like a request, rather than an outright order. The sweetness of his voice was refreshing for my nerves.

My fingers fumbled with the first button on my light pink sweater. They relaxed with the next ones, and I slipped it off one arm. As I went to slip it off the other, Junior whispered, "Slower."

The material slipped from my arm at a much slower pace, as per his request. I shrugged it off, letting it bunch up behind me. I bit my lip, more out of concentration than seduction, but Junior's reaction to it was instantaneous.

"Have I told you how fucking beautiful you are today?"

"You haven't."

"You're fucking beautiful, Mayda."

"So are you."

Junior didn't chuckle at my breathless words, but he smiled widely before nodding, urging me to continue. "Slide down the strap of your dress."

The thin strap grazed the space where my neck met my shoulder. I pushed it aside in the tiniest increments until it slid down my arm then did the same to the other side.

Moving like this, slow, with the intent of seduction, made me feel more empowered with every movement. It chased away the shyness I initially felt. And the soft graze of my fingertips against my own body made a trail of tingles glide down my back.

My breath hitched, and the thrum of my own pulse pounded against my palm as I slid my hand across my neck, my collarbones, down to the top of my dress.

I flicked the top button with much more confidence, my lids fluttering a split second before my gaze snagged on Junior. The way he was watching me... I could feel the heat in his eyes and it burned me through the lens.

"Widen your legs and slide the skirt up."

My thighs spread open, my hands coming down on the tops of them. I slid a path up, the movement causing the hem to glide until it was bunched at my waist.

I could already feel a wet spot on my panties, my desire likely darkening the center of the material.

"Hermosa." His voice was hoarse. "Slide your panties aside. I want to see your cunt."

My fingers met my inner thigh, creeping towards the lacey edge of my panties. I paused before I reached them.

"Are you going to touch yourself, Damián?"

He groaned and the sound echoed through my room. His eyes closed like he was being tortured, and when he opened them again, there was hope. "Do you want me to?"

"Sí." The word whooshed out on a breath. "I want you to feel what I feel. I want to see you too."

"Whatever you want, cariño." He adjusted on the bed, sliding back so I could see his body. "What do you want me to do?"

"Take your shirt off?" Bossing him around didn't come naturally to me. It came out a plea, instead of a command, but Junior smiled and obliged, working with expert slowness. He pulled his shirt off from the bottom, and I despaired that he wasn't here in front of me right then, because the way his arms flexed as he pulled the shirt over his head made me want to lick across his muscles.

"Done." He leaned back against the mound of pillows. "Now show me your cunt."

I hooked my finger inside the edge of my panties and tugged them away from my lips.

"Ay, ay, ay," Junior groaned. "Carájo, Mayda."

Emboldened by his words, I slid my middle finger against my slit.

"Are you wet for me?" he asked.

"Always."

"Play with your clit."

I didn't. Not yet. "I want to see you too, Damián."

"Of course." The buckle of his belt clinked. His zipper slid down, and I was greeted by the sight of his hand slipping into his boxers and pulling his dick out. He gripped it in his hand, his knuckles tightening as he squeezed up and down his length.

Seeing him like that reminded me of how he felt inside me, and my core ached for him right then. I groaned, pushing a finger inside, but it didn't fill the building need.

"Your clit, Mayda," Junior reminded me.

I pressed against it on his command, rubbing circles along the sensitive nub. It felt good, but it didn't compare to his fingers, to his tongue.

"Do you have toys, Mayda?"

His question had my eyes shooting open—when had I closed them?—and staring. A breathless "Yes" escaped me.

"Take out your favorite. I want to see you fucking yourself with it. But get naked first. I want to see every fucking inch of you."

My panties fell back into place as I removed my hands from there. I pulled off my dress and bared my body before him. Clad in nothing but a matching bra and panty set, I stood and made my way over to my night stand, going through the drawer and pulling out my favorite toy.

I held it up for his inspection a brief second before setting it aside.

"What does that one do?" Junior asked, a hint of wickedness in his voice.

"It suctions the clit."

His hand worked over his dick in response. His movements slow and drawn out, taking his time to pleasure himself as he watched me.

"Take everything off. I want to see you."

I was all too happy to oblige, reaching behind me first to unhook my bra and toss it aside. My panties followed just before I went back to the bed, widening my legs so he could see.

"Fuck, you're so beautiful."

I didn't think I'd ever get tired of hearing those words.

"Grab your toy. Turn it on."

My hand closed around the handle, thumb pressing hard down on the button. The thrumming sound filled the room.

"Are you wet enough, cariño?"

"So, so wet."

"Show me."

I used my fingers to spear into my own pussy, parting my lips, smearing my own wetness against myself. I gave attention to my clit, rubbing it in small circles that had me parting my lips and releasing the softest of sighs.

"Use your toy." Junior's voice was rough with want.

Again, I wished he was here with me. But I did as he bade, bringing the toy down between my legs, pressing the rubber cup end against my clit. The sucking sensation brought instant relief that had me canting my hips up to meet the toy. Even with the vibration on low, I felt myself coming apart at the seams.

"Fuck, oh fuck, that's hot."

My eyes were half-lidded, enraptured with Junior's own movements on the camera. His hand worked, knuckles tightening as he squeezed his dick. We fell into a rhythm together, where he thrust into his own palm as my hips rose to meet my toy.

"Damián..." A mewl of pleasure escaped me.

"Sí." His own voice was a breathless whisper. "Say my name, cariño."

"Damián."

"Have you touched yourself, calling out my name in secret?"

"Yes."

He grunted out a curse, his hand moving faster and faster over his length. "Tell me," he panted. "Show me. Show me how you touched yourself."

With the press of my thumb, I turned the vibrations higher and the movement against my clit became a rapid pulse. I swiveled my hips, pressing the toy down hard against my body. I was empty and wanted to be filled, and yet I felt myself fast approaching the edge he always pushed me towards.

"Just like this," I rasped. "I touched myself just like this."

"Beautiful. Fucking perfect. Fuck, are you close, cariño?"

"Yes, yes."

It didn't take long. Junior's voice alone was an aphrodisiac through my system. I was high on it, on him. Every inch of me felt wired, ready, pulled taut like a string. And all it took was the sound of him coming to snap it.

"Oh, fuck, fuck, fuck." His breathless cries filled the room, and I quickly followed after him in release. My whole body jerked as the orgasm crashed over me. His fervent cursing a mirror of my pounding heart.

Breathless minutes passed before I held the button down and shut off the toy. It was hard to hold myself up, my limbs shaking, my skin burning. Sitting up, I smiled at Junior's image on the camera. His own lazy smile curled higher.

"Fuck," he whispered. "I *miss* you."

The words made my heart constrict. "I miss you too."

"How soon can I see you?"

"As soon as possible."

"Tomorrow?"

I melted into my covers, breathless and content as I replied, "I'd like that."

CHAPTER 29

JUNIOR

SEEING MAYDA COME APART on the other end of the phone camera had been the highlight of my day. Yet soon after cleaning off the sticky mess left behind, I had to get back to reality. A reality in which my grades were dwindling because of my duties at the rancho, in which I neglected work to fix that problem and then got chewed out for it.

I still hadn't found a work-school balance, and it felt like every single area of my life was being affected because of it. I knew that doing anything outside of the rancho was probably a moot point. But that didn't matter, because a part of me still thrived to prove my papá wrong.

He'd let Gabi go to college for accounting, because she was a woman and he didn't want his daughter beholden to any man, but also because she wanted to work for the rancho and deal with the numbers, something she'd been doing since we were in high school anyway. My other sisters hadn't needed to chip in when the two oldest were already doing that, so my parents had always been more lenient with them.

I wouldn't lie... I envied the younger girls for that. And I wanted to make good grades, get whatever diplomas I could get my hands on, if only to prove to him that I could do exactly what he never thought I could.

Only, lately, I felt like I was failing even in that.

Mayda was my only anchor.

Maybe I should have listened to her. Talked to my parents about my dreams.

The only problem was, I didn't even know what they were. I was being pulled in too many directions. I loved the rancho, I did. But I wanted more out of it. Something different. Something fresh.

I felt like I was stuck in a rut I couldn't get out of.

So the next day, when I ditched work and school to pick Mayda up after school, I forced myself not to feel guilty about it. I'd given so much time of my life to the rancho already. I could afford one day. Just one to do something that I wanted without the stress.

When Mayda walked out of the school, bag slung over her shoulder, I hopped out of my truck and waved at her. When she approached, the urge to take her into my arms and kiss her senseless was strong, but because we were still hanging around the school parking lot, I decided to curb my desires and offered her a chaste kiss on the cheek instead.

"Hey, how was work?"

She smiled as I went to the passenger side and opened the door for her. "It was fine."

I didn't believe her. Her tone implied something else. I didn't mention it; instead, I helped her up into the truck, closed the door and jogged back to the other side and hopped in.

"Was Principal Jenkins being a dick again?" I asked as I backed out. "Want me to beat his ass?"

Like expected, that got a laugh out of her.

"You can't beat up my boss."

"Maybe not, but I can make you feel better."

Her brows kicked up. "Yeah? How?"

I waggled my own in her direction. "That's a surprise."

She fake-groaned. "You know I hate surprises."

She didn't, not really. She claimed she did, but I'd watched her for years now. She whined about hating surprises right before receiving gifts from Gabi. But I noted the way her eyes lit up, the awestruck and grateful smiles, the pure joy at being pampered even just a little.

I'd always been jealous that Gabi had been on the receiving end of those moments.

And they were moments I wanted to steal for myself too.

"Suck it up, nena," I teased. "Because I'm not saying a word."

"The zoo?" Mayda squealed. "Junior, you brought me to the zoo?!"

The way she was bouncing up and down in her seat, one would have thought that I'd just gifted her with diamonds. She was nearly out of the truck before I'd even put the thing in park and rushing towards the entrance.

I had to jog to keep up with her and thread our fingers together before she got lost in the crowd.

"I take it this is a surprise you like?"

"Junior, I love it! It reminds me of when we were kids."

It reminded me of that, too. At first, I'd wondered if it was lame to bring a grown woman to the fucking zoo on a date, but then I'd remembered all the times we'd come together as kids. The absolute joy she got from something so simple.

I'd wanted to recreate that today.

It was a weekday, and yet I was surprised that the place was full. We waited in line a while and, after getting our tickets, made our way inside. And even though we'd been here before, Mayda still held a map to the place in her hand.

"What do you want to look at first?" I asked, looking down at the map.

"How about we go see the sea lions? There's going to be a show in a few minutes."

"Whatever you want, cariño."

Our hands clasped together as we walked all around the zoo and for a moment, it felt like we were kids again, except we wandered with a different perception of the world and of each other. The reality is I shouldn't have waited so long for this, but I couldn't help but wonder where we'd be if I'd actually confessed back then.

I tried not to dwell on that and instead enjoyed our day together. We circled around until we ended up in the petting zoo area to pause and watch.

The ponies whinnied softly and the kids sitting astride them trembled with nerves, while their parents encouraged them and demanded they smile for pictures from off to the side. Others chortled their laughter as they held their hands out to the goats behind wooden fences and their dark tongues licked out to feed from between their fingers.

My gaze snagged on a particularly shy girl whose parents nudged her forward along the fence. At first, she refused to go, shaking her head adamantly back and forth. Her pigtails slapped her cheeks and her nose scrunched adorably. I found myself smiling as she worked up the courage to do what was asked of her. Crumbling the animal feed in her hand, she pushed her arm forward, through the bars of the fence. Immediately, a goat came and devoured every last crumb. The real joy was in the girl's gap-toothed smile when she turned it towards her mother.

"So cute," Mayda whispered from my side. She'd been as enraptured in the display as I was.

I smirked at her. "You like goats?"

Her eyes rolled. "I meant the kids, but the goats are cute too."

"You like kids?"

"I mean, obviously." She gestured at herself, as if to remind me that she was a school counselor.

"I mean, do you want any of your own?"

"Oh, yeah."

I smiled at that. "How many?"

She shrugged and her own smile fell. "So, a part of me always wanted a sibling when I was younger. It got really lonely, and watching your family always made me crave more. But I figured it was selfish to want to have another kid around when my mom is the way she is." She turned to me, the sun hitting her head, gifting her with a halo of light. "But now that I'm older, I don't know. I want a big family. Kids I can give love to, that I can spoil. I want to give them everything I never had."

My hand gravitated towards hers and our fingers threaded together. "I want a big family too. Comes with the territory, being Mexican and all."

She cackled. "Stop it!"

I shrugged. "What? It's true." We bumped our shoulders together another moment in jest, and I turned back to the animals and the children enjoying them. "But in all seriousness, animals are therapeutic, aren't they?"

"Oh, yeah. I can't remember how many times I'd be feeling down because of something my mom did. Gabi would notice and just...take me to the stables. Like it was a cure for all ailments." She chuckled as the memory swept over her eyes. "And the thing is it was. I think horses can just sense emotions, because they always somehow just made me feel better."

I thought back to all the times the horses had made me feel better when I was in a rut. It was true that they seemed to sense emotions, but I'd always been of the belief that animals were smarter than humans.

"I felt the same," I offered. "Whenever I'd get into it with my papá, the horses would just be there. Like old friends."

I wondered right then, as I watched the same little girl go back up to the goat with renewed confidence, if anyone else felt the way we did, and if they did I wondered if they had the same ease of access like we did on the rancho. I'm sure not everyone did, and it was a damn shame. I thought both animals and children could both benefit from something like that.

If only we had something like that on the rancho...

My thoughts were cut off as Mayda's phone rang from within her purse. Her fingers pulled from mine so she could reach in and take it out. She looked at the caller I.D., eyes going wide. The change went over her swiftly, she answered in a rush, her voice shaking.

"Mom?"

I turned towards her, frozen and unsure at what to do as her voice rose in a panic.

"Mom, where are you? Mom?!" She pulled the phone away from her ear. "Fuck!"

"Mayda?" My worry mounted as tears threatened her hazel eyes. "Mayda, what's wrong?"

"It's my mom. I... I have to go."

CHAPTER 30

MAYDA

I KNEW THE MOMENT I saw her name on the caller I.D. that it wasn't going to be good. Usually, she never called me when she wanted money. When she wanted something from me, she usually crawled back home and stole from my wallet or tried to find something to pawn off.

But then I'd heard her voice. The fear rising in her whispered, hoarse sound.

"Mayda," she'd murmured. "Help me."

Then the line had gone dead.

"I... I have to go." The worry immediately shot to my throat and made me almost delirious. I rushed, twirling and nearly folding my ankle in the process. Junior caught my elbow, wrapping his arm around my waist before I could fall.

"Mayda, cariño, please take a breath."

I couldn't. I couldn't fucking breathe. So many scenarios popped into my head. Had something gone down with one of her dealers? Was she fighting for her life? Was she so strung out that she was on the verge of an overdose?

I couldn't think straight.

My breathing came out labored, sawing in and out of my chest painfully.

"Cariño, breathe with me, okay?" His hand closed around mine and he brought it up to my chest. Surely he could feel my heart pounding, could feel how it was about to burst straight from my chest. "Breathe with me, Mayda."

I tried to focus on the sound of his voice, the way his chest rose and fell against my backside. Focusing on that gave me purpose. It made the fierce pounding of my heart calm into something steadier and manageable.

"She's in trouble, Junior," I said, more calmly than before. "I have to go find her." His hold on me loosened and I turned in his arms, palms meeting his chest. "I have to go."

His thumb swiped against my cheekbone in a comforting gesture. "You're crazy if you think I'm going to let you go without me."

I wanted to step away, to tell him no. He didn't need to be dragged into my family mess. But the logical part knew I couldn't do this without him, and the emotional part didn't even want to.

"Okay," I whispered. "But we need to hurry."

"Do you have any idea where she could be?"

My phone tightened in my hand as I hit redial for what felt like the thousandth time. It went straight to voicemail. Just like it had so many times before. I resisted the urge to throw the thing out the window in frustration. That would have been counterproductive.

"I have no idea," I grumbled. "I... I know her hangouts; places I've had to fish her out of before."

His hand came down against my knee, giving me a squeeze. "We'll find her," he said. "I promise."

I couldn't even manage to give him a pained smile. I wanted to bite out that that wasn't something he could even promise me, but I held back from being spiteful. Having him near helped me. It felt reassuring not having to go out and look for her alone, but...

I didn't want to think about the rest or my own feelings. The most important thing right then was finding my mom.

The rest would come later.

So we drove for what felt like hours. I gave Junior directions in a curt tone, keeping my face plastered to the window. We drove past the highway, past suburbs, even past my own shitty neighborhood and into an even shittier maze of crumbling homes, poverty, and despair.

Junior slowed as we drove through the neighborhood, looking out his own window to see if he could make out my mom's form somewhere among the bodies of homeless people that laid out in the darkening afternoon.

"Drive over here." I pointed towards the laundromat. I could usually find her there, trading cash for weed or little baggies of white powder. "Park here, please."

Junior silently did as I asked. He'd barely spoken the deeper we arrived in this area, but he did now as I reached for the door handle.

"Where the hell do you think you're going?"

I shot him an incredulous look. "I'm going to find my mom."

"No, you're going to stay in the car and I'm going to go look."

"You're insane if you think I'm not going in there to find *my* mother."

"And you're out of your fucking mind if you think I'm going to let you go in there at all. It's too dangerous."

I couldn't help the mirthless laugh that escaped me. It only made Junior frown at me, and I could feel his anger, but at this moment, I didn't care. "I've been picking her up from this neighborhood for a long time, and I've done it without your help before. I can do it again." I reached for the handle, but Junior all but jumped across the space that separated us, covering my hand with his.

"Mayda, stay in the fucking truck."

"No, Junior. And we don't have time for your machismo bullshit."

"Terca," he retorted quietly. I wasn't even mad he was calling me stubborn. "Fine," he said, as if I'd ever needed his permission. "We'll go together."

"Fine."

He eased back. "But let me get out first, okay?"

"Fine," I snapped.

He ignored my outburst and hopped out of the truck, walking around on my side, he opened my door. I ignored his offered hand and hopped out on my own. The chill of the approaching night curled around my exposed legs, sending a chill straight through me.

I didn't wait for Junior as I marched towards the back of the laundromat, but it didn't matter because Junior was at my heels, crowding against my back protectively. We didn't speak, but as the sky finally settled into night, I made my way towards the back alley.

"Mayda," Junior grumbled, grabbing the back of my cardigan. "Wait."

There was a figure at the back of the alley. A body clad in nothing but a thin shirt and jean capris. She was slumped against the wall, half of her body sprawled across the dirty ground.

I let out a curse and rushed forward.

"Mayda!"

I ignored Junior and stepped close to my mom, dropping to a crouch. I was careful to avoid the trash on the ground, careful like I always was. Just in case. My mother's body was skeletal, dirty, and covered in vomit. The stench almost made me gag, and I had to fight the sensation back.

"Mom." I grabbed her shoulder, feeling her bones protruding through the material of her shirt. "Mom!" My fingers flew to her neck. The faint press of her pulse against my fingertips brought a surge of relief. "Thank fuck."

"I'm going to call an ambulance," Junior said.

I didn't turn to look at him as he dialed and his firm voice demanded help. I could only stare at my mother, so pathetic against a half-crumbled wall. Her phone was nowhere in sight, probably pilfered by another druggie so they could pawn it off and make a quick buck.

"Mom." My fingers curled around her shoulder, hard with anger and worry, both raging inside me. I shook her once, hard. She was too still, her body cold and unmoving. "Mom!" She didn't stir as I tried to shake her awake.

So many times throughout my life I wondered if I'd walk into this exact situation. To find her cold and waxy like a corpse. The dark part of me wanted it, and the part of me that still loved her dreaded the day. I wondered if today was that day, the day my darkest thoughts came true.

Everything around me went cold. I couldn't move my hand from her body, keeping it pressed, waiting for the heat to extinguish, for her chest to stop rising, for her heart to stop beating. I wasn't aware of Junior calling my name. Of the flashing lights of the police and the ambulance as they arrived. I was numb as Junior pried me away from her and the medics gave her a dose of Narcan and put an IV in her just before taking her away.

"Mayda. Mayda? Mayda!"

When I finally snapped out of my stupor, we were at the hospital. I wasn't even sure how we got here without my knowing, but Junior was in front of me, his worry palpable. The severity of it finally woke me up.

I took a breath. "Junior..."

"Mayda, the doctor said your mom is okay. She's alive. They pumped her stomach and she's stable now."

His words didn't bring the relief they should have, but they didn't bring dread either. I wasn't sure what to feel. How to feel. I was numb from the inside out.

"Do you want to see her?" Junior asked.

I didn't. I was afraid, but I forced myself to nod anyway. Moving on stiff legs with Junior and a nurse guiding us, we walked to the room where my mom was being kept. I stared at her still body through the glass. Connected to monitors and the rise and fall that marked the steady beating of her heart. She was so still, lifeless. But those lines marked her survival.

"She's sleeping," the nurse said, stating the obvious in a soft tone she'd likely used thousands of times before.

"Will she be okay?" The words came out of my mouth in a dead tone. I had to force my gaze away from the lump of bones on the hospital bed to turn towards the nurse.

She gifted me with a tight smile. "She will be fine. We are keeping her overnight. You can come tomorrow to see her. Visiting hours are at..."

I turned away from her once again, tuning her out and making sure her voice became nothing more than a distant echo in my mind. I refused to retain the information.

My mom... She'd always done her bullshit. She'd always splurged on too much alcohol, passed out in random alleys...

But she'd never overdosed. Or if she had, I'd never witnessed it. Not to that degree. Seeing her on the verge of death and being numb to it? I shuddered.

Junior mistook it for cold and wrapped his arm around my shoulders. "Come on, cariño," he whispered. "Let's get you home."

I let him guide me out of the hospital, leaving behind the sterile scent that clung to the bones of the walls and seeped through your skin even after you left it behind. The stench clogged through me even as I sat in his truck and he drove. The scenery flew by me in a blur, and I didn't react the entire way until he put the truck in park and I saw the dark skeleton of my beaten down house in front of us.

I took a breath and waited as Junior hopped out and rounded the front of the truck to open the door for me. I accepted his help but forced my fingers out of his own to go forward and open the door.

The emptiness that greeted us inside had never felt more lonely than it did in that moment. It was suffocating and I hated everything about it. I threw my purse to the side, not caring when it hit and knocked over a lamp.

"Mayda..."

I peeled off my cardigan and tossed that to the side, needing to get the clinging stench of the hospital off my body. I needed a shower. I needed to scrub the memory and feel of my mom's cold body from between my fingers.

"Mayda!"

I was whirled around, gripped by the shoulders in Junior's strong hands. He stared down at me, a worried crease between his brows.

"Mayda, say something."

Those two words seemed to crash around us. Like a wave tumbling to shore. Like I'd been a fragile piece of glass suspended in the air for far too long, and far too slowly, and was just now falling onto concrete. Everything shattered around me, and my emotions came with an impact that slammed through me so quickly, it hurt.

"What do you want me to say?" My voice broke. "You saw her. You saw—" I broke off, shaking my head back and forth. "Junior, I think you should leave."

He reeled back as though I'd slapped him. His jaw tightened. "I'm not leaving you alone."

That wasn't what I wanted to hear. Why did he always have to act so goddamn stubborn?

"Get. Out." My palms met his shoulders and I shoved. I'd never been prone to violence before, but something swelled in me. The shock of the night finally rippled through my system. All that anger bubbled to the surface and needed an outlet.

And Junior was here, even when I didn't want him to be.

But it didn't matter that I'd shoved with all my might, because he didn't budge. He stood there like a block of a man, glaring down at me.

"I'm not leaving."

"Why would you want to stay after that?" I demanded, my voice rising, emotion spilling out of me.

"What do you mean?"

"Are you here because you pity me? Poor, pathetic Mayda with her druggie mom?"

He sucked in a breath. "I would never think those things about you."

"You should!" Silence followed my shout and it was even more deafening than it had the right to be. "You are too good for me Junior. Do you know why I never let myself get close to you?" I pushed on before he could ask or try to guess the answer. "Because of her. Because her blood flows through my veins. My mom, the junkie." I stepped away from him, my shoulders wracking up and down with sobs. "She's pathetic and I'm no better. Living a lie, covering up her mistakes. My family, my *life*, is a fucking joke and you're so good and kind—" I broke off as the sob caught in my throat. I felt like I couldn't breathe. A part of me didn't want to. I wanted to drown in my own sorrow.

"Mayda." Junior's voice was hard. "Eso es una mierda y lo sabes." *That's bullshit and you know it.*

"Junior." I held my hands up, pleading. "Please leave. I'm embarrassed. How could you ever look at me the same after that? I can't—"

He let out a sound of frustration, and the next thing I knew, I was enveloped in his arms, and he was pressing my face into his chest, holding me tightly to his body, like he could merge our bodies and souls this way.

"No te voy a dejar sola," he whispered against my hair. "I am not leaving you. Ever. I l—I know you, Mayda. I know your heart and you aren't like her."

My eyes burned as the tears flowed and stained his shirt. "She almost died, Junior." And I had felt nothing.

"Cariño, your mom is sick. Her addiction is a disease. She needs help. More than you can provide. You've done more than enough, and I think now is the time you let go..."

His words are like a knife to my gut. I took in a shuddering breath. "I wanted to save her." And maybe in wanting to do it all on my own, it became a thing of pride and embarrassment. I hadn't been thinking about her or her well-being. I'd only been thinking about myself.

First, because I hadn't wanted to be put into foster care, so I hid the truth from everyone. I learned to do everything on my own, and because of that, I'd gotten so used to keeping the truth close to my chest, lying to everyone around me. I became independent and not in a good way. I'd held us together for so long, and now I finally felt like I was falling apart.

"You have, cariño."

"It doesn't feel like it."

"You did everything you could, and everything that never should have been your problem to deal with. You were a fucking kid. She should have taken care of you. You can let go of all that, okay? Fall apart if you need to. I'm here."

He was right. I hated that he was, but… I'd been forced to grow up too fast. I'd been the one who needed love and care, and instead I'd been neglected and forced to be a parent to my parent. And for a moment, it had felt like I was about to bury the one who made me suffer for so long, and yet love for her still flowed fiercely through me.

I wondered if that made me stupid, for loving someone who hurt me? Love was pain, they said, even when it wasn't supposed to be.

My hands wrapped around Junior's waist, and I pulled him to me, inhaling his spicy scent. My cheeks heated with shame at the way I'd acted in the heat of the moment. Suddenly, all that I'd said before fell apart.

"I'm sorry."

His arms tightened around me. "It's okay. Like I said, nunca te dejaré sola."

Words I wanted to say were poised on the tip of my tongue, but right then didn't seem the time to blurt them out, so I swallowed them back and took a deep breath. "Can you stay the night?"

"Of course."

"And can you just... hold me? I don't think I can handle being alone..."

He pulled away and tilted my chin up so our eyes met. In them I found the answers to questions I hadn't even asked and words I was too cowardly to say.

"Of course," he whispered. "I'd do anything for you, Mayda. Anything."

And I'd do anything for him. Those were the words I wanted to reply with. Instead, I wrapped my arms around him, and I held him tighter.

So tightly, it was like I could merge our bodies and our souls into one being.

One entity.

One love.

CHAPTER 31

JUNIOR

MAYDA'S SLEEP WAS RESTLESS. She tossed and turned, and it didn't matter how many times I pulled her into my arms throughout the night, she fought my hold in her nightmares and whimpered and cried out.

Seeing it broke my heart.

By the time morning came, she'd finally fallen into a deep slumber, one I couldn't follow her into.

Last night had been disastrous. What had started off as a date had ended in something terrifying for her. Something I didn't want her to live through ever again.

I feared for her, in more ways than one. She'd looked so broken for a moment there, and a selfish part of me had been absolutely terrified that I was going to lose her. That she'd kick me out and not invite me back in. So I stood my ground. I'd let myself be selfish until she gave in.

She'd carried this weight around for far too long. She didn't deserve that. She needed to be honest with those around her. I was sure if she told Gabi about it, my sister would understand. My whole family would. If only she'd lean on us more...

But I wouldn't give away her secret. Not if that wasn't what she wanted.

But I would help her myself.

Climbing out of her bed, I pulled on my jeans and t-shirt and checked my phone. I tried not to wince at the many messages and missed calls from my papá and mamá. The missed calls from my mamá were far more terrifying than anything else. It took me back to a childhood where she'd yank on my ears for daring to ignore her messages. If anyone decided not to call or text back within moments, we would easily find ourselves on the receiving end of her wrath.

But if I called her back now, she would demand answers.

Answers that weren't mine to give.

I slipped out of the room and walked out to the kitchen, my fingers working to send a mass text to my sisters and parents in our family group chat.

> Estoy bien. I stayed the night with Mayda.

It was early, and the only one who replied back was Gabi.

> :eyebrow wiggle GIF:

I rolled my eyes at her antics. Of course she didn't know the truth. It made me feel weird that I knew something she didn't. I made a mental note to talk to Mayda about confiding in my sister as I pocketed my phone before I could see my parents' disappointed reply. For now, I was going to make Mayda breakfast.

After peeking in her fridge and finding it sparse, I decided to make a grocery run. I shot off a quick text, knowing that Mayda would check her phone when she woke up. Then I grabbed the keys to my truck and set off to the grocery store.

I stocked up on a few things to make her a quick breakfast, then added a few more groceries for the week in the cart. On the way back to her place, my mind kept wandering back to the night before. To the emptiness in her eyes throughout the entire process of finding her mom and getting her to the hospital. The way she'd finally broken down, pushed me away.

I gripped the steering wheel tighter and made an impulsive, split-second decision as I changed courses. I made it to the hospital within minutes, parked, and headed up. I might've lied to the nurses and told them Luciana was my mother-in-law and it was the only reason they'd let me in to see her.

On the way to her room I ran into Officer Reynaldo. He was an older Mexican man with a rounded belly and graying sideburns. I'd known the officer for most of my life. He'd gone to school several times when I was a kid to talk about the dangers of drugs and peer pressure.

"Junior!" he greeted warmly, his brown eyes crinkling at the sides as he smiled. "Haven't seen you in a long time. How are you? How's the family?"

"They're good. Everything is good."

"Where you headed?"

"I'm... Mayda's mom is here..."

His expression changed the moment the words were out of my mouth. He shook his head back and forth, the disapproval already set there. "Luciana," he muttered. "I've had to collect her and lock her up overnight more times than I care to count."

That was news to me. I was sure that would be news to Mayda as well. There was a lot about her own mother she didn't even know. I wasn't surprised. The woman was in and out of the house, and Mayda couldn't possibly keep track of her every minute of every day.

"She's why I'm here," Officer Reynaldo went on. "When we got the call about the overdose, I wanted to come talk to her. Get her set up with some NA meeting information. Here." He dug into the back pocket of his uniform and pulled out a pamphlet, handing it to me. "There's a number there. Maybe she'll listen to you, if not Mayda."

I stuffed the pamphlet in my pocket. "I'll make sure she gets this."

With that, we said our goodbyes and I made my way to Luciana's room. She was sitting up, staring out the window when I arrived. Her entire body jolted with surprise when I stepped into the room.

"Junior." She smacked her chapped lips and her brows furrowed. "What are you doing here?"

Seeing her filled me with the strangest sensation of both pity and anger. Pity at what she was; nothing but a spectral figure lying in a hospital bed, near dead. Anger at what she'd put Mayda through.

There was no question about it. Mayda deserved better than her.

She deserved her mom back.

"Mayda and I found you last night," I said.

She cleared her throat and looked away. Embarrassed? She should be. "Where is Mayda? Didn't want to come see me, I take it."

"She's sleeping, actually. She was up all night with nightmares because she found you near dead in an alley. She doesn't know I'm here."

She swallowed. "Well, why are *you* here?"

I dug for the pamphlet and tossed it in her direction. "You need to get better. For Mayda's sake. For *your* sake."

Her shaking fingers slid across the blanket in their trek to grasp the pamphlet. She smoothed out the crumpled edges, staring down at it with an expression I couldn't read.

"Your daughter loves you," I went on when she didn't say anything. "You love her too, don't you?"

Tears filled her eyes to the brim. "I do."

"Don't you owe it to your family to get better?"

She didn't say anything else, and neither did I. I didn't think there was anything else left to say. I turned and started out the door.

"Mayda is proud, you know," she called after me. "She'll be mad you came to see me."

I didn't turn around. "She'll learn to love me for my stubbornness,"

This earned me a snort. "She's loved you your whole life, fool."

CHAPTER 32

MAYDA

WHEN I'D WOKEN UP the next morning after my mom's overdose, it was to a warm meal made by Junior and him nowhere to be found. I'd slept for far too long. He'd left a quick breakfast of eggs a la Mexicana out for me on the table and text messages claiming his dad needed him on the rancho.

I was glad he was gone, if I was being honest with myself. I didn't think I had the bravery to face him after the way I acted the night before. Besides, I had to go visit my mom, and I'd wanted to do that alone.

The only problem was, when I got to the hospital, she was already gone and none of the nurses or doctors could tell me where she went.

I wasn't surprised. It was her coward's way out of getting her ass chewed by me. Instead of facing me, she ran. The same way I should have ran from her a long time ago. But in the end, she'd be back. Just like always. And I'd welcome her, because she was my mom after all. And there were some relationships that were too hard to let go, no matter how toxic they were.

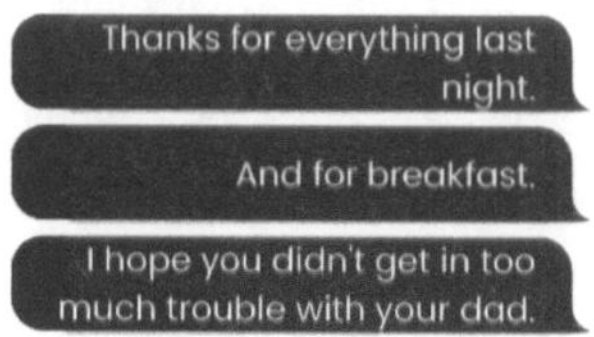

I'd sent those messages immediately after arriving back home from the hospital.

And for days, they remained unanswered.

At least, unanswered in an unexpected way. It was like Junior had gone mentally AWOL or like he was avoiding me. The timing of it didn't make me feel any better. I wanted to have faith and believe that the only reason he wasn't responding was because he was working, but my thoughts gave so many twists and turns that I wanted to cry. What were the odds that he suddenly was drowning in work the day after he played witness to my mom OD'ing in an alley?

I didn't want to think he would leave me.

Not after his words. Not after he vowed that he wouldn't.

But his absence pulsed like an open wound.

I went through my week in a numb state, barely concentrating at work because I was focused on Junior. Whenever I texted him, trying to pull him back to me, he responded with little more than a heart or a thumb's up.

I texted Gabi constantly as well, hoping to get a glimpse of Junior, to no avail. I also didn't want to outright ask my best friend what her brother was up to. If I knew Gabriela Águila-Gutierrez, which I did, I knew she would fish the information out of me by any means possible, and then do worse to her brother when she knew.

"Hey, Mayda?" The words came first, the rap on my office door came second. I looked up as a head full of frizzy hair peeked through the cracked door. The wide, red-lipped smile of Mrs. Angelica Teller met me.

She was another young Latina staff member. She was Colombian, beautiful, with an expressive face and tall limbs. She wore a mischievous smile, her eyes blinking with as much mischief as the diamond on her ring finger.

"Hey, Angie."

"There's a special delivery out front for you." Her smile broadened even further, and it only deepened my confusion.

I pushed to my feet. "A delivery?"

"Mhmm... Come see."

I trailed after her, the scent of her citrusy, tropical perfume clouding pleasantly near my nose. We walked into the wide expanse of the front office and there, sitting on her desk, was a vase of marigolds.

Angie waved her fingers in a ta-dah moment in the direction of the bright blooms of orange. "There's also a card. I may have peeked at it already."

"Chismosa."

She laughed but gestured impatiently at it with her lips and eyebrows. The way she controlled her facial features like that was a talent I never could possess, so I obeyed and plucked the folded card from the blooms.

Mayda, I'm picking you up after school. -D.

I frowned at the note.

"Uh-oh, that's not the expression of a happy woman. Is it a stalker? I thought D was a boyfriend, or a secret admirer."

"No, Damián is my boyfriend." I slipped the card back into the flowers, trying to harden myself against them. Damn Junior and his knowledge of all my favorite things. I wondered briefly if the flowers were a gift to soften the blow of his absence or if they were a parting gift. If we'd reached the end of the line on us.

Fuck, that hurt to think about.

"Ah, lover's spat, then?"

"Something like that."

The problem with the weight of my secrets was that nobody else knew about them. Nobody except Junior. And when he was ignoring me, there was no one else I could turn to about everything I was feeling inside. That shouldn't have been odd. After all, I'd been alone most of my life. While I had Gabriela, I'd never told her about my mom, and I'd certainly never told her about Junior, no matter how hard she pressed.

Things had changed within the span of weeks.

Junior had become mine. He'd learned my secrets, and I'd learned his and now he was the only one I wanted to talk to. To vent to.

And he was ignoring me.

I mean, evidently not anymore if he was picking me up.

If I even agreed to that.

I probably was going to agree to that. I was mad, yes, and a part of me wanted to just curl up and ignore the situation. To pretend like we never happened. To go back to a time before he knew my secrets and before we learned each other's bodies, because then I could avoid whatever heartbreak was coming my way.

But I owed the truth to myself, if nothing else.

And I'd demand it from Junior, too.

CHAPTER 33

JUNIOR

WHAT KIND OF A gift did you give your girlfriend after you practically ghosted her for days?

In my defense, my papá was pissed at me. My mamá too, for that matter. I'd disappeared way past curfew without telling them where I was or where I'd be. I didn't live under their roof anymore, but I still lived on their property, and that meant I had to check in.

"Qué independencia ni qué nada," my mamá had screamed at me. "Te regresas a vivir aquí!"

Panic set in my chest at the words. If they made me move back to the main house, all my carefully constructed lies and secrets I was keeping would have been found out. I'd had to all but beg on my knees to be allowed to still live on my own.

It was only thanks to Ximena and Sofia that I was allowed to keep my place at all. If I moved back, they would have to give up their shared dancing and painting space, and not even I was worth giving that up for. They'd argued as vehemently as I did.

In the end, I'd kept my space, but my papá put me to work.

He didn't rage like my mamá did. She could be all screams and frustration, only to turn around and smile at you five minutes later. No, a Mexican father's disappointment was worse because it was as quiet and as lethal as poison.

His quiet sighs whenever I walked into the room, the penetrating way he glared at me right before ordering me to do something that would take me hours. And it felt like I'd barely get a minute to breathe before he was ordering me to do something else. He kept a hawk-like watch on me, always pushing, never stopping. I barely ate or drank, and by the time the day was over, all I could focus on was speeding through homework until I found the energy to toss myself into bed and fall asleep.

I'd barely skimmed through Mayda's messages, only able to respond with quick emojis. By the time he'd finally let me breathe, I was panicking. I knew she would be overthinking. She would be worried. I'd fucking ignored her for days after I promised I'd always be there for her.

So I arranged for flowers to be sent to her work, with a note and a promise that we'd see each other that afternoon.

Then there was just the matter of my papá. He'd never let me leave. Not after what I pulled last week.

I hated to do it, but I knew I had to lie.

"We're out of feed," I told him. "Gabi needs me to go place the order."

He'd waved me off. I didn't even let out a breath until I was in the truck and the rancho was in my rear view. Okay, so it hadn't exactly been a lie. He knew we needed feed. But Gabi dealt with accounting, which meant she and papá always went over the orders together. I guessed he hadn't called me out on my bullshit because I was feigning an interest in the rancho.

I'd pay for it later, I was sure of it. Just like I was paying for all those late nights trying to turn in assignments before midnight. The dark circles probably shone under my eyes. I didn't care.

It'd been too long without Mayda already.

I missed her with an ache that was unbearable.

And I was finally going to see her.

I arrived at the school just as she was walking out and towards her car. I was glad teachers always seemed to stay a little bit after all the kids had already left, so the parking lot was relatively empty.

I parked and jumped out, walking towards her with my arms wide, ready to pull her into a hug. But the moment I stepped near her, she halted and physically cringed away from me.

That stopped me in my tracks.

I looked over her, my heart dropping and rising and dropping again as her cold expression didn't change. For a second, I was reminded of what she was like before.

Before us.

Cold. Aloof. Mysterious.

"Mayda..."

"Junior," she whispered. "Hi."

I put my hands back down and an awkward pause swept between us. "Did you get my gift?"

"Yes. I left them in my office."

That was it. No smile. No thanks. No flush.

Fuck, fuck, fuck. She was *pissed.*

"Let's go for a drive?"

She gave a terse nod and didn't say anything. She just walked to the passenger side of the truck and hopped in without waiting for my help.

Fuck.

I had so much explaining to do.

CHAPTER 34

MAYDA

I WAS STEELING MYSELF for what felt like the inevitable. Though a small, hopeful part of me wondered if he wasn't here to dump me, to say that he preferred us to be friends. He had been ready to pull me into his arms for a hug, and he'd looked genuinely happy to see me. But this was Junior. He was always quick to offer people a smile.

The first half of the drive we spent in silence. I noted the way Junior's knuckles whitened as he gripped the steering wheel. I also noticed the dark circles under his eyes, and the fact that he was still in his work clothes. He looked... haunted. Stressed. A part of me worried about his health. I had the urge to reach across the space that separated us to grab his hand, to ask him how he was doing.

The pettier part of me wanted to bask in the prolonged silence, to let him witness my own anger, but also I just wanted to protect myself from any hurt that may have been coming my way.

So I didn't say a word. I kept myself firmly seated as he drove. I barely paid attention to where he was taking us, focused instead on gnawing at my bottom lip in worry. It took a while before he finally stopped.

Empty space surrounded us. Nothing but land and crops. Not Los Corazones, but a different spread of land on a high hill that overlooked a deep drop down into woods of dried trees.

He parked and opened his door without a word, jumping out. I followed, not wanting to be trapped inside such an enclosed space while we spoke. My heart thumped uncomfortably in my chest. We rounded the hood of the truck and I leaned my back against it, staring out at the scenery.

I didn't speak. I couldn't. The words were caught in the back of my throat. Did I want to say the words before he could? To give into the instinct to get it out and hurt before I could be hurt?

I wasn't my mother, though. Hurting Junior didn't sit right with me.

Finally, he spoke. "I'm sorry, Mayda."

I let out a slow breath and felt the tears prick the backs of my eyes. I held them at bay and channeled my anger, reminding myself that my feelings were completely valid here. "For what, exactly?"

"This week has been crazy at the rancho. I barely was able to leave without my papá on my ass."

"That doesn't answer my question, Junior."

He turned to face me. "I'm sorry I've been AWOL this week."

"Why were you?"

He rubbed the back of his neck and winced. "My parents were pissed off that I stayed the night at your house without telling them."

It was my turn to wince. "Shit."

He nodded. "Yeah."

I knew what his parents were like when they were mad. Particularly his mom. The woman was as terrifying as she was sweet.

It was a wonder he was still living…

"They wanted me to move back to the main house. You know why I can't do that. They're… *suffocating* me. And then my papá told me I was getting too distracted. He put me to work and between the rancho and homework, I barely had time to breathe, let alone text you."

"Junior…" Empathy swelled in me. Did I think his excuse was flimsy? No. It made sense. I knew the weight he carried. I was the only person who knew. I was glad he hadn't been avoiding me because of what he'd witnessed with my mom, but the way he was going about all of this? It wasn't healthy. "You need to talk to them."

His jaw worked and he huffed a breath. "You know I can't."

"Junior…" Thunder struck overhead. The sky darkened, and a part of me felt like I was witnessing a bad omen about to unfurl. "Junior, are you just going to live like this the rest of your life?"

"Carájo, Mayda, déjalo ya."

Let it go.

But I couldn't.

It wasn't in my nature to let something rest.

A slight drizzle began coming down on us, and we stayed as we were, facing one another. Something between us changed in an instant. A fire that bloomed and threatened something wild and destructive.

"You can't live like this," I urged.

"Oh, you're one to talk."

I jerked back as if he'd slapped me, my face heating.

His arms spread wide. "Your whole life is based on a lie, Mayda. You've lived with your mom's secret forever and you're trying to lecture me?" He scoffed.

And the words? They pierced me. They fucking hurt. "That's different," I whispered, feeling my voice weak in its cadence.

"It's the same thing!"

Thunder crackled. Water became a heavy stream from the sky.

"You haven't been able to talk to your mom or get her into NA. I had to do it for you. So don't come and lecture me about what I have to do with *my* parents."

I felt completely floored by his angry tone. Never, never had I heard Junior speak to anyone with the vehemence he was using against me. A second later, the words he spat registered, and my brows furrowed.

"What do you mean you had to do it for me?"

He froze, eyes widening in an 'oh, shit' expression. He clamped his lips closed immediately, a guilty expression settling over his features.

"Junior?"

He sighed. "I... I went to see your mom at the hospital."

"You did what?!" My mouth dropped open. "When?"

"The morning after..."

"I went that afternoon and she was gone." The shock I felt couldn't be described. "What the hell did you say to her? And why the fuck didn't you tell me?"

"I just went and told her to get into NA for your sake."

Embarrassment was swift as a gust of wind. My cheeks heated and not even the steady beat of rain coming harder could cool them. Bad enough he'd been witness to my shame, but he'd gone to talk to her too?

"Why would you do that?" I demanded, my voice little more than a whisper. "Why would you think doing that was a good idea and why wouldn't you tell me?"

"I didn't want to upset you. You were already so broken—"

"Broken?" My voice cracked on the word. "Is that how you see me?"

"Of course not!"

"You just said it!"

"You know I didn't fucking mean it like that. She's been bringing you down your whole damn life, Mayda. You refuse to drag her ass to NA, so I went and told her to do it for you."

The shame was replaced with rage. They battled within my body and I took a step forward. Our bodies were getting soaked. The rain came down harder. My hair started clinging to my cheeks, but all I knew was there was a storm building inside me, bubbling to the surface. Thunder cracked across the sky as my hands met Junior's shoulders and shoved.

"How dare you?! I went to find her at the hospital and she was gone! Now I know why. You scared her off."

"I was trying to help you—"

"By lying to me! By going behind my back and then ignoring me!"

"I told you why I was busy. I didn't lie to you, I just didn't have time to tell you what had happened."

"Still, none of that excuses what you did!" My shout was drowned out by another cackle across the sky. "You had no right."

He looked shamed, but I didn't let his expression get to me or cause a pang in my heart. It was inexcusable. He stepped close, but didn't reach for me. "I was helping you."

"I don't need your help with my mom, Junior. I've been dealing with her for years by myself. You scared her off and now I have no idea where she is or if she's okay or what even happened. Because you had to go and act machista and take matters into your own hands." He was silent. I should have stopped, but I pressed on. "You're trying so hard to fix my life, but you won't even fix your own."

His nostrils flared. Water slid down his face and he stepped close, his boots squishing beneath the grass. "My life is fine."

I laughed a mirthless sound. "You really think that? You really think you're just fine when you've gone around pretending to be someone you're not in front of your family? At least I've always known what I've been, Junior. I come from trash, I will always be trash. I've never fucking lied about that—" I gasped as his arm struck out, hand encircling the back of my neck. He yanked me forward, plastering me across the front of his body.

"Don't," he warned over the sound of the storm, "insult yourself like that in front of me, Mayda. Ever again."

"Let go of me." The command was whispered across wet skin. I stood on the tips of my toes, the material of my skirt pressing against the skin of my legs.

"No," he replied. "You want to leave me. I can see it in your eyes."

I was. I was going to tell him that this wasn't going to work out. We were too different. We came from different places. We would never understand each other.

I was going to say all of that, and he knew.

He shook his head furiously.

"You can't." His voice cracked with a vulnerability that I'd never heard from him before. "You can't leave me, Mayda."

My heart splintered in my chest. "We aren't compatible, Junior."

His fingers dug into the back of my neck. Not enough to hurt, but enough to send pleasure zinging down my spine.

Despite the anger and words my heart didn't mean, despite the rain and the closeness of our bodies, I wanted him.

"Tell me you were lying," he urged. "Tell me what we both know is the truth."

He wanted words. Words I wasn't strong enough to give just yet.

"Mayda..." His grip on my neck tightened and his forehead dropped to mine. "Tell me you still want me."

I did. I wanted him with every fiber of my being. And he knew it.

"Don't let this break us apart." His hand slid from my neck and down the length of my back, stopping just above the curve of my ass. "Te dije," he whispered, causing bumps of pleasure to rise along my skin. "Te dije que no te dejaré ir."

He turned and pushed my body against the hood of his car. I fell against it, a sound of startled pleasure pushing past my lips. He crowded behind me, wrenching me up by the back of the neck.

"Don't leave me, Mayda." He turned my face towards him. Water clung to his lashes. The storm raged, echoing with the same torment that lived within the both of us.

I wanted to deny him.

That was a lie.

I didn't want to deny him. I wanted to give him everything.

"I won't," I vowed. "I won't."

The kiss that came crashing down tasted like water and tears. His, mine, or both, I wasn't sure. All I knew was the salt as our tongues and teeth crashed together. Of the wild desperation of our entangled bodies and the rain that pelted against us.

Junior's hands were hot, a blazing trail that tracked across the skin at my thighs, shoving my skirt up to my hips. The hood of the truck was a cold contrast to the fingers that tore aside my panties and plunged inside without warning.

My body curved into his chest, bowing back as I screamed, tearing my mouth from his to choke down gulps of air and water.

His fingers scissored inside me, smearing my own cream against my inner walls.

"Fuck," he groaned against my neck. "Estás empapada. So fucking wet for me, cariño."

"Always," I rasped.

"Tell me again." His fingers curved deeper within me. "Tell me you won't leave me."

When I didn't answer, he grabbed the end of my hair and tugged. There was a bite of pain on my neck in which I relished. I wouldn't admit it with words, but I liked this side of him. I liked the brittle, uncontrolled dominance. Something so different from the way he presented himself in public.

"I *won't*," I promised as his lips skimmed across my own. And I knew then that it was true. A vow. Now that I had a taste of him, I couldn't imagine ever being with anyone else.

Junior was it for me. He was who I'd been waiting for, and not even my anger at him could tarnish that.

His fingers left my heat, shoving my panties down to my thighs. I gasped as he fumbled with his own belt buckle between us. I didn't see when he freed himself, but I felt his hard cock slap against my skin. Warm. So warm.

"I need you." He pushed me down flat against the hood of the truck. "Are you on the pill, Mayda?"

I barely rasped out an affirmative answer before I felt the tip of him prod my backside.

"Can I?"

He was asking permission before he entered, and something about it warmed my heart but didn't dim the arousal or urge to have him inside me.

"Yes, yes, yes."

That was all he needed before he plunged into me from behind. My chin hit the metal of the car, and I cried out as he moved. His hips snapped against mine in an angry, brutal rhythm.

He felt too good, and with every shove as he rammed in and out of me, I saw stars. My cries mingled with the thunder overhead, drowned out in the crescendo. My throat pained me and I wasn't sure if it was because I was shouting or holding back tears. Whatever the case, I pushed back against him with every thrust, the pleasure mounting to painful proportions. He gripped my hips, pushing my lower half against the cold metal of the hood.

The contrasts of temperatures sent shock waves through my body. My clit touched the cold while Junior was relentlessly hot from behind me. My orgasm crashed over me like a force then. There was no warning, no build up. It slammed through me as vicious as his thrusts. My body trembled and the rain pelting down against my sensitive skin only prolonged my release.

Junior didn't stop. His length went in and out of me, his hips moving in quick snaps, pushing me harder and harder against the vehicle. I groaned, my hands sliding down against it, trying to find purchase that wouldn't come. Holding my breath. Waiting.

When his release hit him, he let out a cry, stiffening and pumping wildly into me until his body curved over mine, keeping me pinned down against the metal.

I breathed harshly, coming down from the brutality of our love-making, my senses focusing one-by-one on everything around me.

His dick still inside. The cold, hard slap of water. The warmth his body provided to counter the skies. The hardness on either side of me. The sensitivity of my skin...

He huffed a breath near my ear, the warm blow bringing me back to reality. He whispered my name and pressed a kiss to the side of my neck. Slowly his body peeled off of mine. I pushed myself up by my palms and turned in time to see him tuck himself back into his jeans. My own skirt fell back down against my legs, the wrinkled wet material clinging to my skin. I smoothed my hands over them, setting it back below my knees.

Looking at Junior hurt. It built an ache in my chest that threatened to bring every foundation I'd built crumbling down. And yet it also promised to rebuild it anew.

His eyes looked pained, tortured, as he took me in.

I sucked in a breath, feeling the evidence of what we'd just done slide down the inside of my thighs.

"Nos vamos a enfermar," he said after a while. "Let's get in the truck."

He turned away from me and I went to my side. When we were both back in the warmth of the truck, our clothes soaking through the seats, Junior's hands lifted to the steering wheel, whitening as he grasped it.

He turned to me with slow purpose. "I'm sorry, Mayda," he whispered. "I shouldn't have gone to see your mom."

I took a breath. "I'm sorry, too. I shouldn't poke my nose in your business like that."

His jaw tightened, but he didn't say anything. If only because his phone began ringing at that precise moment. He seemed to welcome the reprieve and reached for it with trembling fingers, swiping, he pressed it to his wet cheek, uncaring.

"Bueno?"

The voice on the other end rose. Masculine, the undertone of his dad, I was sure. Junior listened, his eyes growing wider and his jaw tightening further. He didn't say anything again. Just hung up the phone and tossed it back down. A moment later, he was turning on the truck and peeling out of there.

I grappled for my seatbelt as the truck bounced down the small hill.

"Junior, what's wrong?" I clicked my seatbelt in place and held tightly to the door, feeling my gut sink low.

I waited for his response. For him to say something. Anything.

But no words ever came.

CHAPTER 35

JUNIOR

DREAD BUILT A HOME in my gut the entire way back to Los Corazones. My papá's angered, panicked voice on the other end was the only thing that had me pressing heavily down on the gas. I was aware that Mayda had asked me a question, but the sound of her words couldn't seem to pierce through my own panic as I sped back to the rancho.

Something was wrong. Something had happened. My papá needed me. I prayed to Dios on the drive there, scared at what I'd find.

When we arrived, the rain had come down even harder than before. It was a miracle we'd even made it in one piece at all. I barely parked the car before I jumped out. My botas sloshed in the water and mud and I rushed towards the stables.

"Junior!"

I ignored Mayda. The rain blurred the rancho before me, and I nearly slipped several times, before making it up to the stables where we kept the horses.

I was met with chaos.

The horses ninnied and jumped, kicking at their wooden doors while the thunder boomed overhead. Their fear was an almost palpable thing and sent shivers down my spine. And for a good fucking reason. The stables were rapidly flooding due to the water rise and the leaky roof.

I'd been meaning to fix that but hadn't had the time.

Mud squelched beneath me as I rushed to where my papá, Don Beto, and Hector were trying to wrangle one of the more spirited horses. From a far stall, I could make out my sister, Valentina, trying to calm a mother and her foal.

I gripped the reins of the stallion. This horse was one of my favorites, and I always made time for him. I hadn't had enough time for that lately, and as I whispered words of calm to him, he seemed to recognize me almost instantly.

He neighed, tossing his head back and stomping his feet before he calmed.

We led him back to another stall with a working door—he must've kicked his own down—and locked him inside.

"We need to get the water out as much as we can," Don Beto said. "Hector, ayúdame."

The two turned away, grabbing buckets and getting to work as best as they could.

Alone with my papá made nausea churn through my stomach.

"We should—"

"¿Dónde estabas?" he demanded.

"I was—"

"You said you were going on a supply run. You were gone for hours. We needed you here."

"I'm sorry, perdóname, papá. I just—"

My papá's gaze shifted over my shoulder and his eyes narrowed. The expression on his face became even angrier and caused an immediate black hole to open up inside me. It sucked away my emotions, spun me out of control, until everything I'd been feeling changed into something else. Something other.

The way his disappointed gaze roved me said more than a thousand words ever could.

And it broke me.

I turned slowly, seeing Mayda at the entrance of the barn, covered in water, shivering against the cold. She looked from the flooded stables to the horses, her eyes wide and full of compassion, then back up to me.

I forced myself to turn away from her.

"Por eso no estabas," he whispered. "Por andar de novio con ella."

The words were an accusation. The reason I wasn't here was because I was being a boyfriend to Mayda. It was true. And what I thought had been a good idea before became just another stupid thing I couldn't get right.

"You have work to do," my papá said. Like I needed the reminder.

My throat clogged as he turned his back to me in an obvious dismissal. I blinked away water from my eyes. Or maybe they were tears. I couldn't tell the difference as I turned away and walked over to Mayda.

His message had been clear.

He wanted me to focus on the important things. And to him, spending time with my girlfriend wasn't it. Once again, I'd let him down, and it never seemed to settle well within me. I hadn't known it was going to rain. I didn't even think I was going to take that long when I set out to see her.

But now my papá's voice overpowered and shoved away everything else.

Even Mayda.

I stopped in front of her.

"Mayda," I said tightly. "You need to go home."

"Do you guys need any help? It looks like—"

"Mayda!"

She flinched at my harsh tone, gazing up at me with her eyes narrowing. I felt gazes boring into my back, and I realized I must've screamed louder than I meant to.

It was hard to believe that only a short while ago, I'd been buried deep inside her, spilling my seed in such an irresponsible way. But I'd felt like I'd die if I didn't have her right then. I'd needed her more than I needed air to breathe.

And now, I needed her gone, so I could fix things with my papá.

"Go home," I repeated. "I'll call you later."

"*Really*, Junior?"

"Yes," I insisted. "Go home."

She took in a breath but didn't say another word as she turned away from me and walked away. I watched her disappear into the rain for a split second before I turned back around, finding Hector glaring my way.

I ignored him.

I ignored papá too as I went and got a bucket and helped without a single fucking word.

CHAPTER 36

MAYDA

THE TEARS THREATENED TO fall. Maybe they did, I couldn't be sure. The trek back to Junior's truck was almost a blur. I ran across the muddy rancho, my flats sticking into grass and mud with every step. I nearly tripped and fell.

He'd told me to leave. He'd *ordered* me to. It felt like every time we took one step forward, we ended up taking two back. I knew it wasn't because of me, that I wasn't the person he was mad with. He was really mad at his dad, at himself, and I had been an easy target. It was no excuse. It wasn't a fucking excuse. But I wasn't going to stand there and argue with him in front of the others.

If he wasn't brave enough to tell his parents what he really wanted out of life, that wasn't my fault. He didn't need to take his anger out on me. I was supposed to have said those words. We were supposed to have had a conversation, but we'd been derailed completely. We'd gotten lost in a moment of desperation and insanity, and then his dad had called...

My foot sunk into the mud and I let out a growl of frustration at having to pause my exit to pull my foot from the mess.

How the fuck was I even supposed to get home? My car was at the school, and Junior had his keys. Would an Uber come all the way out here in this weather?

My frustration mounted as I made my way to the truck and pulled it open to yank out my purse. I prayed the water didn't soak through the material and wet my phone. Maybe I could go up to the house under the porch and call a ride...

"Mayda?"

I slammed the door with a yelp and whirled to face Gabi. She was in a pink raincoat and boots, the hood of it shielding her face from being pelted.

"Gabi..." A sob broke out of me at the sight of her.

My best friend let out a curse and reached for me. "Let's get you inside and out of the rain," she said.

I was too weak to argue as she led me away from Junior's truck and up towards the main house. I almost dreaded running into anyone else, knowing they'd crowd around me and demand to know what had happened, and I wasn't sure I had the strength in me to explain.

Thankfully, we went in through the back door of the kitchen. Finally out of the cold storm, the warmth of the house felt like a hug wrapping around my legs and shoulders. Doña Gloria was in the kitchen, stirring what smelt like chocolate in one of her ollas de barro.

She caught sight of me and let out a soft gasp. I was glad for the water, because then she wouldn't know that what was on my eyes were tears.

"Ay, mija. You're soaked." She looked at Gabi beside me. "Take her upstairs and get her dry before she catches a chill."

Gabi grabbed my arm and tugged me away without a word. Doña Gloria didn't say a thing about the mud I was tracking through the house or complain that she was going to have to clean them up. I did slip out of my flats at the edge of the kitchen out of consideration before walking upstairs.

When we were in the safety of Gabi's room, she went to her bathroom. She ran the shower water piping hot and led me inside.

"I'll be right out here when you come out."

That was the last thing she said before the door clicked close and I was alone in the steaming room. I sighed and hurried through the motions, taking longer than I probably should have under the burning steam. Mud and rain slid off of me, and the tension knotting at my shoulders fell away too.

When I got out, there was a towel and a t-shirt and pajama bottoms waiting for me on the closed toilet seat. I dried up and slipped the clothes on then went out into her bedroom to find Gabi waiting for me, freshly changed herself, and with two steaming cups.

"Chocolate abuelita." She held her hand out with the offering. "Here, drink it before it gets cold and I'll rub vaporrú on your feet."

I sat on the bed, relishing in the feeling of being pampered for a bit while she dipped her fingers into Vicks and slid the minty gel across the bottoms of my feet, rubbing it in until it warmed my skin. When she finished, she placed a pair of fuzzy socks between my legs in silent command.

I set my mug to the side on her table and put them on. There was something about the taste of chocolate abuelita on your tongue and vaporrú on your feet that could make you feel whole again.

"Better?" Gabi asked.

"Much," I replied with a deep sigh.

"Good. Now, what's wrong?"

I knew it was coming, the interrogation part. I sunk myself into the pillows, exhaustion clinging to my bones.

"Junior and I had a disagreement." That was putting it mildly, but there were things I couldn't say. Secrets I couldn't share. Not even with my best friend.

"A disagreement," she echoed, disbelief coating her words.

"Mhm…"

"Mayda, I found you in the rain. You're rarely ever adventurous, so I know something bigger is up." She nudged my knee with her own. "Talk to me."

The words I so badly wanted to say got stuck in my throat. I was never good at expressing myself. Gabi knew that about me, and she waited a few beats before she sighed.

"Mayda, all our lives you've carried around some big secret, as if I never knew or couldn't realize…"

I felt my heart nearly stutter to a stop at her words.

"I know it's about your mom. I know… she's never there for you. She never was there for you. I think my parents knew something was up too, but you know how they are."

I didn't have a family to call my own, but I could get an idea. No one ever wanted to burst their own perfect little bubble with someone else's problems. They could pray over a rosary for you at mass and ask God to help someone else's shitty life, but when the time came to act, to help someone escape said shitty life, they turned the other cheek.

It was hypocritical, yes. A double-edged sword? For sure. It was complicated and heartbreaking. But I understood. People had other things to worry about, things more important than some stray kid that hung around them sometimes.

"You'd be right," I said. "But that isn't what this is about."

"So what did Junior do? I'll cut off his dick."

I choked, a strangled laugh coming out of me.

"I know things are tense between him and my papá. He wants Junior to focus on the rancho, but he's been distracted lately. I'm sure that hasn't been easy."

"No," I agreed, reaching for my mug of hot chocolate again. "It really hasn't."

"I also know my brother. He'd rather suffer through shit rather than talk about it. It's that machismo shit I've tried to beat out of him. Feels like he has to be strong for everyone else. And I know that's not an excuse, because I hate that shit and you know I don't believe in it, but do you think you could forgive him for being stupid?"

I'd forgive Junior anything.

I wondered what that said about me.

He could rip my heart straight out of my chest, stomp all over it, and I'd still forgive him. Was that pathetic? Probably. But I knew Junior, and I knew myself. I'd been in love with him for so long that I could hardly see him in a new light other than what I'd crafted and what he'd shown me. Did he have his faults? Obviously. He was machista. He was impulsive, and he did keep everything locked tightly behind a vault.

But everything about him ran deeper than those things. He was strong. Kind. Caring. There were so many facets to the man I now called mine, and I'd be a fool to give him up because of one misunderstanding. No matter how angry I was and could be, that I could recognize, at least.

"Yeah," I whispered, taking a sip. "I can."

Gabi smiled at me and wrapped her arm around my shoulder. "Drink your chocolate, stay the night. I'll take you home tomorrow morning. In secret if you don't want to see him right now. And when I get back, I'll kick him in the balls for you."

"Please don't."

Gabi's nose scrunched while her eyes gleamed with wicked delight. "Why? Don't wanna hurt the merchandise now that the two of you are banging?"

My face heated and she cackled at my expense.

"Shut up!"

"It's not like you guys are even discreet. He disappeared all night and nearly gave mamá a heart attack. I covered for you both, told them you'd texted me and told me he was with you, even though you didn't answer my messages that night."

I hadn't answered because I'd been worried about my own mom. They didn't know that part, and I was reluctant to tell them.

"Thanks," I said.

"Anytime. Now drink your chocolate and shut up."

CHAPTER 37

JUNIOR

I T HAD TAKEN US hours after the storm had stopped to clear out the stables. I all but crawled back home, exhausted and with the weight of my papá's disappointment pressing down on my shoulders. I closed my eyes as soon as my body hit my mattress, and when I blinked, it was morning.

And I felt guilty.

The way I'd acted with Mayda was deplorable. I'd been a fucking asshole for days, and I'd chased her away moments after I'd fucked her over the hood of my truck without protection.

Why had I turned her away?

I was embarrassed that she'd witnessed my papá's anger. I was ashamed that I'd let him down in the first place and I'd taken it out on the one person who didn't deserve it. I owed her an apology. No, more than that, I owed it to her and to us to be better when it came to our relationship.

To do that I needed to talk to my papá, needed to ask him to cut me some slack. I was drowning, barely keeping my nose and mouth above water, and he needed to know it.

I knocked tentatively on his office door, knowing he'd been in there with Gabi checking numbers in the aftermath of the storm. I entered even when he didn't answer, only I found him alone.

He grunted in greeting but didn't look up from his paperwork.

"Pa." I took a seat in front of him, feeling millimeters small. "We need to talk." He looked up then, the stern lines of his face a prominent part of him now. "About yesterday, about... a lot of things."

Knots formed in my gut as he stared intently at me, waiting for me to say what I needed to say.

"Papá, I'm sorry I lied about where I was going yesterday. I didn't leave to buy anything. I went to see Mayda."

His jaw tightened with displeasure.

"I know you want me to dedicate every waking, breathing second into the rancho, but pa, I'm suffocating. I need days off. I wanted to spend time with Mayda and..." *And have time to do homework.* I couldn't say that. I wasn't brave enough. I swallowed the words back. "I want to spend time with her."

His eyes narrowed on me. Consuming my words in slow sips like he would a glass of añejo. "Let me ask you something." He leaned forward on his desk, his gaze piercing. "¿Te vas a casar con ella?

The question startled me back in my chair. My eyes widened and I stared at him. Typical. Marriage was on his mind. For him, for my mamá, relationships were about the end game, and you should never go into one without the long term in mind.

But the question didn't scare me. It only made things clearer. I knew what I wanted.

Perhaps I always had.

"Sí," I answered. "I want to marry her one day."

His whole demeanor changed at my response. The frown disappeared, and something like relief crossed over his features. "Mayda is a good girl," he said, tapping his fingers along the desk. "She's your sister's best friend and your mamá loves her like a daughter. I was happy for you, but I had my doubts. I didn't know if you were with her for a moment or if you both were thinking about your futures."

A future with Mayda sounded fucking nice.

"I am," I said firmly. "Thinking about a future with her."

He nodded. "I was worried you were just being...¿cómo se dice? A player."

Was that the reason he'd been so adamant on telling me not to see her? He thought I was going to break her heart?

"It's not like that. It's serious."

"Que bueno." He sat back in his chair. "So, when is she moving into your place?"

I almost choked on my own spit. "We aren't—"

"I was with your mamá for a week before our parents asked us if we were going to get married. Kids these days take too long to decide what they want." His palm slapped down on the table. "Don't let time pass you by. Scoop her up and give me grandchildren before I get old and sick."

"Ay, pa." I shook my head back and forth. "There's plenty of time for that later."

He grunted and looked as though he didn't quite believe me. "Fine, then I will let you have Saturdays and Sundays to be with Mayda. But I want you to stop disappearing around here. This is your legacy, your *emperio*, and I want you to take it seriously."

And just like that, my heart sank to the pit of my stomach.

"And I want grandchildren."

"Sure, pa."

"Soon."

"Whatever you say."

With the go ahead from my papá, I went out to work. I wasn't going to press my luck by asking for the day off after we had a massive storm. Even I wasn't that foolish. He'd bended a little, and I had to meet him halfway. Even if I was still disappointed about the turn of things, even if I hadn't had the balls to tell him that I really didn't want the empire he built for me…

Maybe the real reason I couldn't tell him the truth was because I knew what question would come next.

"Then what *do* you want?"

And how could I answer him when I couldn't even answer for myself?

I was torn from my thoughts when a fist hit me in the chest. The wind left my lungs and I coughed, jerking back and rubbing my chest.

"Fuck!"

That brutal fist came flying at me again, only this time, I caught it in my palm and shoved it away.

"What the fuck?!"

"Don't take that tone with me." Gabi slapped my forehead with her other hand. "I told you if you hurt my best friend, I'd make you pay. Get ready to pay." She assumed a fighting stance, like she was going to karate chop me in the throat.

I stepped backwards, but she only followed.

"Christ, Gabi, let me explain—"

"No explanations. Only pain."

And then the crazy woman did something utterly disbelieving. Wearing inches of heels, a pencil skirt, a collar shirt, and blazer, she did exactly what she promised and *kicked*, sending the toe of her heel grazing against my cheek.

"Fuck!"

All that and she didn't even break a sweat. It was like she ate the patriarchy for breakfast. Her expression was feral and not a single strand of hair was out of place.

"Gabi, stop."

She assumed her stance once again. "No." Her leg went flying in my direction, but this time I dodged it.

"Gabi, *stop*."

"You're going to take your sorry ass out to find her and get on your knees and beg for forgiveness."

"You didn't need to go all Karate Kid on me just to say that. I was planning on doing that anyway."

She smoothed down her skirt and huffed a breath. "I was lenient with you this time, only because Mayda told me not to chop your balls off because she wants kids someday."

My brows kicked up. "Did she say that?"

"It was implied. Now go. Apologize."

"I can't right now. I have to help around the rancho."

"How about I cover for you and you go see my best friend? Right this instant."

I was reluctant to leave and lie to papá again, especially after we'd kind of reached an understanding. If I fucked this up again, he'd never let me live it down and he'd chain me to Los Corazones forever. Then I really wouldn't have time for Mayda.

"Gabi," I started to argue.

"No. You will go. Right now."

"You're so fucking stubborn."

"I *know* you're not talking to me, hermano." She scoffed. "You're the stubborn one. I can't with you. How can you and Mayda both be simultaneously so perfect for each other and so stupid?"

"What's that even supposed to mean?"

"It means you both lock yourselves up. You're both so damn secretive, so alike in many ways. But you're so dumb because you can't even talk to each other. You'd rather choke back your own feelings than lean on each other—like couples are supposed to—and drown in your own misery."

"Wow." I blinked at her. "What a beautiful description."

"Shut up. You know how Mayda is. I don't know what's going on with her, I just know that she's never had a good home life. She doesn't know what a healthy relationship is supposed to look like. You do. Even then you're still too dumb and too machista to lean on her."

"I'm not machista."

"Shut up. You are."

I felt offended. I wasn't. Not the way the old timers were. I didn't expect a wife to wait on me hand and foot. I didn't demand my woman to stay home while I brought in the money and the food. I wasn't a fucking caveman. I knew what century we lived in. I knew women were empowered, and I'd never take that away from my sisters or Mayda.

"You like to take care of everyone, so much so that you don't realize it's to your own detriment. You think you have to have all the answers, walk on eggshells, keep everyone happy."

My throat tightened because my sister was hitting the nail on the head. But how did that make me machista?

"You're too proud," she went on.

At this, I threw my head back and laughed. "Me? Have you looked in a mirror?"

She bristled. Oh yeah, she was proud and she knew it.

"You're the worst one of us." All my hermanas had their faults, and I tried not to compare them, but of us all, Gabriela was the proudest one.

"Am not."

"Are too. Especially when it comes to relationships, so you have no right to preach to me about mine."

"I—"

"Remember Carlo?"

She gave a full body shudder at the mention of her ex-boyfriend. "He chewed too loudly."

"What about Rodrigo?"

She flicked her fingers. "He left crumbs in the margarine."

"Mhm, and Roberto?"

She made a face. "He serenaded me on the third date. Without an instrument, Junior. Think about that."

"Eres odiosa."

"I am not hateful."

"You are. You find fault in everything and everyone."

"Listen, leaving crumbs in the margarine is a punishable offense. Not to mention gross."

"I leave crumbs in the margarine."

"Because you're a crummy, smelly man. Besides, we aren't talking about my relationships and the Curse of the O's. We're talking about you and Mayda."

"The Curse of the O's?"

"All my worst relationships were with men whose names ended in O's. Cursed."

I waved my hands in front of her, wanting to bring an end to the conversation immediately. "Look, this is going nowhere. I have to get back to work." I pushed past her, almost expecting her to lash out at me again.

She didn't. She let me walk away a few steps first before she called out, "You better grovel after work! She might not wait around for you forever, you know."

And fuck if those words weren't motivation enough to fix things with Mayda.

Chapter 38

MAYDA

THE KNOCK AT MY door startled me from devouring my Chinese food in peace. I sighed, setting the container aside and went to answer.

"Junior..."

He looked at me and gave a wince. "Mayda, can I come in?"

I let out a breath and stepped aside. I knew he was going to come. Gabi had all but promised me through text that she'd threatened him to get his ass in gear, against my own wishes. But besides the threats, I knew he would seek me out. That's just who he was.

"Gabi didn't spear your dick with a fork, did she?" I asked after a beat of silence once he sat on the couch.

"Not due to a lack of trying..."

I shook my head. "I asked her not to say anything to you."

"It doesn't matter if she had or not, I still would have come to find you."

"I know."

We sat across from each other, meeting each other's eyes for a long time.

"I'm sorry."

"I know."

"I shouldn't have done what I did. I shouldn't have taken my anger out on you."

"I know." I sighed and scooted closer to him on the couch. I hated the self-imposed distance between us. I hated feeling like we were miles away from each other when we were in the same room. "I'm not mad at you."

His eyebrows flicked up, his mouth dropping open. "I don't know if I believe that."

"I was at first, but I was mostly hurt. And I'm not going to say that what you did was okay, because it wasn't." I reached for his hands and we immediately threaded them together. "But I guess I'm old enough to know that we both have our issues, and sometimes when people have problems that are unresolved they lash out or react in ways they shouldn't." His hand tightened against mine.

I'd actually thought long and hard about this. Did I have a right to be upset? Of course. I thought we both did. But I also knew that we'd said things that were true. I wouldn't pretend to know what it was like to be in his position, just like he could never pretend to know what it was like to be in mine.

"I shouldn't try to fix your life when I have my own secrets, you were right."

"Mayda." He pulled me close, nearly sprawling me in his lap. "I shouldn't have said that. It was such an asshole thing to say."

"It was," I readily agreed. "I'm not saying it wasn't. But you were right, regardless. I don't know what it's like for you. You have so much riding on your shoulders, and I can only give you my opinion from an outside perspective. I think what needs to happen now is that we both move forward from this. We both obviously have our own issues we need to work through. So instead of fighting and arguing, I think we need to listen and be more understanding. Not be so quick to call it quits."

He let out a breath, so heavy I wondered how long he'd been holding it. "Mayda, I don't fucking deserve you," he whispered. "I don't. I've been a huge asshole, I've pushed you away when it's taken me so fucking long to even get you in the first place. You're right. There's... shit I need to get through. Shit I need to work on. I promise I'll try and do better."

"That's all I want," I whispered. "For us to try."

He pulled me onto him then and I ended up straddling his lap. He held me close enough that the beats of our hearts synchronized. Our warmth seeped into each other in a way that felt safe, comforting. My body relaxed against his. We breathed each other in. I inhaled his spicy scent, burying my nose into the crook of his neck.

"I'm sorry I went to talk to your mom without your permission, and I'm sorry I didn't tell you about it right away afterwards," he whispered.

I pulled away with a sigh, closing my eyes against the onslaught of emotions. When I opened my eyes again, I found his filled with regret.

"Even if you hadn't gone to see her, I have a feeling she would have disappeared regardless."

"You haven't seen her since?"

Worry tugged through my gut at the reminder. "No," I said. "But this happens sometimes. She appears then disappears for weeks..."

"But this was the first she's OD'd?"

I shrugged. "The first time I witnessed it anyway. But even so, she does this a lot."

Junior opened his mouth to ask more questions, but I didn't want to talk about my mother right then. I didn't want her phantom presence coming between us. I didn't want to think about her at all. At least not until she showed up begging for money once more.

"It's okay, Junior," I reassured him. "She'll turn up." He looked worried, so I gifted him with a soft smile. "She always does."

Things changed for the better. With school occupying most of my time and the rancho occupying most of Junior's, we found our own bliss on the weekends. Being with him, going on dates, chilling with Gabi and her sisters, hanging at Los Corazones, it was like when we were younger but better. Being at their house only kept me away from my own.

I should have felt guilty for not being there in case my mom showed up, but I was floating too high in my own happiness that I didn't think about her save for the fleeting moments I stepped into the house for a change of clothes. I'd look around, but there was never any sign that she'd been there at all, so I shrugged it off.

She'd be back. I recalled those words to Junior. She always came back.

Her absence didn't leave worry behind in those spaces. My new routine that involved Junior, the Águila-Gutierrez family, and sex—lots and lots of sex—filled the empty parts of me.

Sometimes after I'd climb down from the high of the multiple orgasms Junior gave me, it was to let that cynical voice inside me out to whisper.

This feeling won't last.

I always squelched it before it could grow louder, snuggling closer to Junior like his presence could dispel the negativity my irate mind drove me towards. For the most part, he could, except in those moments when I broached the subject about his career path and wanted to give him suggestions.

He tried to shut down on me, even when I was primed and ready to talk about it. Those were the only moments when things seemed tense between us, but as promised, we worked through it. We talked it out instead of trying to shut each other out, no matter how hard it was to find the words.

Being a part of the Águila-Gutierrez fold as Junior's girlfriend was an entirely different game than being there as Gabi's friend. They treated me with the same veneration they always had, but the looks in their eyes were different. Now, they openly talked about weddings and grandchildren, the latter of which had me choking on my morning café.

It was no secret that I'd been spending the night at Junior's place. If I'd expected things to be awkward because of it, it wasn't. Except for Gabi's inappropriate eyebrow waggling, no one else mentioned the way we stumbled in for breakfast, Junior's arms clinging to my waist like he didn't want to let me go.

That had been this morning. I'd laughed as we waddled into the kitchen, his lips pressing slow, torturous kisses against the side of my neck while I tried to shove him away and preserve a modicum of modesty. He'd laughed against my skin, not caring that his family caught a glimpse of his cheesy, loving ways.

He liked to flaunt our relationship around. Because of it, any unease I might have been feeling about who I was and where I came from dissipated. He was happy with me, and I was happy with him.

I was over the moon with this new life I found myself a part of.

I should have known that good things never lasted.

Minutes after sitting down for breakfast, there was a knock at the front door. After staring back and forth at one another, trying to silently gauge who it could be, Señor Águila stood and went to answer it. He was gone a few moments before he came back, only he wasn't alone.

"Officer Reynaldo!" Mamá Claudia stood up to greet the police officer who found himself in the dining room, a grave, subdued air about the older man. "Sit! Would you like a plate?" She started shuffling towards the kitchen, but the small shake of his head had her stopping.

"Thank you, Claudia, but no. I'm afraid I didn't come for that. I actually came to speak to Mayda. In private."

I froze, spoon halfway to my mouth. Setting it down on my plate, I stood, my gaze flickering over him. His features were etched in grave lines, and while I couldn't exactly read the older man, I could certainly read the tone surrounding him.

Dread curdled in my stomach and I felt my legs pushing me stiffly in his direction. I forced a smile to my lips, but it was wobbly and strained as I led him into the living room. I could feel the curiosity of the others behind me until the door separating the dining room and living room closed.

It wasn't my house, but Mamá Claudia would be cross with me if I didn't mind my manners, so I gestured at the couch. "Would you like to sit?" My voice sounded hollow and far away and I wasn't even sure why.

Growing up, I'd learned to fear police officers, only because my own mom put the fear of them into me.

"They'll take you away from me," she would whisper with her eyes bloodshot and vomit staining the side of her mouth. In those moments, I could have believed she cared about what happened to me, when she wasn't drowning herself in bottles of rum.

I'd known Officer Reynaldo for years, and still his presence made my hands shake. I had to force myself to remember that I was no longer that little girl. That he couldn't take me from my mother and throw me into foster care. I was a grown woman.

"Of course, please sit." Officer Reynaldo didn't sit until I'd done so first, my back straight as I watched emotions war over his features.

"I'm not sure how to say this, Mayda..." He ran a hand over his hair. Suddenly, he looked older than his years, and the solemn tone of his words made my nose sting. "We've been looking all over for you to let you know..."

"Let me know what?" Hollow words that didn't sound in my ears. I felt like a robot saying them. White noise rushed in my ears and my chest felt too tight. Like someone had grabbed it in their fist and was slowly squeezing the life out of me.

The impending sense of dread just rose higher, and I knew, I knew why he was here. I'd waited for this day. I had hoped for it in my darker, more violent and younger years.

But as Officer Reynaldo leaned forward and grasped my shaking hand in his, I couldn't stop the blow his words caused. "It's your mother, Mayda. She was found dead last night."

My world tilted off its axis. One moment, I'd been floating contentedly through the solar system along with the other planets and the next, I was falling, getting sucked into a void. Vaguely, I heard the words Officer Reynaldo continued to speak.

"Overdose."

"Alleyway."

"I'm sorry."

The world slipped beneath my feet, and while a part of me wanted to crumble, to curl up into a ball and cry for the mother I used to know and the fact that she was gone, I could do nothing but sit there with his hand in my own while my mind raged a war I would never win.

I was falling, and there was no one present to pick up the broken pieces of me.

CHAPTER 39

MAYDA

NUMBNESS WAS LIKE THE bitter cold. It invaded your veins, slipped through the cracks and attacked every ounce of warmth within you. I felt nothing, down to my soul. Tears didn't touch my eyes, the heartbreak didn't fester, because it wasn't there to begin with.

There was nothing but a hollow echo where emotions were supposed to live.

The initial truth had shock invading my system and after a minute or two of complete silence, of seeing faces crowd around me, I smoothed my hands across my jeans and stood up, staring down at Officer Reynaldo.

"I want to see the body."

We'd followed him—me and the entire Águila-Gutierrez clan—to see my mother's still body. Pale. Waxy. She looked almost like a doll. I'd never seen her so still, but in that moment, the cold swept over me.

I took a breath and turned away from her. I barely registered Junior's expression, let alone anyone else's.

I began planning the funeral with an almost eerie calm. The only reason I knew that was because Gabi had described my demeanor in that manner more than once.

Preparing for funerals was hard work, work that couldn't be done with tear-stained eyes and a broken heart. So I did it. I continued living, breathing, working. I went home to face the hollow skeleton of a house that felt almost as empty inside as I did, only to get a change of clothes and go back to Junior's place. Even then I only stayed there at his own insistence.

Nothing else mattered except getting through this.

Everyone around me treated me like a fragile thing on the verge of breaking. It was hard to contend with that reality. The reality in which they'd all found out my mom overdosed in an alley and didn't bat an eye. They didn't judge her, but they'd gathered around me like I needed the support.

But I was fine.

I was okay.

That was something they couldn't seem to accept.

When the day of the funeral finally came, I slipped on a black dress that hit down to my calves. Junior was in the shower, but I was ready, so I decided to head up to the main house to see if Gabi was ready too. I slipped in through the back door, finding Doña Gloria in her regular position behind the stove, stress cooking.

She turned when she saw me. Everything about her screamed pity. Her old face softened and she rushed to meet me, grasping my hands and pulling me deeper into the kitchen. "Mija." She sniffled. "How are you feeling? Would you like some chocolate?"

I didn't comment on how it was hot as hell outside. Too hot for a warm beverage. I didn't say anything as she guided me towards the couch and sat me down. She moved quickly, her every movement motherly as she grabbed a throw blanket and set it across my legs, tucking the edges beneath my thighs.

"Wait a second." She rushed back to the kitchen then came back out with a mug in her hand. "Here, drink this. It will help make you feel better."

It felt like only a few days ago when I'd been drinking this same chocolate in Gabi's room, letting her rub vaporrú on my feet. Then, I'd felt whole after sipping the sweet liquid.

Now, I felt nothing.

Yet dutifully I sipped.

Then Gabriela came downstairs and she was followed by her sisters. Usually the storm of women were enough to bring a smile to my lips as they chatted animatedly. Today, they were morose. Dressed in black, the color subdued their vibrant skin tones. It looked like it didn't belong on their bodies. Neither did the matching frowns all four of them wore.

Gabriela's hair was pulled back into a tight bun, giving her a severe expression as she searched me for a hint of emotion I wouldn't show. Ximena's usual pigtails were tamed back into a ponytail, though some curls escaped their elastic and curled over her cheeks. Sofia wore her hair in a long braid down her back. Valentina's hair waved down her shoulders, though she looked very mature in her black, high-necked dress.

"I just came to see if you were all ready." I set the mug aside on the coffee table, pushed aside the blanket, and stood. "It's almost time to leave. Junior was in the shower."

Gabriela stared at me. Her sisters stood a little ways behind her, deferring to her almost, in their actions. They stared at me with equal wariness. Maybe that should have annoyed me, but I didn't feel anything. Nothing at all.

"You okay, Mayda?" Gabi's brow lifted a fraction.

"I'm fine. Are your parents ready to go?"

Her sisters looked back and forth between us like they were watching a soccer match.

"Almost."

There was silence, and I took a moment to count through the list of all the things I had to do in my head. I'd tried to give my mom a decent funeral, though it required heavy expenses, expenses Junior and his family helped me cover. In the end, I'd decided to cremate her and toss her ashes onto her own grave.

She wouldn't have wanted a huge fanfare, and there wasn't anyone besides us heading to her funeral anyway. She'd lost all her friends at the bottom of a booze bottle so long ago. And now she was finally gone too.

The silence was eventually broken when their parents and Junior came to the living room. Doña Gloria and Hector soon followed. I'd tried to convince Señor Águila not to cancel work that day, but he'd ignored me, giving me a weird look as I'd said the words.

"Ready to go?" Junior asked, wrapping his arm around my shoulders. He'd been clinging to me ever since the news was given to us. Careful not to leave me alone for too long, though never crowding too close. He was there in case I needed his shoulder, however unnecessary that was.

"Ready," I agreed, leaning into him.

The funeral itself was a quiet affair. The father was only there for Mamá Claudia's and Abuelita Mari's benefit. I wasn't even sure if my mom actually believed in God. She'd never made us go to church before, but it felt necessary to have him there, whispering a few words about how Heaven had gained another soul.

I wasn't sure anyone present believed that.

I certainly didn't.

When it was done, and the father said his final blessing, I walked over to the urn that held her ashes. There was a tombstone she wouldn't be buried beneath, carved with nothing but her name, date of birth, and date of her death.

Did it make sense to have a headstone with no body beneath it? I wasn't sure. Junior had insisted, though, despite knowing about the cremation. He said I might want to visit her in the future.

I wouldn't but hadn't argued. It was easier to just go along with it. Get the whole affair over with.

I held the urn in my hands. It was heavy, weighing my arms down.

I stared at it. At the porcelain that held the ashy remains of my mother.

"Let's get back to Los Corazones," Mamá Claudia suggested. "We can get some food in you. You look skinny, mija."

I went to pull the top off the urn.

"Mayda," Junior whispered, appearing at my side quietly. "Are you sure you want to do that?" His voice held more pain than mine ever could.

I looked into his distressed face and gifted him what felt like my first smile in weeks. "I'm sure," I replied. "I want this over with."

Pulling the top off the urn, I walked towards the tombstone and proceeded to dump the contents across the grass.

Gray ash blew with the wind, spreading over the blades. Like snow settling over the earth. Like the white powder my mom liked to snort through her nostrils.

As the ash finally settled against her stone, I stared one last time at the engraving.

LUCIANA JIMÉNEZ

Then, I turned away. Finally, it was done.

My mother was gone.

Following the funeral, I busied myself until exhaustion settled down to the bone. It was easy to fall into a routine that occupied most of my time. I spent day and night pouring over documents on my students, meeting with them against the principal's better wishes, with an almost burning, desperate need to help them.

In the evenings I returned to the rancho and ate dinner with Junior's family, and I tried to ignore the glances they all sent me from across the dinner table like I was some fragile creature at the point of breaking. Nobody brought up my mother, or maybe that was because I didn't give them the chance to do so. As soon as I inhaled my meal, I went back to Junior's house where I'd taken up residence. Just the idea of going back home to an empty house made me cringe.

I wasn't sure why. It wasn't like my mother was ever there when she was alive, so going back there shouldn't have mattered. For some reason, it did. It mattered. And like everything else, I shoved it down into that same place below the numbness.

At nights I laid next to Junior, our bodies barely touching, and I stared into the darkness until a dreamless sleep claimed me. Then I'd wake up the next morning and do it all over again.

And again.

And again.

It felt easy to fall into nothingness when the ground beneath me became a black hole, something I could fall through with flailing hands and there was no wall and no rope and nobody there to catch me.

Until they were.

The door to Junior's house opened. Tonight, he'd told me he wanted to eat in instead of at the main house with his entire family; he was working late at the rancho, so I promised I'd make a meal for the both of us. The kitchen was being filled with aromatic spices and arroz and carne de guisado.

My mom had never taught me to make it, but I'd found a recipe online from a Boricua who made Puerto Rican dishes that looked divine. I found calm in cooking.

"Hey," I greeted with a soft smile over my shoulder. "Food's almost ready."

He was silent and the quiet unnerved me, making me turn. He was in his work clothes, a t-shirt and jeans, boots, and a vaquero hat perched on his head. With his elbows pressed against the countertop, he leaned forward.

"You look cute with that hat."

He didn't reply.

"You okay?"

"Mayda, we need to talk."

Nothing good ever came from those words. I tried not to freeze up like instinct demanded. Instead, I slowly turned off the heat of the stove and turned fully in Junior's direction. I steeled myself, searching his face for an inkling, a hint of what this could be about.

"Is something wrong?" I could feel my heart beating faster. After days of shoving feelings aside, that single sentence put me on the edge of a panic attack.

"Yes." He gave a pause. "Something's wrong with you."

I blinked, unsure I'd heard correctly. "What?"

"Mayda, it's been days. Days since your mom died and has been buried, and I haven't seen you shed a single tear."

"So that means something is wrong with me?" I scoffed. "Very nice." I wanted to turn away from him and this whole conversation, but his gaze demanded my attention.

"I've just never seen you act so cold. I'm worried about you. Like you're shoving everything down. It's not healthy."

I wanted to snap at him, but I was careful as I measured my words. "I'm fine. Just because I'm not crying doesn't mean I'm unwell. Besides," I tried for levity, "I thought guys didn't like it when girls cried anyway."

He gave me a scowl and pulled his hat off. "You know I'm not like that. I just don't want to see you keep it locked in. I don't want you to shut me out. Talk to me. Please."

My hands waved helplessly through the air. "What do you want me to say?"

"I want you to be honest with your feelings. I won't force you to talk to me if you don't want to but give me *something*, Mayda. Anything."

"Junior, there's nothing to say." A knot formed in my throat, one that had no business being there in the first place.

"Of course there's plenty to say, Mayda. Your mom is dead."

"You think I don't know that?!" I exploded. I hadn't meant to raise my voice, but the shout came out of me, days of shoving down anger and frustration and so much more finally bubbled up. I'd tried to keep my composure, but I couldn't. Everything I'd pushed and pushed rose up and poured out of me. All of my heartbreak shoved between the cracks of my heart, dripping sadness in my voice. "You think I don't know that she's gone?! I tossed her ashes on the ground. I saw her body. I—" I broke up, feeling hot, fat tears splash against my cheeks. I used the back of my hand to wipe them away, and I tried to gather myself before I faced him again. "She's dead, Junior. She's dead and I think the worst part about it is that I don't feel anything at all."

There it was.

The terrible secret.

The one I'd been too ashamed to say out loud, finally out in the open.

"Mayda..." His face contorted into an expression of pity, shock, and remorse.

"No, you wanted me to talk? That's the truth. I knew this day would eventually come. It didn't matter how long I wished it, I knew she wasn't going to get better, be sober. I knew it was only a matter of time for someone to call me and say they found her body." Now that the words were flowing, they couldn't stop. And with every shout, I stepped closer to Junior until I was nearly a step away. "I have been preparing my heart for this moment for years. That's the ugly truth. I mourned the loss of my mom a long time ago. Seeing her body? I felt nothing. Nothing except relief."

There was a moment of silence as those ugly words sunk in. The reason I pushed forward. The reason I was numb. I'd spent my entire life feeling. I'd spent my entire life worrying about her, crying over her. When I'd seen her body, it felt like I had no more tears left to shed.

It was shameful. What kind of a daughter was I?

"That's the truth, Junior. The truth is, I'm a monster. She's dead, and I'm numb, and it's like nothing has changed except for the fact that I don't have to worry about my shit getting stolen anymore. So if I haven't spoken about it, that's why. Because you'll know what a bitch I really am deep down."

Junior shook his head and stepped close, crowding me with his presence. He cupped my chin and tilted my head up, swiping away at my tears with his thumbs, but still they flowed.

"You have a right to your feelings," he said. "You aren't a monster. You aren't a bitch. Do you hear me? It doesn't matter what you say, I know you loved your mom. No matter how much you pretend to be unaffected. No matter how much you pretend you don't. I know you loved her, cariño. I also know that despite that, you deserved better, and you never got it. But you can mourn her. You can feel guilty. You can love her, hate her. You can feel all the things at the same time."

A sob choked out of me and I dropped my head against his chest, feeling the beat of his heart. Everything poured out of me. Every word I didn't say, he read between the lines. It didn't matter how often I tried to push him away, to prove what kind of a monster I felt I was inside sometimes, Junior was there to pull me out of that.

I sobbed, shoulders wracking up and down. I felt like I had finally landed on the ground, suffering the aftermath of days within the darkness. Of pain and broken bones. Maybe this feeling was what I was trying to avoid. This agony clawing out of my chest.

Junior's arms eased the ache as they wrapped tightly around me. His kiss against the top of my head grounded me to earth, but the tears never stopped flowing.

"She's dead," I whispered against the material of his shirt. It smelt like sunlight, hay, and horse, and that special spicy scent that was all him. "She's dead, and I never got to say goodbye."

"She knew you loved her," Junior whispered.

"The last thing I said to her was really mean."

That day in the kitchen, I'd thrown my money at her. I'd insulted her.

And I would be forced to live with that forever.

"It's okay, cariño."

"I loved her."

"I know you did."

"I didn't want her to die."

"I know you didn't."

And Junior spent the rest of the night holding me as I let the tears flow, finally allowing myself to feel what I hadn't dared before.

Finally letting myself mourn.

In the only way that I knew how.

CHAPTER 40

JUNIOR

MAYBE GABRIELA WAS RIGHT. Maybe I had a proclivity for trying to fix things, but it was because of that I was able to break through to Mayda and get her to open up to me.

She all but lived with me since we discovered what had happened to her mom. Slowly, the empty space in my closet was occupied with stacks of her clothes. Her toothbrush sat next to mine in the bathroom. Even her favorite mug had taken up a permanent residence on the counter next to mine.

It was nice sharing that space with her. It reminded me of my papá's words. About marriage and grandchildren. It warmed my chest to know that if there was one thing certain in my future, it was her.

My career choice was still up in the air. I was reaching the final dregs of school and spent weekends and late nights cramming for exams with Mayda's gentle help. I was exhausted more often than not and tried not to dwell on the fact that soon I'd graduate and I still didn't know what I wanted.

"I sense a darkness on the horizon," Abuelita Mari whispered, pulling me from my thoughts.

She was bundled on the couch with her crocheted scarf, even though it was hot out. She wrapped the thing closer around her shoulders and shivered.

She'd been like this since the funeral. Distant. Muttering on about superstitions that nobody else believed.

I sighed, indulging her. "What do you mean, abuelita?"

She turned to look at me, a haunted expression in her eyes. "People die in threes, mijo. That's the rule of things. Dios is coming to claim more lives. Mark my words."

A chill slid down my back and I tried to shove the sensation away. Her words felt like an omen. Like scary stories meant for the dark.

"Ay, abuelita, don't talk like that."

She made the sign of the cross and dug into the pockets of her sweater to pull out a rosary.

"I'm going to pray," she whispered. "Care to join me?"

Eesh.

I wasn't a nonbeliever, but there was something about being forced to go to church as a kid, being pulled by the ears and forced to sit and confess on my knees to a father who looked down his big nose at me, that put me off of prayer.

"No gracias, abuelita. I'm going to head home and wait for Mayda."

She nodded in distraction, her fingers sliding over the white beads as her mouth began to mutter her Padre Nuestro.

I left the main house. It was relatively quiet with Ximena and Sofia locked away in their room and Gabriela out in her office crunching numbers. I wasn't sure where mamá was, but Doña Gloria was in her domain, preparing a late lunch and dinner.

I waved to her as I left, turning down her offer of agua fresca as I went. Beads of sweat trickled down my temples from the afternoon sun. While work was still on full blast, I'd decided to take a break and greet Mayda when she got home.

It was probably for my own reassurance rather than hers. She was healing these past few weeks as well as could be expected. That numbness that had lived within her since the funeral had disappeared and she'd allowed herself to actually talk about her feelings.

She'd told me she wanted to see a therapist, to heal her hurt inner child and get rid of the bitterness that was left behind.

I knew she still hadn't talked to Gabi or my parents about her mom. At least, not in detail. I didn't push, but I had a feeling she was embarrassed with them knowing who her mom really was.

But they hadn't looked at her any differently. In fact, they looked at her with much more reverence than before. As in awe of her as I was. That someone who had such a hard life had become so kind herself.

She was resilient. Sometimes too much. But I knew she would be okay.

I walked up the small walkway to my place, pushing my way inside. I still wore a smile on my face as I went to my living room, but the smile immediately fell the moment I saw my papá, standing over my laptop.

"Papá?"

He whirled to face me, every contour of his face marred in anger. I was taken back by the expression.

"¿Me puedes explicar qué es esta mierda?" He shoved my laptop across the table, the screen facing me.

Open on an email from my school.

An email about my upcoming graduation details.

My heart dropped at the sight of it. My stomach tying in knots. A rush of shame swept over me, quickly followed by anger.

"Why are you going through my things?"

I'm not sure where I found the audacity. As far as I saw it, as far as anyone saw it, I was living on my papá's property. He'd given me life. This house. It was as much his as it was mine and he had every right to go through my shit as he saw fit.

"Don't take that tone with me, cabrón. I came in to borrow your laptop because mine isn't working and then I catch this mierda. I didn't go to school, but I'm not stupid. I know what this is."

I felt cornered, put on the spot. My mind worked on overdrive trying to come up with an excuse, anything I could use to explain my way out of this, but all I did was come up blank. What could I even say? The truth was glaringly obvious.

So I did the only thing I could think to do. I deflected.

"You had no right to go through my things."

He glared, the creases between his brows an obvious sign of anger, the veins standing out against his dark skin. "I had every right," he ground out. "You may not be living at the main house anymore, but you live under my roof. You're my son, and you've been lying to me!"

"I've been lying because I don't have any other choice!" I shouted.

I couldn't help the words tumbling out of me. Like a glass being filled for too long, I reached the end of my limit and was spilling forth everything I'd ever been too afraid to say.

"Yes, I got myself a college degree in child psychology. What's wrong with that?"

"What's wrong is that you lied to me. Why do you even want a degree when you have the rancho? You have everything you need."

He ground his teeth together. "Is this why you've been lying to me? Going off at all hours, ditching your responsibilities? For this?" He gestured at the laptop. "You've been neglecting the rancho for what? A community college degree?"

"This is why I couldn't tell you!" I waved a hand through the air, in his direction, the scowl on his face. The one I knew would be there if he ever found out the truth.

Everything I ever feared was coming true, and he wondered why I couldn't talk to him. Because when I did, he judged. Immediately. Why couldn't he be the type of parent to ask what *I* wanted? Why couldn't he be the type of father to guide me towards my dreams instead of on a pathway he'd set out for me?

And why had I just taken it all these years?

"You're judgemental," I went on, not caring how his cheeks reddened. "You wouldn't have taken me seriously."

"Taken what seriously? W*hat*, Junior? You think you have a future in this? What would you even use this degree for? You've wasted your money!"

I let out a growl of frustration, yanking at my short hair from the roots. "That's exactly why I can't talk to you or tell you anything. Because you will always put anything I say down. You don't believe in me."

"I believe in you," he argued.

"No, you don't! You believe I can run the rancho, but you don't think I'm good for anything else. But this is *my* life."

"Your life?" His dark eyes gleamed with a challenge. "And what will you do with your life? With your fancy psychology degree?"

The dreaded question came up. As inevitable as it was. I knew he was going to ask it, and yet somehow it still floored me completely. What was I going to do with my degree? My heart beat faster against my chest, and every single thought fell away because the truth has always been there.

I had no fucking idea what I was going to do.

I'd wanted that title so desperately, and I had it. But what would I use it on? That was the question. And because I didn't have an answer, my papá knew that meant I didn't have a plan. And to him, that was as unprepared as I could get, which made every dream and idea worthless.

He clicked his tongue and shook his head at my lack of response. His big arms crossed against his chest and he huffed a breath. "You don't even know what you want for yourself. You've been irresponsible, leaving your duties for this, for dreams and uncertainty, when you have a whole rancho that needs you."

"I don't want it!"

His eyes widened at my shouted words. At the vehemence. At the anger and resentment I'd accumulated for years for him and his precious rancho. For thrusting me into something without taking the time to ask me if it was really something I wanted.

"I want to be more than a stupid farmer," I spat out, the bitterness laced on my tongue. "I want to be more than what you conformed to."

The words sounded ungrateful. I knew that. But I couldn't stop myself from saying them. Because, as ungrateful as they sounded, they were the truth. My papá wanted me to be a better, more successful version of him. Unfortunately, our definitions of success were different. We wanted different things, and he thought that if I didn't take what was being offered, I would surely fail.

"That's what I am to you?" he whispered. "A stupid farmer?"

"Not you. Just—"

"No, no. Te entiendo. I understand exactly what you mean. I worked my ass off to give you a better life than I had. Forgive me for wanting to make your life easier than I had it."

I rolled my eyes, stepping back on the balls of my feet. "Here we go again. You're going to tell me how hard you had it, how grateful I should be. I never said I wasn't, pa. I love you. I admire you. But this?" I waved a hand through the air. "This isn't my life. It's not for me."

His face reddened with anger. He uncrossed his arms and stepped forward. "You won't be anything if you pursue that career. You don't even know what you want to do with it. Dejáte de pendejadas, Junior. Stop with the nonsense and get back to work. Do something that actually matters."

My anger rose. There he was, dismissing everything I was telling him. Like it didn't matter. Like my hopes and dreams were less than his, than anyone else's. We only mattered when we were following him around. When we wanted a slice of his demands.

That wasn't fair.

"No," I spat. "I'm done with farming. I'm done with crops. I'm done! It's time I found my happiness instead of listening to you!"

"Don't talk to me that way!"

"I'll talk in whatever way I want! I'm done!"

My papá stepped forward, opening his mouth to speak, but all that came out was a gasp. His cheeks puffed and his hand shot out to grab at his shoulder. He doubled over, body toppling to the floor.

In that moment, I forgot about my anger. I forgot about my frustrations. I shot towards him, holding his body up as he gasped for breath.

"Papá!"

His eyes rolled and fluttered closed.

"Papá! Papá, can you hear me?" I grasped him tightly, unsure of what else to do.

"Junior?" Mayda's voice drifted towards me. "Junior, what's wrong?"

"Call an ambulance!" I shouted, cradling my papá's body to my chest, rocking him back and forth. "Hurry! Please hurry!"

I heard her dialing and speaking in the background. For a moment, taken back to a time when I'd done the same for her and her mom in an alleyway. My abuelita's words came back to me in that instant.

"People die in threes, mijo."

I sucked in a breath, shutting those words out of my system, cradling my papá closer, and I whispered, "Diosito, por favor. Mi papá no. Mi papá no."

God, please.

Don't take him.

Please.

CHAPTER 41

JUNIOR

BLINDING WHITE LIGHT AND the smell of bleach and antiseptic. Of life and of death. The hospital bustled with activity, life scurrying along around me while I sat with my head hanging low between my legs and my family around me while we waited on news of my papá.

The tears burned behind my eyelids but didn't fall. The knot in my throat was a constricting force that threatened to choke me.

"People die in threes, mijo."

My abuelita's words haunted me, swirling around my head like buzzing pests I couldn't get rid of. So again, I prayed. To someone, anyone who would listen to my pleas, joining in on my mamá's and Doña Gloria's whispered words low enough that no one could hear me. No one but God, that is.

My sisters paced the hospital floor, each of them wearing their own worry in different ways. Ximena by twisting her paintbrushes in circles, Sofia by biting her nails down to the quick, Valentina by bouncing on the balls of her feet, while Gabriela walked and glared like an army commander, all but silently demanding news from any passing nurse.

Hector sat near me, his presence and support something I needed desperately. And Mayda...

Her hands slid across my back, offering comfort that wouldn't come.

We'd heard no word since we'd arrived, no reassurance, and the lack of any information made me want to scream.

"Family of Damián Águila?"

I shot to my feet. We all crowded around the unsuspecting doctor, who took a cautious step back as we descended on him. My mamá pushed to the front of the pack, her eyes red-rimmed but her shoulders back, head tilted up.

"I'm Damián's wife," she said shakily.

The doctor offered her a smile. "Your husband is a very lucky man. He's going to be okay."

My mamá's knees buckled, and I felt my own relief crash against my body like a wave to shore. I nearly fell to my knees to thank God right then. He was okay. My papá was okay, and that was all that mattered.

"Gracias a Dios." She made the sign of the cross and clasped her hands together.

"Your husband isn't out of the clear just yet, though. Unfortunately, he had a heart attack. We were able to treat him, but there were complications that required surgery."

"What kind of surgery?" Gabi demanded.

"We found a build-up of plaque in his arteries. This prevents the blood from flowing and pumping the way it needs to. We performed the surgery to remove the build-up and get his heart pumping again. This problem is caused by diet, alcohol, and even stress."

The room went in circles that wouldn't stop or slow down. I couldn't remove my tongue from the roof of my mouth, too heavy to even speak.

"He was very lucky to arrive when he did. He's out of surgery now and is resting. He's stable but can't receive visitors quite yet. The hardest part is going to be recovering."

After exchanging a few more words with the doctor, he left and we all breathed a collective sigh of relief. I almost melted to the floor but kept myself upright. I had to force myself to be strong, even if I didn't feel it inside. My sisters and mamá needed me to keep my shit together. While he was in this hospital, I had to take the mantel. It was up to me to be the man of the house.

I took a breath. "I'm going to stay here," I declared to everyone, drawing their attention towards me. "I'll stay and wait for him to wake up. There's nothing you can do now except go home. Get some rest."

My mamá scoffed and shook her head. "Damián is my husband. If anyone is going to stay and wait for him to wake up, it's me."

I wanted to argue. It was my fucking fault he was lying in this hospital bed in the first place. We'd argued. I'd yelled. His heart hadn't been able to handle it. I'd been too cruel. Too selfish. And these were the consequences of that.

But I bit hard enough on my tongue to draw blood. My mamá didn't deserve my ire, and I couldn't bring myself to fight, too frightened that what had happened to my papá would happen to her too.

"Take your hermanas home," she continued. "I'll stay the night and call you all when he wakes up. Go back to the rancho and rest."

I swallowed past the lump in my throat and nodded. We all said our goodbyes to her, giving her hugs and kisses on the cheek before I led them out. I'd rushed here in my truck and Gabi had driven my other sisters, Doña Gloria, and Hector, all of them crammed into her car.

We divided ourselves into the two vehicles, and drove away from the hospital in silence.

At the rancho, my footsteps were heavy as they carried me up to the main house. I could hardly focus when Hector pressed a hand to my shoulder, offering me a squeeze and a nod of strength.

Doña Gloria stopped me with a fierce, motherly hug. "I'll pray for him." She whispered the promise right before making the sign of the cross on me. I kissed her fingers when she put them up to my lips and let out a small breath of relief when she turned away and waded through the walkways up towards their home.

"Junior?"

I blinked and Mayda was in front of me. I wasn't sure how long I'd stood there and stared, but Hector and Doña Gloria were no longer in my line of vision, so it must have been for some time.

"Your sisters went inside and up to bed, though I don't think they'll be getting much sleep tonight. I checked on Abuelita Mari, too. She's fine and finally resting after I gave her the news."

I couldn't find it in me to say a word. I turned from Mayda and began the walk back up to my place. I was supposed to see how my sisters were, but she'd taken care of that, and now that I was faced with the actual task, I couldn't bring myself to face them. Not after what I did. Not when it was my fault he was set up in that hospital in the first place.

I'd caused the stress that made his heart go out.

Me.

Seeing their tear-stained cheeks would be a stark reminder of that, and I already carried the guilt with me. I likely would forever.

I could hear Mayda's feet shuffling behind me as we made the trek up to my place. Each step forward surmounted my rage, making it build. By the time we went inside, I couldn't stop staring at the spot it had happened. At the spot where he doubled over.

That could have very well been his last moment alive. And the last thing I would have said to him would have been far too cruel.

The knot in my throat became even more constricting.

"Junior..." Mayda's hand came down against me and I yanked myself away, the rage exploding as I gripped my laptop from the coffee table. With a cry, I tossed it, sending the device flying against a far wall where it cracked and broke to pieces.

Mayda jolted, a gasp piercing out of her.

"Junior!"

I whirled to face her. "Soy un pendejo!"

She flinched at the harshness in my tone. She didn't deserve my ire either, and I wanted to temper it, but everything was too much. I was too overwhelmed, and everything was bubbling over.

"Don't say that."

"It's the truth! He's in that fucking hospital because of me and I—"

"Junior, it's not your fault. You had an argument. You couldn't have known—"

"But I should have! I should have known, Mayda. I should have known better. I should have just nodded and told him I'd take over the rancho like a good son. Instead, I screamed at him. I told him he was a stupid farmer. The things I said..."

"You didn't mean any of it." She reached for me, grabbing my arms like an offer of comfort. They slid up, reaching out to cup my cheeks. "You didn't mean it, and I'm sure he knows that."

I couldn't be sure. I wasn't sure of anything. Nothing except this burning inside me. To forget all that had happened in the past few hours. I couldn't take it. I couldn't take the feelings swelling inside me. My skin itched and everything inside me screamed.

Grasping for the ends of Mayda's hair was an instinct, only my movements were sharper, harder. I yanked, tilting her head back. A gasp left her lips, one I'd learned to recognize intimately.

"Junior..." Her hands slid down to my chest, palms pressing against the rapid beating of my heart.

There was a need raging a war within me and I needed her. Desperately. Like her touch was a balm to my senses, something that could always quiet the storm of my mind.

I dropped my forehead to hers, inhaling her scent. Her essence. My heart was a pounding beat in my ears, and while the world around me swayed, she was the only thing steady in my life. And at least for a moment, I wanted to bask in it as much as I could. Because when I let go, I knew what would come next.

I knew what I needed to do.

"None of this was your fault," she whispered against my mouth.

The words pricked at my anger.

"Stop talking," I snapped, tugging against her hair once again. "No more talking. Please. I—I don't want to talk about it anymore."

"Then what do you want?"

"You."

Because only she could pull me from the darkness of my spiraling mind. Only she could temper the rage. Save me against my own waking nightmares. So I did the only thing I wanted to do. I unleashed my ire against her body in the form of pleasure and temptation and caresses.

I walked her backwards until she slammed against the wall, rattling a picture frame behind her. She winced, gasped, and her eyes searched mine, a furrow between her brows.

I didn't want her psychoanalyzation. I didn't want to talk. I didn't want to bare my fucking feelings. I just wanted this. The heat of her body against mine and to lose myself in the only way I knew how.

My hips ground against her waist and I leaned down until my mouth skimmed hers. "No more talking," I whispered, though my voice broke. I hated that weakness most of all. I pushed her harder against the wall. Almost like my own debilities were her fault. They weren't. At all. But I wanted the release regardless. "Please, Mayda?"

"Please what?"

"Please let me fuck you until I forget."

"Yes."

The confirmation was little more than an expulsion of breath. One I claimed with my lips as soon as it left her mouth. I kissed her like I'd die otherwise. I felt like I would. Like without her I was nothing but specks of dust that would vanish with the wind. Insignificant, small.

With her, I was much more than I could ever be on my own.

I moved with little to no finesse, too lost in my need to be with her. Fragile and on the point of breaking, and only she could fix the shattered bits of me. It was unfair to her, and yet my cock fucking wept to have her, possess her. To sheathe inside her because it was all I could think to do.

Her own fingers fumbled between us, pulling at my belt and unzipping my jeans. It was a struggle to get the material past my hips, but as soon as she freed my cock, I tore at her panties from beneath her skirts. Her warm skin branded me. Marking me as hers.

I tore my mouth from hers and she gasped for breath, moaning as I slid my tongue and teeth against her neck, biting, marking. Every move I made was rough, rougher than usual. Her hair threaded between my fingers and I gripped, keeping her tethered to me because that's where she fucking belonged.

"Put me inside you," I ordered, biting down against her rapidly beating pulse.

She groaned, taking my cock in her palm, guiding me against her folds. She was warm and wet, and I surged forward with a cry, sheathing fully inside her. She cried out, but I swallowed the sound, releasing her hair to grab her by the hips. Her body slammed against the wall over and over again as I pounded into her. I pulled out and lifted her into my arms before surging back into her. The picture frame rattled behind her with every thrust. Her warmth pulled me in and our joining became nothing but a desperate rhythm that I couldn't stop once I started.

She shuddered around me, her orgasm pulling her apart at the seams. She spoke, but I couldn't hear what she was saying. It was all white noise and my own hips surged forward over and over again until my release finally claimed me.

My whole body trembled against hers and I held Mayda close, basking in her for a little bit longer before reality came crashing down on me once again. The reality where my papá almost died because of me.

There was no coming back from that. It didn't matter what she said, and even if I'd found comfort in her with the briefest of seconds, it didn't matter. None of it did.

Because it had happened, and that guilt was something I would never be rid of.

I pulled away from Mayda then, the sorrow once again crashing over my body like a freight train. Her legs unfurled from around me as I set her to her feet. I sucked in a breath, righting myself and turning from her. I hated to do it, but I couldn't stop the suffering from wanting to drown me whole, and I didn't want to take her down with me.

"I think you should leave," I whispered, all but choking the words out.

And looking away prevented me from seeing the expression on her face, the one I knew would be there as I whispered those words.

"Go see Gabriela. I just…I'm sorry, cariño. I need a moment alone. I need to process everything."

I ached to reach for her, but in my guilt, I felt I didn't deserve more than what she'd already given me.

"Okay, Junior. I'll be at the main house. If you need anything from me."

I held my breath, waiting for the sound of my front door to click closed as she left.

It wasn't until she was gone that I stared at that cursed spot once again. The spot where my papá had doubled over.

I went there sitting myself on the floor.

And I wept.

CHAPTER 42

MAYDA

I F COMFORT WAS WHAT Junior needed, I was more than happy to provide that for him. If he needed my body to forget about the turmoil that went on within his own mind, I'd offer myself up on a silver platter. Because one thing I hadn't told him was that I loved him and would do anything for him.

I kept those words buried close to my chest, though. They were on the tip of my tongue before I turned and walked out of his place. The rejection stung, I had to admit that, and I didn't want saying those words to feel like a ploy of any kind. And it most definitely hadn't been the right time for them at all. I didn't want to say them while his mind was swirling with dark thoughts, even when a part of me burned to let him know he wasn't alone.

I understood guilt probably more than anybody. But I wasn't going to tell him how to process his pain. If he needed to be alone, I had to respect that.

And he was right. I needed to see Gabi. My best friend was strength incarnate, but I knew her dad nearly dying would have shaken her up. She would be strong for her sisters, but she wouldn't be honest with them about how she was feeling.

She'd be honest with me, though.

So I crept up to the house, letting myself in through the kitchen door. The emptiness of the house sent a chill down my back. It was late already, and they would have been asleep regardless, but the entire place felt cold and mournful. Like my own place did with my mom's ghost haunting the halls.

Taking a breath, I went upstairs and slipped into Gabi's room. I didn't bother knocking. And the inside held a sight I never imagined I'd ever see.

Gabriela was curled on the floor in the fetal position, her entire body wracking through with painful sobs.

In all my life, in all my time of knowing her, I'd never seen Gabriela break down. I'd barely ever seen her shed a tear. It was easy to associate her with strength with her tightly coiled hair and suits she wore like armor.

This vulnerability was rare, and it shattered my already fragile heart to pieces.

I dove to the floor and wrapped my arms around her. Soaking her sadness down to my soul. With her hair unwound, dressed in her pajamas and makeup running down her cheeks, she seemed more vulnerable than I'd ever known her to be.

"I've got you," I whispered as I rocked her back and forth. She only cried harder and clutched onto me like her life depended on it.

I wondered if this is what I looked like. To hold on so long to your strength, that when you finally broke, you unraveled completely.

At one point, that must have been me. And the Águila-Gutierrez clan had always been there for me.

Now it was my turn to do the same. To be their rock. To hold them together like they'd held me together for so long in my youth and in adulthood.

"I've got you," I repeated.

The door to her room creaked open, and I looked up to see Valentina on the threshold. The youngest sister looked so small right then, with tears tracing a path down her cheeks and her arms hugged around her middle.

"Can I come in?" she whispered, voice breaking.

Gabriela sniffed and tried to pull herself together. I knew if she did, she'd lock away her feelings once more. She'd pretend to be strong. So I held her tightly with one hand and lifted the other in invitation to Valentina.

Valentina walked in and curled on the floor next to us, wrapping her arms around Gabi. I gave them room to hug. To grieve. No, they hadn't lost their dad, but I was sure it was traumatizing for them just the same.

The door to the bedroom creaked once again. This time, it was both Sofia and Ximena seeking entry, their hands clasped tightly together. They didn't wait for permission before entering, squeezing into the pile we had going. Ximena's pillowy body cushioned mine, and I wrapped my arms around the sisters a moment before they lost themselves in each other. I pulled away, watching as they eventually fell asleep where they were. I placed a blanket over their bodies, and they barely stirred; if anything, they pushed closer. Wrapped together.

While I watched from the outskirts.

Like I always tended to do.

CHAPTER 43

JUNIOR

WITH MY PAPÁ AND mamá at the hospital, it was up to me to take care of Los Corazones. I was up earlier than usual the next morning, my uniform and sombrero perched firmly on my head, and I began to work. Falling into the tasks papá had groomed me to take over felt like stepping into a second skin. One that didn't quite belong to me, but I was forced to mold onto my body just the same.

His office was pristine and well-organized, so at least finding things was an easy task. I knew Gabriela probably wouldn't come in to work, so I pulled out the ledgers and began looking over the numbers and inventory myself, making notes on a separate sheet on what we needed for the week. The horses needed more feed, buckets for the cows needed to be replaced, some of the shovels and farming materials were in bad shape...

I wasn't sure how long had passed before Don Beto was knocking on the office door, peering in at me with worried eyes.

"Junior," he greeted. "Most of the trabajadores are here and waiting for news."

It had been late afternoon when my papá had his heart attack, and a lot of the workers had been witnesses to the ambulance coming to take him away.

I sighed and pushed myself away from the desk. "Vamos."

Don Beto walked at my side, and it felt strange that he was deferring to me. It should have been my papá at his side. I felt like nothing more than a cheap replacement. A farce. One they'd see from a mile away.

My palms began to sweat and my heart thumped as we arrived to face the trabajadores. They all stood expectantly staring in my direction, some of them shuffling around nervously. I wanted to recoil in fear. The immense pressure that pressed against me, threatening to beat me to the ground.

I wasn't made for this. I wasn't made to control their fates. To give them any kind of news.

But the image of my papá doubling over and gasping in pain had me straightening my shoulders. I wasn't made for this, but it was something I had to do.

"As most of you probably know, my papá had a heart attack yesterday afternoon." Gasps and murmurs rang out. "He's fine now. He went through surgery and is in recovery. He's still at the hospital and will probably be there for a while." I felt my throat begin to constrict, so I pushed through before I could choke up. "We know what the jefe would say. We are the heart of this rancho, and even while he's resting at the hospital, we have to keep going. So I'll be taking over his duties while he's unavailable and in recovery."

Saying the words felt like bringing an ax down on the back of my own neck.

"So any questions, concerns, or complaints, please come to me or Don Beto. The office is always open."

With that, the meeting was over. I still had to wait while several workers came up and offered both their condolences and relief that my papá was okay. Their support made the backs of my eyelids burn and the trust they placed in me made me want to turn the other way and run.

But I couldn't.

I didn't have any other choice except to take the role I didn't want.

The one that was always meant for me.

I stared at my opened email for a long time, my mind traveling too far away until a blurred hand waving in front of my face pulled me out of my thoughts.

"I've been calling your name for five minutes."

"Mayda." I blinked at her, surprised to see her at all during the middle of the weekday. "What are you doing here?"

She was dressed in a floral skirt and cardigan, her hair loose over her shoulders. My fingers reached for the strands on instinct, tugging at the ends lightly before flicking them over her shoulders.

"I took the day off," she said. "You guys needed me."

My breath caught. She hadn't even taken off when her own mother died, but she'd taken off to be here for my hermanas? For me?

I didn't fucking deserve her.

My hand clasped over hers. "You're too good to us, cariño."

She gave me a soft, pained sort of smile. "I love you guys. It's no trouble."

My heart skipped at the words she'd just confessed. Before I could ask her if that included me too, she waved in the laptop's direction.

"What has you concentrating so hard?"

My face flamed like I'd been caught doing something I wasn't supposed to. But it was too late to close the laptop shut. She was already staring at the screen, and while I was sure her eyes were picking up the words, she kept turning in my direction, waiting for me to explain.

I swallowed past the sudden thickness in my throat.

"It's the college," I explained. "I... finally graduated. One of my professors said he was impressed with one of my projects. He offered me a job."

Mayda's entire face lit up and she clapped her hands together with excitement. "Junior, that's wonderful! I'm so happy for you!" She leaned down, kissing my cheek. When she pulled away, a frown creased her eyebrows as she took in my own pained expression. "What's wrong?"

I cleared my throat and closed the laptop softly. "I'm not taking the job."

"What? Why not? Is it not something you're interested in? I thought since it was in your career field..."

I shook my head, wanting the conversation to be done and over with immediately. "No," I said, putting too much force on the word. "I can't go anywhere else. Especially not now. Los Corazones needs me."

My papá needs me.

"I have to stop with the bullshit," I said more firmly, finally turning to face her. I forced myself to harden my emotions against what I knew I would read on her. What she would want to say. "I've been playing around enough. It's time I got serious about my future and focused on Los Corazones."

Mayda blinked at me, and I couldn't stand the pity I saw.

"But you wanted this."

I forced myself to my feet, shoving my chair back. "I don't know what I want, Mayda." I stepped around her, letting our fingers graze as I walked past. I gave into the final urge to let my hands glide across the bottom of the ends of her hair. But for once, the action didn't bring me comfort like I thought it would. "I have to get back to work, okay, cariño?" I started to walk away.

"Junior?" Mayda called after me, stopping me in my tracks. "Just don't shut me out, okay?"

"Nunca," I promised. "Nunca te dejaré ir."

I'd let go of my dreams for Los Corazones, but I would never let Mayda go.

In the absence of my papá, I dedicated almost every waking hour to the rancho. He was still holed up at the hospital, under the watchful eye of the nurses and doctors in recovery—and my mamá's eagle eye. I still hadn't gone to see him.

A part of it was because I had so much to take care of at Los Corazones, and I knew he'd want me here putting up a brave front for the trabajadores. A bigger part of me knew it was because of my own guilt.

It was eating me alive. Or rather, becoming an ingrained part of me. So much so that the only thing I did nowadays was work like the devil was nipping at my heels. I barely saw my family except in the mornings during breakfast. Things with Mayda were still rough if only because I needed space to process my thoughts and to wrap my head around this new work schedule. She was nothing if not patient and understanding.

Every day her hopeful eyes watched mine as I left for work. She tried to bring up conversation regarding my schooling and job opportunities, but I always shut the conversation down. I didn't feel the need to talk about it, especially when I'd already made up my mind.

I was giving up the foolish notion I had called a dream to pursue a life on the rancho. She knew this, and I knew she wanted to try and convince me otherwise. It was why it was easy to run away. From the conversation, and drown myself in what needed to be done.

"Hey mano, how are you holding up?" Hector asked.

"Fine."

His piercing gaze swept over me, and for once, there was no humor in it.

I didn't want to talk about it. It had been days, and my papá was still at the hospital.

I knew my best friend only cared about me, and asking me was his way of showing it.

"You sure?"

"Sí. I'm sure."

I could tell he was about to call me out on my shit. He would pry the truth out of me by force if he wanted to but at that moment, Don Beto appeared to interrupt us.

"Jefe," he said to me. The name felt mocking, even if he didn't say it with that intent. It was with reverence, one I didn't quite deserve. "Señorita Gabriela sent for you. Says she has to go over some numbers with you."

Saved by the bell.

I thanked him then turned to Hector. "See you, mano."

Gabi's office door was open and I walked in to see her hunched over her desk, pouring over a sheet of numbers. Just seeing them gave me a headache.

"What's up?"

She looked up. There were dark circles beneath her eyes. The sight of the strain and red-rimmed eyes hit me like a punch to the chest. I'd been so busy drowning out my own guilt that I hadn't checked on my sisters. I had no idea how they were faring. How they felt.

Mayda had been there for them and I hadn't.

I really was a piece of shit.

Gabi stood. "I lied, I don't need to talk about numbers."

"Then what—"

"Why are you avoiding Mayda?"

"Christ, is that why you pulled me away from work? For a lecture? I don't need one."

"Answer the damn question, Junior."

"I'm not avoiding her."

One of her trimmed brows kicked up. "You've been avoiding everyone."

It was true, but I feebly protested anyway.

She rolled her eyes. "You haven't gone to see papá at the hospital, either. You know he comes home soon."

I clenched my jaw and looked away from her.

"You should go visit him. He's been asking about you."

The guilt felt like an all-consuming monster. I hadn't been able to face him and she knew it.

I was afraid of what he would say, the blame he'd put on me. Seeing him frail in a hospital was something I didn't think I could stomach.

"Junior," Gabriela admonished. "Go see him. Today."

I had to face the consequences of my actions sooner or later.

She was right.

I *had* to go see him.

"Okay," I said. "I'll go today."

Papá was sitting up among a mound of hospital pillows. I expected him to look fragile, but he didn't. Even connected to machines that monitored his heart, he looked like a force. Strong and hearty. It was hard to believe he'd even had a heart attack, let alone a surgery.

Still, my guilt wasn't assauged.

If anything, it incremented. In one mere moment, I'd brought this strong man crumbling down.

"Junior."

Torn away from staring at his figure, my papá forced my gaze to his face with that single word.

I stepped deeper into the room, and there was a tense moment of silence as we each took the other in. Neither of us said a word, and I wasn't sure if it was because we just didn't know what to say, or if he was upset. If he blamed me.

I wouldn't be surprised if he did.

My knees almost gave out and I tried to speak, but my throat was too tight. I cleared it, tried again.

"Papá."

Another moment of silence passed.

"Sientáte." He nodded in the direction of a spare chair.

I did as he asked, legs spread, my hands clasped together. I couldn't take my eyes off him. And he seemed to be assessing me with just as much fervor as I did him.

Finally, he said, "How's the rancho?"

My body threatened to seize up at the question. It was perfectly innocent, and I knew he wouldn't directly address what had happened to him, or what we'd argued about right before he'd fallen to the ground. Sometimes, for him, it was easier to shove the bad stuff beneath the rug. Maybe then they'd go away on their own. I wondered if that was something he truly hoped or if it was a form of manipulation. Whatever it was, it worked.

"Good," I told him, faking a smile, though it felt more like a grimace. "I went over our inventory and checked through the materials. What we have should hold up for another month or so, but I went over the numbers with Gabi and we'll be ordering some more supplies since we can swing it. The trabajadores are working extra hard, too."

"Good," he replied. "They haven't been giving you trouble?"

I swallowed past the lump in my throat. "No. Everything is good. They're listening to me."

He smiled at me. "They know who the jefe is."

The denial came instantly. "I'm no jefe..."

"Claro que si."

Of course he would think I was.

It was why we sat where we currently did in the first place. And it didn't matter how many final, feeble attempts at denying it I gave.

The truth was, Los Corazones was my destiny. I was a fool to try and fight it in the first place.

"Papá... I just wanted to let you know..." My words caught, the tears evident in my voice. "I heard what you said. And you're right. I'm going to stop wasting my time on the unimportant stuff and take my place at the rancho, like I should have done this entire time."

Finally, finally, my papá beamed at me, only it didn't bring joy to my own chest to see it. It brought nothing but dread.

"I'm glad to hear you came to your senses, mijo." He reached out, his warm hand clasping against my shoulder to give me an affectionate squeeze. "You'll see once you get into the swing of things. The rancho is right where you belong. Tending to the crops, overseeing the workers. There's nothing better in this world than that."

"Yeah," I agreed. "Nothing better."

He looked happy at the proclamation, and I should have been too. So why, instead, did I feel like I was dead inside?

CHAPTER 44

JUNIOR

THE DAY PAPÁ CAME home, everyone awaited him in the living room of the main house—even Mayda. I'd driven him and mamá from the hospital in the car and resisted the urge to help him walk up towards the house. He was a proud man and wouldn't appreciate the help. It was embarrassing enough to him for my mamá hovering over him like a hen.

The doctor had ordered rest, diet, and a healthier lifestyle. It meant no more greasy foods and certainly no more tequila. He'd grumbled the entire time the doctor was giving the orders, but I knew my mamá and Doña Gloria would enforce the rules with an iron fist.

Valentina all but smothered him when we walked through the front door. He let out a soft grunt when she threw herself at his body, wrapping her arms tightly around his waist, her cries muffled against his chest.

"Vale—" I admonished. "Ease up."

She pulled away with a sniffle.

"Ay, mija." Papá wiped at her tears. "No llores. I don't like to see you cry."

Soon my sisters had crowded around him to give him hugs to welcome him back home. I stood on the outskirts, my eyes meeting Mayda's over the display before I quickly looked away, embarrassment heating my cheeks.

"Welcome back home, señor," Doña Gloria said. "And thank God you're okay. Come, sit. Eat. I prepared some food for you."

My papá rubbed his hands together. "I'm starving. Hospital food is bad. I'm happy to be rid of it."

"Yes, well, remember, you're on a new diet," my mamá reminded him. "So Doña Gloria prepared a special meal just for you. Vegetables and plain chicken."

Papá groaned. "What am I, a gringo?"

Mamá gave him a sympathetic pat on the back. "You're going to have to eat like one from now on."

He groaned but followed everyone into the dining room regardless.

It was nice to see him up and about, though the doctor had ordered him to stay off his feet for a while and to avoid stressful situations.

That meant taking over the rancho would be in my duties from here on out, and papá would get his dream, after all.

"I'm glad your dad's okay."

Mayda's voice made me startle. I'd almost forgotten she was here as well. I was so lost in my own thoughts, I'd completely spaced out and ignored her presence.

"Thanks," I said. "Me too."

"Will he be okay?" She played with the hem of her pink and gray cardigan. The color was pale against her own tanning skin and it somehow brought out the shadows beneath her eyes.

"The doctor says he needs to avoid stressful situations from here on out, so I'll be taking over Los Corazones."

She opened her mouth like she wanted to say something and thought better of it, clamping her lips closed. She took a breath. "As long as that's what you want."

"It is."

We stared. I hated this, this distance I'd put between us. But if I was going to take over, my papá had been right. Los Corazones deserved my entire focus. It was the least I could do for him. Still, this chasm the rancho created between Mayda and me wasn't one I enjoyed. I hated avoiding her. I hated not talking to her. But the truth was, I was embarrassed. I couldn't look her in the eye, because I knew I'd find expectations staring back at me. She'd expect me to pursue my dreams. She'd encourage it, actually, and it made me so much more of a coward because I couldn't. And she wouldn't be able to understand that.

Like my papá, it was easier to push the discomfort under a rug. Not talk about it. Not talk to her about it, and hope it went away. But Mayda was stubborn, and I was embarrassed.

"I guess I should go," she said hesitantly. "I just wanted to see if your dad was okay."

She waited a beat, maybe waiting to see if I would stop her. I wanted to, but a bigger part of me didn't want her to stay to see the truth I'd hide from everyone else but couldn't from her.

I was afraid of Mayda. I was afraid of the truth she could wrench from my soul and the feelings she wreaked on my heart. She'd break down my walls and pull the truth from me, and it was one I couldn't face.

So I did the only thing I could think to do.

I nodded and said, "Okay."

CHAPTER 45

MAYDA

I KNEW WHY JUNIOR was avoiding me, but that didn't make it hurt any less. Every text I sent went unanswered, and those that did receive a reply were disguised in emojis and one word.

We'd regressed back to a place he promised we wouldn't go back to, and instead of feeling angry, I felt tired.

There were only so many texts I could send, only so many times I could stay the night with Gabi trying to get Junior to notice me at the breakfast table the next morning. The rejection stung every time he smiled before he stood up and went to work at a job I knew he hated. Sometimes, his hands would slip against the ends of my hair, giving me the lightest of tugs. But where I'd learned to relish in the gesture before, now it felt like old times.

When we both barely spoke to the other, too afraid to take the first step. This time was different. Now it seemed like we'd bulldozed past, and were in one anothers rear view mirrors.

The pain of that reality had me slinking back to my own house day after day, feeling emptier than I'd ever felt in my life. With no mom to worry about, and no late nights waiting for her to come home, I was living within a shell almost as empty as my soul.

My phone chimed with a text.

Let's go out tonight.

I sighed as I read her message and leaned back on my couch. I wasn't in the mood for much lately, and my best friend was starting to notice. I didn't want to go out. I wanted to spend my nights wrapped in Junior's arms, our legs twined together, naked bodies pressed close. I wanted to wake up to him filling me in slow, loving movements. I wanted his laughter trickling through my ear and breakfasts with his family while he traced hearts on my leg from beneath the table.

I'd grown too used to him. Too used to what we'd had. I had let it fill my every waking moment, and now that he was no longer there, it felt like I was crashing without him.

I hated that feeling. I was strong before him, and I could be strong again without him.

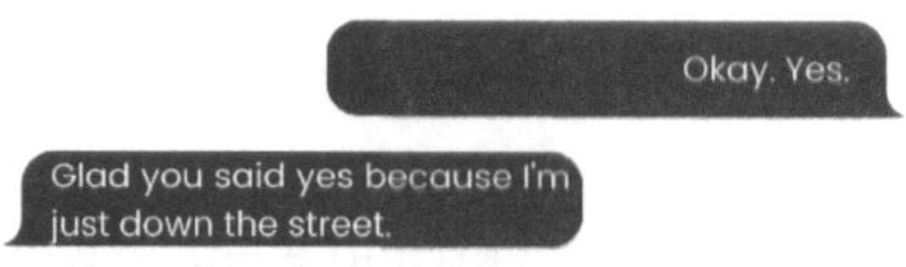

I chuckled and got up to open the door just as she pulled into my driveway. Once she was inside, she followed me up to my room so I could pack an overnight bag.

"It feels bigger in here," she whispered as she took a seat on the edge of my bed.

"Funny, I was feeling the same thing."

"This might not be the time to think about this, but have you thought about selling the place?"

I paused, hand stuck on a night dress. "I hadn't, actually."

She shrugged. "Something to think about. You might not want to be paying for something so big if it's just you." Her nose scrunched. "Besides, you should move to a better neighborhood."

"There are some apartments over in Oakland that I was eyeing. They have a swimming pool and a gym."

"I meant at Los Corazones."

I sighed. "Gabi, I don't think that's going to happen. Your brother is..." I trailed off, unsure what to say.

"He's a dick. I know."

"Not that. He's going through a difficult time."

"Yeah, well, he needs to get his head out of his ass. You're too patient, Mayda. If that was me, I would've marched down there and shown him who his girlfriend, boss, and future wife is."

I rolled my eyes, zipping up my overnight bag. "If it was you, you would've dumped him the minute he didn't text back."

"You're right. So why haven't you?"

The question was cutting. A knife to the chest to wrench out the truth.

I sat next to her on the bed and kicked my legs out in front of me. "Because I love him," I whispered.

Gabi reached for my hand and squeezed it. "I know you do. But sometimes, you have to love yourself more."

I leaned my head against her shoulder, feeling the emotion clog through my system. It was a vicious cycle, it seemed. Like I was destined to give all of myself to one person and receive scraps in return. But that ended today.

Gabriela was right.

Loving someone was okay. It was good. Love made the world turn and hearts beat. But it could also be a poison, one that could slowly kill you over time if you weren't careful. I'd let my mom poison me down until the day she died. And now I was letting Junior do the same. Biting my tongue when things upset me, letting him do as he pleased, not asserting my place.

"You're right," I whispered, as the steady sinking realization came over me. "I need to love myself more."

Ximena was a miracle worker. I thought that every time she took makeup to my face and morphed me into a whole new person. She went with something smokey and sexy, all dark tones, glitter, and red lipstick that highlighted the heart shape of my upper lip.

I walked down the stairs in heels in a cluster among Gabi and her sisters. My spirit felt lifted, more than it had in weeks. Maybe it was because of my talk with Gabi, but I knew it was because I was determined. I had to let some things go. The negative cycles I found myself in were only detrimental to my life and my spirit.

I needed to stop locking myself away. I needed to stop seeing myself as lesser than others and undeserving of love.

All my life I'd thought myself on the outskirts of their family, but I finally realized that was never the case. I'd always been a part of their unit, I'd just been too stupid to see it clearly. But it was staring me in the face now as Ximena slipped her arm through the crook of mine, laughing affectionately.

We were all dressed in different shades. Gabriela wore black, her heart-shaped neckline doing wonders for her boobs. I was in pink, something demure that offset the bold makeup. A fantasy,

Ximena had called me. Angelic and sinful at the same time. While Ximena herself wore a bright yellow dress that was loud and attention-grabbing but made her look like sunshine. Sofia wore a long, red dress with a slit down the side and a flower in her hair.

Valentina, meanwhile, grumbled among us because she wasn't old enough yet to go clubbing.

"Ma, pa!" Gabi called out. "We're leaving! We'll be back later!"

Her parents came out into the living room. Señor Águila walked around at a slower pace than he usually did, and I assumed it was because of his surgery, though he looked perfectly healthy. I knew, more than anyone, that looks could be deceiving.

"Go with God," Mamá Claudia said. "And be careful. Call if you need anything."

"Yeah, yeah," Gabi waved her off. "We know the rules."

Just then, Junior came into the living room. The smile he wore dropped as soon as he set his eyes on me. The easy expression twisting into something dark. Sensuous. Heated.

It made my face flush and it felt like the room heated a couple of degrees. Despite what I'd told myself, it was very hard to ignore his presence. A big part of me cried, wanting him to notice me. Wanting him to grasp the ends of my curled hair to pull.

He did step close to me, though, close enough to touch, but he kept his hands to himself. "Where are you going, Mayda?" he asked.

"I thought it was obvious."

He blinked as if I'd slapped him, but the heat never once left his gaze. His eyes raked over me. I knew the expression well. I knew what it was he wanted to do to me. What he would have done, had we not had an audience at the moment.

I wondered if I would have pushed him away or pulled him closer in that event.

I guess we'd never know.

"I didn't know you were going with them." His tone felt accusatory, and it instantly made me angry.

"Well, maybe you would have known had you bothered to text me back at all these past few weeks."

He frowned. "Mayda—"

"You know what, Junior? Save it." I whispered the words, low so nobody else could hear. I didn't want to make a scene in front of his family. Gabriela knowing we had problems was enough. "You don't have a right to tell me anything right now or ever."

"What's that supposed to mean?"

"It means I've been waiting, Junior. And I am tired. I'm tired of giving and getting nothing in return. So you don't get to look at me like that, and you don't get to be upset that you don't know what's going on in my life when you haven't made the effort to reach out and find out. So I'm going out tonight, and I'm going to have a good time instead of pining after you any longer."

He jerked back, but I didn't wait to see what expression he would make or what he would say. I'd waited for a long time for him to give me the words I'd wanted to hear, and I knew if I waited then, I'd just be disappointed.

I plastered on a sweet smile. Luckily, everyone was engrossed in their own conversations and hadn't noticed Junior and I arguing. I smiled and kept on smiling as we got into the car and drove to the club. I smiled through the music, through the dances. I smiled as I turned men down, and I smiled as Gabi snapped pics of us all together.

I smiled.

Even though it hurt.

CHAPTER 46

JUNIOR

I SHOULDN'T HAVE ACTED possessive upon seeing Mayda. But seeing the way that pink skirt hugged every curve I already had memorized made me into a neanderthal. She was right, though.

I'd been avoiding her. Because she was the only one who would make me give in to the truth. The only one who could make me confess everything I'd otherwise tried to keep hidden.

I was a coward. I knew it. But her words resonated loudly down to my soul. I didn't want them to, but the minute she'd said those words, I'd gone back to my place to brood. To open up my desktop computer and stare at my emails from my professors, to look at my final graduation information with emotions clogging through my throat.

Fuck.

I'd given it up because of my papá. Because my own selfishness had almost cost me his life. Even as the longing tugged through my gut at the sight of those emails, I couldn't give in. I had to remind myself that my family was important. More important than my own wants and my dreams.

Nothing was more important than keeping my papá healthy. Nothing.

I went back to the main house with heavy steps. Between being stuck working the rancho and other duties, I'd been sticking near my papá as often as I could. My own worry making me hover as much as my sisters and my mamá. More than once he'd growled, "Ya déjame." Demanding I leave him be didn't stop me, though.

I needed to assure myself he was okay as much as I needed to talk to him about the duties I was fulfilling. To make him proud. So he didn't live on the edge of worry that I was running his rancho to the ground. Even after mamá tried shushing us and getting us to talk about something else, conversation always came back around to work.

And how proud he was of me.

If that pride kept him from another heart attack, I'd sacrifice anything it took to keep him happy and healthy.

The main house felt empty. I looked around but didn't see anyone. Abuelita Mari sat on the couch, watching her nightly telenovela.

She beamed at me when I came in. "Sit with me, mijo."

I did as she asked, looking at the screen and overly dramatic acting. It was a new novela and the actors on the screen were on a rancho, two lovers pressed together in a passionate embrace.

It only made an ache grow in my chest.

"Junior, I want to ask you a question," Abuelita Mari said out of the blue.

"Sure, abuelita."

"What do you want out of life, mijo?"

The question caught me off guard. For a moment I didn't know what to say, how to answer. I found myself staring at the telenovela on screen once again. The scene had cut to something new. A shot of horses and a young girl riding one.

Longing gripped me like never before.

I cleared my throat and turned back to my abuelita. "To run the rancho."

"You're lying."

"Abuelita!"

She shrugged. "Everyone can tell you're miserable, mijo. Except for your papá. The rancho has always been his dream and he wants to pass it off to his son, so it blinds him to the truth."

Her words caused my chest to nearly cave in. "It's my duty," I whispered. "He was hurt because of me—"

"Don't blame yourself for that," she argued in Spanish. "He drinks too much and eats junk. He also stresses himself out for no reason. It was a culmination of everything piling up, but it wasn't your fault. You have to understand that." Her fingers touched the rosary around her neck. "God works in strange ways, but I believe this was a sign."

"A sign of what?"

I almost feared the answer.

"Que tienes que aprender a hablar con la verdad."

But speaking with the truth was hard when the consequences could be brutal.

"Y tienes que aprender a amar, Junior."

"What do you mean I have to learn to love?"

"Learn to love yourself enough to go after what you want and believe you deserve it as much as anybody else does. Even if it's hard."

I sat back against the couch as I let my abuelita's words sink into my system. Learn to love myself. I did love myself. But maybe... maybe I hadn't ever loved myself enough. Maybe she was right. Loving oneself didn't just mean self care or exercise. I supposed it could've also meant being brave enough to give yourself the happiness you deserved, unapologetically. Even if it meant going against your papá's wishes.

Suddenly, an idea dawned on me as I watched the novela on screen and the horses rush across a field.

Perhaps the idea had been there all along, and I'd only now been awake enough to see it.

Weeks went by. Weeks since I'd actively seen or spoken to Mayda. Since I had a talk with my abuelita. Sure, I'd seen Mayda around the house, but she barely spoke a word to me. Not even after I'd texted and apologized for my behavior.

She left me on read.

But what she didn't know was that I wasn't avoiding her. At least, not like I had been before. Since talking with my abuelita, I felt as though a fire had sparked beneath me. One in my mind that refused to be put out.

Once one idea sprung to my mind, several more followed until a plan began forming in my mind. it occupied every waking second. Even as I went about the rancho, overtaking papá's duties, it lived and thrived inside me.

Weeks became months and my plan finally fell into motion. Once a week I met with a therapist online to help get me through the worst of my insecurities. With their help, I realized I'd clung so much to the idea that I owed everything, even my happiness, to my papá, to my own detriment.

Seeing someone about my issues had been difficult, at first, but it helped me open up, in ways I never thought I would, and muddle through my most intimate thoughts.

I kept it to myself, wanting to be a better man. One that was deserving not only of Mayda's love and time, but of my own dreams as well.

Dreams I was itching to put into motion.

My knuckles rapped along the wood of Gabi's door before I burst inside without waiting for an answer. "Gabi, I need your help with something."

She leaned back in her chair, a malicious look crossing over her features. I knew what was coming and tried to suppress an eye roll.

"Well, well, well, so you want a favor?" She hummed. "What do I get in return if I help you?"

"The joy of helping your brother."

She cackled. "I think not. What does joy for you get me?"

I rolled my eyes. "Look, this is serious."

"I'm being serious."

I pushed my way into her office and sat down despite her noise of protest. The folders I carried were slapped on her desk and curiosity sparked in her gaze at the sight of them like I knew it would. She reached for a folder, pulling it closer to herself by the edge, but my palm stopped its trajectory, slapping down against it.

"You know every number, every coin, that passes through Los Corazones, right?"

"Okay, color me curious. I'll bite. Yes, I know the exact number of coins that passes through Los Corazones."

"You know how much the rancho earns from business with restaurants and small grocers and every little penny it has saved up in the bank, right?"

Her eyes narrowed. "Yeees?"

I smiled. "I have an idea. Something I've been cooking up for a while now, and I want you to help me run the numbers and probabilities of success."

She straightened into what I called her business posture, making a gesture with her hand so that I continue. My breathing grew labored and my palms started sweating. A small voice in my head demanded I run away and take my ideas with me. It was stupid. There was no way she would think it was a good idea. I was wasting her time and mine. I should focus on the rancho and leave these dreams behind me...

No.

I forced those thoughts to a stop. I took a breath, doing the exercises my therapist taught me to do. I started naming all the reasons it was a good idea and let those take hold in my mind instead.

It was a good idea.

A damn fucking good one.

Confidence restored, I flipped open my folders. Every bit of painstaking research was in these pages. I'd invested so much into it, knowing that if I was going to bring it to fruition, I needed an actual business proposal. And the first thing I needed to do was convince Gabi. Only then could I take it to papá. If it didn't pass by her keen eye, I'd have to start all over with something new.

But I was determined. And the passion for this project bled through my voice as I began explaining my idea to Gabi. I slid papers to her, everything from graphs, to statistics, to an elaborate business plan with logos, phrases, and so much more.

I'd tried to cover every angle I could and had gotten it mostly perfected.

When I finished explaining, I sat back. There were several beats of silence as Gabi's eyes slid over my pages.

"I just need to know if the numbers will allow it," I whispered.

Finally, she looked up at me. "You did all of this yourself?" she asked.

I nodded, feeling a flush rise up my neck. "I did."

"Let me get this straight; you've been getting your degree in secret and this is what you plan to do with it?" There was no judgment in her voice. Only a bone-deep curiosity.

This must have felt like a bomb being dropped on her. No one had known. No one except Mayda and papá, and it seemed like he'd kept that secret to himself as much as I had.

"I did."

She whistled. "Damn, hermano. I'm... impressed. And this?" She nodded at my plan arranged on top of her desk. "It's very thorough. That's good, but if you want to convince papá, you'll need my help." She opened one of her drawers and pulled out an enormous ledger, slapping it down against the table.

"So, you think it's a good idea?"

"While I loathe to give you a compliment, yes, hermano." She smiled softly in my direction before flipping the ledger open. "It's an amazing idea. Now, shut up while I run the numbers."

We spent hours in near silence and I watched her work, pouring over number after number. When she finally finished, she slammed the ledger closed and looked up at me, a serious expression on her face.

My heart sunk to my stomach. It was no good. Fuck.

"I don't know how to tell you this..."

My hands tightened into fists.

Gabi broke out into a smile. "But your plan is going to work."

I gave a grito that made her laugh. She pointed the end of her pen at me. "You owe me," she said with mock-vehemence. "Dessert at La Concha whenever I fucking want."

I stood up and grabbed her in my arms, pressing a sloppy kiss to her cheek.

"Ew, get off."

"Thank you, hermana. Thank you."

"Yeah, yeah. I'm the best. I know."

"You are. And now, the real battle is just beginning."

"Papá, can we talk for a moment?"

My papá looked up at me through his small spectacles. He was reading a book, marking his place with his finger. My mamá was knitting next to him and pretending not to eavesdrop.

"Of course, mijo. Is there something wrong with the rancho?" He started to get up, but I held my hand out.

"No, sit. Don't work yourself up, okay? The rancho is fine."

He chuckled and leaned back. "Old habits. Guess I won't have to worry much about that now that you're taking over."

I almost lost my nerve right then but plowed ahead. This conversation had been a long time coming and I needed to be brave, even if I felt the fear inside.

"That's what I wanted to talk to you about."

His bushy brows kicked up on his forehead as I handed him my laminated proposal.

"What's this?"

"Open it."

He did, slowly going through the first few pages of my introduction. His face went red as he started reading. He didn't finish the page before he looked up at me, surprise, accusation, anger, betrayal... It all lived in his gaze. The way they had the day he'd had his heart attack.

My mamá must have sensed his distress, because she set her knitting aside and grabbed the proposal from his hands, flipping back to the first page to read.

She looked confused when her gaze met mine. "Junior, what is this?"

I smiled warmly at them. "My dream." I looked to my papá, begging him with my eyes. "Please hear me out."

"We're listening," mamá said, hand coming down against papá's knee. His entire body relaxed and he looked at me. Stern but open to listening.

That was progress.

"I know you've dreamt of giving me your empire all my life, and I know these past few months I've been doing what you've asked, but I want to be honest with you once again. I don't want it."

My papá huffed a breath. "You don't want Los Corazones."

"I want you to understand that I love the rancho. I love what you've built. I love the trabajadores, the land, the animals, but I don't see myself running it the way you do. I love it, but it isn't my dream. This is my dream." I gestured at the proposal. "And I don't think your job is unimportant. I don't think you're just some farmer. But this, papá, this is what I want to do with my life."

And I began to explain.

I explained the same way I had to Gabi, but with her help, I was even able to point out the numbers aspect, calculating a return and the benefits we would reap if we implemented my plan.

They both listened, only interrupting with questions that I was able to clear up as soon as asked.

"So you see," I said. "I love Los Corazones and I want to be a part of it, but in this way. Not yours."

Papá closed the cover of my proposal with a huff. It felt like déjà vu watching stew in the silence. With Gabi, I hadn't felt this nervous dread, though. Such an aching want.

"You really put in the work," my papá said. "I'm surprised. This was very... se me fue la palabra."

I chuckled. The word escaped him. I was all too familiar with that happening.

"I'm impressed," he went on. "You did your research."

I nodded. "I want this."

"I can tell."

Once again silence descended, making me nearly squirm with discomfort.

"I thought you wanted Los Corazones," papá eventually said.

How to tell him the truth without riling him up? I needed to be honest, as honest as I possibly could be.

Slowly, I shook my head. "No, papá. I never did. And I think, deep down, you knew I didn't. Los Corazones has always been your dream for me, and I didn't have the heart to tell you otherwise. Then when you found out and got hurt—" My throat tightened.

I'd spent hours and many sessions talking about this to my therapist. About how hard it was to go against him, not only because of everything, but because of his heart attack.

"My heart attack wasn't your fault." His brows pulled together. "I am sorry if you felt like it was. I just thought... no lo se, I thought we had been on the same page." He looked down at my proposal, perfectly laminated. Every detail and hours of work put into it obvious. He sighed and looked back up at me. "It's a good idea, mijo."

Maybe a part of me hadn't expected his acceptance. Getting it felt like my heart grew wings that lifted me into the air. I almost didn't believe this was real.

"Yeah?"

He nodded. "I like it. The numbers don't lie. This would benefit Los Corazones and the community."

Mamá nodded at his side. "I think it's a good idea, too. When do we start?"

I blinked. "We?"

She chuckled. "Of course, mijo. Did you think we would let you do this on your own? We are familia. Familia supports each other." Her hand reached out, squeezing papá's and then mine. She became a thread between us. A tether. "No matter what. I wish you would have been honest sooner, though."

Papá nodded his agreement with that, but there was nothing I could do except offer them a sheepish smile.

"I need to work on that."

They both nodded. "We all do, I think."

"Mijo?"

I looked at my papá. "Yes?"

"What can I do to help with your dream?"

My throat clogged with emotion. He wouldn't apologize. He wouldn't say he was sorry, he was too proud for that. He wouldn't bare his feelings, either. But this? This offer, it *was* acceptance. It was support.

It was everything I needed. An olive branch he was extending and there was nothing left for me to do except hold on tight.

"Just be here," I said finally, tears swelling in my eyes. "I just need you to be here."

CHAPTER 47

MAYDA

I LOOKED AT THE shelter I had once called a home. Something, I realized, that had never really been a home to me at all. A home wasn't just a roof over your head. A home was where you left your heart. It was the people you surrounded yourself with. It was the love you gave and received.

This place had never really been my home. That had been the rancho. It had been with the Águila-Gutierrez family. With Gabi and her sisters. And for a while, it had been with Junior.

We hadn't spoken in a while, and I'd be lying if I said I didn't miss him. I did, with every fiber of my being. He had sent me a few texts asking about me, but I hadn't replied. If only because I had vowed to myself to be strong. I refused to be pushed to the sidelines every time things got hard. I refused to be that person. I refused to be seen and not heard when things got hard.

I had to love myself more than that.

It was why I'd kept my distance. It was why I'd made Gabriela promise she wouldn't tell me anything about him, just like she wouldn't tell him anything about me.

If he wanted me back, I was right here, but only if he promised to change.

I wasn't bitter about it. Bitterness was a poison, one I didn't feel like ingesting. Just like the heartbreak was too, and I could stave that easily enough by keeping myself busy.

I did that too. First, by selling the house.

It had gone quickly to a family who needed it. All my things had been taken out, the walls fixed, a coat of paint slapped over it. It looked new. Empty.

Like the bones had been given sinew and form to a place that no longer belonged to me.

Gabi offered up a place in her room until I found myself an apartment. I wasn't sure I could live so close to Junior without feeling the heartbreak, but I'd taken her up on it. Not because I wanted to see him, but because Gabi was my family, and it'd only be for a short time until I got approved for an apartment anyway.

Leaving this all behind felt surreal, but it also felt like closing a chapter that had run on for far too long in my life.

It wasn't 'the end' as most stories liked to conclude.

This was a 'to be continued.' I had to figure out how to live my life. Without the heavy weight my mother caused pressing down on my shoulders. I had to piece myself back together anew. And for the most part, I felt like I was succeeding.

The last of my belongings rattled from within a box as I made my way to my car. Getting rid of everything, from my mattress to the appliances in a garage sale felt therapeutic. I wanted to start from scratch, keeping only the most essential things.

Outside, the sunlight hit me and I squinted against the harshness of it, catching sight of a truck pulling up towards my place.

My heart did several dances in my chest. I tried to tame it into submission, but the moment the engine cut and Junior hopped down and stood there, I was a goner.

I set the box on the hood of my car. "Hey."

His piercing, dark eyes regarded me. They ate me up from my head down to my toes and stopped on my face. They were searching, though for what I couldn't be sure. I wanted to analyze everything I could from a single glance, but if I began weaving stories now, I'd never stop, so I calmed my emotions. I let myself feel them, because there was no point in pushing them behind a wall.

I was sure he could read the love I had for him on my face anyway.

Finally, he spoke. "Are you moving out?"

So Gabi had kept her promise to me and told him nothing. The genuine confusion in his voice was ragged and real.

I nodded. "Yeah. I sold the place. Too many painful memories here, ya know?"

He nodded, and I felt my face flush. I hadn't meant to say that, but being with him felt easy even if we hadn't spoken in weeks. Months. It was like we picked up right where we left off even with a chasm of words unsaid between us.

"I'm sorry," Junior blurted.

Genuine confusion filled me. "For what?"

He pushed away from his truck, slapping a hand across the back of his neck and rubbing. It was a nervous gesture, one I'd come to recognize. Genuine regret filled his eyes as he took me in.

I wondered what he'd find. A scared, unsure woman, or would he see the new me? I'd remolded myself once again. Come out stronger on the other side. Would he see that version of me? Would he find me in all my facets?

"For not being here for you when you needed me. I am a terrible boyfriend."

Am.

Not *was.*

My heart pounded faster.

That meant in his eyes, we were still together.

"We aren't together anymore, Junior."

He closed his eyes against those words, like they pained him. They pained me, but they had to be said. He didn't get to abandon me for months and come back thinking we were still a thing.

"I'm sorry."

I just shook my head. I knew the past few months hadn't been easy for him. I could give him a little bit of grace, but I wouldn't bend. "I know you had your own stuff going on."

He shook his head. "That's no excuse, Mayda. You forgive me too easily and I don't deserve it."

"You're right," I agreed. "You don't. But I won't argue with you. What you did to me was shitty. You broke my heart. But I know you had your reasons. I just hope you can work through them. I want you to be happy, Junior. That's all I've ever wanted for you."

His face contorted. "Why does it sound like you're saying good-bye to me?"

Was I? I shrugged. "Maybe I am."

He took a prowling step forward. His energy was electric and zapped through me the closer he got. Every nerve in my body felt alive with his presence. More alive than I'd felt in weeks.

"What if I told you I didn't want that? That I'm here to get you back? To make up for my mistakes?"

My heart screamed and every instinct told me to jump into his arms, but I held my ground. "I'd tell you that unless you changed—with actions, not words—that there's no chance of ever having me back. You made promises to me before and broke them almost at every turn."

"I know." He sighed. "There aren't enough words to ever express how sorry I am for what I did to you. But what if I told you that I've been seeing a therapist for months now?"

That answer floored me. "W-what?"

He prowled closer. "What if I told you that I heard you? That I listened. That I'm working every day to be a better man? Someone worthy of you." He was close enough to touch me now, and he reached into his back pocket. I looked down as he produced something between us.

A flier.

"What if I told you that I took your advice and went after my dream?"

I took the flier he was offering me and read it over. The words were big and bold. Opening it revealed an image of Los Corazones and its animals.

Los Corazones

Horse Therapy for Underprivileged and Disabled Children.

I stared at the words, wondering if they'd rearrange before my eyes. There was a full program on the flier with dates and times and the types of therapy offered.

"I don't understand." I knew for a fact this wasn't a thing. Gabi would have told me if it was. I was sure of it. This wasn't something Los Corazones did. They had animals, sure, but they focused mostly on crops and distributing produce.

"Remember when we went to the zoo? Something you said at the time sparked something in me. How animals can be very therapeutic."

"Yeah..."

"Did you know there are no programs or places that offer Equestrian-assisted psychotherapy?"

"I did not know that."

"It's true. I checked. I also checked, and I'd just need to complete an online course, an onsite training program, and pass an exam in order to be able to open this. I've enrolled into the program already. My parents—particularly my papá—are excited to open up a new business venture on the rancho."

"You mean you talked to your dad?"

His eyes shone and I wondered if it was unshed tears I saw there. "I did," he whispered. "He said he's proud of me and supports this idea. It helped that I presented it to him like a business with the numbers to back it up, too. Thanks to Gabi."

I felt my own tears threaten to run down my cheeks. Slowly, I handed the flier back to him. "I always knew you'd do great things," I whispered. "I knew you had it in you."

He took the slip of paper, holding it between us like a shield of some sort. His eyes were searching, tender, as they took me in.

"That's the thing, Mayda, I couldn't have done it without your wisdom. And this whole time we've been apart has been agony."

My tears fell. "Junior, it's been hard for me too."

"You know what I realized while I was putting together this proposal?"

"What's that?" I sniffed.

He reached for my hand, threading our fingers together. "I realized that my dreams mean nothing if you aren't there to share them with me."

I began crying in earnest. Junior leaned forward, brushing my tears away with his fingers.

"I love you, Mayda," he said. "I've loved you since we were kids. I've loved you since the first moment I saw you. My fingers crave the touch of your hair, your attention, your smiles. And I fucking miss you. Can you forgive me?"

The answer came easily. "Yes."

"I want you back, but I don't want half measures. Move in with me. You're my family, and I am sick of wasting so much time. We've wasted enough of it already. Be mine, be a part of this project. Let's share our dreams and build our own legacy. Together."

And really, when a man showed you how much he loved you by going into therapy to better himself, by listening, by finally reaching for his dreams? When he changed for the better and came to you with tears in his eyes asking for another chance—as if you wouldn't have given it to him regardless—and telling you all that you'd ever wanted to hear from him?

Well, there was only one thing a girl could say to that.

"Yes."

Epilogue
6 Months Later...
JUNIOR

THE SIZZLING SCENT OF carnes asadas floated through the air. Caps of coronas hissed as they popped open. Tongues burned as that first bite of salsa hit. Laughter rang through Los Corazones just as the sun set across the horizon, basking it in that all-too familiar glow.

The pulsing of laughter and dancing feet across the ground, of peace and convivio, was the very pulse that kept Los Corazones going.

The heart of the rancho was family.

And we were one big ass family.

From my parents, to my hermanas, my abuelita, Doña Gloria, Hector, the trabajadores, and of course... Mayda. We all made the rancho thrive. I loved it here, now more than ever.

Now that I was officially an Equine Therapist, we had begun construction and were expanding on our acreage. More horses, more stables, and a track. So much was going into this project, and even though we hadn't opened yet, there was already interest in what we were building.

I was proud of it.

I was proud of me.

I took a swig of my beer, glancing out at everyone having a good time. Hector was leading Valentina through a dance amidst a sea of bodies, my youngest sister's head thrown back in raucous laughter. Mayda was dancing with my papá, her smile a radiant thing that tugged at my insides.

She'd moved in with me six months ago and things had never been better. I woke up with my fingers curled into her hair, our legs twined together. A full smile always graced her lips when she woke, and it felt like my life had finally fallen into place.

Los Corazones was thriving like it never had before. My life had changed completely.

And I wouldn't have it any other way.

One Year Later...

MAYDA

"That's very good, Livvy," I praised.

The young girl beamed at me from atop her horse. Her dark curls hidden beneath her protective helmet. Her gap-toothed smile tugged at my heart.

Los Corazones Equestrian Therapy had been open for months and it was already a huge success. So much so that they got children and teens from all around involved. Not to mention, Junior had gotten the idea—and the funds—to create a scholarship program to help involve underprivileged kids who couldn't afford it.

Things were going well, and I was proud enough to be a part of it.

After Livvy did a final lap around the track with her favorite horse, Starfire, I helped her down while one of the trabajadores took the horse away. Livvy ran to her awaiting parents, words of praise already gushing from her lips.

Everything was running smoothly, a fact that brought a smile to my face. I wasn't always able to help since I had my own job during the weekdays, but on the weekends I loved giving my time to the children and Junior when I could.

I walked up to the front offices, stopping by to say hi to Gabi. The moment I entered her office, she let out a scoff and an annoyed huff before slamming her laptop closed.

"What's up with you?"

She gritted her teeth. "Saint Enterprises."

"Ah."

Saint Enterprises had been the bane of her existence ever since Equestrian Therapy had started booming. The corporate company was constantly in Gabi's emails, demanding an audience with the Águila-Gutierrezes, wanting to buy them out or merge. Or both.

Gabriela had sent several scathing emails telling them where to shove it, but they always pushed back more intently each time.

"Infuriating, condescending assholes. As if we'd ever fucking give in to gentrification," Gabi seethed.

"Of course not," I humored her.

"They think they can just sign a check and we'll hand over our hard earned work to them. Fuck that."

"Yup. Hey, have you seen Junior?" My stomach twisted into knots. "I have something I have to tell him."

Gabi cut off her oncoming rant and narrowed her eyes on me. She didn't make a comment though, simply waved her fingers. "At the main house, I think."

I thanked her and left. She'd been complaining about Saint Enterprises for weeks, and I knew if I entertained her, she'd just go on and on. Usually, other businesses were wary of Gabi's cunning, strict persona. I wasn't sure what was different about S.E. They probably had a death wish or something.

I walked up to the main house and found Junior pacing the living room.

"Hey. You okay?"

He whirled and his face broke out into a smile upon seeing me. That smile had been warming me every day for a year since I'd moved in with him. We had our problems, like any couple, but nothing nearly to the scale as they had been before.

Therapy had helped guide us both through our problems, and I liked to believe we'd come out stronger for it.

My stomach gave another heave as Junior came towards me.

"How are you feeling?" he asked.

"Good." My stomach told another story. I hadn't been this nervous in months. "I've been looking for you."

"I've been looking for you too."

My brows kicked up. "Oh?"

He raked a hand through his short hair. "I don't know how to say this. I probably should have chosen a better way, but I honestly can't fucking wait anymore."

"You're confusing me."

"You know I love you, right?"

I smiled warmly. "I love you too."

"We wasted way too much time our whole lives avoiding each other, and I don't want to waste any more." Junior dropped down to one knee and I nearly jerked back from the surprise of the action. And when he pulled a velvet box out from the back of his pocket and opened it to reveal a ring, I felt I would faint.

"Junior?"

"I don't want to waste a moment more. Marry me, Mayda. Be my wife. Be my everything. Let me love you until we're old and in the ground. Be my best friend until the days we take our last breath. Please. Marry me. Marry me."

Tears fell down my cheeks and a sob escaped me. I barely looked at the ring, when all I could do was nod vigorously.

Junior breathed a sigh of relief and slipped the ring onto my finger as he stood. Then his fingers gripped the ends of my hair and tugged back so he could take my mouth in a scorching kiss.

"I love you," he whispered when he pulled away.

"I love you too. And... I have something to tell you."

He dropped his forehead to mine. "Yeah?"

"I'm... pregnant."

His entire body stilled one second before he wrapped his arms around me, hugging me tightly against his chest. His entire body shuddered. And when he pulled away, there were tears in his eyes.

"¿En serio?" he asked.

"Yes."

He let out a grito that drew his entire family into the room. They all clapped along with him, offering up their congratulations as they pretended they hadn't been eavesdropping from the other room.

But I knew the Águila-Gutierrez family. They'd been listening. And as they all took me into their arms with hugs and congratulations, welcoming me into the family, I smiled through my tears.

And I knew that this, right here, was the one place I'd always belonged.

About the Author

J ADE HERNÁNDEZ IS A proud Mexican-American woman who strives to bring more Latinx stories to life within the contemporary romance genre. You may know her as Aleera Anaya Ceres, the USA Today Bestselling Author of diverse fantasy and paranormal works. Under this new penname, she aims to represent her culture by writing sweet, dark, gritty, and fun stories for all. As an introvert, Jade prefers to stay inside with a good book, collect tarot cards, and she's recently found a love for book boxes! She currently lives in Tlaxcala, Mexico with her husband and children.

ALSO BY JADE

Los Diablos Motorcycle Club Series
Ink Me (*coming soon*)
Miguel (*coming soon*)
Mayan (*coming soon*)
El Rancho Los Corazones Series
Learn to Love You
Los Corazones #2 (*coming soon*)